Sherlock 1
and the Chocolate Menace
by Suzette Hollingsworth

The Great Detective In Love #3

Sherlock Holmes solves the most perplexing mystery of his life—
unlocking the human heart.

To

Gloria Stookey

who understands, as I do, the power of chocolate

and, incidentally, who understands the power of
hard work, perseverance, loyalty, and dreams come true
But that is for another book

And to

Lieutenant Commander
Michael Dascenzo

For his many years of service
patrolling the seas in a submarine
Undetected by and threatening to those who would wish us harm

PRAISE FOR
SUZETTE HOLLINGSWORTH'S NOVELS

"Best Holmesian Book of 2015" – Amazon customer

"This is an excellent, gifted writer, with a true future ahead of her." – CHARLOTTE CARTER

"Sir Doyle would enjoy. It has all the classic trappings of one of his novels. From the language to the descriptions of London and its denizens, it is historical fiction at its best." – Christopher Gallagher

"A Sherlock tale with Hepburn and Tracy flair . . . It had the feel of a classic old Hollywood mismatched romantic comedy to me.... Hepburn and Tracy. It was charming and would really appeal to people who love the idea of a kind of Jane Austen meets Conan Doyle mash-up." - RaynaRed, Audible reviewer

"Cumberbatch/Sherlock meets his match!" - Jan, Audible reviewer

"Sherlock in Mr. Darcy mode . . . " - PandaRS, Audible reviewer

"Irene Adler has competition" - Mary, Audible reviewer

"This is a very fascinating novel. All the characters are very vibrant and come to life while reading them." - Coffee Time Romance & More

"Her humor is refreshing, I laughed out-loud on a few occasions, shed a few tears, and sat on the edge of my seat for most of it." AnaMaree Ordway, owner Ye Olde Bookshoppe

***

"Sherlock Holmes and the Case of the Sword Princess" was a 2015 Chanticleer Mystery and Mayhem finalist

"Sherlock Holmes and the Dance of the Tiger" is a 2016 Chanticleer Mystery and Mayhem finalist

Also by Suzette Hollingsworth

Sherlock Holmes & The Case of the Sword Princess
Sherlock Holmes & The Dance of the Tiger
Sherlock Holmes & The Chocolate Menace

published by Bookstrand

THE PARADOX: The Soldier and the Mystic

THE SERENADE: The Prince and the Siren

THE CONSPIRACY: The Cartoonist and the Contessa

To be released in 2017:
Sherlock Holmes & The Vampire Invasion

Sherlock Holmes
and the
Chocolate Menace

Sherlock Holmes and the Chocolate Menace
Copyright © 2016 by Suzette Hollingsworth
Imprint: Mystery with romantic elements

Cover Design by Fiona Jayde Media
Inside artwork by Clint Hollingsworth
Cameo of Sherlock Holmes and Mirabella Hudson
by Clint Hollingsworth

PUBLISHER'S NOTE:
This is a work of historical fiction. As such, there are historical figures
who actually lived contained within the pages of the book; the author has
attempted to represent them honestly, but some leeway must be given as she
has never met them in person. There are also fictional characters within the
book who seem more real than historical figures, namely those created by
Arthur Conan Doyle. For all the remaining characters, names, places, and
incidents, they are either the product of the author's imagination or are used
fictitiously, and any resemblance to actual persons, living or dead, business
establishments, events, or locales is entirely coincidental. So what is real and
what is not? We no longer know.

Published by Icicle Ridge Graphics. For permission requests, write to the
publisher, addressed "Attention: Permissions Coordinator," at the following
website address
http://suzettehollingsworth.com/contact/
ISBN: 978-0-9975170-2-6

Acknowledgements

Naturally, first and foremost, I must acknowledge Arthur Conan Doyle, who created the captivating characters of Sherlock Holmes and Dr. John Watson, who are so real in our minds that many consider them as historical figures rather than as fictional characters.

I wish to thank my editors: May Peterson, Kim Runcinan, Gretchen Stiller, K.J. Charles (an award-winning author), and Ashley Davis (also a Ph.D. in astrophysics).

This book would not be possible without my husband, Clint Hollingsworth, who is an exceptional artist/writer/editor. Both of his books, "The Sage Wind Blows Cold" (wilderness thriller) and "The Road Sharks" (science fiction) are Chanticleer finalists.

If I could, I would kiss the feet of the voice actor who produces my audiobooks, Joel Froomkin, but I haven't met him. Joel is a phenomenal talent who brings my books alive and truly turns my books into theatre. He is an amazing actor and director (Joel has directed Molly Ringwold and Charles Shaughnessy, of "The Nanny" fame.)

And to those persons who have believed in me throughout: my husband Clint, my BFF Charlsie Sterry DDS, Susan Bartroff (also a great editor!), Virginia Hashii (who first told me I was a writer and got me started on this journey), Amy Brazil (who encouraged me to keep going), Harvey Gover (who was the rock of my childhood and in my heart forever), my mother Mary Denison, my grandparents Omah & Marvin Hewitt, and readers and friends SueAnn Green, Rena Kohr, Kem Dawson, AnaMaree Ordway, Rex Gordon, Patsy Cantrell, Denae Lancaster (also an excellent colorist), Jill Delabano, Michelle Berry, and all the Beach Angels!

And, of course, to all true friends everywhere who keep our dreams alive when they falter in our hearts.

Dreams are more real than reality itself, they're closer to the self.
--GAO XINGJIAN, *Dialogue and Rebuttal*

CHAPTER ONE
Chelsea Street, London

"The Devil take the lot of you! Hold him down, he's only one man!" he muttered, taking a puff on his cigar with pleasure, as if he were enjoying a smoke and brandy in his study after dinner rather than torturing a kidnapped victim.

"You bastards!" The captive's face was twisted and red, his breathing rapid and labored, his eyes bulged and jutting everywhere in obvious fear, the cigared gentleman could see through the slit in the curtain.

"He won't stay still, boss!" exclaimed Babbitt, the strong arm. "He's thrashin' batty-fang here and there!"

"Inject the drug." He made a mental note to buy *La Intimidad* cigar again at Hardham's tobacco shop on Fleet Street: the blend was particularly fine, a fair contender to his Turkish cigars.

"I have friends in the queen's government!" the captive screeched.

"Do you, Mr. Hamilton? That's precisely what I was counting on."

Moriarty only allowed his cigar to be visible protruding from the curtain. Even hidden, with his nod and the resulting slight movement of his cigar, a needle was injected into the now-secured man's arm.

"ARGHHHH!"

Moriarty smiled to himself. *This is the power I wield.*

The struggle had been entertaining; it had taken three men to keep the young gentleman still long enough to do the dirty deed. For a government official, the man was surprisingly fit.

"Very good, Mr. Hamilton," Moriarty smiled from behind the curtain, well hidden in the dark. "It should only be a few minutes now."

"NO! No! Stop, you fiends!" the prisoner shrilled.

"We will stop when you answer our questions. Then you are free to go." *If you are still able to go, as it were.*

"You fiend! Why are you doing this? Are you a Tory?"

"I have no particular political affiliation," Moriarty replied from the shadows, taking a puff on *La Intimidad.* "But that will change shortly. Just think of me as the power behind the throne."

"What do you want?"

I want to rule, naturally. What else? "Ah, what do I want? That is for me to know and you to assist me with."

"You're insane!"

A prerequisite for the ruling class, I should say.

"You'll never get away with it." But Hamilton's speech was becoming slower.

"Ah, but I think I shall." *I am British. Great Britain rules the world: the sun never sets on her colonies. To rule England is to rule the world. And I, as it so happens, am the best and brightest of her queen's subjects.*

"Not on my watch!" the captive wailed.

"Make all the noise you wish. No one will care about your caterwauling, Mr. Hamilton," Moriarty said as he sat comfortably in a powder-blue velvet Louis XIV chair only a few feet from the captive.

"Where are we?" the bound man asked, still imagining that he could procure his freedom with enough knowledge. *Just like a politician to think he could talk his way out of anything.* Moriarty smirked, shaking his head in amusement.

"One of my best money-makers, as a matter of fact. Let's just say that shrieks are not uncommon in this particular locale."

Moriarty looked about the room at the maroon embossed wallpaper, the fresh flowers, the crystal chandelier, and the mirrors—for those who liked that type of thing. It was no wonder the clientele included prominent businessmen and politicians. Even King Leopold II was a client at this upscale brothel catering to the wealthy.

Chelsea Street was completely respectable; no one expected this here. And the rooms were well padded, deafening the troublesome noises.

Mary Jeffries, the madame, had done an exceptional job at giving the place an appearance of respectability—allowing the patrons to pretend they were something other than they were.

Whoremongers.

He himself channeled his passions into more elevated endeavors. He was not common like them. Moriarty pursed his mouth in disdain. Even royalty was commoner than he.

"Why? Why am I here? I never went to such a place in my life!"

"Inject the morphine, Babbitt. It will increase the effect of the drug," Moriarty said.

"Aeeeee!" Hamilton screamed in protest.

"Never?" inquired Moriarty. "You've never been to a brothel before, Mr. Hamilton?"

"I mean . . . once I . . . well, maybe twice . . ."

"That's better. Tell the truth." *Good.* Hamilton's tone was becoming quieter — and more agreeable.

Kings and paupers together at last. It gave their vices the impression of being high class.

Moriarty frowned. Except for the white slavery and child prostitution, which could never be made to look acceptable, however talented one might be. It was distasteful.

In truth, Jeffries was a devious and manipulative woman, which would ordinarily make her a person after his own heart. But she didn't know where to draw the line. One could have whatever one wanted—power, fame, riches—if one understood the rules of society: what the public would accept, and, most importantly, how to label something evil as 'good.'

There was no line for Mary Jeffries. She even arranged the abduction of children, as well as the kidnapping of unsuspecting women and the smuggling them to foreign countries—far away and out of the jurisdiction of their beloved Mother England.

Moriarty looked about the elegant room. Despite his regard for Jeffries' talented subterfuge, he did not approve of the latter two activities. It was not gentlemanly. It was *unsavory*. Even those who frequented cocaine dens did so willingly—and hurt no one but themselves. A high-class prostitute who entered into the profession willingly was one thing, but forcing women and children against their wills?

For mere money. There were much simpler ways to get money if one were intelligent. Why, he could make more money in one day on the stock market than Mary Jeffries made in a year inflicting suffering on the unwilling.

Murder and torture must have a higher purpose.

"Owwww!" his victim yowled.

"For pity's sake, Hamilton! *Damnit*, I know you're not in any pain! It's all in your head." All the noise was disruptive when one was enjoying one's smoke.

He himself had a code. *I only give people what that they themselves desire in the darkest corners of their hearts.*

I do not create those desires, I only fulfill them.

He enabled people to realize themselves. Moriarty knew that he could not be blamed for the evil in men—he did not create it, and it would not end with him.

I am a genius. But above all I am a gentleman.

Maintaining his image was all-important to him. He had a job to do here, but waiting for the drug to take effect, combined with his view of the extravagant décor, was an unpleasant reminder of his labor concerns.

"Such a lovely crystal chandelier," Hamilton said. "I'd like to have one like that in my home."

Good. The drug is working.

"I could procure one for you, Mr. Hamilton," Moriarty said.

"Could you? What would I have to do? I entertain important people you know."

"I'm sure you do." *Why else would I have an interest in you?* And yet, you are not so very important yourself; you would not be much missed. "I only want to ask you a few questions, Mr. Hamilton."

"What do you want to know?"

"I'd be very interested to know where the submarine plans are."

"The submarine plans?" Hamilton smiled. "Whoever has the submarine blueprint rules the seas."

"Oh my goodness, I hadn't thought of that," Moriarty muttered.

"Honestly, you should," Hamilton chided. "There is no other submarine design with a working torpedo in existence. Currently England is number one on the seas, but if someone else were to have those plans . . ."

"Someone like Germany?"

"Oh, that would be dreadful if the Kaiser had those plans in his possession."

"Indeed, we must keep them safe. And where are the plans?"

"Where are they? Would you really like to know?"

"More than I can possibly say."

"I don't think I should tell you. I'm not supposed to tell anyone."

Moriarty leaned forward. "But you feel compelled to, don't you, Mr. Hamilton? As if the words just flow from your brain to your mouth. *Where are the submarine plans?*"

"They're in the war secretary's home."

Moriarty sat straight up in his chair, his cigar paused in mid-air. "Hugh Childers. The Secretary of State for War. Why not in his office safe?"

"Mr. Childers has a much bigger staff in his house."

There are several ways to dispense of the staff. "Yes, there is a surprising lack of security at the Parliament building. And what is the combination to Childers' safe?"

"Ha ha! Do you think I would know that? I'm merely Childers' private secretary." He added somewhat bitterly, "No one tells me anything."

"Ah, but you are far more informed than you realize, Mr. Hamilton." Knowing the location of the plans was a great help. He had several expert safe crackers on staff. This drug was proving to be even more useful than anticipated.

It could be used to amass information—and erode reputation. "You work for one of the fourteen men in the prime minister's cabinet: his most trusted inner circle. Tell me more about the prime minister's whereabouts."

"Gladstone?"

"Unless you know of a different prime minister. Good Lord, yes!" *Clearly the drug doesn't increase intelligence.*

"Gladstone is a great man."

Yes, yes. But that's not much to work with, is it? Moriarty sighed heavily. "Mr. Gladstone has his flaws, doesn't he?"

"All men do."

"I am interested in one man in particular: Gladstone. Have you seen him in the brothels?"

"Everyone has. He's helping the prostitutes—as is his wife."

"I need names," Moriarty commanded.

"Shall's I makes 'im talk, boss?" Babbitt asked from behind the curtain.

"Stay out of it, Babbitt! Can't you see that Mr. Hamilton is quite agreeable?" *If not very helpful.*

Yet.

"Of course, why shouldn't I be? There is Lucinda, whom we attempted to place in a position, but she did not have enough education even to present herself as a maid." Hamilton sighed. "She was a beauty. And the other servants didn't like her. Probably for that very reason. But so lovely. Why, I myself would have hired her if—"

"We're not interested in your licentious tendencies, Mr. Hamilton, only in Gladstone's. Did the P.M. ever take advantage of Lucinda?"

"No! I mean . . . he spent a great deal of time with the ladies, but I never had any reason to suspect—"

"Didn't you? Tell me more about the girls who were particular favorites of the P.M."

"There was Danielle, who died."

"Now we're getting somewhere!" Moriarty leaned back into his seat as an idea began to form. "The P.M. had her killed to cover up his having his way with her."

"Of course not!"

The truth has very little to do with it. Moriarty smiled. *True or not, it could work.* It was only a matter of creating the "evidence".

"It was no such thing! Danielle was too far along with the disease."

"Tell me, Hamilton," Moriarty interrupted, "was Gladstone ever alone with the girls?"

"Probably."

Now we're getting somewhere.

"And what is the name of one of the younger girls now in the prime minister's home?"

"Emily."

Moriarty tapped his chin as he envisioned a scenario. "Could Emily be the child of an illicit affair?"

"Certainly not!"

"Further substantiated by the fact that she is in Gladstone's home." *Any lie would always be believed by the sheep—and those whose fear and hate* embraced the lies.

But how many sheep were there in England? That was the question.

"Zzzzz . . ."

"He's closing his eyes, boss," Moriarty heard from the other side of the curtain. That would never do to have the victims sleepy; the formula must be adjusted.

"Damnation! Right when we were getting somewhere! How much more morphine did you inject? You gave him too much! Do not ever make the same mistake again. Do you understand me?" Moriarty did not like to lose his temper—a gentleman always maintained his calm.

"zzzZZZ . . ."

Bloody hell! Hamilton was asleep. This would never do. Moriarty pulled the curtain open with a strong pull.

And then there was no more sound. Moriarty checked his pulse. "You idiot! He's dead."

Killing someone was always the last resort. A man of intellect never killed unless it was the logical thing to do. And the only option available to him.

I am not a common criminal. It was a source of comfort knowing that he was blameless when he laid his head on the pillow each night.

"*Hang it all*, Babbitt! How could you make this mistake?"

"I was careful, boss, I was. Maybe it was the other drug what killed him."

"That's a possibility." Moriarty considered these words. "It is imperative to keep records of the body weights and the quantities of each drug given. Next time use your brains!"

"Heh, no one's as smart as you, boss." Babbitt reflected on his own words for a minute. "Excuse me, Professor, but there is one what is almost as smart as you. . . . and he is askin' questions."

"Indeed he is. But we shall dispense of him shortly. I shall get Holmes where it hurts."

"Where is that boss? I should like to know!" Babbitt growled, as if he would like to be the one inflicting the pain.

"*The girl.*"

"What girl?"

"The young assistant, just out of the schoolroom."

"Har! har! You think Sherlock Holmes cares about some gull? I thought his bird was Irene Adler."

"You thought wrong, Mr. Babbitt." *Imbecile.*

"So he's a tendre for the chit? Who is the gull? Is he in love wif' her?"

"Nothing so extreme for Sherlock Holmes, but it is enough for a man who is more machine than human. I wouldn't say Holmes is in love so much as his heart has been touched. First there was Watson, and now the girl. I never thought to see it."

"Tsk tsk!" Babbitt shook his head, but a smile formed on his lips, even as he reflected on the possibilities.

"Indeed. Once the heart is engaged, it is over. All efficiency is gone. Holmes will not be able to function in the same mechanical state as he was heretofore known for. His judgment is compromised."

"But if we hurt her—won't Holmes be mad?" Babbitt asked in a surprisingly perceptive manner. "I've seen him angry. Didn't like it. Not worth it."

"If we hurt the girl, all the better." In fact, she would be an ideal candidate for white slavery: so lively, so shapely. That one would fetch a pretty penny.

Moriarty reflected that perhaps he would keep Jeffries around a bit longer.

"Unless he comes back an' hurts you, boss. You'se better off to just kill him."

"That's why I do the thinking." *Birdbrain.*

"Yes, sir." Babbitt swallowed hard under the professor's glare. Moriarty found his employees hungry and destitute—and gave them just enough respect that they would die for their employer. Precisely as it should be.

Moriarty smoothed his tie, glancing at the victim lying on the table. "And, naturally, if Holmes is no longer a challenge for me, he shall be killed as well."

But Moriarty knew the half-wit was right. Just as Holmes' friends were the Great Detective's Achilles heel, Moriarty knew his Achilles heel was Sherlock Holmes.

He should have already killed Holmes. But then what would be the point of living?

The game would be over.

Thankfully, Sherlock Holmes felt the same way. Their acquaintance was of a relatively short duration, but ultimately satisfying.

There was a quick tap on the door, flung open before Moriarty had the opportunity to respond. Quite without hesitation Mary Jeffries walked inside.

Moriarty felt a fury rise up inside him as she glanced at Hamilton lying on the bed. It was rare that he experienced his passion to this degree. "How dare you enter this room without permission, madame!"

"Oh, I'm so sorry." But her eyes said that she had entered for information, which she now had. "I only wish to be of help. Will you be needin' a cab?"

CHAPTER TWO
Au Rocher de Cancale, Paris

Sigh. The oysters had sounded so elegant, but they were a great deal more effort to consume than she generally liked in her meals.

Several weeks working in the Cirque d'Hiver—the Paris circus—in the most strenuous employment of her life had left her, well, *hungry.* Attempting to eat these oysters was making her, well, *hungrier.*

Paris is not what it seems. The City of Light shrouded a hidden complexity beneath its glitzy surface. Just as working in the Parisian circus had sounded so glamorous—when, in fact, it was fascinating, exhausting, and, above all, life threatening.

"Mr. Holmes, I wonder . . . if you're not . . . would you mind?"

"Yes I would mind, Miss Hudson." Sherlock observed her eyeing his plate. He moved the white china plate utilized by the popular sidewalk café of *Au Rocher de Cancale* closer to himself.

How selfish. "You have no intention of eating your lunch, do you, Mr. Holmes?" Mentally Mirabella Hudson, Sherlock Holmes' laboratory assistant/chief bottle washer and now tiger trainer, calculated the distance between her plate and Sherlock's, but she didn't think she stood a chance of a successful outcome. Sherlock Holmes was an expert at fencing, boxing, and *Jiu-Jitsu* and though he had taught her as well, she was still the master's student, merely going undercover when the Great Detective needed a female operative.

"Probably not," Sherlock said.

Mirabella glanced at the unfailingly handsome Dr. John Watson seated with his back to rue Montorgueil, a significant street in the Châtelet-Les Halles district of Paris.

I can't expect any charity there. Beautiful to behold but eager to part with his food the former army doctor was not. He was attacking his repast of mushroom omelet, sausages, champagne, and orange scones with the characteristic enthusiasm of a military man ready for the fight. Or perhaps as one who was still recovering from army food, which had been his main fare only one year prior.

Before her eyes returned to the laborious task which was her lunch, Mirabella eyed the cod on Sherlock's plate, the beautiful golden breading glistening in the sunlight.

"May I ask why I mightn't have what you do not want, Mr. Holmes?"

"Because I wish to save you from yourself, Miss Belle," her mentor pronounced.

Save yourself, Mr. Holmes, that should provide you with more than ample avocation. The man consumed more drink, tobacco, and drugs than he did food. He was progressing much better with his Battersea Park ale than he was with his meal.

"We are not alone in our rooms, Miss Belle," Sherlock added. "We must have a care for social decorum." He arranged the lavender and white striped silk sash around his neck, shown to advantage by a navy corduroy jacket.

Social decorum? She stifled her smile, afraid that she might never stop laughing if she allowed herself even a giggle.

Sherlock Holmes was the last person in the world to pretend to have superior knowledge in not deviating from the norm! In spite of his elegant dress and the conductor's hat he wore ornamented with silver embellishments—or perhaps because of it—everything about his appearance was disturbing. Almost deranged. Arched angular eyebrows, midnight-black overlong wavy hair fighting for freedom beneath his hat, and a pronounced unshaven jaw line boldly displaying a cut indicating that he had recently been in a fight. Perhaps more than one.

The man was the embodiment of social effrontery.

And yet—he was mysterious, entrancing, provocative. How could he not be with those silver-grey eyes which observed everything and pierced one's soul? Sherlock could connect with one on the deepest level. He could excite, invigorate, awaken, ignite.

And crush.

How someone so rational and unemotional could connect with one on such an emotional level was the greatest riddle of her existence.

It was disturbing. *And confusing.*

"Although etiquette is generally not Holmes' forte´, he is right, for once, Miss Mirabella." Dr. Watson chuckled, leaning towards her which caused his blond-streaked hair to fall into his eyes. "We are amongst Parisian high society. Would you truly wish to be the laughing stock of Paris?"

"Well, no, of course not. I had only wished to eat lunch," she replied, gazing into gorgeous eyes the color of the Mediterranean.

Stop it, girl! she admonished herself. John Watson was the dearest of friends—but that's where it ended. She knew very well that her heart was no longer engaged in that court.

But neither am I blind.

And yet, John Watson had done her the great service of teaching her young heart what she wished for in a beau. She knew what she didn't want: someone who enjoyed the company of women and was not ready to pick one. Someone for whom she wasn't enough.

For which the good doctor could not be blamed. It made all the sense in the world that she wasn't enough: she was unfeminine, awkward, and plain. She had a gift for putting her foot in her mouth. And she was more interested in books and experiments—even cadavers—than in social events, needlepoint, or playing a musical instrument.

Still, if she were to someday have a beau—which wasn't looking likely at this point—she did wish for one, like John Watson, who was gentle, kind, sensitive, loyal, brave, patient, even-tempered, complaisant, relaxed, and amenable.

Mirabella glanced at Sherlock. And *not* vexing, overly demanding, unpredictable, provoking, extreme, opinionated, intense, zealous, tormenting, and unrestrained.

And psychotic.

"What ho?" said Sherlock, his eyes suddenly alighting on an exquisitely fashionable brunette in a maroon satin walking suit. She had only just been seated next to the street some tables away from them, a magnificent purple feather protruding from her maroon velvet cap.

Who is she? Curious, Mirabella turned to look in the direction of Sherlock's gaze.

A slow smile began to form on the Great Detective's lips.

Oh my! It was not too much to call the young woman in red a *femme fatale.*

The dark-haired beauty turned to smile at Sherlock while chatting amiably with her companions: a man of average appearance in a brown tweed suit—he seemed familiar, perhaps because he was so ordinary—and another beautiful woman with strawberry blonde hair wearing a lavender silk gown. Whereas the brunette was stylish, the blonde was ostentatious, adorning herself with lavish sapphires and diamonds. Mirabella wouldn't have thought such jewelry appropriate for daywear.

But the bigger question in her mind was: how did such a man as that, who looked intensely boring and as if he might be a bank examiner, warrant two such ravishing ladies?

Even more disturbing was Sherlock's reaction. His expression was wistful, and the air was, well . . . *charged.*

The air was always charged when Sherlock was present, but this was different.

Currently the electrical field was between Sherlock and the lady in red who had turned to smile at him. That dangerous charge which Sherlock wielded was a disruptive, uncontrolled energy which propelled him into every manner of disturbance and trouble.

And this woman was trouble.

Now that Mirabella caught a glimpse of her face, something about the woman in red looked exceedingly familiar as well. How strange that two people who looked so familiar—the gentleman and the lady in red—were completely unknown to her. Mirabella knew with a certainty that she had never placed eyes on the beauty before. No one could have forgotten that face or that figure!

"Blazes to hell!" One of Sherlock's instantaneous fits overtook him. "I should have put Miss Belle in disguise!"

"Disguise?" she asked, perplexed. "But we're not on a case. We solved the Russian spy's—I mean, Miss Janvier's—murder."

"Even so, I don't want the group which has just been seated to take notice of you, Miss Hudson," Sherlock replied curtly, adding in a tone of voice that she knew to be an order, "Cover your face with your hat as long as they are here."

Heaven help us! Would this case ever be over? But she did as Sherlock commanded—she dare not do anything else!—angling the rim of her large headdress so as not to reveal her face while catching glimpses of the trio. She had only just purchased the fashionable hat from a Parisian milliner with Mycroft's assistance, so she knew it must be quite the thing.

"God save us," she heard John mutter under his breath, even as he fingered the revolver she knew to be in his jacket, his champagne brunch momentarily protected from the onslaught of his appetite.

"What is it, Dr. Watson?" she asked, alarmed.

John leaned close to her again and whispered under his breath. "The gentleman is . . . *Moriarty.*"

Very distracting when John does that. The masculine scent of tweed and earth mingled with the odor of fresh fish. *Heavenly.* Lovely fish and beautiful man, but none of it for me.

"Professor Moriarty?" That dull-looking man in tweed? Suddenly the name registered in her brain and she felt her hand shaking even as she clenched her fist.

In her alarm, Mirabella jabbed her fork into the shell. This action was a bit too much force for the oyster on the half-shell with which she had been struggling, flinging the delicate morsel into a spin upwards into the air before embarking upon a journey across the sidewalk of *Au Rocher de Cancale,* just missing a nearby woman's peach silk dress. The oyster then slid some two feet, skidding to a halt in front of the nose of an Afghan Hound accompanying his master at the well-known sidewalk café, who obligingly consumed the evidence of the disastrous faux-pas.

She looked about, assuming as much innocence of expression as she could muster. An action such as this in British high society could destroy one's social standing. Permanently.

Thankfully she was neither in Britain nor in high society.

Dr. John Watson momentarily covered his eyes with his hand, his stylishly long sideburns accenting a perfect jaw line. John's alarmed expression, only visible for an instant but now forever embedded in her memory, contrasted starkly with the touch of amusement in Sherlock's eyes.

"That wasn't precisely what I meant by keeping a low profile, Miss Hudson."

"I'm so sorry, Mr. Holmes." She motioned with her chin to the party of three. "Is that Moriarty. . . the *criminal?*"

"The most dangerous kind of criminal. One whom no one suspects."

"But *you* suspect, Mr. Holmes."

"The astute and intelligent observer suspects, thereby excluding Scotland Yard," Sherlock said. "Professor Moriarty of the University of London. He wrote a treatise on the binomial theorem which gained him the position of the chair of the mathematics department at the University of London."

"*One* treatise?" she asked. "That was very easy work to have gained such a notable position in academia."

"The professor would have liked his post to have been Cambridge or Oxford, but rather than applying himself to gain the post he desires, he dissipates his energy in fiendish endeavors."

"He wastes his genius," Dr. Watson added, staring pointedly at Sherlock.

Studying the professor she realized something else. "That's the street vendor! I saw him on the day Miss Janvier died!"

"Naturally. And you're just now noticing this, Miss Belle? You must learn to recognize people in different settings and even in disguise." An expression of fear crossed his countenance, not ordinarily seen on the face of Sherlock Holmes. "It could save your life, Miss Belle."

"Who is the woman in red?" asked Mirabella with only a moment's hesitation.

"The woman," Sherlock replied with obvious admiration, smiling to himself, as he took an unnecessarily large gulp of Battersea.

"Yes, I can see it is a woman, but who?" she asked as cordially as she could muster.

"*The* woman," he repeated, not meeting her eyes, as if it were suddenly a matter of complete indifference to him whether or not she were there. When only a moment ago he had been focused on her, giving her an expensive bottle of perfume in appreciation for working on the case.

"The brunette is one Miss Irene Adler," Watson said under his breath.

"Oh, my!" exclaimed Mirabella. "Not the one in the police record?

Where you were chained . . . in the hotel—"

"No, in spite of all belief to the contrary, that was a different female altogether," emphasized Sherlock, raising his right eyebrow. "And it is completely irrelevant."

"Chains? A hotel? Different female? Irrelevant?" Mirabella thought she might choke on her own saliva. "Are you quite serious, Mr. Holmes?"

"I am always serious, Miss Belle, I thought you might have learned that by now."

"Bloody hell!" the generally good-mannered John Watson muttered under his breath with uncharacteristic hostility. "Irrelevant to whom, Holmes? Are you saying Irene Adler was not the woman in the police report?"

"I am," Sherlock stated unequivocally.

"Then who—?" Watson demanded.

"Oh, I suppose the time has come." Sherlock sighed resignedly. "Recall, Watson, that the woman in question wasn't present when the maid arrived and found me chained to the bed. I never identified her."

"But Holmes, you have always said that Irene Adler is *the woman*," John objected, in a rare state of agitation.

"None other."

"Are you saying you were with another woman?" Watson exclaimed in a forced whisper. "And you who don't hold the fair sex in high esteem!"

"Of course I do. The highest. I place women on a pedestal: pure, chaste, innocent, refined, helpless. And generally naïve and requiring our assistance." He nodded to Mirabella. "I am pleased to place Miss Hudson in an altogether different category."

Different from the 'woman' category. How lovely.

"Who was the woman in the hotel then?" Watson demanded. "And why would you let the police believe it was Miss Adler?"

"I never said one way or the other. The false conclusions of others cannot be placed at my door, particularly one so incompetent as the London police," Sherlock said. "Besides, the lady in question is married. I would not wish to ruin her reputation."

"Holmes! Most improper!"

"Improper? That astonishes me, coming from you, Watson."

Mirabella was in a state of extreme bewilderment herself. This man who perceived the world in an unequivocally logical fashion—almost mechanical in his approach—clearly had a tender spot for someone. And a mystery woman, no less! She twisted her lips in annoyance.

Why should it concern me?

"Furthermore, my friend, you don't know everything about me, you see." There was a wicked gleam in his silver-grey eyes. "Kindly consult your notes on the case. *A Scandal in Bohemia*, I believe it is?"

"Refresh my memory, Holmes."

"I must have failed to share the resolution with you, old boy."

"You seem to have overlooked a great deal in the retelling of the story."

"Ah, well, I didn't wish you to sensationalize the narration, and, in the interest of Miss Adler's privacy, I might have kept a few of the facts to myself."

"Do tell."

Sherlock dabbed his lips with his handkerchief while casting an approving glance at Miss Adler, who returned the glance with a sly smile. "Irene Adler led everyone to believe that she was a loose woman and was blackmailing the King of Bavaria after a sordid affair. Perhaps for money or perhaps for revenge, that was the only part of the case which I hadn't concluded. Of one thing I was certain: Miss Irene Adler was a schemer and a contortionist."

"As I said," Dr. Watson interjected.

"She even fooled me. When, in fact, the king was the heel, he had used her and tossed her aside. He wished to marry a *suitable* woman and Miss Adler was in his way. He thought that because she was a stage actress and he a king, he could do as he wished."

"The cad!" Dr. Watson exclaimed.

"Just so!" Sherlock agreed. "The picture on her possession of the two of them together was her only protection."

"Hmph!" Mirabella exclaimed, indignantly. "You must re-publish *A Scandal in Bohemia* and set the record straight, Dr. Watson, for the sake of working women everywhere! Just because Miss Adler is a woman who must earn her living does not mean that her feelings are any less important."

"Precisely." Sherlock nodded. "His Majesty wished to keep the affair secret, or better yet, to sweep Miss Adler under the rug for good. Irene was holding the only card available to her—the incriminating photograph—as insurance to her own safety. Recall that she was dealing with a man of immense power and riches."

"What did she do?" asked Mirabella, leaning forward.

"In the end she married a solicitor, a Mr. Godfrey Norton, and escaped to America before she could be silenced. The king is now married and she is therefore no longer a threat to him."

"And yet here she is," said Dr. Watson, waving to her table.

"Every value of devotion, loyalty, and ethics she holds dear," Sherlock continued, "and yet Miss Adler had the brains to ensure her own survival and that of her fiancé while deceiving us all as to her true nature." His expression was one of utter admiration.

"Miss Adler has a turn for disguise, as I recall," John Watson added.

"She is a stage actress, which she put to good use," Sherlock agreed.

"And she anticipated and outsmarted the great Sherlock Holmes!" Mirabella felt dazed. She had never met anyone who had outsmarted Sherlock.

"As well as the King of Bavaria and all his paid mercenaries," Dr. Watson added.

"To be sure. Both pure of heart and a superior intellect. Irene Adler represents all that womankind should be—and is not." Sherlock agreed. "Hence, *the woman.*"

"So . . . are you in love with Irene Adler, Mr. Holmes?" Mirabella asked hesitantly.

"Don't be foolish, my dear Miss Belle." Sherlock chuckled. "All emotions, and romantic love in particular, are abhorrent to a mind which values logic and reasoning above all else. Becoming entangled with a woman is like throwing grit into a well-oiled machine. A great distraction and a waste of time besides."

"And what about the lady in the hotel room? Are you in love with her?" Mirabella pressed, surprised at her curiosity. She knew it was completely unladylike to ask, but one wished to know.

"Definitely *not*," he replied definitively.

"Then who is the lady from the hotel room, Holmes? *And why were you there?*" Dr. Watson repeated.

"That remains to be revealed, does it not? That lady was, in fact, all that Irene Adler appeared to be and was not: a schemer, a jezebel, and a controller of men. Her entire life is a charade—and a duplicitous game."

"If our Miss Adler is such a saint, why is she with Moriarty?" Dr. Watson asked pointedly.

"I believe it is the other woman who interests Miss Adler." Sherlock took his pipe out of his pocket and began to fill it with tobacco.

"And who is the strawberry blonde?" Mirabella asked in a whisper.

"Fantine Noel, the Countess of Florentine—and a violin virtuoso," Sherlock said. "It appears, my dear Miss Belle and Dr. Watson, that there is yet an unfinished element to the case centering on our beautiful Russian spy."

CHAPTER THREE
The Woman

"Mr. Holmes." The raven-haired beauty's greeting carried a shockingly familiar tone of voice as she approached the party of three.

"Miss Adler. Or should I say Mrs. Norton?" Sherlock rose and took her hand, smiling into blue eyes, twinkling as she beheld him. Mirabella had never before seen Sherlock distracted by anything. Astonished, she studied Irene Adler as best she could through the linen-weave rim of her hat: a brunette, small and petite, so unlike herself. She was elegantly dressed, with dimples which made the actress' face light up when she smiled.

"Yes, Mr. Holmes. I am now married." Her smile was warm and her manner gracious, indicating that their marriage was a happy one.

"I must surmise that your husband has business in Europe, Mrs. Norton?"

"Indeed, Mr. Holmes." She looked surprised. "How did you know?"

"I know you are no longer performing on the stage, so it must be your husband's business which brings you here. The King of Prussia is now married as well, and is therefore no longer a threat to you. Consequently, you can travel where you wish."

"Very true. My husband received a favorable offer of a position in France, and we were delighted to return."

"Speaking of the theatre circuit," Sherlock continued, motioning to the other woman, "I presume that is where you met Countess Florentine?"

Irene's lilting laugh was delightful. "I wonder why we bother speaking since you already know everything, Mr. Holmes?"

"For the benefit of your charming company, of course."

"Naturally, I was an opera singer and stage actress, and Fantine a—"

"—concert performer taking the continent by storm with her unequaled talent." Sherlock completed the sentence, taking the dazzling Fantine's hand and kissing it.

Oh, my! Mirabella almost shook from the magnetism between the two. She had thought it was directed towards Miss Adler, but perhaps it was this

Fantine . . . countess . . . *person. Who is she?*

"Sherlock," Fantine murmured in a shockingly familiar—dare one think *flirtatious?*—tone of voice as her eyes moved from the young and handsome detective to rest upon the bottle of Lorenzy-Palanca's *Nuit d'Arlequin* perfume placed on the table.

I should have put the expensive gift away, Mirabella knew at once. Until this moment it hadn't seemed important that the divine perfume with secondary scents of pink orchid and vanilla was an inappropriate gift from anyone except one's intended. Its blatant display made one's character appear questionable.

Of course, it was only Sherlock who had given the perfume to her in appreciation for her work on the case, so it meant precisely nothing, but to the eyes of the world . . .

"Dr. Watson. Mr. Holmes."

"Professor Moriarty." Sherlock nodded, his tone suddenly stiff.

Mirabella took advantage of the five staring at each other to catch a quick glimpse at the gentleman who was the two beauties' escort.

The man in a three-piece brown tweed suit and a plaid scarf didn't look like a criminal mastermind. The man they called Moriarty had auburn hair and a neatly trimmed beard, with intelligence in eyes that somehow looked dark and frightening despite their pale green, translucent color.

He looks to be the dullest individual imaginable. Except for his eyes, which had a surprising intensity which was somewhat startling.

Dr. Watson was silent. Almost rude.

The tables were strangely reversed. John Watson was always the polite gentleman and Sherlock so blunt, one who could care less about social convention, except when it suited him.

Mirabella glanced down at her pink linen suit and cream-colored lace blouse in which she had heretofore felt quite the thing. Everyone said that pink was her color with her chestnut brown hair, but naturally the color which best suited her was far from sophisticated. She felt like a schoolroom miss next to these ladies.

"And who is this young lady?" Miss Adler extended her hand, which Mirabella accepted while keeping her face hidden with her hat, although she could tell that the tone of Miss Irene Adler's voice was favorable.

"This is my laboratory assistant," Sherlock replied, not revealing her name. As annoying as it was to be swept over, she had to trust that Sherlock had his reasons: he always did, and she had learned to follow his direction. "Washes my jars and such."

"I see. Is there a great need for washing jars here in Paris? Away from your laboratory?" Fantine asked.

"An astonishing need," stated Sherlock decisively.

At this moment Miss Adler begged their forgiveness, kissing Fantine on the cheek. "I must be going. So nice to see you." She turned towards Sherlock. "I can't thank you enough, Mr. Holmes. I hope that there is no ill feeling between us as there is only gratitude on my side."

"Because you outwitted me, Miss Adler? To the contrary. It was an honor to be made the fool at your hand." He bowed his head reverently, and there was genuine admiration in his voice. "Every value of ethics, courage, and intelligence which I hold dear I find in your character."

The woman! Before her was the woman Sherlock Holmes held in the highest estimation of all womankind. Mirabella bit her lip as her mind raced.

This was the woman whose photograph Sherlock treasured. Irene Adler had used everyone's misguided notions and prejudices, their desire to see the worst in everyone, and fooled them all. She had even fooled *Sherlock Holmes!* He who was notoriously unobstructed, who walked into a crime scene with his mind a blank slate.

Mirabella remembered the way the countess had looked at Sherlock. Irene Adler might be *the woman*, but Fantine Noel was *the seductress*.

Once Miss Adler had taken her leave, Sherlock turned to Moriarty who watched the proceedings with interest. "And how do you get on, Professor?"

"To be perfectly frank, Mr. Holmes, I am most displeased with you at the moment."

"That is dreadful news, Professor. And what, may I ask, have I done to win your censure?"

Moriarty pulled a chair out for Mrs. Noel, though neither were invited to do so, followed by seating himself. "I believe it is your existence on the planet which disturbs me."

"And does your assistant have a name, Sherlock?" Fantine coo-ed, moving closer to Sherlock who was seated beside her.

"It is no concern of yours, my dear," replied Sherlock with a forced but alluring smile.

"Oh, Sherlock, you are mistaken," pressed Fantine. "If it is important to you, it is important to *me*."

"What you mean to say, Fantine, is that if something is my private affair and absolutely none of your business, it is important to you that you should disregard my wishes on the matter." Sherlock grew suddenly stern and distant. "Let me be clear on whose wishes shall prevail in this instance."

"Marvelous!" Countess Florentine took out her fan even as she ran her hand along the bottle of *Nuit d'Arlequin* perfume. "The mystery lady must be a very good jar-washer."

"Excellent, I should say," agreed Sherlock.

"I can't help but notice, Sherlock, that, in addition to washing jars, she receives gifts of expensive perfume," said Fantine, her voice shaking as if embarrassed for the younger woman.

Mirabella bent her head even closer to her chest, feeling the awkwardness of her situation, and the sting of Countess Florentine's implication. Whereas she had previously been made to feel like a schoolroom miss, she now felt like a dance-hall girl pretending to be a lady of quality.

It isn't true! Mirabella wanted to scream. She wasn't being "kept" by Sherlock Holmes! If anything, she was being worked to death—and starved!

Peculiar that the inference, though far from the truth, still hurt. Why should the words disturb her if they weren't true?

Worse than the insinuation, Sherlock had made it very clear that he wished her a hundred miles from here. *But why?* Possibly Sherlock was so awed by Fantine's beauty that he wished his bumbling assistant would disappear.

"If it can be any concern of yours, Countess," Dr. Watson said, clearly inflamed that Mirabella had been slighted.

"Oh, do you disapprove of me, Dr. Watson?"

"In every way," he stated in a low tone, tapping his chin. "I believe that your identity has suddenly become clear to me. And, if I am correct, it has something to do with a police report."

"I couldn't say, not having seen the report." Her laughter had a nefarious quality to it.

It is she! Fantine Noel is the woman from the hotel room!

This is very bad.

"You are a dangerous woman, Countess," Dr. Watson added.

"Some consider that to be my best quality," she said provocatively, glancing at Sherlock.

Mirabella bestowed an appreciative glance upon Dr. Watson, who had succeeded admirably in re-directing Countess Florentine's attention away from her, which had no doubt been his intent.

"And as to a police report, the countess is a concert violinist by trade. There is no secret to her identity," Moriarty said. "Fantine is a performer of some renown on the concert circuit."

"And no doubt you travel in the highest social circles, Countess Florentine?" John Watson asked.

"Naturally. I travel in both society and academic circles." She glanced at Moriarty. "I open doors for James, and he opens them for me."

"And what doors are those?" Dr. Watson asked.

She fingered her diamond and sapphire necklace.

"Fantine is interested in beautiful objects. And Moriarty is interested in her connections," Sherlock said. "And how is the count, Fantine? Is he still alive?"

"I'm no longer with Count Florentine," Fantine replied lightly.

"She's already killed him," John Watson muttered under his breath.

Fantine glanced at Dr. Watson. "The count is very much alive."

"You're not currently married, Countess Florentine?" asked Sherlock, bemused.

"I didn't say that, Sherlock."

"So thankfully you retain the title, Countess," Sherlock said.

"That must be a relief to us all," Dr. Watson said, clearly not besotted with her beauty.

"After the count there was a charming government official of some type," Fantine said.

"It didn't work out with the government official, I take it?" Sherlock asked as he filled his pipe with tobacco, stopping abruptly as an idea obviously occurred to him. "Let me guess. Your former lover is now deceased."

"How did you know, Sherlock?" she exclaimed, surprised.

Sherlock turned suddenly to stare at Moriarty. "And what was the cause of death?"

Moriarty shook his head somberly. "Why do you look at me, Holmes? How should I possibly know?"

Fantine shrugged, her voice somewhat reflective. "Tragically, I don't know. He was quite young, so it seemed odd to me that he should be taken ill. At any rate, though I don't wish anyone dead, I fear the affair would have ended soon anyway. I simply find myself easily bored." She glanced at Sherlock. "But I shall no doubt remedy that."

"It is unlikely," said Sherlock, lighting his pipe. "Sadly, you are, my dear Fantine, unlucky in love."

"It is her partners who are unlucky," muttered Watson.

"Quite the opposite," she asserted, her eyes transfixed on Sherlock. He glanced up and his eyes met hers with a suddenness which was disarming.

Mirabella fought the desire to convulse. *Please, please may we leave this place?* The idea of Sherlock and this woman together was disturbing to her in the extreme!

"I expect that you caught the Cirque d'Hiver while you were in Paris, Professor Moriarty," Sherlock said.

"Naturally."

"It comes as no surprise that you had some interest in the circus," Sherlock said.

"Oh, and why is that?"

"One of the performers, a Miss Joelle Janvier, was a spy dealing in Russian and French intelligence."

"The *late* Miss Janvier," corrected Professor Moriarty, bowing his head. "A tragic loss."

"And how did it affect you, Professor?" Watson asked, setting down his beer with a bit too much force.

"I understand that you, in particular, must feel the effects of her loss, Dr. Watson," Moriarty said consolingly.

"I am sad to see anyone lose his—or her—life." Dr. Watson added with a degree of venom, "*Almost* anyone."

"Perhaps the world would be a better place without some," replied Professor Moriarty amiably, his penetrating eyes fixed on John Watson. "Or perhaps . . . it might go *unnoticed*."

"Did you have anything to do with Miss Janvier's death, Moriarty?" Dr. Watson demanded.

"You wound me, Doctor," said Professor Moriarty.

"In point of fact, I believe that our illustrious professor very much wanted the divine Miss Janvier alive. She was an invaluable resource to him." Sherlock said. "Is it not so?"

Moriarty frowned. The implication was clear: there was information the professor wanted which he had not been able to obtain due to Miss Janvier's death.

"And your assistant?" Dr. Watson tipped his head in the direction of Fantine Noel, remaining seated as he began attacking his meal again. "Did Countess Florentine take an interest in Miss Janvier?"

"Certainly not!" exclaimed Fantine with indignation. "James has better things to do than going about killing women. And I am most certainly *not* his assistant!"

"True on both accounts," said Sherlock. "Professor Moriarty would never have performed the act himself even had he desired to do so: he would take care not to implicate himself in that fashion. Bad for business."

"And what business might that be?" asked Moriarty in an unconcerned manner.

"The criminal machine which you run, of course. I had hoped it to be confined to London, though I never believed it. Now I see that you are extending into international territories, Moriarty. I don't advise it."

"And yet Scotland Yard has no belief in such an extraordinary operation," said Moriarty.

"The absence of a belief does not make it untrue," said Sherlock. "There are many murders which can be placed at your door as if you had pulled the trigger yourself."

"Oh, my! Such accusations!" exclaimed Fantine.

"I realize that you are in the business of petty theft and breaking hearts, my dear Fantine, along with making exquisite music," Sherlock said. "Nothing more."

"The fame and connections are marvelous—I know simply everyone of importance—but the pay is not as much as you might think," she said demurely, stroking her necklace.

"Professor Moriarty here has much higher stakes. I'd advise you to stay clear of him and to seek other companions—and occupations."

"Oh, I am not much interested in James' business. It is far better not to know. However, I should like to discuss that with you further, Sherlock. And when shall you be returning to London, darling?"

"If you are not the professor's assistant, then what is your connection to him, Countess Florentine?" Dr. Watson asked.

"Didn't you know? I am his sister."

CLANG! Dr. Watson's fork dropped onto the pavement.

CHAPTER FOUR
A Matter of National Security

"Blast!"

"What is it, Holmes?"

"Another incident of state secrets being revealed," said Sherlock, studying his copy of the *Pall Mall Gazette* from the comfort of his fireside chair at 221B Baker Street. "The plans for the *Abdül Hamid* have gone missing."

"The only submarine able to fire a torpedo while submerged?" John asked in alarm, looking up from his book.

"Precisely," Sherlock said.

"Who do you think has them, Holmes?"

"I have every intention of finding out," Sherlock said, pointing to the *Pall Mall*. "Do you recall that the war secretary's assistant was found dead in his bed of a drug overdose?"

"Very sad for a promising young man, but it isn't uncommon. What was the drug?"

"Morphine according to the report, but I think we should determine that for ourselves."

"Holmes . . . you don't mean . . . ?"

"Indeed I do. Don't you find it a bit coincidental that the submarine plans in the care of the war secretary go missing at the same time his assistant is found dead?"

"But the newspaper doesn't draw that correlation. Surely it would have been evident if there had been foul play involved—"

"Ha! ha! My dear fellow, if we waited for those in power to come to the correct conclusions, nothing would ever be solved. Is it settled then? Tonight?" Sherlock grew somber. "This bodes ill for England if those plans are not recovered. It is a matter of extreme national security. Would you want those plans to fall into the hands of the Germans?"

"Naturally I would not! Of course I am with you, Holmes! But frankly, I'm more worried about the French and the Russians." He cleared his throat. "But there's something else, isn't there?"

"Indeed." Sherlock said. "My sources tell me that Mr. Hamilton was lately seen about town with a glamorous musician."

"*Fantine Noel.*"

"None other. The question in my mind is," continued Sherlock, glancing out the window onto Baker Street, "what is Fantine up to?"

"That is easily answered," said John, a pipe dangling from his mouth as he scowled. "No good."

"Obviously."

"*Bloody hell!* What are you about, Holmes!" John punched his fist in the air, allowing his book to drop to the floor beside his chair. "You know the woman is a viper! Why do you insist on keeping her company?"

"A beautiful viper—and a violin virtuoso. She speaks five languages and hobnobs with the wealthy and influential. Moriarty is most jealous of her, you know. He was never able to gain notoriety outside of the academic circuit. Fantine, on the other hand, is charismatic, beautiful, and mixes with everyone of note."

"Are you insane having an affair with Moriarty's sister? If you break her heart, Moriarty will kill you!"

"That presumes a great deal not in evidence. And he might very well kill me anyway, Watson. It also presumes that Fantine and Moriarty are on good terms. For two devious, conniving, competitive, power-mad people who want it all for themselves, it isn't difficult to surmise what their childhood relationship must have been. I guarantee they will each of them maintain the relationship only as long as it is advantageous."

CHAPTER FIVE
Murder

There are certainly more enjoyable places in the world to spend one's time than in a foggy, damp graveyard, particularly when one is forced to exhume a body from that same graveyard.

Sherlock leaned the shovel against the dirt pile and jumped into the grave, still breathing hard from doing the majority of the digging. He examined the face of the body and sniffed. His grey eyes flashed with intense recognition.

Watson lifted the eyelids as Mirabella held the gas lamp over the face, the moonlight not being sufficient. "The pupils are the size of a pinpoint and the lips are blue. It is certainly consistent with a morphine overdose."

"Respiratory failure?" Sherlock asked. He nodded to the night watchman, whom he had bribed. It served him well that he was on good terms with those from every station in life, Mirabella considered. Still, it was going to be a long night before they returned the body to its permanent resting place.

"It appears so. But we won't know without testing the blood," Watson said, taking the needle out of his bag.

"Not yet, Watson. We're going to have to move the body to Baker Street and bring it back in the morning," Sherlock said. "We have no way to keep the samples from becoming contaminated here."

Mirabella groaned. "Where will you put the body?" she asked, but she knew the answer.

"On my laboratory table, naturally. There is no other surface."

"Aunt Martha will kill you if she finds out."

"She won't."

"Yes, Mr. Holmes," she said, nodding. This was not a part of the position that she particularly liked, but anything they could learn assisted in bringing the victim's murderer to justice.

Sherlock bent down to study the clothing more carefully. The body was outfitted in a surprisingly stylish suit. He took another sniff.

"Moriarty," Sherlock said. "Moriarty is behind this."

"How do you know, Holmes?"

"Because the victim's teeth are white, naturally. Didn't you observe it, Watson?"

Mirabella fought the urge to convulse. Sherlock turned towards her. "What is the matter, Miss Belle?"

"Nothing at all, Mr. Holmes. I am simply not accustomed to grave robbing."

"Ah, but the work is only beginning. We need to open the organs and the tissues. And once we have all the samples, we will have the data."

"It's going to be a working night," Dr. Watson said.

***

Having the body safely transported into a cab Sherlock had hired, they began their return journey to Baker Street, covered in dirt and smelling none to well themselves. This in itself was going to cause a problem as Mirabella was accustomed to bathing herself in her wash basin in the privacy of her own room, a decided luxury compared to the cracked clay bowl she and her older sisters had shared in Dumfriesshire.

But she would require the copper tub to clean up from this night, which would alert her aunt to their outing. Martha Hudson's lodgings at 221 Baker Street had on the premises a large copper tub which the landlady placed in her kitchen every Sunday morning before church. Aunt Martha then heated the hot water, allowing for a bath for herself each week.

Mirabella sighed. Every day working alongside Sherlock Holmes was making her less modest. Some might go so far as to say that living under Sherlock's influence was turning her into a disrespectable young lady.

Only those objecting to grave robbing, she supposed.

"Is something amusing, Miss Hudson?" Sherlock demanded.

She bit her lip. "Not in the least."

"Good." Sherlock returned his attention to the body. "What does Moriarty want—and *why*?" Sherlock mused, as if talking to himself. "Why did this man need to die? Why did Moriarty kill him? Of what possible benefit was killing a cleric in the war secretary's office?"

"For information?" Dr. Watson asked.

"A dead informant is not very talkative," Mirabella said.

"Agreed. Perhaps Moriarty got the information he was seeking," Sherlock said. "No doubt the location of the *Abdül Hamid* plans—or a sufficient hint. Still, something doesn't set well with me. Moriarty doesn't kill for no reason, and Hamilton was a valuable informant."

"If there were drugs involved, perhaps Hamilton was killed accidentally," Dr. Watson said. "It is next to impossible to know each person's fatal dose."

"But why were drugs utilized?" Sherlock considered. "Torture or the threat of death is the more common venue. One wishes the victim to be cognizant, after all."

"It does seem strange," Mirabella said. "Why was he killed?"

"And let's not forget 'how,'" Sherlock said.

"I thought you said it was morphine—" Mirabella said.

"We don't know that without the data," Sherlock said. "And it might not have been the only substance in his system. I detected another scent, in addition to the cigar smoke, however faint. I think a mistake was made, and Hamilton died. I must find the other substance. This holds the clue to the man's death."

"Holmes, what did you mean when you said the white teeth revealed that Moriarty was the murderer?" Dr. Watson asked.

"I smelled *La Intimidad* on the victim's suit," Sherlock said. "There's not a handful of men in London who can afford that cigar, Hamilton not being one among them. He was a cleric in a politician's office. Besides, there is nothing to indicate that Hamilton was a smoker. His teeth were white."

CHAPTER SIX
A Hidden Message

Sherlock picked up the latest edition of the *Guardian*, pushing the *Pall Mall Gazette* off to the side of his marble end table momentarily. "Listen to this Watson: a Mr. Thomas Heaphey stated that he saw the apparition of a lady not once, but thrice, and the third time she asked him to paint her portrait. Such a strange request from a ghost, don't you think, old chap?"

"Damn you, Holmes! Listen to me!" Watson stood in front of him. "Moriarty and his sister appear to be on excellent terms."

"I assure you I am listening, my good man," said Sherlock, his eyes returning to the paper as he leaned back into the satin rose wingback chair next to the fire. "You were speaking of Fantine Florentine, formerly Fantine Moriarty, but I thought a ghost who wished her portrait painted far more interesting. Whatever do you think the specter's purpose was in doing so?"

"Think, Holmes! I must assume that Fantine is the woman in the police report?"

"Correct."

"Then the last time you saw the woman she attempted to poison you! And then chained you to a bed!" The sleeves of his white cotton shirt were rolled up, and as his hands tightened around his leather suspenders.

"Oh, that was only because I wouldn't cooperate," Sherlock shrugged, glancing up. "She didn't mean to hurt me."

"She didn't mean to hurt you? What did she mean to do . . . *precisely?*"

"Obtain information," Sherlock stated, his eyes glued to the *Guardian*. "Use your brain, old man."

"So because her *intent* was not to hurt you, the fact that she *did* hurt you is of no consequence?" Watson demanded.

"Precisely." Sherlock nodded. "Besides . . . all she did was drug me. It is very unlikely I would have died from it."

"True, her brand of poison is candy to you and the usual drugs you ingest. But she did not know that."

"Hmmm. . . . what? . . . No, I suppose not," said Sherlock. "Though I do expect the lovely Fantine administered a full strength dose of whatever it was she gave me. No doubt she thought it was so, at any rate."

"Holmes, pay attention! You may be a scientific genius, but when it comes to women, I have the superior knowledge."

"You shall get no argument from me on that point, my friend."

"And you are like a lamb to the slaughter, Holmes. You're as naïve as a schoolroom miss at her first presentation."

"Really Watson! All because of a failed date? Are you telling me that you have never had an encounter with the opposite sex end in disappointment?"

Watson leaned forward in his chair. "No, Holmes, I have *never* had a date poison me. And I have *always* held the upper hand where women are concerned."

"Your matrimonial state is evidence to the contrary," Sherlock murmured, picking up his pipe.

"I should say it is proof of my success. But let us return to your obsession with Fantine Noel, if we may," Watson replied curtly, assuming a superior stance. "If you cannot discuss it as a friend, let me address it as your doctor who is interested in your continued existence."

"Unnecessary. It was actually a delightful interlude. Perfectly enjoyable." Sherlock smiled at his friend.

"Delightful? Enjoyable? Have you lost your blasted mind, man? You awoke chained to a bed."

Sherlock raised his eyebrows at his friend as he lit his pipe. "Have you tried it, my dear Dr. Watson?"

"If Fantine had wished to, she could have murdered you, Holmes."

"Indisputable proof that the lady meant me no harm."

"But why, Holmes? Why would you cavort with a sorceress?"

"Excellent question, Watson. It's difficult to say."

"Try."

"Perhaps I love the danger. The mystery. The absolute uncertainty." Sherlock leaned back in his chair. "Also, Fantine is an excellent contact for me. She may yet lead me to Moriarty or give me some clue which will aid in my entrapment of him."

"Or she may kill you."

"There is that."

"Honestly, Holmes, for such an intelligent person, you are sometimes a complete idiot. You're playing with fire."

"I assure you, of that I am well aware." A slow smile formed on his lips. "That is precisely why I'm involved."

Sherlock glanced out the window when he heard the first floor door of the flat open and close. *Ah, Mrs. Hudson has a guest.*

"Holmes, have you ever . . . have you known . . . have you ever *been with* any other woman?"

"I wouldn't precisely call Fantine Moriarty a woman."

"What would you call her then?"

"A siren. A witch. A villainess. A lovely interlude." Sherlock sighed. "And anyway, no *real* woman would have me."

"Very likely true."

"Nor would I wish to be entangled." Sherlock neatly folded his paper and set it on the marble-topped end table, glancing up at the clock on the mantel as the bells began to chime. *Noon.* It wouldn't be long now. "Besides, Irene Adler is *the* woman."

"I beg to differ, Holmes. There *are* other women, and Irene Adler is far from the exemplary model of the species. Give me five minutes and I can find one better."

"Hello!" exclaimed Mirabella as she entered the rooms. "And what do you have for me today? Oh, your laboratory is a disaster. I marvel that you haven't fainted from the fumes. Oh, my goodness, how many times have I told you to place the lid tightly on the sulfuric acid?"

"Make that five seconds," said Dr. Watson.

"Excuse me?" asked Mirabella, placing her package on the table.

"Nothing, Miss Mirabella." Watson smiled and looked up from where he was now seated beside the fireplace.

"Have you had lunch?" She turned to face the gentlemen after firmly tightening the lid on the jar, before moving to wipe her hands on a dishcloth.

"Not yet," Sherlock replied, studying her unusual gown. She wore a simple gown quite elegant in it's execution. The design mimicked fancier ball gowns at the same time it was *almost* suitable for movement and work. There was a brown silk underskirt, covered by a burnt orange layer form-fitted in the bodice, quite flattering to her actually, with the material gathered on both sides at the hips, forming a layer of material gathered in folds between the waist and the knees into a bustle. A third layer of lace was strung around the waist. Pearl buttons accented the form-fitted bodice.

All in all it shows Miss Belle's shapeliness to advantage.

If the truth be told, he found her figure most appealing: feminine, but not frail, as so many women of the day were. He liked a woman who looked like she could stand—or run—beside him. A delicate woman was about as much use to him as a screaming baby.

"That's a lovely gown, Miss Mirabella," Dr. Watson interjected softly.

"Thank you, Dr. Watson." She curtseyed.

"A bit dressy for day wear," Sherlock said. "I prefer a simple maid's costume."

"No doubt you do, sir," she said while unwrapping the brown package and laying it on the kitchen counter. "For your lunch I have a delicious tongue. Would you care for a sandwich with mustard and tomato?"

"Sounds perfect," replied Dr. Watson. "And are you pleased to be back from Paris, Miss Mirabella?"

"I can't say as I miss the tigers. I met some interesting people, but *that* was no holiday. Although . . ."—she sighed—"I would like to return to Paris someday if I were there on pleasure rather than on business."

Sherlock glanced at her, imagining a holiday with Miss Belle before he put the thought out of his mind. *Ridiculous.* There was little more revolting than a lecherous old man: he eight and twenty and she eighteen years of age.

He smiled to himself. Besides, there was no reason to place the French in danger. Miss Belle could be a bit accident prone.

"Did you hear the news that the plans for the *Abdül Hamid* have gone missing, Miss Belle?" Sherlock asked.

She turned to face him, her expression suddenly somber. "It's very bad news, isn't it?"

"Exceedingly bad, I should say. It could usher in a tyrant."

Mirabella gasped. "Is it really so bad as that?"

"World domination by an unscrupulous power? Most certainly. It is critical that we recover those plans. And quickly."

"Why are we all sitting about here then, Holmes? Shouldn't we be *doing* something about it?" Watson demanded.

"Tonight," Sherlock said. "Acting in the daylight is an impossibility."

Sherlock turned to Mirabella. "I have a question for you, Miss Belle. A very important question." He noted that she looked at him with grave apprehension. "Why does everyone take me for an ogre? I'm actually a delightful fellow. Fair, just, witty, charming, *brilliant.*"

She placed her hands on her hips. "Is that the question?"

"No, that was a statement of fact."

"And the question?" She tapped her foot on the floor. He might have been annoyed by this a month ago, but he surprised himself that it struck him as amusing.

"Yes, it has distressed me for some little time now." He glanced about at everyone staring at him suspiciously. "And I must say that I don't know why when I am in a good mood everyone is so uncharitable. It would seem that all my associates wish me to be miserable."

Watson shrugged. "It's all we know."

"Do tell? And what is the question?" She pursed her lips. He had to admit she looked quite fetching in her gown, wisps of hair on her cheeks, with a touch of flame in her eyes.

"If you were a ghost, Miss Belle, what possible reason could you have for wanting your portrait painted?"

"If I were . . . a *ghost?*" She stared at him as if he had lost his mind.

"You heard me, Miss Belle, please answer the question." He pointed to the newspaper. "I'm in something of a rush and I don't have time to repeat everything as you generally require."

"Well, I . . ."

"Do answer the question, Miss Mirabella," Watson pleaded. "Or we shall never have any peace. Pretend that it is a reasonable question rather than the incomprehensible babbling of a madman."

"Oh, yes, yes, I see," she said, Watson's words obviously channeling her confusion into action.

"A ghost who wants her portrait painted?" Mirabella repeated. "Well, let's see. . . I suppose it is conceivable that one could be more beautiful as an apparition than one was in real life—perhaps if one had blemishes in life and the skin were smoother."

"Smoother skin when one is dead?" Watson repeated, his dismay apparent.

"Or maybe one has a glow about one—as a ghost, I mean."

"Undoubtedly," agreed Watson. "Goes without saying. Take a note of that, Holmes, because once your lady friend has killed you, it will be your comfort."

Mirabella's mouth dropped open. "Lady friend? *Mr. Holmes?* You can't be serious!" Suddenly understanding appeared to dawn on her. "You don't mean the woman at the sidewalk café in Paris, do you? The countess?"

"Precisely," Dr. Watson said.

Mirabella shivered. "She made me nervous. And isn't she your arch enemy's sister?" Mirabella shook her head. "Do you really think that wise, Mr. Holmes?"

"You see, everyone thinks you're a fool, Holmes," Watson muttered under his breath.

"No," Sherlock disagreed. "Only those who know me well."

Mirabella placed her hands on her waist. "And, honestly, Countess Florentine didn't seem very nice."

"Not at all," Sherlock agreed.

"My father says never to start down that thorny path," she added. "You might get so entrenched in the weeds that it is difficult to extract yourself from them."

"Very eloquently put, Miss Belle. So you think the only reason for the apparition's portrait request could be one of vanity?" Sherlock persisted.

"Naturally I do not! You didn't give me much time to reflect on the answer, Mr. Holmes. It is not a question I have often considered."

"I should hope not," said Watson.

"A detective must think on her feet," said Sherlock. "There is rarely any time for reflection."

"D-do you believe in ghosts, Mr. Holmes? I wouldn't have thought it.

You're so eminently logical."

"To be intelligent one must be open to all possibilities. To configure one's world in one's own small image is the mistake of most," stated Sherlock. "One can have the most brilliant mind on the Earth—I am only in the top ten, mind you—but if one does not consider every possibility, one has nothing."

"Top ten? Do you mean to say, Holmes, that you consent that there might be nine people in the entire world more intelligent than you?" Watson asked.

"Certainly not." Sherlock chuckled at the humor of the remark. "But I don't wish to appear conceited."

"It's a mental exercise, nothing more, Miss Mirabella," said Watson, returning his eyes to his newspaper. "Holmes doesn't believe in ghosts any more than Lestrade believes in fairies. When Holmes doesn't wish to discuss a particular topic, he always invents these ludicrous games."

"I am most impressed, Watson. You do make progress despite all evidence to the contrary." Sherlock nodded approvingly. "But I find the game interests me. Continue, Miss Belle, answer the question."

"Maybe she wished to be remembered and there were no portraits in life," she reflected, sighing. "Maybe she was quite *lonely* in life. . ."

"Very sad. Holmes, I never thought I'd say this, but do get out your violin and play along," suggested Watson.

"Or maybe . . . maybe it was to get a message to someone. A *secret message*." Mirabella's eyes lit up as she easily entered into the spirit of the thing. An endearing quality actually, her romantic imagination combined with her sweetness and eagerness to enjoy herself. "Something in her appearance you know—a locket, perhaps—which bore a secret message that only the viewer would know."

"Certainly it's a possibility." Sherlock nodded.

"If one is an addle-headed idiot, it is," agreed Watson. "And a love-sick puppy."

"But often doesn't one wish to have one's portrait painted because one is in love with the painter?" asked Mirabella dreamily. Sherlock half expected her to twirl around the room in her lovely gown, her hair flying here and there.

"Read that in one of your novels, have you, Miss Mirabella?" Watson smiled for the first time.

"And I think it the most likely explanation," stated Sherlock approvingly. "Excellent work, Miss Belle."

"Mr. Holmes, are you feeling quite all right?" she managed to utter.

"No, he's not," uttered Watson. "He's a bloody fool."

"Shall I get you a sherry, Mr. Holmes?" Mirabella pressed, concern now written across her face. "This conversation—it *isn't like you*."

"There you've hit the nail on the head," said Watson.

"I won't be here for lunch," Sherlock stood, arranging his white silk tie. He glanced in the mirror over the fireplace and combed his hand through his hair. "I have a lunch date."

"A lunch *date*?" she asked peering around the corner where she had hurried to procure a glass of sherry.

"Are you asking me for more information, Miss Belle?" Sherlock asked with raised eyebrows.

"Of course not! You're my employer, of what possible right would I have to quiz you?"

"This would be the first time you haven't, Miss Belle."

"Although—" she began.

"Here it comes," said Sherlock, bestowing a rare smile upon Watson.

"It would only be common courtesy to let me know if you won't be here for lunch as I do plan my life around your every need not to mention your every whim, Mr. Sherlock Holmes."

"No matter, I'll have the tongue for dinner," he replied, shutting the door behind him as he exited the room.

He waited for an instant outside the door, counting on his hand. When he reached "five" he began to hear her voice through the door, commiserating with Watson.

It appears I'll have the tongue now and later. He chuckled to himself, taking the steps two at a time.

CHAPTER SEVEN
Cadbury's Chocolate Factory

Bridge Street, Birmingham

CLICK! CLICK!

"Ah, there's the lock," Babbitt said, smiling. The grey fog grew dense around them, making their nefarious goals easier to achieve.

Babbitt opened the dark brown door. "What's this place, boss? An opium den? A gaming house? I know it ain't the morgue. That's me favorite. Sometimes I go there on me afternoon off."

"No doubt. One wishes to be with family on holiday."

"What do you mean, boss?"

Professor Moriarty pointed to the sign over the door they had just broken into. *Cadbury's Chocolates.* "Can't you read, Babbitt?"

"Nah, never had the time to learn."

Moriarty swatted Babbitt's arm with his ebony walking cane, shaking his head. *I wish I could get another like Colonel Moran.*

"*Ouch!* What were that fer?" Babbitt exclaimed.

"Perhaps you had best take the time to learn to read now. Talk to Flanders and he'll arrange it. I won't have any idiots working for me." Not that being able to read would help this one. Moriarty looked him up and down. "And while you're at it, get a new jacket. That one is threadbare."

"Sure, boss." Babbitt smiled, apparently liking the idea of a smart jacket.

"And don't kill anyone. I'll buy it."

Babbitt's face fell. "If you say so, Professor."

Moriarty looked around at the large chocolate vats, the assembly lines, and the ribbons and decorative boxes.

"What are we doin' 'ere, boss?" Babbitt stared at his boss in surprise. "Are you 'ungry? Har! Har!"

"Shhh! Be quiet." Moriarty motioned to some of the 'fancy boxes', elaborate heart-shaped velvet boxes with ribbons, often kept as keepsakes by their recipients even after the confections were gone. The expense of the boxes alone put chocolates out of the range of most pocketbooks. "Get thirty of those."

Another of Babbitt's associates moved to collect the boxes.

"We ain't goin' for the big stuff no more? I love the big capers."

"Not at all. Theft, pickpockets, smuggling, rail hold-ups—that's all penny-ante stuff."

"I know you go in for what looks legal but what makes more money, Professor." Babbitt took his index finger and tapped his brain a few times. "That ways the law can't go after youse."

"Indeed, very observant of you, Babbitt." Like the run on the stocks from last week after his purchase only to have the stocks triple in value. Moriarty had made enough to retire on that one. But naturally he wasn't discussing his exploits with anyone who didn't need to know.

And it was all on a need-to-know basis.

"Then what is we doin' here in a chocolate factory?"

We're taking over the world, you idiot.

"We're collecting thirty fancy boxes of the world's finest chocolate," Moriarty replied under his breath. "Pay attention and do your job."

"Yes, sir. Why don't you jus' buy 'em? You're rich, gov'ner!"

"So there is no record of the transaction, imbecile!"

"I'll bet somehow it's for money," Babbitt insisted as he placed the boxes in the bag he had carried along. "It's always for money."

"The strange thing about money is that you think it will satisfy you until you have it. You would do better to mind your own business and to perform your job," Professor Moriarty said. "If you weren't so capable at breaking into everything, and so willing to murder anyone, be it your own mother or the Queen of England, I'd have been done with you long ago, Babbitt."

"But you wouldn't kill me," Babbitt laughed.

"No, I wouldn't kill you," Moriarty agreed. *As much as I might wish to.* Only a fool went about killing his own employees—word got around quickly about that sort of thing and one was without employees.

Pure idiocy. Moriarty hadn't built a criminal empire being a fool. He actually paid his employees well and had a reputation for being a prince among men with the underclass.

Unless he were crossed. Unless everyone knew the fellow had it coming. Then he had the reputation of being a ruthless shark. That was another way one maintained control: punishing those who were traitors.

Or those who were made to look like traitors.

"How much money is there in chocolate?" Babbitt insisted. "I know it goes for a pretty penny, but—"

"—I have plenty of money," Moriarty replied. *I am revered in the criminal world, but I am forgettable in society. Outside of academia, no one has heard of me.*

I am the most brilliant man in the world and everyone thinks I am a dead bore.

Moriarty was fed up with the empty-headed lords and ladies, those persons of importance, looking at him as if he didn't exist. A duke or a prince walks in the room and everyone almost trips over their own feet to obtain a glimpse of His Royal Highness.

I'm smarter than any birdbrain royal child of first cousins. I may never be adored and worshipped—but those idiots will someday be my pawns.

Moriarty glanced at the pastry tubes used to squirt decorations on the chocolates. Those might come in handy. He pointed to the tubes, indicating that he wished his minions to confiscate them.

I will change the course of history. How is that for power?

"Now shut up and stop asking questions, Babbitt!"

Babbitt appeared a bit dejected momentarily. "Say, boss, that reminds me. Someone else has been asking questions."

Moriarty turned his full attention on his stooge, receiving the reaction Babbitt clearly wished for. Softly he asked, "Who?"

"The madame."

"Jeffries?"

"Uh-huh."

"She's beginnin' to think that she runs London, boss."

This was Moriarty's opinion as well, but he wasn't about to say so.

"London is my town." There was no major criminal in the city who did not answer to him in one way or another.

Except Jeffries.

Worse than that, he was linked to her, and Moriarty cared about his reputation above all else. Every success he had was based on his ability to lead a double life and to present a certain image to society. *Everything* was based on this.

Jeffries was a master of blackmail. She had it down to an art form. She dealt in the ruination of reputations—someone who did not hear the cries of children would not hesitate for an instant to take *anyone* down with her into the depths of hell.

What is there to stop her from taking me?

Mary Jeffries was an astute woman and he admired her for that. Very clever indeed. And her blackmail information had proven interesting reading as well.

"She will have to be removed," Moriarty muttered. He didn't like to do it, and it was a rare thing to dispose of one's own. But the woman had no taste. No breeding.

"Can I do it?"

"She's out of your league, Babbitt. Perhaps Colonel Moran." His number-one man and an expert with a long-range rifle was the one to stop Jeffries one of these late nights when she was returning home.

Babbitt looked so disappointed that even Moriarty felt sorry for him. "Never fear, there will be something for you to do. One might manage to pin the murder on one of the Bobbies as well."

A double win.

CHAPTER EIGHT
A Dubious Association

"Did you see how Mr. Holmes was dressed, Dr. Watson?" Mirabella pressed, resuming her dusting as she pretended to work.

"Cleans up well, doesn't he?" considered John, tapping his fingers on the marble tabletop beside him.

"*Surprisingly so*," she whispered as she dusted the skull on the mantelpiece, even as she glanced at the photo of Miss Adler on Sherlock's desk, the handcuffs beside the photo.

Mirabella stared at the closed door in perplexity. "I have never before seen Mr. Holmes so light, so airy, so . . . *happy*."

"So silly," muttered Dr. Watson, pretending to read his newspaper.

"Precisely!" She turned to stare at him. "I would have sooner thought the world flat than to ever expect to call Sherlock Holmes *silly*."

What kind of ridiculous question had the Great Detective asked her? Why would a ghost want her portrait painted? Sherlock never uttered nonsense. In fact he was always so darn serious.

I like it. As much as she hated to admit it.

Then why did she feel so disturbed?

"I'm afraid there is much more afoot than our friend behaving a bit giddier than usual," John added with foreboding.

"Oh? Whatever do you mean, Dr. Watson?"

"*Danger*. Pure and simple. And who will combat the danger if the great Sherlock Holmes is indisposed?" He flapped his newspaper in an irritated fashion and flung it on the table. "Leaping through the fields, picking daisies, as it were."

Mirabella looked at the good doctor, who was staring at the closed door with an expression of disapproval.

"Do you truly think it is that serious, Dr. Watson?" she asked, pausing from her dusting momentarily. "And do you think Mr. Holmes could be in *love*?"

"Love?" scoffed Dr. Watson. "I guarantee it is not love. But that is not what worries me. It is the utter change in personality. His dress, for example. I mean, Holmes is a handsome enough fellow, but he never pays the slightest attention to his appearance."

"Unless it is to deceive a criminal," she considered.

To be sure, it had been quite a remarkable difference in Sherlock, oh yes. He had been dressed impeccably in a dark blue brocade vest with turquoise threads embroidered throughout, a white silk ascot tie, and a white cotton shirt with blousy sleeves. He wore neatly pressed dark trousers along with a long dark frock coat which almost reached his knees. His black boots were expertly polished.

All that was enough to shock one, but Sherlock did have an excellent tailor and Mrs. Hudson kept his clothing pressed, so it was not entirely unprecedented.

But there was much in his appearance that was uncharacteristic. He had sculpted a goatee beard and a moustache—with all the appropriate places of his face *clean-shaven*. And, as if that were not enough to cause one's heart to stop, his lustrous, dark curls had been fashionably trimmed atop his head!

Sherlock Holmes is behaving more like a dandy of fashion than a police detective.

"Ah, deception. I suppose courting a young lady could be considered a deception of sorts."

"Not for Mr. Holmes." She shook her head in disagreement while straightening the stacks of Sherlock's medical papers. "He is genuine in all things."

In a sudden movement, John arose and walked to the gasogene, where the ginger, sugar, and water were already in the lower compartment. He placed a cup beneath the spout, adding tartaric acid and sodium bicarbonate to the upper compartment. The experiment began, and the carbon dioxide forming which would produce a gas to push the liquid in the lower compartment through the spout in the form of a carbonated ginger beverage, he returned to his seat.

"I've never seen him like this with anyone else," Watson said.

"I've never seen him like this—*ever*," she whispered, leaning against the fireplace mantel. "The Great Detective, the one who cannot be bothered, has succumbed to the services of *a barber*!"

"Yes, Holmes has truly attended to every detail—not for a disguise, but to present himself in the best manner possible." John Watson closed his eyes momentarily, adding, "For that *vulture*."

And then the memory of dancing with Sherlock at Miss de Beauvais' Christmas ball washed over her. Being held in his arms while they danced the waltz. The excitement of dancing the mazurka.

Sherlock smiling down at her.

"Like a moth to the flame," John Watson replied.

"Excuse me?" She reluctantly came back to the present.

"Holmes is a moth to the flame where Countess Florentine is concerned," John repeated.

"Oh, yes. Sorry." She felt herself blushing.

She beheld Dr. John Watson, so concerned for his friend, and it warmed her heart. So much about John was admirable: faithful and loyal to his friends.

John Watson had his own demons, to be sure, as a result of his time spent as a military doctor in Afghanistan. That was no doubt why he took so many risks with Sherlock; throwing himself into the Great Detective's cases kept John's memories at bay—until the night came. Mirabella knew that John often paced the floors during the sleeping hours, the young doctor's bedroom being on the third floor above Sherlock's room.

"What is Fantine Florentine like?" asked Mirabella.

"Like a viper," said Watson. "She is everything that Irene Adler appeared to be and was not: a schemer, a jezebel, a controller of men. Beautiful, amusing, extremely intelligent. I gather that Countess Florentine is a petty jewel thief and uses her contacts on the concert circuit to move in high society: where she also obtains information for her brother, who lacks her charm and charisma. But Fantine, like Moriarty, loves the game, and for that she would gladly throw her mother to the wolves."

"So unlike Mr Holmes."

"True. Holmes is excessively loyal to his friends. He would die for them. Though he does not give his heart freely." John smiled at her, setting his cup on the table. "Forgive my gloominess, Miss Mirabella. It serves no purpose and is most ungentlemanlike to be such a bore in a lady's company."

"I don't want Sherlock to be hurt either," she sighed, plopping down in the basket chair opposite him, her duster hanging from her hand. "For one who is so perceptive, he can be childlike and naïve in some ways."

"Indeed."

Dr. Watson stood and stretched his back, rubbing his injured leg momentarily.

"Miss Mirabella, it's a beautiful day out."

She glanced out the window. "It is."

"Don't you think we should take advantage of this break in the dreary London weather? Would you care to go for a confectionary?"

"I would love it." She threw the duster to the ground and grabbed her hat and coat. She hastened to put on her gloves in a few seconds flat before the most handsome and eligible young doctor could change his mind. They were friends only—and that's how it would stay—but certainly a lady didn't mind the company of a dear friend.

Particularly if he were exceptionally handsome and charming.

CHAPTER NINE
Cadbury's Chocolate Shoppe

"Would you like to be my next husband?"

Sherlock laughed, leaning back in his chair and displaying his polished black boots before him. "Should you like that, my dear countess?"

"I think it would be heavenly," Fantine pronounced with beautiful red lips.

"And how long would that marriage last?" he asked as he brought the teacup to his lips, amused.

"I assure you, darling, that you would be safe. I never kill my husbands."

"Very admirable. Though I venture to say there is always a first time with you."

"You are quite despicable, Sherlock." She placed her gloved hand in front of her lips as her eyes danced. "I have other ways of getting what I need."

"Not what you need, Fantine, what you *want*, let us be honest." He raised his eyebrows at her. "And the count? What would he say to your marrying me while you are still married to him?"

"Oh, I have no doubt he will have the marriage annulled in a short time. We have only to reach a . . . *settlement*."

"Have a care, Countess. Is it good for business? Always enmeshed in scandal, as it were. You are on the concert circuit."

"To the contrary. It adds to my allure."

"You don't need any assistance there, my dear." Sherlock glanced about Cadbury's café, a favorite of the fashionable for coffee, tea, and hot chocolate.

"Why are you here, Fantine?" Sherlock asked. "Or should I say Countess Florentine? I presume that you went to a great deal of trouble to obtain the title."

"Trouble? No, I enjoyed every moment of it." Her lustrous strawberry-blonde curls were arranged atop her head, and from there cascaded down her shoulders. A powder-blue velvet cap was tilted to one angle, from which a magnificent white feather protruded, just tapping her shoulder.

Every eye in the place had glanced her way at least once despite their less than prominent location.

For Sherlock, her allure wasn't because she was a beauty—which she was, make no mistake—but there was many a beauty in London. Combined as it was with her intelligence she was suddenly the woman who had everything.

Well, everything except a conscience. Even that had its advantages.

"May I bring you tea or chocolate?" the waitress asked, curtseying in her dark uniform accessorized with a white apron and white cap. Cadbury's staff was well known for its attentiveness, being trained to treat customers as guests and to make them feel welcome for the entirety of their stay.

Sherlock would have preferred a bit less attention on this day.

"Do you have the Chun Mee green tea?" Fantine asked.

"Yes, miss," the waitress said with an additional curtsey.

"A pot, please," Fantine said. "And you, Sherlock? As I recall, you like your hot cocoa in the morning."

He frowned at her indiscretion before turning to the waitress. "I believe I shall have a pot of cocoa. Cadbury's is the best, I understand."

"I see you have been to Singapore of late, Countess," Sherlock posed once the waitress had left.

"However did you know, Sherlock?"

"You have obviously developed a taste for the little known Chun Mee tea, which is only produced in the Chinese Jiangxi province. In addition, your gown is of an exquisite silk which I expect was made in that same province."

"Hmm, that is scanty evidence. There is more is there not?"

"I do happen to know that the barrister who recently held your interest was employed by the Jardine and Matheson firm, a major exporter of both products. And—he was stationed in Shanghai."

"I am a married woman! I have no personal interest in a barrister." Fantine glanced at him slyly.

"Not unless he were very rich." Sherlock shook his head. This game was almost too dull. "Or had excellent contacts with the very rich."

"I am disappointed in you, Sherlock." She smiled demurely at him. "This is information which is not in evidence on my person and which warranted further research on your part."

"Not precisely. I did notice the Jardine and Matheson emblem on an envelope when you opened your purse."

I wish I might see something in her purse that will lead me to the plans for the Abdül Hamid. Even so, Sherlock knew that if he stayed with Fantine long enough, she would eventually unwillingly lead him there.

"Even so, Jardine ships out of both Hong Kong and Singapore. How did you know which port I was visiting?" she asked.

"That is a simple matter," he replied nonchalantly, bored with the ease of the deduction. "There is more money in Singapore."

"I thank the heavens I do not have your cynical view of things, Sherlock!" She giggled.

"Fantine, do be straight with me for once." He leaned towards her, lowering his voice. "What is your association with Professor Moriarty?"

"He is my brother, of course."

"Is there anything else?" Sherlock demanded. "Why do you lie when I will discover the truth?"

She touched his hand with her gloved hand. "It is the discovery I enjoy."

He pulled his hand away. "You waste my time, Fantine."

"You worry too much, Sherlock." She placed her fan on the table and ran her hands along her slim waist, making a deliberate—and successful—effort to return his eyes to her, the blue satin gown with velvet buttons and lapels adhering perfectly to her exquisite figure.

"I realize, of course, that Moriarty is very jealous of you, Fantine, a violin virtuoso who has both respectability and fame. The professor was never able to gain notoriety outside the academic circuit—and there only in a limited capacity. You, on the other hand, are charismatic, beautiful, and socialize with everyone of note. Moriarty is a background person, a person to be overlooked, which he does not like."

"If James applied his genius to mathematics instead of diverting it to everything else, I expect he would have acquired the chairmanship at Oxford or Cambridge which he desires." Fantine shrugged. "One must decide what one wants and not dissipate one's energy."

"You are one to speak, Fantine. Your music is heavenly. And yet you use the circuit to gain contacts—and to steal: jewelry, information, whatever is handy."

"It is a little hobby of mine. My music is my focus."

"Take care Fantine. You have everything anyone could want. And yet you could throw it all away with your greed." *It runs in your family.* "Why would you jeopardize your musical career? Why don't you instead enjoy the life that you have?"

"You are one to speak, Sherlock. I never saw anyone so gifted with a more self-destructive nature."

"I bring criminals to justice. That is a far different thing from self-destruction."

"The end result is the same."

"Perhaps. But I was speaking of your tendency to self-ruination, not mine." Sherlock fixed his gaze on her. "And your brother's. Moriarty even masterminds mathematics like he does everything else—utilizing his advanced students to do the work rather than doing it himself once he formulates the concept."

"And your point is?"

"Fantine, you're a thief, nothing more. You deal in jewels, valuables, and blackmail when it suits you. Moriarty is cold-hearted and ruthless. I can trace a half a dozen murders to him. You should not associate with him, brother or not."

"He pays well. The concert circuit is not so profitable as you might imagine." But she was no fool, and only a fool would dismiss James Moriarty's danger. "Why don't you put him in jail if you know all this?"

"His web is too intricate and his barristers too clever." He put the porcelain cup to his lips and enjoyed a sip of steaming chocolate. "Don't align yourself with the devil, Fantine."

"James' game is so much more fun. So ingenious." She leaned forward and touched his hand. "And *lucrative*."

"Ah, so now I know. You enjoy being a criminal—just as your brother does."

"I wish you wouldn't put it that way, darling." She lowered her aquamarine-blue eyes, even as she smiled, her lightheartedness restored.

"You are an exceptional talent, Fantine, but I wonder how much you love the money and the fame." Sherlock glanced about the dining room, mentally assessing all the occupants. He was unable to stop himself from doing so even in the presence of such captivating company.

"Naturally I do," she said sweetly.

"Have a care, Fantine," he replied coolly, his eyes still on the shop's inhabitants. It was a small shop, crammed to overflowing with patrons. The shop front was painted white with purple trim, but inside the surroundings were much more neutral, with white walls, beige trim, and black furniture. It was always crowded—too crowded—with a decor very like a home.

"I don't know why I go anywhere with you, Sherlock. No man ignores me like you do."

"No doubt." He returned his eyes to her. "Do give up the idea of marriage to me, Countess, if in fact you ever considered it. I do not have sufficient money to tempt you."

"But you do have other things to tempt me." She glanced at him with mischief in her eyes, running her eyes along his torso.

"And inevitably I would have to put you in jail," he added, ignoring her flirtation. "That would be the greatest loss to the concert circuit. I myself could not bear it."

"Nor I. The money I can get for myself. But jail—oh no, that would never do."

"Better that than the hangman's noose." He raised his teacup to her.

"And better to be enemies, I think, Countess."

"It is much cleaner," she agreed.

"That is why you don't care for it."

She smiled, her red lips seductive as she took a sip of tea. With delightful enemies such as this, who needed friends? Sadly, he enjoyed Fantine Noel's company more than that of most, despite knowing that she rarely spoke the truth and was generally playing him for a fool.

As a bearded gentleman approached them, and Sherlock observed a slight discomfort in Fantine's countenance.

"Countess Florentine. Mr. Holmes." Richard Cadbury bowed to the countess, his long white beard reaching almost to his waist in the process, missing her brief expression of discomfiture which she was unable to hide. He was balding but had no shortage of facial hair. He wore a dark frock coat and a white cotton shirt which somehow complemented his long beard.

"That new confection you have developed is absolutely divine, Mr. Cadbury!" she exclaimed with a bit too much enthusiasm.

Sherlock's interest was piqued, as Fantine was obviously on good terms with the second son of Mr. Cadbury and the founder of the shop. Richard and George had taken over the firm in 1861 and made it the success it was today.

"Chocolate candy?" asked Mr. Cadbury, chuckling. "Is that which thou refers to, Countess Florentine?"

"Oh, yes, I love it," she said.

"I thank thee, Countess Florentine. Many people do love the confections, it seems."

"And what is the secret to the *divine* flavor?" she begged. Though it seemed to Sherlock that she was attempting to distract Richard Cadbury. Sherlock knew that quality of Fantine's intimately.

"I grind the cocoa beans and then mix them with the sweetened condensed milk," replied Mr. Cadbury without further adieu. "It sounds quite simple, but it is actually a complex process requiring expensive machinery."

"How clever." She reached for her reticule. "Well, I think we must be going."

"I want to thank thee for thy recent order, Countess Florentine," said Richard Cadbury.

A frozen smile crossed her expression.

Mr. Cadbury continued, "It is strange. I had heard from several that thou had made a gift of a fancy box to them—and yet I have no record of such an order."

This is it. This is the key to Fantine's dealings with Moriarty—and the submarine plans. Sherlock looked at his hands momentarily as if he were bored by the conversation, but he kept his eye on both parties.

Fantine appeared unconcerted. "My assistant picked up the chocolates naturally—not on my account. And paid cash."

"There was a theft of thirty boxes out of your warehouse, was there not, Mr. Cadbury? I believe I read about it in the *Gazette*."

Richard Cadbury appeared alarmed. "I meant to draw no correlation! I was merely curious as to who picked up the boxes she distributed." He bowed to her. "I beg thou wouldst forgive me. I never meant . . . "

"Ah. A large order, Countess?" Sherlock asked while tapping his fingers on the table as if the answer were of little interest to him. "I did not realize you had such a weakness for sweets."

"Oh, the chocolate delicacies were not for me." Fantine laughed lyrically, revealing her musical roots as she bent close to Mr. Cadbury.

"Who were the confections for then?" persisted Sherlock.

"You surprise me, Sherlock! I have many friends in London, and what better way to express my affection and incite reciprocation than with a box of chocolates?" She pouted. "Everything I do is not a devious plot."

"You don't say," Sherlock murmured.

"Oh, look! Mr. Darwin!" she exclaimed. She motioned with her eyes to Mr. Cadbury.

"Sir Francis Darwin, the esteemed son of Charles Darwin," Richard Cadbury smiled with interest. "And my customer."

"This is certainly the meeting place for all of London," said Sherlock. "So many religious groups take great offence at Mr. Darwin's scientific theories. Do the Quakers find them objectionable?"

"Is thou asking if I will refuse to sell Sir Francis Darwin chocolate because of the difference in our religious beliefs?" Mr. Cadbury grinned. "No, we do not differentiate there. We are all God's children. Above all the Quakers believe that the Light of God is present in every person of every faith, and even present in those who profess to have no faith."

"A radical notion to be sure," Sherlock said. "Some do an excellent job of ignoring that light. I make their acquaintance daily."

"That wouldst be free will," nodded Mr. Cadbury. "But the light is there nonetheless."

"This is where we enter theory without any evidence of scientific fact," said Sherlock.

"Please do not argue with the best chocolatier in London, Sherlock," Fantine pleaded.

"I wonder, Mr. Cadbury, if I may ask for Countess Florentine's sake, who struggles daily with her love of riches," pursued Sherlock. "You are clearly a religious man—and yet so wealthy. Does wealth pose a difficulty for you?"

"Wealth? A difficulty?" laughed Fantine. "Honestly, Sherlock, I have heard you say some ridiculous things, but that—"

"I am asking Mr. Cadbury, not you, Fantine. You make no secret of your love of riches, but I venture to suppose that Mr. Cadbury worships Another. And yet, the great irony is that I suspect he is wealthier than you are, my dear."

She frowned at Sherlock, apparently not liking the idea that anyone should be wealthier than she.

"It is quite a paradox, isn't it?" Sherlock smiled as he removed his pipe from his pocket. "He who doesn't seek wealth should have so much—and you who live for riches can never have enough."

Her frown deepened.

"I shall answer thee, Mr. Holmes," Mr. Cadbury began solemnly. "As Quakers, English law bans us from university to study law or medicine. Education is most important to us, but it was denied us. Business and agriculture are the only professions open to us."

"And yet you show no bitterness to those who persecute you."

"He merely takes their money," mused Fantine. "If they want the chocolate, they must pay."

"To take was never the intent. We only wished to serve according to God's will," continued Mr. Cadbury calmly. "We began by looking for an alternative to gin which has done a great disservice to the poor. So, we started our coffee and tea business. The exotic cocoa bean intrigued us."

"That bean has done very well by you," commented Sherlock, motioning about the shop.

"There were many lean years at the beginning. Still I always sought to do God's will in everything I did." Mr. Cadbury bowed to his guests. "I don't wish to keep thee any longer, I shall return to my work."

As Richard Cadbury walked away, it struck Sherlock that he had been in the company of the pure of heart. Not something he often encountered in his line of work.

"I don't think I would care for the morning prayers and daily Bible readings," whispered Fantine to Sherlock once Richard Cadbury was out of earshot.

"The bigger problem, my dear countess, is that thievery is against the Quaker belief," considered Sherlock reflectively.

"Very closed-minded, indeed. I do hate a religion with too many rules, don't you, Sherlock?" She shook her head. "Perhaps it is not the religion for me."

"Very true, Countess Florentine, you need a much more forgiving God."

"I assure you that God delights in my existence, Sherlock," she whispered, adding, "as do *you*."

"Your existence, yes. Your behavior—questionable. Oh, no!" said Sherlock, looking towards the door. "What are *they* doing here?"

CHAPTER TEN
The Party Grows

"Holmes," acknowledged Watson coolly, approaching the party of two with Mirabella on his arm, looking quite dapper in his pecan-brown top hat with brown satin trim.

"Well, if it isn't Dr. Watson and Sherlock's illustrious bottle washer," mused Countess Florentine. "My she does get about."

Sherlock was clearly annoyed that Fantine had identified her. But Mirabella refused to let anything diminish this marvelous day. How were they to know that Sherlock was at Cadbury's Shoppe? That is the last place she expected to see the Great Detective.

She felt a stab of jealousy as she beheld Sherlock's ravishing lady friend.

"Sherlock, you really must introduce us formally." Fantine Noel turned to her distinguished companion with indignation. "This is becoming quite absurd."

"It will go no further than here, do you understand, Fantine?" Sherlock replied with a sternness which was severe even for him.

Countess Florentine momentarily opened her mouth in surprise, covering perfect red lips with a white glove before replying, "Well, of course, Sherlock, if you wish."

"I do."

"As you have surmised, this is my laboratory assistant."

"And her *name?*" Countess Florentine demanded.

"Miss Mirabella."

"And her last name?" Countess Florentine leaned forward.

"Miss Mirabella will suffice."

"Miss Mirabella. I really must say I am quite astonished. Sherlock is quite protective of you."

"He hasn't always been so, I assure you, Countess Florentine," Mirabella replied, curtseying. "This is a recent development and likely to be revoked at any moment. I have no doubt that he will throw me in harm's way at the earliest opportunity."

"Oh, she is amusing!" Fantine laughed.

"What are you doing here?" demanded Sherlock in his unfailingly direct manner, indicating that the opportunity for harm's way was soon approaching.

"It occurred to me that Miss Mirabella might enjoy a visit to Mr. Cadbury's shop," remarked Dr. Watson offhandedly. "Didn't know you were here, old boy."

"Didn't you? It appears everyone is," said Sherlock.

Mirabella seated herself without an invitation, Dr. Watson following suit even as he nodded stiffly to Fantine. Mirabella continued chattering happily while intermittently looking about the shop and smiling to the waitress. *Oh my, what a treat this is!*

"There is no need to be seated, Miss Belle. Perhaps it is time to take some exercise. I should think a chocolate would do unwanted damage to the waistline," remarked Sherlock.

"Would you, Mr. Holmes? Well, I shan't come to this shop without having a cup of tea—and I shall save the chocolate sweet for later." In all honesty, she didn't know when she had had a lovelier day, and she refused to let Sherlock Holmes in one of his sour moods spoil it.

Besides, no employer provided more unwanted exercise than Sherlock Holmes, and well he knew it. If she wasn't escaping man-eating carnivores, she was engaged in a knife fight with kidnappers or searching a murderer's room. The only thing she hadn't done yet was jump into the mouth of a volcano, but no doubt that would be required in time.

Still, she wouldn't give up her life for anything. *Almost* anything.

She turned to Dr. Watson and asked amiably, "What would you like Dr. Watson? A hot chocolate perhaps?"

"English tea, of course. I don't wish to drink my dessert."

Mirabella laughed liltingly. "How clever you are, Dr. Watson."

"Exceedingly clever," remarked Sherlock with a raised eyebrow as he glared at the two of them. "I can't recall when I've been more amused."

The waitress took their orders, returning quickly with the steaming beverages.

"What a delightful time this is," sighed Mirabella. Of the party of four, the two ladies appeared pleased with the company and the surroundings and the two gentlemen anything but.

"I presume you have finished your work, Miss Belle."

"Oh, I'm taking a holiday today," Mirabella said, smiling demurely.

"Are you?" asked Sherlock pointedly. "What a lenient employer you must have."

"The Saturday half-day, you know." She nodded definitively.

"It isn't Saturday," Sherlock said.

"It isn't? How foolish of me!" Mirabella giggled.

Countess Florentine smiled at her, clearly enjoying the show. "Oh, let the child have a bit of fun, Sherlock."

Mirabella bit her lip. She didn't like being called a child, although she hoped rather than believed that it was meant kindly. She was beginning to think she could like this Fantine Noel despite the beauty's earlier frostiness—and her obvious hold on Sherlock. Mirabella couldn't like that, though she wasn't certain why.

At any rate, Mirabella wouldn't have purposely defied Sherlock had he informed them where he was going, but since they were here she had best acquaint herself with the countess. In the interest of the case of course.

Mirabella felt her determination rising. Sherlock had once called her 'the first lady detective,' and she had best behave like one.

"It interests me excessively that my employee should be taking a holiday without my approval, regardless of the day of the week. At any rate, the half-day off is Mr. Cadbury's invention, not mine, which makes it entirely irrelevant where *my* employee is concerned."

"Of course it wasn't yours, Mr. Holmes," smiled Mirabella. "That would require an act of good will."

"And the abandonment of logic," Sherlock added.

"Oh, I don't know," considered Watson, leaning back in his chair and running his hands along his leather suspenders. "It has everything to do with logic. A happy employee is a productive employee."

"It is quite obvious that there is a nonexistent productivity amongst my employees, excluding the Baker Street Irregulars," said Sherlock solemnly. "And seeing as how Miss Hudson appears excessively jubilant, I must conclude that there is an inverse relationship between happiness and productivity."

CHAPTER ELEVEN
Unfinished Business

"I have a job for you, Moran," Moriarty said.

"The madame?" Colonel Moran, formerly of the 1st Bangalore Pioneers, expert long-distance shooter, and Moriarty's chief of staff, took a long puff on his cigar.

Moriarty nodded. "It can't be helped."

"It might have to be."

"What do you mean, Moran?" Moriarty grew alarmed as he stared at the colonel's frozen expression. The colonel was a gentleman, after all. "Do you have an aversion to shooting a woman?"

"In most cases, yes. But not in this one. She is more serpent than woman."

"What then?"

"Jeffries has a letter with her lawyer, a Mr. Reynolds, to be opened in the event of her death. It pinpoints you, Professor, and outlines everything she knows about your operation. She wants to be a partner, you see."

"How do you know all this Moran?"

"She told me. No doubt knowing I would tell you. I have confirmed it with Mr. Reynolds."

"*Blazes to hell!* I wish I'd never crossed paths with her." It was rare for Moriarty to feel that anyone had any power over him, and it was not a feeling he cared for.

"Everyone who knows her feels the same." Moran tapped his cigar into the ashtray. "And what about the submarine plans?"

"I have the original in my possession," Moriarty said.

"Have you made a copy?"

Moriarty shook his head. "The original blueprint penned by its designer, Thorsten Nordenfelt, is the only credible design. Even the slightest alteration in the measurements can make it worthless. Remember, there are others who have tried and failed. The *Abdül Hamid* is the *only* submarine plan with a working torpedo. All the others failed the test. A reproduction would be worth a fraction of the original."

"Still, it is a necessary precaution. You have several good forgers on staff. Why don't you use them?" Moran took a puff on his cigar, blowing circles into the air. "You might be able to convince someone that the copy was the original."

Moriarty stared at his second in command with disbelief. "The temptation is too great to steal it for themselves. Surely you can see that, Moran."

"I'll keep an eye on them." Moran's expression was intense. "I am not one to be trifled with."

"The blueprint is more valuable that the queen's jewels and represents a great deal more power. No, I can't trust anyone but myself. When I have time, I'll do it myself, but right now I have bigger fish to fry." Moriarty fixated his gaze on the colonel. "And even you don't have eyes in the back of your head, Moran. At any rate, I want those eyes on Jeffries. While I represent a threat to the queen, Jeffries represents a threat to *me*."

"What will we do if we can't dispose of her?" Moran asked bluntly. "Make her your partner?"

Moriarty frowned. "That would be like welcoming the Black Plague into one's home."

"She's a loose canon, to be sure." Moran nodded in agreement. "And a threat to me as well. I am mentioned in that letter to Reynolds."

CHAPTER TWELVE
Scandal

ARE WE A GODLESS NATION?
How long will Great Britain remain "great"?
PM COVORTING WITH LADIES OF THE NIGHT

Will I be able to stop Moriarty? Or is England doomed?

Even though Sherlock had been expecting it, the headline scattered across *Punch* sent chills down his spine. It was like a dark mist building through-out England.

Moriarty was awaiting the right moment of pageantry, Sherlock had no doubt.

A dead body, missing submarine plans, and an infiltration of government. There was no time to waste.

Now the real work begins.

***

Mirabella was unaccustomed to seeing an expression of concern on Sherlock's countenance while reading *Punch*, so her interest was immediately piqued. *Punch* was a gossip periodical he often purchased for amusement rather than for information, she knew.

"What do you see now, old chap?" asked Watson, leaning towards him in his chair opposite.

Sherlock read aloud,

WHO RULES THE KINGDOM?
Queen still in mourning
twenty-three years after death of Prince Consort
HAS THE MONARCHY SEEN ITS DAY?

"How terrible to insult both the queen and the P.M.!" Her curate father was absolutely appalled at the insults now being published in the newspapers veiled as information. "Perhaps we truly are a Godless nation."

"Undoubtedly, but I can live with that," muttered Sherlock. "However, being an immoral nation is a concern."

"I never realized that immorality was a concern of yours, Mr. Holmes." Mirabella smiled sweetly as she arranged the dusted the skull on the mantel.

"It is. Though perhaps not as much as being a nation under the control of a foreign power," Sherlock added. "Does someone wish to bring down our system of government—or give someone else a foothold to do so?"

"But you never take anything in *Punch* seriously, Holmes," Dr. Watson said. "On more than one occasion you have said that there is no more than a grain of truth in the entire publication."

"I might say so, but that doesn't mean the rest of the country disregards it," Sherlock said.

"True, most people don't read the intellectual papers," John added. "*Punch* could do much more damage than the *Pall Mall*, simply because it has a wider readership."

Sherlock appeared deep in reflection. "First the country is threatened with the leak of the submarine plans, and now the queen herself is attacked."

Disturbed by the headlines, in her distracted state Mirabella glanced out the bay window looking onto Baker Street to see an organ grinder singing and boys running in and out of the pedestrians. A cabbie stopped in front of the flat and someone unusually tall stepped out, but she could not make out his identity as his top hat blocked her view of his face.

Is he coming here? She couldn't tell as the stranger had stepped out of her view. And why would a gentleman be in attendance? She smoothed her orange silk gown and glanced at the clock.

Six o'clock. Early for dinner but far too late for visiting. No gentleman of any breeding would attempt such a thing—unless it were a desperate matter.

"Miss Hudson, have you forgotten something?" observed Sherlock quietly. "Our dinner perhaps?"

Unfortunately, I have forgotten nothing. Mirabella looked over her shoulder at Sherlock as she moved to the door.

Knock! Knock!

"Ah, so you were paying attention," said Sherlock, a sudden light in his steel-grey eyes as he ran his hand through his raven curls. "Did you hear the footsteps on the stairs?"

"Yes, I did, that's why I went to the door," she said under her breath. *Your powers of observation are slipping, Mr. Holmes.*

"What? Speak up! Really, my girl, you are most disturbingly inattentive of late."

Mirabella bit her lip even as she reached for the doorknob, pulling it open a bit more forcefully than was necessary.

"Mr. Holmes!" she exclaimed. There before her was the more charming of the Holmes brothers.

By a long shot.

She had only encountered Mycroft Holmes briefly—at the *Cirque d'Hiver* in Paris—but he was not one who was easy to forget.

"Miss Hudson." The elder Holmes brother nodded cordially, a lock of black hair falling onto his forehead as he did so, acknowledging her even before turning to the gentlemen present. *None* of Sherlock Holmes' other guests had ever shown her that courtesy.

"How do you do, sir?" she gushed, taking their guest's black top hat and white silk opera scarf, sighing as his gloved hand brushed her hand.

I am not man crazy, truly I am not. But neither am I blind. She knew very well that there was not a woman in the world whose head would not be turned by Mycroft Holmes.

Mirabella was also quite aware that the debonair Mycroft Holmes meant to take no particular notice of her. It was mere amiability: Mycroft was congenial to everyone. But no gentleman treated her with as much reverent politeness as did Mycroft Holmes. In fact, most gentlemen would ignore a servant girl. Good looks were a common enough thing among gentlemen, but a working girl was unaccustomed to respect and kindness from such a man. His charm was definitely not lost on her.

"You do look well, Miss Hudson. The burnt orange silk is most becoming with your chestnut brown hair." Mycroft smiled warmly at her, his resonant baritone voice trailing off in a most inviting manner. "Very few women can wear orange to advantage."

"Thank you, sir." *Don't let it go to your head, girl.* Mirabella reprimanded herself for feeling a bit heady over the compliment: she reminded herself that if she were a high-born girl instead of a servant girl, she would not be able to be alone in this room with three gentlemen without a chaperone.

And that's all she was: a servant girl. The only difference between her and a domestic was that she wasn't wearing a black dress with a white apron and hat—she was allowed to wear her own clothing.

For now. Her attire was recompense for the two cases she had assisted Sherlock with. Whether or not there would be other cases remained to be seen. Sherlock had twice now inferred that she was the world's first female detective, but he very soon relapsed into treating her like the scullery maid and intimating that she was not capable of handling the danger.

Perhaps it is for the best. As exhilarating as working on the cases was, Mirabella had been alarmed to discover just how dangerous detective work was. Her dream had always been to study science at university, and she did hope to someday attend with a body. She didn't wish to be the ghost in

Sherlock's story attending university.

Mycroft handed his cane to her, a gesture that very quickly reminded her of her place.

"Is something amiss, Miss Hudson?" Mycroft asked. "You're shaking your head. Do you dislike my gloves? You know, I have had the same thought myself. I don't believe the gloves quite realize the claims that were made about their superb quality."

"Oh, no, the gloves, they are . . . *very fine.*"

She stole a glance at Mycroft. As was their owner. And yet, everything about Mycroft Holmes was, well, *too perfect.* He always moved as if he were conserving energy, while Sherlock had much in common with the gnat, zipping here and there. Make no mistake, none of Sherlock's movements were unnecessary, but there was never even a second's hesitation in doing that which needed to be done.

Mirabella positively could not envision the elder Holmes brother running along a railroad track, scouring the sewers, getting on his hands and knees in the dirt to look for clues—and certainly not in the boxing ring.

"You have saved my glove-maker's reputation for yet another day, Miss Hudson. I thank you and he thanks you." Mycroft bowed reverently before turning towards the men in the party.

Sigh. She curtseyed after setting the elder Holmes' brother's hat on the table beside the door.

"I've been expecting you, Mycroft. Do come and join us," remarked Sherlock impatiently. "Miss Belle, another sherry for my brother please, do cease standing there gawking and attend to my guest. We have matters of the utmost importance to discuss."

It is no wonder manners appeal to me; they are in such short supply.

"You are very good, Mr. Holmes." She curtsied again, this time towards Sherlock. *Except when the moon is full.* "Yes, sir, once I have seen Mr. Mycroft Holmes comfortable I shall do so immediately." She motioned with her hand to the settee.

"Mycroft can find his way around the queen's government, he can find his way to the sofa."

"I can see that you are not at your best this evening, Shirley," Mycroft drawled.

"I am not. I am quite concerned, in fact."

"As am I," Mycroft agreed.

Mirabella's fingers tightened around the crystal neck of the sherry decanter as she poured another glass. Sherlock Holmes—incorrigible, annoying, critical tyrant.

Fascinating, amazing, and to whom I owe everything that has meaning in my life.

Without Sherlock Holmes she would very likely be a chamber maid somewhere emptying bedpans—if she were lucky enough to have not lost the position. Sherlock might agitate her to death, but she knew it was because he had very high expectations of her performance.

Above all she must not lose this job. Instead of being cast off as unemployable and unmarriageable, a burden on her relations, she was learning from the most skilled detective in London.

She glanced at Mycroft whom even the queen herself confided in. Most illustrious company indeed for one who had been dismissed from her first position.

The only problem was that every day a new layer of her incompetence was revealed. Sometimes one feared to choke from it.

"Have you seen the paper, Shirley?" Mycroft asked, his smile fading quickly as his gaze met Sherlock's.

"Most certainly. I expect you refer to the *Abdül Hamid* plans gone missing?" Sherlock nodded gravely, even as Mycroft delicately positioned the tails of his tuxedo as he moved to sit in the dark purple velvet settee beside Sherlock's wingback easy chair.

"Naturally. And have you seen the headlines this evening? Very bad business." Mycroft ran his hand through his hair, causing a lock of hair to fall forward on his forehead. "Do you have any idea where the submarine plans are, Shirley?"

"I have a hunch. Let's hope that hunch is correct."

"Good. If I can be of any assistance, do let me know."

"My investigation will be entirely illegal, so I can't ask for your help at this time, Mycroft."

"One must do what one must." Mycroft shrugged. "As you have no doubt surmised, Shirley, we have an unsolved mystery." He added under his breath, "Of the greatest importance."

"How you can breathe is the greatest unsolved mystery of all," said Sherlock. In truth, the elder Holmes brother's black formal attire was offset by a white shirt of Egyptian cotton with an extraordinarily high, stiff collar that made one gasp for air merely to look at it.

As she moved to deliver the glass of sherry, it startled Mirabella to realize that she was following the train of Sherlock's thoughts in watching where his eyes alighted. Outside of science, she did not wish for their minds to be so closely aligned.

Mycroft opened the edition of *Punch* which he had pulled from his overcoat and began reading aloud:

DISRAELI LIBERAL AGENDA
Tory MP sides with liberals

"It isn't very specific," considered Dr. Watson, pursing his lips.

"The worst thing you can say about a Tory is that he is a liberal in disguise," said Sherlock, lighting his pipe.

Mirabella had listened to enough conversations in this room to know that Benjamin Disraeli, the Earl of Beaconsfield and the conservative MP, would take great exception to the headlines.

"And further down in the article it is stated that Disraeli dresses like a dandy—which, of course, he does," Mycroft said.

"Naturally," agreed Sherlock. "There is always a grain of truth in slander. It will set the stage for the complete annihilation of the target."

"Are they criticizing the Tory MP because of the way he dresses? How absurd! Every woman loves a man of fashion," Mirabella said, glancing approvingly at Mycroft. "And everyone knows that the Tories are the conservative party."

"The inference to fashion is much bigger than which side of the political spectrum the MP falls on," said Sherlock. "More likely which side of the fence his romantic interests lie."

"Oh, my," Mirabella whispered.

"Do you think Moriarty is behind this?" Dr. Watson asked.

"Of course he is. And it is going to get much worse, I guarantee it. *Much worse*," Sherlock said somberly. "No other criminal in the country has such a lust for power and attention. Anyone else would be delighted to simply take the money to the bank. The professor would willingly lose it all for the gratification of being bowed down to."

"Could blackmail be the intent?" Dr. Watson asked.

"Very unusual for blackmail. Ordinarily we would have seen secrecy and demands for pay-offs," said Mycroft.

"You would not have known if it had been blackmail," Mirabella said. "It would all be secret."

"Miss Belle makes an excellent point," considered Sherlock, taking a sip of his sherry. "Instead of a blackmail demand we see the hints and leaks in the newspaper."

"As if the perpetrator were anxious to spread the word," said Dr. Watson. "Once the word is out, there can be no payment."

"Unless it is a different pay-off," Mycroft added with deliberation. "What I propose is that there is scandalous information out there—and that the holder of that information wishes to use it for some personal gain. What that gain is, we are still investigating."

"It is possible that the sole purpose of these attacks is to rise in the government," Sherlock suggested.

"True. All of the victims of the attacks thus far have been public officials."

"And it hasn't all been words," Sherlock said.

Mycroft raised his eyebrows, turning suddenly to face his brother.

"Hamilton?"

Dr. Watson cleared his throat. "Yes, we're intimately aware of Mr. Hamilton's death."

"So it was murder. You have confirmed my suspicions," Mycroft shuddered. "It is dreadful to think of Hamilton's being killed over information. No one is privy to more information than *me*."

"Think on a much larger scale, Mycroft," Sherlock said, his expression grave.

"Larger than my own safety?"

"Submarine plans gone missing. Slander in the papers. A dead body. If the submarine plans were all that was wanted, there would be no reason for the slander. Perhaps the person or persons behind the newspaper slander wishes to take over the government," suggested Sherlock. "Perhaps even . . . destroy the monarchy."

"Heaven save us," Dr. Watson said.

Mycroft shook his head. "And yet I have feared the same."

"Destroy the queen? What an absurd notion, to be sure!" Mirabella's mouth flew open in shock. "How is it possible . . . How could it be done?"

Clippity-clop. FWEEEEE! The sound of horses' hooves hitting the pavement outside, followed by the shrill whistle of a policeman.

"Are you feeling ill, my good man?" Dr. Watson asked as he studied Mycroft.

"Quite ill, Dr. Watson," replied Mycroft, obviously coming to some conclusion in his mind. "We have difficult days ahead."

"Indeed, it is most serious." Sherlock nodded, pointing to the newspaper. "It is life and death. *Queen and country*."

CHAPTER THIRTEEN
A Midnight Snack

"Miss Hudson, before you retire for the evening, could you whip us up a little something?"

"But you've already eaten." Not that she objected, but how many meals could they eat in one evening?

"I don't wish for food. I wish for an explosive. One that could break open a safe. Your chemistry is coming along is it not?"

She spun on her heels to face him. "What are you going to blow up, Mr. Holmes? Please tell me it isn't a bank."

"Of course not, Miss Hudson. I am in the business of catching criminals. I am on the side of the law. Or did you forget?"

"It does slip my mind at times. And what do you wish to explode?"

"A safe. At the University of London."

"The University of London? Which I one day hope to attend? Are you so determined that I should stay in your employ, Mr. Holmes, that you are going to destroy the school?"

"Miss Hudson, will you make the explosive, or shall I?"

Heavy sigh. "Honestly, I should think dynamite would serve you best, Mr. Holmes. Nitroglycerin is very unstable, as you know."

"Dynamite it is, then. I believe you shall find some in my bedroom closet, if you could please fetch it here while I finish my smoke."

"Actually, I'll wait until you're finished smoking before I bring the dynamite."

"There's no time to waste, my girl. Moriarty has a safe at the University of London. I'm of a mind to return something belonging to the British government. Are you with me?"

"Naturally I am." She held her chin up high. "I don't wish to see my country invaded by foreign powers."

***

"Very good, Miss Belle."

Mirabella opened the lock on Moriarty's office door in under three minutes. Dr. Watson entered first, with a lit candle that they might see. Sherlock entered with two sticks of dynamite in his pocket. Dr. Watson moved to the window and opened it.

Looking about the office, Sherlock saw that Moriarty's desk was entirely clean and that the walls were lined with books.

"The professor doesn't spend much time here. It's far too neat. Not a working office," Sherlock said.

"Let's get this done and get out of here, Holmes," Watson said.

"Indeed." Sherlock moved to the back of the office and quickly found the safe. "I would stake my life that Moriarty has the submarine blueprints."

"How many dynamite sticks?" Watson asked.

"Two. But before we use them, Miss Belle will take a stab at opening the safe herself. She did quite well with the door and she's becoming a decent cracksman," Sherlock said. "We've been practicing this very thing."

She moved forward and, starting with zero, began turning the lock, quietly calling out each number where there was tension as she moved the dial, which Watson wrote down. "0 . . . 3 . . . 4.5 . . . 7 . . . 8.5"

When she was finished, Mirabella took the paper and began studying the numbers, scribbling her formulas.

In the meantime, Sherlock took a chisel and hammer and began hammering on the handle of the safe.

Click. The door was open in precisely one minute.

"Mr. Holmes! How did you—"

He reached inside and pulled out the papers, examining each as Mirabella now held the candle, peering over his shoulder.

"This is nothing more than simple mathematical formulas." Mirabella became momentarily excited. "This one is interesting. It's about ultraviolet light."

"*Focus*, Miss Belle."

She continued scanning the papers for anything relevant. "There isn't anything here."

"Aha! We have it!" Sherlock reached inside again, to pull out . . . a crisp, new deerstalker hat.

Attached to the hat was a note: "Your old one begins to look worn."

Sherlock felt his heart fall in his chest. The sting of failure was great, particularly with the stakes so high.

But there was no doubt in his mind now that Moriarty had the plans for the *Abdül Hamid*.

"Shhh! I hear someone coming!" Mirabella whispered. Sherlock blew out the candle, nudging her to the window that she might go first. Sherlock placed the new hat on his head and the old one inside the safe, shutting the door, as he returned the dynamite to his pocket.

Sherlock followed her through the window just as the door was opened. But Watson was still in the room—and he walked with a slight limp, easily detectable. Nor was Watson as fast a runner as his flat-mate or, very likely, as fast as the university security.

A guard holding a lantern peered inside, casting light about the room.

At just that moment a loud ruckus was created by *someone* yelling in the yard outside the window.

As the guard moved to the open window, Watson, who had moved to the other side of the door, slipped out of the room, the loud noises providing a cover for his exit.

CHAPTER FOURTEEN
The Cloak of Invisibility

"We have to find those plans. For the safety of Britain—and subsequently, the world." Sherlock said, cracking his three-minute egg on the following morning, only just delivered by Mirabella, along with a single piece of toast. Such a light meal constituted a feast for the Great Detective in the early hours.

"To be sure, this is a submarine with a working torpedo," Watson agreed. "It cannot be seen from the surface."

"It has every advantage of invisibility without detection," Sherlock said. "The submarine is a perfect weapon. It could literally choke supplies to England in time of war. She is a great power, but we forget that Britain is still a small island."

"Moriarty has probably already copied the plans." Mirabella poured another cup of tea for the gentlemen and one for herself as well, seating herself at the table to eat her breakfast now that they were served. There was a time when she wouldn't have thought to seat herself with the gentlemen. She might still be their employee, but she welcomed the easiness that had developed between them.

"He hasn't had time yet." Sherlock shook his head. "I have it on good authority that certain parts of the plans are in code; it will take some time to decipher the key. In addition, any buyer would only want the original. One incorrect reproduction and the plan is worthless. But I agree that we must find them soon." Sherlock took a bite of his toast. "One thing in our favor is Moriarty's tendency toward being lazy—as well as arrogant."

"Moriarty is certainly prideful," said Dr. Watson. "But I question that a criminal mastermind is lazy. And how does that help us, if indeed it is true?"

"Nothing is truer. Moriarty would only trust the copying of the plans to himself. Wouldn't you think he would burn the candle at both ends if need be, to the exclusion of all else, to ensure the blueprint is copied? But the professor is so sure of himself, and so lazy, that he will attend to it when he finds it to be convenient. In the meantime, he enjoys his evening brandy and excursions to the opera as usual."

"He's going to the opera when he has in his possession plans which could change the course of the world?" Dr. Watson asked with disbelief.

"I have it on good authority. Wiggins is on the case." Sherlock tapped his chin with his forefinger.

"You have a *child* trailing the world's most powerful criminal?" Mirabella asked with incredulity, her teacup pausing in mid-air.

"Wiggins effectively commands an entire troupe of detectives, which I guarantee you no one at Scotland Yard has accomplished. Moreover, I'll pit the Baker Street Irregulars against the Yard any day of the week, Miss Hudson. Wiggins is in possession of intelligence, bravery, and the ability to take direction as well as to lead."

"Excuse me . . . I never meant . . ."

"To be sure, Gregson is the smartest of the Scotland Yarders, and yet he still can't hold a candle to Wiggins. As for Lestrade, he is not a bad sort: he has the drive, but lacks imagination. Athelney Jones is, of course, an imbecile." Sherlock gave a nod in the direction of kind acceptance. "Still, Jones has the tenacity of a lobster, which is sometimes what is needed. As for Hopkins—no, he is *never* what is needed." Sherlock returned his stern expression to Mirabella. "But let us return to the subject at hand."

"Yes, sir." Mirabella swallowed hard. "So you believe that Moriarty wishes to sell the plans, Mr. Holmes?"

"They must be worth a fortune," Dr. Watson said.

"There are two ways to look at this. Not only would it be terrible for these plans to fall into enemy hands, but this does not bode well for the continued confidence in the British prime minister. That's the second occurrence of a leak this month. Gladstone could indeed be ousted with a vote of 'no confidence,'" Sherlock said.

"Which would, in turn, be quite serious for the safety of England. There is no greater statesman than William Gladstone," said Watson.

"Precisely. Combine the theft of the plans with the slander in the newspapers, and the missing submarine plans could lead to a change in the power at the helm." Sherlock took a sip of tea.

"You don't seriously think the submarine plans were stolen in an attempt to oust Gladstone?" Watson asked.

"It is a possibility." Sherlock nodded somberly. "But I fear it could be even worse. Perhaps these are the actions of a man who wishes to rule England."

CHAPTER FIFTEEN
The Madame

"I'd be happy to watch her for you," Mary Jeffries said, smiling to the parents of the blue-eyed, blonde child.

Such a lovely girl. About ten years old. Precisely the type of child who would yield top dollar with that long blonde hair and large blue eyes, so happy with the promise of life.

"How kind of you," the mother said. "We'll just collect our luggage. We can't afford a porter."

"I'll take good care of her."

And the minute the parents were around the corner, Mary had the child by the hand. "Come with me. We'll just go get an ice cream."

Her hansom cab was waiting. The girl was whisked into the cab, never to see her parents again.

She would soon be black and blue everywhere, screaming and crying, which was precisely what some men liked.

***

There was a special place in Hell for Mary Jeffries.

And for the rich politicians who protected her.

Inspector Jeremiah Minahan resigned from the Metropolitan police force when senior officials refused to prosecute Jeffries.

The only conclusion: those senior officials had either been paid off—or were her clients.

Minahan was a disillusioned man; he had always thought good would prevail. Still, he couldn't give up, not while there was a chance to end the suffering of even a single child.

The former inspector utilized his early retirement to compile reports for journalist William Thomas Stead outlining the widespread corruption involving his colleagues, cabinet members, and prominent men of the day. Stead subsequently wrote a series of articles for the *Pall Mall Gazette* exposing Jeffries' prostitution rings in the Eliza Armstrong case.

Minahan had finally been able to convince Jeffries' former housemaid to testify, who had witnessed a thirteen-year-old girl being whipped with a belt and thereafter raped by a customer.

I finally have her. Minahan waited for the verdict, smiling.

"Come to the bench." Jeffries went before the judge, accompanied by several wealthy army officers.

The judge spoke. "Mary Jeffries, you are ordered to pay a fine of two hundred pounds. In exchange, because you have pleaded guilty, all the evidence against you will remain undisclosed."

He hit the gavel, even as Minahan's jaw dropped.

Jeffries paid her fine—in cash—smiling at Minahan as she left the courthouse. Her young escorts, all girls in her employ, formed a circle of protection around the madame as she left the courthouse and entered her cab.

Jeffries went free, her freedom paid for with the torture of children, and William Stead went to jail for three months for "abduction" because he had purchased Eliza Armstrong from her chimney-sweep father in order to save her.

CHAPTER SIXTEEN
The Punch Line

TORY MP DISRAELI FAVORS THE COMPANY OF MEN
In more "chambers" than Parliament
CAN WE TRUST HIM AT THE HELM OF OUR GOVERNMENT?

Sherlock's eyes returned to the latest edition of *Punch*. Fear gripped his very being, an emotion to which he was unaccustomed.

VICTORIA MIRACLE BABY?
The Duke of Kent never fathered any children with his mistress, Madame de Saint-Laurent

These headlines seen together were suicide.

Moriarty was laying the groundwork for something so terrifying that the moment it occurred it would not seem remarkable but rather believable.

GLADSTONE OLDEST PRIME MINISTER ON RECORD
Is he too old to lead the country?

"*How dare they!*" exclaimed Watson. "It's bad enough to question the prime minister's morality, but no one can argue with his abilities!"

"The bloody bastard!" Sherlock threw the paper on floor.

"Gladstone, Victoria, and Disraeli are possibly the three greatest leaders England has ever had at one time," exclaimed Watson, equally outraged.

"Though any two of them cannot stand each other," added Mycroft, glancing at the clock on the fireplace mantel. He straightened his tie as if preparing for departure. The world might end but there was still opera.

Mycroft had arrived just as they were sitting down to dinner—as seemed to happen a great deal lately. They had all been served after dinner sherry in the living room and were enjoying tea cakes—as much as anything could be enjoyed.

"Moriarty must be stopped." Sherlock was disgusted with himself that he had let it get this far. He had seen it coming, he knew what Moriarty was about, and yet he had failed to stop him. "It is a cursed disaster."

"I have to agree," Mycroft said solemnly.

"This is *Punch* which is publishing this," Mirabella argued, not often swayed by the opinions of others. "Everyone knows this newspaper publishes gossip heard in London coffeehouses and has as its audience persons of strong zeal and weak intellects."

"And yet, we have a copy, don't we, Miss Belle?" Sherlock posed.

Prior to this Sherlock had always barreled straight ahead as he knew one must: this was his tried and true method. When he had worked alone, he never feared for anything.

But now, with his association with Watson and Miss Belle, he had let his fears for the safety of others influence him—which he should never have done. *He had gotten soft.*

"What are these lies against the prime minister?" Dr. Watson asked, perusing the paper. "Gladstone is a great man who has more than once saved Britain from bankruptcy."

"True, but many find it difficult to tolerate his company," said Sherlock, taking a puff on his pipe.

"Precisely," nodded Mycroft. "Whatever the personal failings of the current rulers—which only adds to their appeal, as far as I am concerned—they do an excellent job. In fact, Gladstone has balanced the budget. England has *no debt*. And we are the wealthiest country in the world. Astonishing."

"Gladstone is a financial genius," Sherlock said.

"So we come to the rumors and the gossip which is floating about it," said Mycroft, taking a sizable bite of a lemon teacake.

"Indeed. What is being said, what is the implication, where is it going—and who started the rumors?" Sherlock said.

"It's pretty obvious the direction this is going," said Mycroft, his expression severe, as he helped himself to a handful of walnuts. "Why don't you take a stab at it, Shirley?"

"Ah, let's see." Sherlock frowned, taking a puff on his pipe. "Victoria is not the true heir to the throne. Disraeli, the head of the conservative party and the former prime minister, is a sodomite, which is against the law and punishable by imprisonment. And Gladstone, the prime minister, definitely does not favor the company of men and is cavorting with prostitutes."

"Precisely." Mycroft nodded.

Mirabella almost dropped her teacup, as she stared at the others. "You don't mean it!"

"*Bloody hell!*" Watson exclaimed.

"I didn't say it was true," Sherlock drawled. "*Necessarily.*"

"But it is, nonetheless, fatal," Mycroft added. "The three most important people in the ruling class of England."

"The most powerful country in the world," added Sherlock. "This could take down the British government."

"Excuse me," Watson interjected, making no effort to hide the impatience in his voice, his complexion somewhat ashen. "What was that first one?"

"The first what?" asked Mycroft.

"The first state secret you mentioned. Concerning Queen Victoria?"

"Oh, right. She is not the true heir to the throne," Mycroft recollected. "Do you have any salami, Miss Hudson? I have such a craving for salami."

"Mycroft, what the deuce are you talking about?" demanded Watson.

"Well, I don't know how many ways he can say it, old boy," replied Sherlock, tapping his calabash pipe of African mahogany on the table. "Really, my good man, let us move on. We have work to do."

"I truly would like some salami, I'm not jesting with you," reiterated Mycroft. "Do you have some spicy mustard? Maybe a small roll?"

"I have no idea. And I'm not getting out of this chair to serve you, Mycroft. Nor is Miss Hudson, who is surprisingly quiet. I wish you might bring tales of scandal more often." He motioned to the teacakes. "Besides, you have had more than enough food—and will be dining after the opera."

"It is difficult to remember the details when one is so thirsty," Mycroft said, taking a sip of his sherry. "I'm positively *parched*."

"Have you all gone mad?" sputtered Watson.

"I don't think so," Sherlock shook his head. "I haven't. Have you, Mycroft?"

"Not to my knowledge," said Mycroft, shaking his head. "That was King George. In some ways it would be most advisable and a good thing if Victoria were *not* related to mad King George. Outside of losing the throne, of course, it bodes well for her and her numerous offspring."

"But Victoria is called the Grandmother of Europe," Mirabella exclaimed with a gasp, finally re-entering the conversation. "If she is not the true heir, then . . ."

"Indeed, her offspring are on most of the thrones of Europe," said Watson.

"Very sad though that she introduced hemophilia into the royal family," Mycroft said, shaking his head.

"What manner of treason—" interjected Watson, almost in a whisper. "Good God! What are you talking about? Whatever do you mean by saying Victoria is not the true monarch?"

"Calm yourself, Watson," Sherlock advised. For one who lacked intensity, John Watson had taken a decided interest in this case. More than interest, he appeared agitated. There was a time when Sherlock had thought the good doctor's damaged nerves were on the mend—but, in his opinion,

Watson's nervous system had gotten far worse since they had moved in together. There was no accounting for it.

"I AM EXCEEDINGLY CALM," managed Watson between gritted teeth. "I am merely outraged, which is quite different."

"Outraged at what?" Sherlock asked as politely as he could manage.

"At your lack of patriotic feeling, to be sure! Victoria, of course, is the daughter of Victoire, Princess of Leiningen, and of Prince Edward, Duke of Kent and the fourth son of George III."

"Naturally," said Mirabella, who appeared to be as dazed as Watson was provoked.

"Natural it was not," said Mycroft. "It was no love affair between the stunning thirty-two year old princess and the pot-bellied, balding fifty-year-old Duke of Kent."

"I wouldn't say too much on that score, Mycroft," said Sherlock. "You won't be long behind the duke."

"I can still cut a dashing figure, though it's questionable whether you can say the same, brother dear," Mycroft drawled, raising his sherry glass to Sherlock. "As to Victoire and Edward, they could not even converse with each other, Victoire speaking only German. Princess Victoria did not speak any English until she was three years of age."

"It is not unprecedented nor does it prove that Victoria was not fathered by the Duke of Kent," argued Watson.

"No, but there are three facts in evidence, two of which are well known," said Mycroft. "One is that King George III suffered from porphyria, hence the 'Mad King George'. This condition, which has many outward and easily identifiable symptoms precluding the madness, stopped abruptly with Victoria. There is considerable evidence among Victoria's staff to confirm this conclusion. Anytime one is heavily waited on, as is royalty, there are those servants who know one's intimate details."

"Ah, yes. Any chambermaid employed in the palace would know. Every good doctor knows that the chamber pot reveals all," Watson said, his voice shaking.

"And second?" Mirabella asked in a whisper.

"Second," replied Mycroft "is that Queen Victoria is a carrier for hemophilia."

"You understand the implications better than I do, Watson," stated Holmes. "The fact is that in the prior seventeen generations of the British royal family there are no cases of hemophilia. *None.*"

Watson appeared to be steadying himself, even though he was seated in a chair. "Either a gene was newly mutated, the odds being one in twenty-five thousand at best . . ."

"Or Victoria was not in fact the daughter of Prince Edward, the Duke of Kent," said Mirabella in a dazed state, stirring the sugar into her tea for about the one-hundredth rotation. "It can't be . . ."

"Victoire was determined that her line should be on the throne," Mycroft proposed.

"One might speculate that she drew certain conclusions from the fact that Prince Edward had never fathered any children with his mistress, Thérèse-Bernardine Montgenet, Madame de Saint-Laurent—a conclusion we might draw as well—and Victoire took matters into her own hands," Sherlock said.

"It is a little known fact that Victoire and her secretary Conroy had every intention of being the power behind the throne when Victoria became queen," Mycroft added.

"An intention never realized," said Watson.

"Ah, yes. Victoria surprised everyone by booting the two conspirators out of the palace on her eighteenth birthday," said Mycroft.

With a slight smile on Sherlock's lips, he added, "A great deal of spunk has our Queen. Reminds me of Miss Hudson."

Mirabella glanced up at him, her expression still one of shock. But at least she stopped stirring her tea and took a sip, however mechanical the movement.

"Have you seen a photo of Victoire's secretary, Sir John Conroy?" Mycroft said. "A case could be made for his resemblance to Victoria in countenance and stance."

"In my opinion, Victoria doesn't look a thing like Sir John," argued Watson. "She is short and plump and he is tall and dashing—as is Victoire."

"I speak of similar mannerisms," Mycroft said.

"Which could be a learned behavior regardless of paternity," Sherlock said. "And yet—if Sir John Conroy were Victoria's father—that would explain her complete and unequivocal hatred of her mother's secretary and the tumultuous relationship she had with her mother."

"There are many reasons to hate a person other than the fact that he is one's father," Mirabella protested.

"Indeed," agreed Watson. "If Sir John Conroy were an ass, which I understand he is, that would explain it as well."

"On the other hand, one might suppose that Victoria saw her mother and Conroy in a compromising situation," said Mycroft. "Explaining her hatred of Sir John *and* supporting the theory of her parentage."

"My guess is that you have it on good authority and it is more than a supposition, Mycroft," Sherlock posed.

"Very good, brother dear, I cannot lie." Mycroft smiled. "I never believed the derogatory things our mother said about your lack of sophistication, and now I see that my confidence was well founded."

Sherlock frowned. "And who is it who reported that Victoria came across

Victoire and Conroy together? Stop beating around the bush, Mycroft, though I know you love to increase the suspense."

"A good story-teller always does. And I am only attempting to show some respect to the lady present." Mycroft nodded in reverence to Mirabella.

"Yes, Holmes, please be aware that Miss Mirabella is present," admonished Watson.

I am always aware when Miss Belle is present. "All conversation is appropriate to the detective." Sherlock commanded, "Spit it out, Mycroft. Who is your source?"

"Baroness Spaeth."

Watson whistled. "Victoria's governess."

"So the queen's governess is in contact with you, Mycroft?" asked Mirabella, somewhat disbelieving.

"In a manner of speaking. Isn't everyone?" Mycroft's countenance was confident. "But have no worries there. The baroness would never do anything to harm our queen."

"If this is true," said Mirabella with alarm, "most of the thrones of Europe are a farce. Victoria is the royal grandmother of Europe! If she doesn't belong on her throne, do any of Europe's royals belong on their respective thrones?"

"It is only Victoria's right to be on the throne of England which is in question," said Mycroft. "Not her royal blood."

"Quite so," agreed Sherlock. "Whatever the truth of her paternal parentage and her legitimacy to the throne, Victoria is still of royal blood through her mother."

"And many of her granddaughters married the legal heirs to their respective countries," Mycroft added. "And yet, there is truth in what Miss Hudson says. It would indeed be a farce if Europe's princes had married who they believed to be princesses and the granddaughters of the queen of the world's most powerful country—and it was not true."

"I call it quite unpatriotic!" protested Watson, his anger rising. "Do you propose to overthrow the Queen of England?"

"Not I," stated Sherlock. "And you, dear brother?"

"Certainly not!" said Mycroft. "If Victoria had not become queen, the throne would have passed to Prince Ernest, the Duke of Cumberland. Lady Lyndhurst claimed he attempted to rape her."

"The wife of the lord chancellor?" said Watson.

"Lady Lyndhurst was attacked by an heir to the throne? One of the *king's* sons?" Mirabella gasped.

"It is only rumored," Sherlock cautioned.

"I can't imagine Lady Lyndhurst would make the claim if it weren't true. Such a claim alone could ruin a lady's reputation, causing the cessation of all social invitations. One would have to have great incentive to say such a thing," Mirabella said.

"True or not, Queen Charlotte herself banned Prince Ernest from all his sister's rooms," said Mycroft, illustrating the reason he was invaluable to the government, "There is talk that Cumberland fathered an illegitimate child with his own sister."

"Definitely not king material," Sherlock said.

Mycroft turned to Mirabella. "Please forgive my plain speaking, but there is no genteel way to say it."

"And was Prince Ernest ever tried and convicted?" asked Mirabella.

"Peers can only be tried by other peers," Mycroft corrected, "and they cannot be tried for anything except treason or for a felony. Only one peer has ever been convicted of any crime, and he was mad so it could not be ignored. Subsequently, a prince of the realm would never be tried for assaulting a woman, much less convicted, which is neither treason nor a felony."

"Assaulting a woman is not so important a crime." Mirabella bit her lip.

"Not legally," Sherlock stated matter-of-factly. "Certainly not in this day and age."

"Shirley is right. I do not agree with it myself, being a proud honorary member of the Victorian Women's Suffrage Society, but it is so."

"I know it is true, but I think it is despicable," Mirabella objected. "A royal should not be able to do things that are illegal for everyone else."

"Just because his purported actions were legal *for a peer* does not mean that the general public approves, Miss Hudson. Lord Lyndhurst put an account of the duke's actions in a London paper. Prince Ernest insisted that a retraction be printed—but Lord Lyndhurst refused.

"What a blackguard! I am a proponent of torture for that type, myself. I would happily deflower him myself," stated Watson emphatically. "Unfortunately we are in the business of upholding the law and cannot attend to it ourselves."

"It is unnecessary, since Prince Ernest died in 1851," Sherlock said. "However, if the Duke of Cumberland had ascended the throne—or descended it, as the case may be—his heirs would now be the heirs to the throne."

"Heirs which would be much more manageable by certain powers than our Queen," Mycroft said somberly.

"You shouldn't be discussing such matters—not here, not anywhere," objected Dr. Watson. "Do you wish to overthrow the government?"

"We don't," replied Sherlock with a tone of foreboding in his voice. "*But someone may.*"

CHAPTER SEVENTEEN
Planning for the Future

"I have the prime minister and the leader of Her Majesty's opposition under attack," Moriarty considered, tapping his fingers on his large oak desk, mathematical formulas sprawled across the large chalkboard behind him. "But I must look to the future. Who will take over the government when Gladstone and Disraeli are gone? And will they be allies, or must they be *retired*?"

And how are they to be controlled?

"It seems to me you have also attacked the queen's reputation—which I cannot abide," the Earl of Alsop objected, clearly disturbed. He was one of the more influential members of the House of Lords and one to keep an eye on.

Alsop's heir, and the next in line to sit in the House of Lords, was a touch more agreeable—and more in debt, Moriarty considered. Always something to keep in mind.

"It was necessary in order to discredit Gladstone and Disraeli. Never fear, my lord, all will be well in the end," Moriarty said in his scholarly voice.

"I suppose." Lord Alsop nodded in reluctant agreement. "You'd hardly be able to replace the queen."

Moriarty smiled at the peer.

"However, a vote of no confidence against the prime minister is a common enough thing," Lord Alsop added.

"I'm counting on it."

"But Gladstone is very popular."

"No one is invincible."

"Have a care, Professor," Lord Alsop warned. "If one were to disengage the prime minister and the leader of Her Majesty's opposition party, one must look to who stands to be the next prime minister."

"I believe that is precisely what I initially said. And who do you think would come to the forefront with those in power removed, Alsop?" Moriarty asked politely.

"Very likely the Speaker of the House of Commons." Lord Alsop's lips tightened as if he had just eaten a lemon.

"You don't think much of Henry Brand, I take it?"

"The country is going to hell in a hand-basket. It used to be that the prime minister was always chosen from the House of Lords. Now, for God's sake, the P.M. is often from the House of Commons! Someone with no royal blood whatsoever! What is happening to our country?"

"A terrible development indeed." Moriarty shook his head in dismay. "We will put an end to all that." *Once I am the P.M. via the House of Commons.* "I have the connections and the money to do so. We will expand our borders and return England to the great country she once was."

"It can't be soon enough for me. And I'm not alone in that sentiment."

Thomas Ecclestone, the Earl of Alsop, might not be the brightest star in the sky, but he was a most excellent ally. It was surprising to Moriarty how many peers were actually amenable to his plan—or to as much of his plan as he was willing to reveal.

Not as surprising how eager men were to believe the slander about others. Moriarty had long known that fear and hatred were much more powerful than empathy and compassion.

And it would be their undoing in the end.

A platform built upon the basic survival instincts was almost invincible. Love, which necessarily required thinking about someone other than oneself, was not as powerful as appealing to one's desire to kill the enemy, perceived or otherwise.

Always evil was crouched in heroic language.

Moriarty smiled. He was not a supporter of either political party, but he was definitely a member of the "I've got mine, to hell with you" party.

And the peers made the best allies: those who had been raised on large sums of money and who didn't know how to exist without vast wealth. The professor could help them there.

Those men who had thought themselves to be above him were now eating out of his hand. It was as if the world came to an end when the peers lost their funds to gambling, poor land management, or whatever the cause might be. They were ready to end it all before Moriarty came along—with his cash infusions.

Still, it might come to ending their own lives if, for example, they were to lose their entire fortune in a game of cards. And, in fact, and it was a way to keep his own hands clean.

"You know that Brand is a liberal."

"It's not a sin." Moriarty chuckled, taking care to hide the full extent of his amusement.

"In some circles it is," muttered Lord Alsop. "Damned progressives."

Liberal or conservative, Moriarty didn't care; he cared about having the control. And the easiest way to control was to set them against each other—and subsequently to control the minds of the populace. *A house divided against itself cannot stand.*

In all honesty, Moriarty merely intended to control the power and the money for himself. Initiate a few wars and control the companies which supplied the weapons. The Zulu in Africa had been a stroke of genius: they had diamonds. One could take the diamonds—and make money doing so.

"It is definitely a time to return to traditional values," Moriarty agreed. *Like diamonds.* "So much change in the world, it is staggering. I have no doubt we will go down in history as the age of industry."

"Our country is slipping away from us," Lord Alsop pronounced, puckering his lips as if he had eaten a lemon. "Into the hands of *the common man.*"

"Not if I can help it," Moriarty said. *It is a fact that your country will slip away from you. Into my hands.*

In all honesty, Moriarty did despise the common man. But even more did he despise royalty.

"What has happened to England? God and country, religion and family?" Lord Alsop was becoming agitated now. "The peerage has controlled England for centuries."

Ah. Now we get to the real issue. It has nothing to do with God and country.

"Indeed. It is an affront to God." Moriarty tapped his fingers on his desk. "What do you know about Brand?"

"He is married to Eliza Courtney, the Duchess of Devonshire's illegitimate daughter with Lord Grey," Ecclestone said with disdain.

Marvelous.

"Indeed. I think we can work with that." Moriarty smiled, a plan formulating in his mind.

CHAPTER EIGHTEEN
A Flattering Condescension

"Do have another chocolate, Baroness Spaeth," Fantine said, offering Cadbury's chocolate fancy box to the baroness, clearly unaccustomed to the attention.

"Thank you kindly, Countess Florentine. I must say, your visit is unexpected."

"Oh? Surely everyone must be in awe of the woman who raised our current queen."

Baroness Spaeth blushed, looking down, even as she enjoyed her second chocolate. "I did spend more time with sweet Drina than her own mother did."

"That cannot be uncommon among royalty." Fantine laughed liltingly, as if to make light of her companion's remarks, a tactic that generally resulted in full disclosure.

A bitterness crossed the baroness' expression, in contrast to the pleasure afforded by the chocolate. "It is not. But the more important point is: for whom did Princess Victoire make time?"

Fantine leaned forward. "Who indeed?"

CHAPTER NINETEEN
The Holy Scripture

"Do you seriously think that Disraeli is a . . . ?" Watson pointed to the headlines as he cleared his throat. "Has a preference for men?"

"I could care less. And it's none of our damned business," said Sherlock. "Outside of stopping Moriarty."

"Naturally it is none of our business," Dr. Watson said. "But don't you feel even slightly *repulsed* by the idea?"

"Not in the slightest," Sherlock said definitively.

"I would say whether or not Disraeli prefers men is debatable and not a fact in evidence," said Mycroft. "Although the best evidence comes from Disraeli himself and his published works."

"Why would Lord Beaconsfield reveal himself in his writings?" posed Watson, shaking his head. "The sexual act between men is punishable by imprisonment."

Mirabella had only just re-emerged from the kitchen. "What is punishable by imprisonment?"

"Consensual sex between men," replied Sherlock nonchalantly.

"Holmes!" Watson protested. "There is a lady present!"

Mirabella reached out to steady herself, the alarm apparent on her face. "Do you mean a god forsaken *sodomite*? Do you know someone who is one?"

Sherlock raised his eyebrows at her. "We do. And it's very likely you do as well, Miss Hudson."

"Oh, *no*! I'm sure I don't." She shook her head, returning to the basket chair.

"So you object, Miss Hudson?" asked Mycroft with obvious amusement, as he spread his arm across the velvet settee.

"Certainly I do! It is not *natural* and it is against the laws of *God*."

"It is not natural for you, Miss Belle, but it might be entirely natural for someone else," said Sherlock.

"But a . . . a . . . *sodomite*!"

"A very disturbing term," said Mycroft. "With an unpleasant connotation. Could you not use another, Miss Hudson? The inference is one of a rapist, which anyone must consider a far different thing from consensual relations." Mycroft shook his head in disapproval, patting his forehead with his handkerchief. "Whereas a rapist is someone who assaults another sexually against his or her will. A deplorable type of person."

"And what term should I use?" Mirabella asked.

"The French, they say, *mignon*, which would be my preference. But I have also heard *mandrake*, *Margery*, *pansy*, and *poof*, none of which I like, but all of which are preferable to *sodomite*."

"I will not make light of it nor apologize for being a God-fearing girl," she said. "I am very proud of my family, my upbringing, my values, and my love of God."

"You seem to have forgotten some of the finer points of the origin of the term, Miss Belle. When the men of Sodom came to Lot's door, these Sodomites asked to see the angels visiting Lot that they might rape the new arrivals. Lot refused, offering his two virgin daughters to his neighbors instead. Thankfully, the angels stopped their host from his ill-conceived generosity. Later, God smote down Lot's wife for merely looking back at her home town as she exited, turning her into ashes, offering no punishment to Lot for offering up his daughters to rapists. Moving forward, these same virgin daughters got their father Lot drunk in order to bed him, that they might become impregnated. I'd say, whoever wrote Genesis 19 had his own disturbing sexual fantasies not to mention a debased opinion of women." Sherlock leaned back into his chair. "Not all sacred texts are sacred. Love God, Miss Hudson, fear God even, if you wish, but question any doctrine which enables you to play God yourself."

"Personally, I would question any religious text which encourages you to hate another," Mycroft said. "Certainly you should hate those who inflict suffering and unkind acts against others, but hating someone simply because they are different from you is murky waters. If in doubt, consult the Golden Rule."

"That would be Leviticus 19:18," Mirabella murmured.

Sherlock's eyes softened as he looked at her. Indeed she did have a loving and caring heart, as well as a desire to learn. She was both intelligent and curious—and a product of her upbringing and the time in which she was born. Overall, her upstanding parents had done right by her. "I understand, Miss Belle. Until you have loved someone who is of a certain persuasion, it does not become real to you. When the object of your judgment is someone you love, it does open one's mind."

"You love someone who is a sodomite, Mr. Holmes?" She gasped, as if she thought him incapable of love.

He frowned, feeling the unexpected sting. "My mind might be far stronger than my heart, but I am not without one. To be sure, there are very few people I love." He could not admit his feelings for Miss Belle at this moment, particularly since she had only just stabbed him with her words. Proof that one should never feel too much.

"It all begs the question," said Mycroft somberly. "Our concern is how such a revelation, true or otherwise, would affect the government. If not for that, we would have no business whatsoever in Disraeli's private life."

"For the conservative party leader of the most powerful country on earth to be revealed to be a *Margery* would be a scandal of the highest degree," said Watson. "Besides being illegal."

"Quite so," added Mycroft. "And if Prime Minister Gladstone were removed along with Disraeli, the leaders of both the Whig and the Tory parties respectively, the government could be thrown into complete disarray."

"And subsequently, the world," mused Sherlock. "The British Empire encompasses the globe."

"The prime minister is cavorting with *men*," moaned Mirabella. "Oh, no, say it isn't so!"

"Not at all," said Sherlock. "The prime minister is cavorting with prostitutes. *Female* prostitutes."

Mycroft said consolingly, "I hope you will rest easy, Miss Hudson, knowing that all is right in the world and that all sex scandals involve the opposite sex."

"Ohhhhh!" moaned Mirabella. "But that would be . . . that would make the prime minister . . . a *pervert*."

"Welcome to the government," said Mycroft.

"Miss Hudson!" commanded Sherlock. "Pull yourself together! Am I too understand that you are so opinionated, biased, and—worst of all—*emotional* that you cannot work on this case? You had assured me that your private opinions would not interfere with your professional behavior. We most certainly cannot give you the particulars if this is to be your attitude."

"Oh, no, it's not that, Mr. Holmes. I promise you that I can detach from my feelings and do what needs to be done," pleaded Mirabella. "I do want to work on the case!"

"I fail to understand, Miss Hudson, why in this great country it is a scandal to have relations with a consenting adult—while children are dying in the workhouses, starved and working fourteen-hour days? Why is that not a greater scandal? Or that poor woman Isabella Walker who was put on trial for the erotic entries *in her private diary* discovered by her husband when her actions were above reproof?"

"Or the British subduing the natives of India by addicting them to opium?" added Mycroft. "I would think the private actions of two consenting men would be of little comparative interest to you, Miss Hudson."

"Oh, no," she whispered, a tear rolling down her cheek.

"What is it, Miss Mirabella?" asked Watson, moving to take her hand. "Do stop vexing the girl, Sherlock. Can't you see she's upset?"

"Now I understand." She was staring at Sherlock. "*You* are a . . . a . . . *poof.*"

"As usual, Miss Hudson, you understand nothing." Sherlock threw back his head and engaged in a rare bout of laughter. "And you apparently have no desire to learn anything further."

"I most certainly do—wish to learn."

"And what have you learned, Miss Belle?" Sherlock asked with feigned patience.

"I know that you are not a mandrake, Mr. Holmes! . . . *I think.*" Patting her eyes with her handkerchief just pulled out of her pocket, she stopped abruptly, a look of horror on her face, before she turned to Watson.

"John, are you . . . would you?" she whispered, her complexion ashen as her glance moved between Holmes and Watson. "You're such *good friends.*"

Watson joined in the laughter, even as he gulped out a response. "No, Miss Hudson, I am *not.*"

How any woman could have observed the way Watson looks at her and still wonder if he played the other side of the fence is a mystery. Sherlock began to truly wonder about Miss Belle's powers of observation. Proof that emotion was one's worst enemy.

"Miss Hudson, I see that giving you time to reflect is not such a good thing. Pour yourself a glass of sherry and take a seat," commanded Sherlock. "Regain your composure at once!"

Watson turned to Sherlock. "Do you seriously think someone is intending to bring down the British government?"

Mirabella's eyes grew wide, but, in her defense, she remained silent, the taking down of the government appearing to be less disconcerting to her than her employer's romantic orientation.

"I do," nodded Sherlock. "And I don't think we're any closer to stopping him."

"Or *her,*" said Mycroft, his expression intense.

CHAPTER TWENTY
A Dangerous Liason

"Sherlock, do come sit beside me," Fantine purred, leaning towards him and revealing her milky white breasts framed by black lace, making no effort to ensure her dressing gown fully covered her body. The sitting room of her hotel room might be separate from her bedroom, but her manner did not distinguish.

"I think not, Countess Florentine." He removed his pipe from his pocket while he glanced out the window to observe the glass ceiling of the railroad station, its two hundred and forty-three foot span forming the world's largest enclosed space, attached as it was to the Midland Grand Hotel. Magnificent that one could see the glass atrium of the train station from her room.

"Are we still on such terms, Sherlock? Call me Fantine."

"I do not wish to abandon all sense of propriety, my dear Mrs. Noel."

Sherlock heard the blast from the steam whistle of an approaching train, sounding as if it might barrel through the room they were standing in.

"I can honestly say that I have never wanted a man to kiss me more than I want you to, Sherlock." She smiled at him, positively alluring despite the fact that he would very soon be deaf.

"I regret to inform you, Countess Florentine, that you might not get what you want."

"I always do." She moved to him and tapped her fingers along his solid chest, before placing her index finger on his lips.

Click-clack Click-clack! He heard the wheels hitting the gap in the rail joints. Astonishing to be joined with the rail station as it were. One felt to be in the engine room of the train.

"This is the staircase suite, if I'm not mistaken?" he inquired. His eyes moved to the spiral staircase which connected her sitting room to her bedroom.

"You rarely are," she said.

"Almost never," he agreed. He could now hear the orchestra playing on the rooftop intermingling with the whistle of the train arriving in the station. Though he personally found the sound of a train both intoxicating and comforting at the same time, he wondered if the in-house theatre found the performances challenging with all the competing noises. He glanced about the exquisite room decorated in gold leaf and maroon, bringing to mind the setting for the sheik's harem with its chiffon fabrics, stenciled walls, mosaics, mahogany woods, and high ornamental ceiling. "This must be a very expensive room."

"Naturally," she said.

"Of course. It must be the Midland Grand for Fantine Florentine; it can be no other. Rich, lavish, and expensive." *Gothic, mysterious, sumptuous, and exotic.* "Not to mention excessively extravagant."

"One can never have too much of a good thing," she pronounced.

"Yes, one can, Countess." He glanced at her. "In fact, the difference between happiness and misery is often in the excess." No one knew this better than he.

"Kiss me, Sherlock," she whispered, leaning towards him. He could feel her warm breath on his mouth.

"Why, so that you might take out your knife and stab me in the back, my dear?"

Hiss hiss! He heard the brakes applied.

"Why don't you long for me as I long for you, Sherlock?" she demanded, but her eyes were laughing.

"Having to be on the watch for a knife attack, poisoning, head injury, and attempted murder tends to dampen my ardor, Countess."

She pushed him down on the couch and her lips came down on his, filled with need. In his experience, Fantine was always filled with need for something she could not name. That would account for her insatiability.

Not always a bad thing.

Fantine Noel would never be fulfilled, he knew that. The longing that ran through her veins gave her a desperation that was, to say the least, stimulating, however he might protest to the contrary.

"Sherlock . . ." she whispered, running her hands along his chest and then his hips, reaching for his belt buckle.

"Fantine," he protested hoarsely, pulling away from her. "Why are you doing this? You'll get nothing from me."

"Oh, I think I will," she whispered, her eyes alight with mischief, always her best look, a glossy pink curl escaping to land on her forehead. "I expect to get precisely what I want."

"I've heard the Midland Grand even has a smoking room for ladies," he mused, maintaining his balance on the couch with some difficulty. "Most progressive."

"Sherlock, you know I don't smoke," she said.

"Oh, yes, you do, my dear." He smiled at her before pulling her towards him, his lips sliding along hers before capturing her mouth.

Oh, she is divine.

How well he understood the need that would never be fulfilled. Particularly by the woman he truly wanted.

But Fantine Noel kept his mind off all that—for a little while at least.

"You know, Countess . . ." he kissed her neck, gradually moving downward. "Why do you continually flirt with me when we both know what this is about?"

"Oh. And what is it about?" She was beginning to breathe heavily, positioning her body so as to give him little chance of resistance.

"To distract me from what you are doing." He lost his face in her glorious breasts.

"I have no wish to distract you, I assure you," she whispered breathlessly. "And I think you know what I am doing."

He pulled her lips to his again, delighting in the taste of her mouth. "Countess, why do we go on this way?"

"What other way is there to go on? Oh, do stop talking Sherlock and take me to the bedroom."

He picked her up in one fell swoop and obliged her, negotiating the spiral staircase of wrought iron balustrade in steps of two and three.

CHAPTER TWENTY-ONE
Answers

The woman is insatiable. She ran her hands along his chest at the moment she should be completely satisfied, and she seemed more interested than ever, although one could not discount the pleased glow in her expression.

"Do you think me a complete fool, Countess?"

"Naturally I do not."

"And yet, I am always your plaything, without exception, doing precisely what you wish."

"And I am your plaything," she whispered. "It is entirely mutual." Ringlets of her lustrous strawberry blonde hair fell loose to her shoulders. He treasured these moments when she was the least regulated and contained. Her lace robe fell back, and, more than the beauty of her shape, he cherished the lack of calculation of her impetuous state. To simply *be* rather than crafting her next move.

So rare for either of them.

He could not help it, she was irresistible: clever, voluptuous, manipulative, devious.

Desirable.

And intelligent. It was her intelligence that sparked his desire. He was invariably able to resist women—it was a pointless exercise with unwanted consequences. He made an exception for Fantine.

"You know very well that there can be no other woman for you, Sherlock," she added.

"There is *no* woman for me," he replied definitively.

"You *stayed*, Sherlock." She pulled her satin robe around her slim waist, but she did not pout, which he found all the more inviting. "Do not pretend with me, it is futile."

"If I were interested in women—which I am not—I should like to find one like you, Fantine—clever and vibrant—unfettered shall we say."

"Why not me then, Sherlock?" she purred.

"One like you—but with some goodness in her," he said. He glanced about the exquisite room in dark blues decorated in a revivalist Gothic style only absent the spires and gargoyles to gaze into the fireplace.

"You would be bored to death with goodness, Sherlock." She ran her index finger along his chin. Her brain was now fixed on a desired outcome, and he could not like it. Every action had a purpose in mind where Fantine was concerned.

But when she was simply smiling at him in amusement or delight it was glorious.

"You need a bit of unpredictability in your life," she added.

"It seems I do, although the experience is something new to me." Granted, part of Fantine's appeal was her ability to manipulate him to her own ends—to outsmart him and deceive him—so rare in his experience.

And yet, those even rarer moments, almost nonexistent, when she desired nothing of him but his mere presence was intoxicating. Sherlock was unaccustomed to one who wanted nothing from him or was not awaiting his performance.

"Hmmm . . . You should like to find someone *good*," she considered.

"Not all good of course. But she should at least be on the *side* of good," he said. Though perhaps a good woman would not have me.

"Whereas I have the devil in me." Her tempting lips formed a wicked smile.

He took her in his arms. "One of the reasons I like you, Countess."

"Like me? You adore me, Sherlock, admit it." She looked away when there was no response. "We have just made love, and you still cannot call me by my first name?"

"Oh, that wasn't love," he replied, running his finger along her lovely white cheek and then along her warm lips.

"What was it then?"

"It was a fantastic ride into the world of ecstasy, I should say."

"That will trump love any day," she replied, suddenly moving to straddle his body.

"I would not know, I have nothing to compare it to," he said, even as he dismissed her advances. "I shall go no further unless you answer my question."

"And what question is that?" she asked.

"Why do you align yourself with Moriarty? He has stolen plans that compromise our country's security. As if that weren't enough, he is amassing state secrets in an attempt to threaten our government more directly. Why would you assist such a person as this?"

"Sherlock, you are so unromantic." Her breath was warm in his ear.

"As I said, this has nothing to do with romance, do not lie to yourself or to me."

She pulled away from him as quickly as she had pressed herself to him, rising to pour two glasses of sherry, her beige silk gown floating as it hugged her body clothed in sheer black lace, her movement particularly inviting, which was no doubt her purpose. She wished to increase his anticipation.

And it was beginning to work.

"If all of your actions are evil then that must make you so."

"Evil? Not at all. I merely do it for money."

"Redeem yourself. Tell me, Fantine, where are the missing submarine plans?"

"Do you suppose that I would tell you if I knew, Sherlock?" she purred.

Ah, but you've already told me. You've just come from Holborn Street according to the cabbie I've bribed to always be available when you desire a cab. Holburn is too far west for the businessmen of London, thereby devoid of first class shops and warehouses, and too far east for the fashionable world—in other words, you. What possible business would you have there? Being of a suspicious nature, you changed cabs when you arrived at Fleet Street, but I would wager there is a large warehouse in the vicinity for Moriarty's contraband—and I anticipate the submarine plans are there.

"No, I don't suppose you would, Fantine."

"And should you be discussing this with me? Aren't you afraid I'll run to James and tell him that you are apprised of his plans?"

"I certainly hope that you do, Countess. I wish him to think I am on his trail. It might distract him a bit."

"As you are distracting me?" She set down her glass. She returned to the bed and began kissing his chest.

"Please, Fantine. I am not a machine."

"Truly? I have often heard you described as such." She sighed, looking up at him through fluttery eyelashes surrounding alluring jeweled blue eyes, striking against her pale hair. "And I find that I must concur."

CHAPTER TWENTY-TWO
Indecent Behavior

"I am absolutely appalled! You have sunk to some low things in the time I have known you, Mr. Sherlock Holmes, but this is beyond indecency!" exclaimed Mirabella, almost slamming the tea tray on the table before him.

"I am gratified to know that it is still possible to surprise you, Miss Belle," he considered, leaning back in his chair, clearly waiting for her to pour his tea.

He was so disheveled that he looked ridiculous as he held his teacup in a genteel manner, his dark curls in disarray, his face unshaven, and his navy silk tie looped half-heartedly mid-way down his chest, an unbuttoned shirt revealing a boxer's muscular build.

"Oh! How can you sit there so smug when you know very well that you have crossed the line?"

"It is certainly not a line which I drew, so I don't know why it should concern me to have crossed it."

"I see," she managed, raising her nose into the air.

"And what is it that you see, Miss Belle?" he asked far too politely for Sherlock Holmes—which was all the more aggravating.

"I see that you are devoid of godliness and propriety—and are the most self-absorbed creature imaginable! You imagine your opinion to be the only one which matters."

"Very true. I find that we are in agreement, Miss Belle, as surprising a circumstance as that might be."

"Obstinate man!"

"True again. And that should concern me because?"

"Because . . . you know very well that . . . you . . . you didn't come home last night!" said Mirabella, her anger turning to dismay. "What do you have to say for yourself, Mr. Sherlock Holmes?"

"I am often out all night, why should this warrant your attention, Miss Belle?" he asked, sipping his tea.

"First of all, you generally come in much earlier than nine in the morning. And you most certainly would have not already eaten breakfast!"

"You are laying guilt at my door because I was not hungry?" he asked, smiling with a smugness which was annoying as he replaced his teacup on the tray, adding more sugar and cream.

"Second, you don't ever have the scent of perfume on your clothes!"

"Not true. Particularly when I am playing the part of a woman."

"And, third, after you have been on a case all night, you don't come in here floating about on a cloud."

His eyes shot up to meet hers. "I am definitely not floating!"

"You are, by comparison to your usual self," she insisted. "Generally you would be flurrying about here in an excited state attempting to solve the case which has absorbed you all evening."

"I am relieved to see that your powers of observation are improving, Miss Belle." He leaned back into his chair and shut his eyes momentarily, the well-defined muscles in his arms evident. He had the unmistakable look of contentment in his expression, alarming to see on the countenance of Sherlock Holmes. She longed to see him in his usual agitated state, generally a source of great annoyance to her. "Allow me a short nap, Miss Belle, and I shall be right as rain. I am positively spent."

"Why do you let her use you like that?" she asked, barely able to keep her hands from shaking.

He opened one eye to look at her. "Why is it a concern of yours that someone *uses me*, as you put it, Miss Belle? Do you feel that it is your exclusive right?"

"Concern of mine? Certainly not! Don't you have a care for virtue and . . . and . . . *morality*?"

"Definitely not. I try to avoid morality whenever possible."

"Mr. Holmes, this is not the way proper people live! What about society and respectability?"

"Oh, do you think I should save myself for marriage, Miss Belle? I am a confirmed bachelor." Sherlock chuckled, holding his teacup in mid-air. "At any rate, it was not that long ago you were afraid I was a *Marjery*. I should think you would be relieved."

"Fantine Noel is not good for you, Sherlock. She doesn't love you."

He raised his eyebrows, clearly noticing that she had slipped and called him by his first name. But, for once, he didn't correct her.

"Oh, so I see you've been talking to Watson," he mused, a smirk on his lips which she found terribly annoying. "Of course she doesn't *love me*, as you say. But she does have a certain affection for me—in her own way."

"And her way is to poison and injure you?" Mirabella asked.

"It is a way that is uniquely Fantine's."

"True love, indeed."

His expression grew serious as his eyes looked intently into hers. "I never professed to be in love, Miss Belle."

"It's just that . . . well that . . . you deserve better than that, Mr. Holmes!" Having poured her own tea, she plopped herself down opposite him, blowing the lock of curl that had fallen into her eyes.

"Do I?" he asked, raising an eyebrow. "And what does a self-absorbed, insufferable man truly deserve? I might have surmised from the comments you have made, Miss Belle, that what I *deserve* is to be carried off by a family of vultures."

"I only said such a thing because you make me so angry sometimes."

"Oh, and why should you be angry? It is not your place to be angry. Moreover, you are in the employ of one of the most brilliant men in England—and the world's only consulting detective. My knowledge I gladly share with you. I also tolerate your tirades and unprofessional demeanor. You are a most fortunate young lady."

"That is true." She clenched her teeth. "And yet you have thrown me into every manner of danger. In your employ I have been shot at, engaged in a knife fight to the death, corseted to the point of fainting, chained to a tugboat, and almost devoured by man-eating tigers!"

"Don't be discouraged, Miss Belle. I have every expectation that the excitement will pick up once you become more familiar with your duties."

She placed her hands on her hips. "In addition, I have no doubt lost both my reputation and my place in heaven in parading about half-naked before spectators."

He yawned. "Do get to the point, Miss Belle."

"The point is, a threat on my life I can bear, but this . . . this behavior of yours, I cannot. Why am I angry, you ask? I shall tell you."

"Then do so."

"I cannot."

"Why?" asked Sherlock.

"Because I am too angry." She stood and moved to stand before him.

He raised his eyebrow at her but was otherwise calmly composed. "Most illogical, Miss Belle. Incoherence I cannot tolerate above all else."

"You shall have to tolerate it, just as I have to tolerate you."

"You are mistaken, Miss Belle. You have to tolerate me because I am your employer, as you so often forget. I, on the other hand, do not have to tolerate you."

"Do you not see, Mr. Holmes? Do you not see how unkind you are to one who serves you?"

"Not in the least. All I see is insubordination."

She added under her breath. "And to one who cares about you."

"Who cares about me in what way?" he asked softly, the anger suddenly erased from his expression.

"In the way . . . in the only way . . . well, as a friend of course!"

"Of course." He closed his eyes momentarily.

"At any rate, we were not speaking of that but of why on earth you would allow that woman to take advantage of you for her own nefarious purposes."

"*Or mine.* So, we're back to that again? Very well, I shall humor you. Why do you concern yourself? Let us be honest, Miss Belle. What is your primary objection to my relationship with Fantine Florentine? Could it be that you are offended that I should have an entirely carnal relationship? Which is entirely none of your affair."

"It isn't *the thing*," she managed to utter under her breath, biting her lip and looking away.

"It isn't the thing *for you*, Miss Belle."

"It isn't in your best interest either," she said softly.

"Oh? You might have fooled me. And since when have you been an expert on what shall best serve me, Miss Belle?"

"Don't you wish to be loved, Sherlock?" She sat beside him.

He reached forward in his seat and placed his hands on her shoulders, gazing into her eyes for a moment. It was mystifying as he looked at her, as if time stood still for a moment, as if they were not employer and employee—but something else.

"What an antiquated notion," he stated finally, his voice raspy as he released his hold on her shoulders.

She felt a tingling where he had touched her that would not subside. "You are brilliant, Mr. Holmes." Nervously she picked up her cup of tea and took a sip.

"I didn't think that was in question. Countess Florentine appreciates my brilliance, I assure you." One again, his gaze penetrated hers. "She prefers to show me her appreciation rather than to speak about it, however."

Egad. It made her stomach tie into knots to think of it, the woman leading the great Sherlock Holmes around like a puppy dog. And his begging, rolling over, and playing dead at the countess' command! At least Mirabella hoped he was only *playing* dead.

"Fantine isn't much of a conversationalist unless one is talking about her," Sherlock added.

"And does the countess appreciate your loyalty to your friends, your commitment to justice, your service to your country, and your devotion to truth? Does she appreciate all the qualities that make you not just the great detective Sherlock Holmes, but—*you?*"

"I assure you she does not. Fantine Noel, though beautiful, devious, and intelligent, has no understanding of such principles."

"Do tell." She leaned back into her chair. "How can she appreciate someone who knows right from wrong since she herself does not?"

"Precisely. Indeed Fantine Noel would sell me for a farthing. She has no loyalty and therefore does not understand it. She is devoted to nothing except herself."

"What do you see in her?" Mirabella demanded. "She is a *criminal*." How revolting that he should be in the arms of such a woman as this!

"Yes, that is most unfortunate. But, honestly, if she were good it would diminish her appeal."

She almost spit out her tea. "What do you mean, Mr. Holmes?" How could one so brilliant say such idiotic things?

"Someone who is entirely good and adheres to a code learned from society lacks a certain spontaneity. As opposed to someone who feels no confines, no barriers, no need to be anyone except who she is."

"Ah, I see. The same could be said about Satan: someone who is simply true to himself, without guilt or compliance to any other man."

Sherlock laughed. "There is a certain devilishness about Countess Florentine that is refreshing. Someone who lives outside the normal sphere of society—like myself—who is unfettered by such constraints."

"You wish for spontaneity, Mr. Holmes? I am quite certain you could find that in someone with a modicum of morality."

"Morality is over-rated. It is precisely what I object to in this instance. I thought I made that clear."

"Honestly! You are positively incomprehensible today!"

"Calm yourself, Miss Belle." He chuckled. "I am not going to settle down with Fantine. Marriage is out of the question. I like her, she likes me; it is merely an affair de coeur."

"Or an affair, at least," she said. An affair of the heart was definitely stretching the truth.

"And why does the physical disturb you, Miss Belle?" His penetrating gaze was quite discomposing as he held her eyes for a moment, the rawness of his expression ever evident in his disheveled state.

"It d-doesn't," she managed to whisper as she looked at him, so naïve and childlike with his tousled hair, and yet so masculine. Her teacup was shaking in her hands so she set it down as best she could. "But you deserve *more*, Sherlock."

"Perhaps. But I assure you that what I had was sufficient. And, if one didn't know better, I'd say you were jealous, Miss Belle."

"Jealous?" she gasped. "How absurd!"

"Then why would you concern yourself with how I am being treated? Not to mention passing judgment."

"I told you, I . . . well, I . . . I never . . ."

"Judgment is often a veil for a different emotion. There is no reason for you to care—unless you do care, Miss Belle."

"Dr. Watson shares my concerns, and he is certainly not jealous."

Sherlock rose from his chair with the clear intent to retire to his room.

"Make certain that your concerns are all that you share with the good doctor, Miss Belle," he pronounced with a sudden sternness.

She flung the *Gazette* under his nose. "Since you have been too busy to stay informed of the case, I have taken the liberty of finding the relevant articles for your perusal."

"A Russian diplomat, a Mr. Perminov, is coming to London for the queen's celebration," he read. "I am not surprised. Any number of dignitaries will be here as the queen's guests. And this shall interest me because?"

She stared at him long and hard, but only had to wait a moment before Sherlock threw the paper on the floor. "Great Scott! I have been a fool!"

"I know that you believe the submarine plans are intended for the Germans, but what if Moriarty intends them for the Russians?" she asked softly, having no great confidence in her idea. But she couldn't in all good conscience keep her conclusions from him. "Or perhaps, as misdirection, the Russians plan to sell the plans to the Germans in turn?"

Sherlock leapt from his chair , pulling her up. He began waltzing about the room with her, twirling her here and there to her absolute astonishment. "I have been on the wrong trail, but I see it all clearly now. Excellent work, Miss Belle!"

He held her tightly in his arms and, for the first time, she wondered if Fantine Noel might be a positive influence after all.

CHAPTER TWENTY-THREE
A Social Butterfly

"When do I get to kill him, Professor?"

"I never like to kill anyone unless it is absolutely necessary. Very uncouth." Moriarty sighed. *Sometimes I am simply too good.* It wouldn't do to shoot oneself in the foot over sentiment. "However, we must look to the future. Which is . . . the Speaker of the House of Commons."

"Who is that?" Babbitt asked.

"Henry Brand, you idiot."

"I thought 'twas Peel?"

"Indeed, Arthur Wellesley Peel is one to watch out for as well."

"When can I kill him?"

"Now is not the time."

"Shall I ship them off to America then?"

"Oh, the Americans wouldn't know what to do with Brand and Peel. The white wigs are very confusing to the colonials."

"Might be a good idea then."

"Patience, my man." Moriarty tapped his chin with his finger. "The reward is thus all the sweeter."

"What about the leader of the opposition, Professor? Can I kill him?"

"Sir Stafford Northcote? No. It is necessary to first determine if he is an asset or not." Moriarty smiled in his most gentlemanly manner, adding softly, "I have ways to force the issue."

"I does like the force." Babbitt was grinning now. "You knows, I was thinkin' . . ."

"Spare me."

"Professor, why don't you get elected to the House of Commons? Anymores, the P.M. is from the House of Commons."

Moriarty stared at Babbitt, surprised. *Believe me, that is precisely what I intend to do.* "And how do you propose that I do this, Babbitt?"

His minion beamed. "How will you win? Hmmm, let's see. There ain't no more rotten boroughs is there? Old Sarum had only six voters for two

MPs, y'know."

Moriarty's frown returned. "You don't think I can win without rotten boroughs? I have more brains than the entire House of Lords put together."

"Well, sure, but . . ."

"But *what?*"

Babbitt shook his head. "You're an apostle o' culture, to be sure, boss, but you can be, well . . . "

Moriarty ground his teeth. It was everything he could do to keep from hitting the man upside the head. "Spit it out!"

"Y'know. *Stodgy.*"

"You're saying I'm a dead bore."

"That's it, boss."

"I'll have you know I am exceedingly interesting." Above all, Moriarty prided himself on being a gentleman of culture and education. When he ruled the country, let's see how unexciting people considered him to be.

"Oh, yeah. Right. I forgot. You're a regular haw-haw toff, boss."

Moriarty frowned. Social situations were indeed challenging. It was difficult to make conversation about children, family, marriages, country homes, and parties—all things that didn't matter to him in the least. He could discuss mathematics for hours, but the general population was comprised of idiots. As for politics and power, which he did care about, people tended to get a bit frightened when he discussed those subjects. Consequently, it would never do to reveal his true opinions.

Moriarty regained his composure. Why should he care for the opinion of an imbecile? Babbitt worked for him, after all.

"The only way youse can win, boss, is if you find a golden boy to be the front man. Then, you can control him like you do everyone, see?"

Even a fool if he persist in his folly can become wise. William Blake may have had the right of it. Moriarty kept his expression staid, but inwardly the wheels were turning.

"Ah, rotten boroughs. Those were good old days. But never fear, where there's a will, there's a way. Ha! Ha!"

Babbitt joined in the laughter, though he didn't appear to know why he was laughing.

CHAPTER TWENTY-FOUR
Lady of the Night

"Do have another chocolate, my dear," Fantine murmured, holding the fancy box as far from her body as she could. She made a mental note to throw the box away once this girl had touched its contents. Thankfully she had worn her thickest gloves.

The younger woman's ungloved hand shook as she reached for the chocolate. She was grey in pallor. Quite revolting to look at actually. She put the candy in her pocket.

"What are you doing, Miss Emily? You must eat the chocolate."

"I only want it for my sister."

Fantine frowned. "You will offend me if you don't eat it. You may have another for your sister." *Although I wonder that your sister would wish to have it now that it is contaminated. Perhaps she is already as revolting as you.*

Emily suddenly appeared even more ghastly, if that were possible. "I would not want to give offence, ma'am! You have been so kind."

Despite her revulsion, Fantine felt a pang of anger for Emily's state: this was the result of those in power being men.

That shall never happen to me. I shall always be the one in control.

Emily reluctantly took another chocolate, momentarily closing her eyes in pure bliss. "Oh, I has never eaten anything like it." She opened her eyes. "Why are you being so nice to me, ma'am?"

Clearly the frail girl was not accustomed to kindness. "You have had a difficult time of it, haven't you, dear? Have another chocolate."

"May I have another for my sister?"

Fantine felt a bit of annoyance at the girl's goodness. Certainly she herself had a certain affection for her brother, but, if the truth be told, she did this work for her own benefit. And to prove to James that there were things she could do better than he. "Yes, yes. She must be very important to you."

Emily nodded. "I will sell me teeth and me hair before I die so as to give the money to me sister Sarah. I don't want her to be so 'ungry that she did what I did."

Fantine knew that the selling of hair and teeth was not unheard of among girls dying of diseases. She shuddered. The extraction would be done without any type of drug to dull the pain—a drug would only increase the cost and therefore reduce the proceeds. And it would be done while the invalid was still alive in order to ensure that the money was given to the intended recipient.

"What is it you don't wish Sarah to do?" Fantine asked.

"To sell her body." Emily sobbed. "I'm going to Hell. I don't want that for her."

"There, there, dear. Hell is a story made up by someone with the intent to make us behave. I wouldn't give it a second thought. And, if Hell does exist, it is the men who will go there, not you."

"Oh, no! Men are what they are." The poor girl showed a reverence for those who had taken advantage of her.

"The prime minister. Did he do this to you?"

"Mr. Gladstone?" Emily asked in alarm. "I've met him. He's kind of scary—at first—he never smiles or laughs. But he never touches. He tries to help."

"I'm sure he wanted to." Fantine sought to hide her disappointment. "The P.M. didn't do this to you?"

"No, ma'am."

"Who did then?"

Emily sought to hold back the tears. "I can't say. It could have been anyone."

Fantine held the box out to the girl. "Give me a name, dear." *I can work with that.*

"I have a feeling . . . but I don't know . . . it would be unkind . . ."

"Tell me."

"It might have been . . . I think . . . Lord Alsop." Emily swayed, and fainted.

Excellent.

Momentarily it occurred to Fantine that Emily would consider it a treasure to find the box of chocolates when she awoke—if she awoke.

Fantine glanced in the girl's direction before leaving, carrying the fancy box. As she exited the building, she threw the fancy box in the alley. She then removed her gloves and handed them to a beggar child, whose face was alight with pleasure. Those gloves would no doubt feed her family for a week.

Fantine shrugged. They were easily replaced.

CHAPTER TWENTY-FIVE
Warehouse Headquarters

"This is it, Watson," Sherlock said, crouched down behind the greenery as he watched Moriarty alight from his carriage and enter a seemingly abandoned building in Old Bailey Newgate. "Moriarty's warehouse. I warrant the submarine plans are hidden somewhere in that building."

"It's going to be difficult to search the warehouse with so many of his henchmen swarming the building at all times. Perhaps we should procure your brother Mycroft's assistance."

"And get the government involved?" Sherlock asked.

"It *is* a matter of national security."

"Which is precisely why we shouldn't involve the government." Sherlock shook his head. "Moriarty has eyes and ears at all levels of the government. It would have to be the only option left to us."

"I'd say we are there. What are you going to do then? We can't give the professor time to decipher the plans."

"Moriarty needs the key. The question is, who has the key? Naturally, it would be the Swedish arms manufacturer Thorsten Nordenfelt and the Reverend George Garrett, who designed the plans. I have telegraphed both of them and instructed them to go into hiding. Now that Moriarty is involved, they are in imminent danger. This is where Mycroft can be of assistance. In the meantime, Moriarty no doubt believes he is clever enough to discern the key on his own."

"Maybe he is."

"That is why we must recover the blueprints. There is so much else I need to be doing—Moriarty has a dozen irons in the fire to put out—but this must be my first priority."

"Holmes, you're running yourself ragged. You're barely sleeping; it's a wonder you're able to function."

"I fear I have no time for sleep presently."

"Let me help you," Watson whispered from behind the brush. "I might be a doctor, but I do have military experience."

"Not possible, Watson. It's too dangerous."

"Holmes, you might be brilliant but you're only one man. You need to get us all on board with this—me, the Baker Street Irregulars, Miss Mirabella, and Mycroft."

"Moriarty will stop at nothing. I can't involve Miss Belle—or even you—and I can't involve children."

"And how is this different from other cases? You're burning the candle at both ends, Holmes. Right now I'd put my money on Wiggins over you."

***

"Careful w' that, Hornby!" growled Babbitt. "Don't drop it!"

"Eh, gov'ner, I'm movin' it just where's you said," the ugly-faced thug said. The work at the Old Bailey Newgate warehouse was hard physical labor, but the new recruit was up to the challenge.

Hornby kept his eye on the room which appeared to be Moriarty's office, keeping his eyes averted when Moriarty was present.

Hornby saw that there was a safe in the warehouse, but it could be nothing so simple as that.

"Get busy, you lazy ass!" Babbitt yelled. "What are you starin' at?"

"Nuffin, sir! I was thinkin' these boxes should be moved over by the boss's window so as the water drippin' through the roof don't damage 'em."

"Oh, you were thinkin', was you? You ain't paid to think!" Babbitt growled, but he glanced at the window and then at the roof. "Aw' right then! Go do it!"

Hornby began moving the boxes, watching Moriarty through the loose weave of his worn hat.

The luck was with him today! Moriarty had the blueprints on his table and was studying them while writing formulas on his chalkboard. Clever to do it away from his office at university. No one here would have the slightest understanding of what he was doing.

And yet, this was the perfect use for the laborer's photographic memory as he determined to show Miss Belle the formulas that evening. He anticipated there would be some difficulty in recollection as he was not as familiar with the mathematical symbols as she was.

"Hornby! Get over here!"

Damn it! If he might only stay about the window long enough to determine where the plans were hidden. Then he might arrange a police search. So much of detective work was long hours of waiting and watching.

At that moment Moriarty rose and pulled the curtains. Sherlock continued to move the boxes as directed. At least he was on the same floor. In about a half hour's time, Moriarty left and locked his office, heading for the warehouse door.

Sherlock studied Moriarty's three-piece suit and saw no sign of anything bulging from his vest. On the other hand, Moriarty favored his left-hand side as he walked. It was subtle, but it was there. And he was carrying a cane.

Of course! Moriarty has no need for a cane. He was not leaning on the cane or using it in anyway, nor was he twirling it as some men did for show as an embellishment—and yet he kept the cane close to his body, as if it were of great importance to him.

He has the blueprints on him, rolled up tightly in that rather thick walking aid!

Sherlock longed to jump Moriarty then and there for the plans. Sherlock would have happily given his life for them, but he would need to procure the blueprints in the process and pass it on to the appropriate person. If he were to attack Moriarty, the professor's thugs would murder him on the spot.

And there was no way to contact anyone in order to follow Moriarty. He would have to slip out and do so himself.

He had a cab waiting a block away. Even so, he needed more back-up. Moriarty had any number of goons surrounding him, and Sherlock knew he wouldn't be able to lift the plans off the professor.

I was a fool to think I could do this alone. Watson was right, he could not continue to work alone. He must accept the assistance of those who had chosen this work of their own free will, regardless of the danger. *I must truly embrace Watson and Miss Belle as my partners—and, yes, even the Baker Street Irregulars.*

Sherlock hated to admit it, but Miss Belle might have been right when she said that, just like Moriarty, pride was his un-doing. He had thought it was his emotion, but emotion was manageable if the mind was stronger. He was a young detective, but he would yet become a successful detective— and the man he was meant to be.

At least something good had come out of this: he had seen the plans with his own eyes, he had verification that the blueprints were with Moriarty, and he knew that the professor had not yet discerned the key.

And he knew something else: he might have trouble lifting the plans off Moriarty, but also would the professor have difficulty handing the plans to Mr. Perminov.

After observing Moriarty alight at his private residence, Sherlock headed straight for Mycroft's office without changing, initially having some difficulty in entering the government building. Once alone together, Sherlock told Mycroft what he knew: the plans were indeed with Moriarty, they were currently in his cane, and under no circumstances should Moriarty be allowed in Mr. Perminov's vicinity.

"It is a tricky wicket to keep a close watch on a foreign dignitary without giving offence," Mycroft pronounced, tapping his finger on his lips. "But I guarantee it shall be done. Mr. Perminov arrives tomorrow for the queen's party, the anniversary of her ascension to the throne. Both he and Professor Moriarty will be under the closest scrutiny at all times. No one shall be allowed near our Russian friend who has not been personally approved by me."

Some moments later, Sherlock arrived at Baker Street, reproducing what he had seen on Moriarty's chalkboard for his employee. "Bloody hell! I do not have a doctorate in mathematics!"

"You should have taken me with you," Mirabella admonished. "Although, like you, I am stronger in chemistry than in mathematics." She stopped speaking abruptly as she studied the symbols. "And yet . . . these are trigonometric functions. I wouldn't think that would be of any difficulty for the professor to solve. But there is something else. . . Oh, my goodness!"

"What is it Miss Belle?" Sherlock demanded.

"Some of these symbols are actually Hebrew, Mr. Holmes! It makes perfect sense! The submarine was designed by a Reverend George Garrett and Nordenfelt, and the key represents their combined knowledge: mathematics and Biblical references."

Sherlock felt his mood escalate. "Moriarty might be an expert in mathematics, but his knowledge of the Bible is no doubt limited." He grew somber. "Could you solve this key, Miss Belle?"

"If I had the original—it is possible I could. I was educated at home by my curate father, you know." Mirabella added shyly with virtuous feminine humility, "And, frankly, I was the best of his students."

CHAPTER TWENTY-SIX
Job Promotion

"Dash it, Your Excellency, you've got to stop cavorting with prostitutes!"

"*Cavorting*? Is this what the moronic are calling charitable works these days?" barked the great Gladstone, the prime minister of a world-wide empire, Great Britain's golden age. He stood up from behind a monstrous mahogany desk, his terrifying stare launched over the infamous beak of a nose which would have made a puddle out of a lesser man than Mycroft Holmes. "Define *cavorting* for me, you impertinent denigrate!"

"However innocent it might be, observing—rather, spending time with—that is to say, lavishing your Christian hospitality upon these unfortunate but beautiful and seductive ladies, it clearly takes up a great deal of your valuable time, Your Excellency." Mycroft rubbed his square chin pensively, clearly unconcerned at the wrath which was being unleashed upon him. He glanced overhead at a simple, un-ornamental chandelier with disapproval.

"The only one who is wasting my valuable time is you, Mycroft Holmes. Take your party and see your way to the door!" Gladstone commanded. Even at seventy-three years old the British liberal statesman was as commanding a presence as ever with the unequivocal appearance of a bird of prey, an impression which had only become exaggerated with age. His stare was fierce, and his presence both terrifying and magnetic. So charismatic was the P.M.'s presence that he had been known to hold an audience in rapture for a six-hour speech on as tedious a subject as the country's finances.

"This is a government issue, or I should not be here. Being a man of intelligence, you must know that, Your Excellency," Mycroft replied with an unconcerned air of sophistication, seating himself in a leather chair while taking special care with the tails of his superbly crafted jacket.

"My brother's inquiries have a broader scope than you appear to be comprehending, Prime Minister," interjected Sherlock.

"What is your precise title, Mycroft Holmes, and what are you doing in my office?" Gladstone demanded, ignoring the interruption.

"I am but a minor government official," Mycroft answered, lowering his chin in humility. "And I am here to serve."

"I'll serve your head on a platter if you don't answer me!" promised Gladstone, his face turning red. "WHAT IS YOUR TITLE?"

Sometimes it was difficult to believe that someone so harsh was truly God-fearing—that he feared anything, in fact.

"You know, I am not certain of my exact title from day-to-day," reflected Mycroft, unperturbed as he tapped his chin in as warm and personable a manner as if he were being lavished in compliments. "I began as an accountant in Her Majesty's treasury. I have never applied for any promotion, and yet I am continually moved from office to office. It is exceedingly difficult to keep up with my current precise title, even for a learned man such as myself."

"You are a clerical worker, then?" Gladstone emphasized.

"I would say a public servant," Mycroft replied, nodding, a warm gleam in his eye.

"You are no longer in the Treasury Department, Mycroft," corrected Sherlock before turning to the prime minister and adding in a hushed tone, "It does not interest my brother overmuch, as long as he knows where to report to work."

"I am astonished to learn that he reports to work," declared the P.M. "He doesn't appear to know his title or even his department."

"He has a team of underlings who deliver him to his desk daily," Sherlock explained. "There was a time when my dear brother was found wandering about, chatting with everyone, not arriving to work until noon. It was determined in everyone's best interest to send a carriage for him."

"Ah, yes, now it comes to me. I was transferred to the Scottish Office as a secretary to the permanent secretary," Mycroft recollected, nodding in apparent thought.

"So you're in the Scottish office?" pressed Gladstone.

"No," replied Mycroft, shaking his head.

Gladstone appeared to be grinding his teeth, his knuckles turning white.

"When the permanent secretary in the Scottish Office saw that he was in great danger of being replaced by Mycroft, he had my esteemed elder brother transferred again," explained Sherlock. He added under his breath, "It showed a commendable degree of foresight not often seen in a politician."

"Do you even know what department you are in?" screeched the prime minister, suddenly on his feet.

"Certainly I do," replied Mycroft, non-plussed. "Though, granted, it is a large and complex labyrinth and a very recent promotion of no more than several weeks duration."

"And what department is that?" insisted Gladstone as he wiped his forehead with his handkerchief, slowly lowering himself back into his chair.

"Why, I am in the foreign office," replied Mycroft. "Ah, now I recall. If titles have any bearing, I believe that they call me the permanent secretary."

"The former permanent secretary was not as fortunate as his counterpart in the Scottish Office," added Sherlock somberly.

"And neither am I," muttered the prime minister. "So. You are in administration, Mycroft Holmes. Again, I ask you why you are in my office demanding information when the prime minister does not answer to a secretary in the foreign office!"

Dr. Watson cleared his throat. "If you could but answer Mycroft's questions, Your Excellency, however personal they may strike you, they have to do with the safety and continued existence of our beloved England which I know is near and dear to your heart."

"Of course it is!" said Gladstone. "And who the hell are you?"

"I am Dr. John Watson at your service."

"More like a thorn in my side if you have anything to do with these two."

CHAPTER TWENTY-SEVEN
No Good Deed Goes Unpunished

"What I don't know is who is after the prime minister," considered Mycroft, beginning to pace Gladstone's office with a familiarity not particularly welcome to His Excellency. "And why."

"Who is after me?" The great Gladstone laughed with uncharacteristic joviality, his ferocity momentarily subdued. "The more pertinent question is *who isn't?*"

"Everyone knows about your charity work, sir," mused Sherlock, waving today's copy of the *Daily Telegraph*. "But this imparts additional information."

"I read it, dash it all!" snarled the prime minister, his expression returned to its predatory state. "It's just the conservative party attempting to make the liberals look bad rather than pitching in to help. Selfishness is the greatest curse of the human race."

"We believe it is more than that," considered Sherlock, seated across from the prime minister with Watson who sat rigidly in his chair. "*Far more.*"

Sherlock glanced about the large chamber adorned with cream-colored marble columns encased in silver filigree, a flattering contrast to the mahogany furniture and brown leather chairs. There was otherwise not much decoration, nor was there any need for it given the magnificence of the furniture and the architecture. The room was somewhat taken over by an enormous green marble table, the center of discussion for Gladstone and his fourteen-member cabinet while making decisions which would impact the entire world.

"The information is more personal," added Mycroft, stopping in front of the prime minister's desk. "The article goes into detail about your work with prostitutes and lists information that only someone in your household would be privy to."

"This is much more than malicious gossip," exclaimed Sherlock, slapping the newspaper on the massive walnut desk. "There is a purpose to it."

"Hmph! I will answer your questions in the hope that it brings your departure nearer—and as I have nothing to hide." William Ewart Gladstone never doubted his own principles, and his devotion to them was complete. Sherlock knew very well that the estimable Watson had used the only card which could have incited the P.M. to reply: *England*.

"The ladies are in my home under my wife's supervision while she attempts to find jobs and residences for them. Many have died of abominable diseases; we are attempting to save those still living from a terrible fate."

"Forgive me for saying so, sir, but if you keep on as you have been, both you and England shall suffer a terrible fate," remarked Mycroft. "And, as I'm quite sure you are aware, England needs you. What are you working on now, Your Excellency?"

"The budget," replied Gladstone. "The balanced budget is the cornerstone of finance. Spending that which one doesn't have can only lead to ruination."

"It is no accident that Britain is the most powerful country in the world and that her people are enjoying every manner of advancement," added Watson with emphasis.

"Which might mean increased taxes at this time?" asked Sherlock, tapping his finger on the desk.

"Only until the budget is balanced, then we reduce taxes," stated Gladstone. "Taxation is for revenue only, not to control economic transactions."

Sherlock knew Gladstone to be a man of his word. The P.M. had succeeded in steadily reducing the income tax over the course of his tenure as chancellor while balancing the budget.

"Ah, you're a free trader, sir," mused Dr. Watson.

"There is the little matter of the tax on paper," mused Sherlock.

"I wish to abolish the duties on paper, naturally, so that the working class people might be able to purchase the news more readily."

"The news that is now blaspheming you," considered Watson.

Gladstone shrugged. "My work is not about being popular. It's about England and what is good for her people."

"Nor is your stance popular in the House of Lords," said Mycroft.

"I should say not!" Gladstone burst forth in rare laughter. "Afraid that it will lead to the spread of radical working class ideas."

"Such as fair wages and working conditions," said Mycroft. "Could be dangerous. And I heard you gave a speech on the closing down of the workhouses. An expensive proposition."

"It is a lamentable fact if, in the midst of our civilization, and at the close of the nineteenth century, the workhouse is all that can be offered to the industrious laborer at the end of a long and honorable life, society will not have discharged its duties to its poorer members."

"In addition, the prime minister's foreign policy of peace and no alliances has kept Britain free from European wars," added Watson.

"If you want war and imperialism, go with that fop," advised Gladstone.

"You speak of the conservative MP Benjamin Disraeli?" asked Mycroft.

"He's the one who sent you here, isn't he?" asked Gladstone. "To ruin my reputation."

"Oh, no," replied Mycroft. "Disraeli knows nothing of our visit."

"Well, if there is some gossip being bantered about, you can be sure Disraeli is behind it," stated Gladstone with conviction. "Do you know, when I first met that tulip, it was 1826, he was twenty-two years old seeking political notoriety, and he was wearing a bright orange waistcoat, red trousers, *and a corset*! A corset, mind you, to effect the wasp waist! Now he could use that corset, so fat from a life of overindulgence is he, but then Disraeli was skinny and thought to be a man of fashion. That wasp waist was his claim to fame! Are you not appalled that such a *man* as this would have risen in the queen's government?

"Benjamin Disraeli is as much a victim as you are, Your Excellency," stated Mycroft, moving to sit next to Sherlock. "Surely you've read the papers."

"Of course I have," Gladstone muttered under his breath. "Orange waistcoat, indeed."

Sherlock took out his pipe, glancing at a box of Cadbury's chocolates on the prime minister's large wooden desk. He recognized it immediately as one of the fancy boxes.

Gladstone's eyes followed Sherlock's. "Hang it all, man! Why do you keep looking at my fancy chocolates? Are you hungry? You act like someone who hasn't eaten in days."

"Do forgive me, Your Excellency," Sherlock replied, but he was calculating how to get some of those chocolates. He doubted explaining that his interest was solely professional would be in the least helpful.

"I shall forgive you for nothing, and I'll thank you to nose into someone else's business," the P.M. retorted.

Sherlock's eyes met Mycroft's who appeared to appreciate his dilemma. Mycroft might not know why he wished the chocolates, but he could have no doubt of his younger brother's intent.

"We wish to save you from yourself, Your Excellency," added Mycroft, an utterance which might have been better kept to himself from the look of the steam coming out of Gladstone's ears. For one who was considered far more socially polished that himself, Mycroft said the worst thing possible at times.

There must be a reason.

"You had better save yourself from my wrath, Mycroft Holmes!" warned Gladstone. "I have always followed my conscience and my principles — even when no one was on my side — and I deuced well won't stop now for the likes of you."

Sherlock considered the man before them, knowing full well that Gladstone addressed the Queen of England in much the same manner as he was now addressing them, which might account for her intense dislike of him.

Gladstone was the same before everyone. Unlike his rival, Benjamin Disraeli, the leader of the conservative Tories, who knew how to play the political game, particularly where the queen was concerned.

"A man who can stand with his peers, every one of them against him is a strong man," said Watson, sitting in a stiff position next to Sherlock. "You're not called *The People's William* for nothing."

"I didn't do it for your approval, and I don't need that now," replied Gladstone, turning momentarily to glare at Watson, who gulped so suddenly that Sherlock thought his ordinarily fearless flat-mate might develop the hiccups.

"I have often wondered, Your Excellency," Sherlock asked, "Did you wish to extend the electorate because you believed better decisions would be made by the people?"

"It is irrelevant," said Gladstone. "I wished to give the common man the vote because it is just that he should have it. Nothing which is morally wrong can be politically right."

Mycroft moved to follow the path of his brother's eyes. Upon reaching the fancy box, he ran his hand along the velvet case and breathed deeply, adding, "The fancy box: a veritable journey into delight."

Then Mycroft surprised even his younger brother, removing the lid of the chocolates *sans invitation*. Even from across the desk the delectable aroma of almond marzipan was evident, along with the zest of oranges, dark chocolate whipped into a truffle, and fresh strawberries dipped in a thick chocolate. The box was covered in velvet and lined with silk and a mirror.

"You cursed intruder! Take your filthy hands off my chocolates!" growled Gladstone. "And sit down! Or you will soon find that the permanent secretary isn't as permanent as you had thought!"

"I mightn't have one, sir?" asked Mycroft, his silver grey eyes expressing longing.

"You mightn't!" roared Gladstone.

Mycroft studied the now opened chocolates. "But the box is practically full, sir. Only one piece is gone."

"I've seen barmaids with better manners, Mycroft!" blurted out Watson.

"For God's sake, we're in the company of the greatest statesman in all of England. Let's get on with our business before he throws us out!"

Gladstone glanced at Watson with something approaching approval but which never arrived before his eyes returned to Mycroft, with the look of the henchman who anticipated lowering the blade.

"Tell me, Your Excellency," Sherlock considered, "and this is important: did you eat the one chocolate which is gone?"

"I did, if it's any business of yours. Which it ain't."

"And did you eat it in the company of anyone?" asked Sherlock. "With a Countess Florentine, perhaps?"

Gladstone dropped his jaw, and the answer was obvious.

"And why did you not eat any more?" Sherlock pressed.

"Too delicious. It's ungodly."

They are opposites. Sherlock glanced from Mycroft to the prime minister. Gladstone was a religious evangelical who never rested and who lived entirely by his principles. It was easy to see why he did not particularly take to Mycroft, whose religion was hedonism.

Mycroft was in love with his own person and with life, completely at ease with himself and devoted to pleasure. Not adverse to God if there was fun to be had in the Almighty's presence.

Mycroft set the box of chocolates down, moving towards the P.M. "I remember when you visited the north, Prime Minister, travelling the River Tyne, twenty miles of people were lined on the river banks to cheer you on. Men stood in chimneys, factory roofs were covered with workers, and women held up their children to see the Chancellor of the People."

"And look where it's got me," said Gladstone, leaning back in his chair behind his massive oak desk. "Idiots barging into my private chambers. These false accusations against me when I am trying to do right."

"Put someone else in charge of it, don't visit the women anymore," said Mycroft.

"No one's going to tell me—"

"Ask yourself why you can't give this up, sir?" Mycroft was now leaning on Gladstone's desk, debonair in a striped satin vest in navy blue and grey. Mycroft had the Holmes' aristocratic nose, strong jaw, raven hair, and steel-grey eyes.

"It's none of your business!" snapped Gladstone.

"It is my business if it has to do with England, sir." Mycroft suddenly became as hard and formidable as the prime minister, leaning closer to Gladstone and partially blocking the P.M.'s view of the other two men in the room.

Quite on purpose, Sherlock knew. As they were engaged, Sherlock moved to the uncovered fancy box and placed three of the chocolates in his pocket. He then returned the lid to the box. Watson watched with obvious dismay, but thankfully had the good sense to allow no sound to escape his now opened mouth.

"I cannot help but wonder, sir, if you are deriving some amount of pleasure from frequenting the brothels, sitting there for hours gazing upon the women. And roaming the streets in search of such women."

For a moment Sherlock thought that Gladstone would leap out of his chair and take Mycroft by the throat.

"Never mind that you wish to purge the demon from your soul," Mycroft continued as he moved away from the desk, seeming to sense when Sherlock returned to his seat. "I realize that it is the very thing a medieval saint might have done, to expose himself to temptation, but it shall never do to face your demons in Satan's den."

"And why not?" Gladstone demanded.

"As you face them, you incite and invite them. If you truly wish to dispel your demons, you must avoid them altogether. Either indulge or avoid—there is no middle ground."

The prime minister stared at Mycroft in shocked annoyance. But Sherlock thought his brother had used the only argument which might work: appealing to Gladstone's religion.

"I only tell the truth, sir. We who have our demons have something in common."

Sherlock raised his eyebrows at his brother. Sherlock was the one who knew what it was to have demons; he should be carrying on this conversation. True, Mycroft had his as well, but they didn't vex his older brother, who clearly delighted in them. Mycroft accepted and embraced temptation without concern. He had no desire to rid himself of his passions.

"You know that you go because you have a craving you do not like. And you know as well as I do: immersing yourself in the temptation will not remove it." Mycroft laughed with abandon. "Do your good deed from afar. For England *and God.*"

"I have spent my life serving England and God. How dare you—!"

"Sir, you are the greatest financial authority yet living today," Sherlock interjected, lighting his pipe. "England needs you."

"Don't light your dratted pipe, Sherlock Holmes. You're not staying."

"If you were like Mycroft and felt no guilt, your actions might be advisable and acceptable," said Sherlock, taking a puff on his pipe. "But you are not made that way, Your Excellency."

"And how am I made?" asked Gladstone of Sherlock.

"Simple," replied Sherlock, shrugging. *"You, sir, are a man of God."*

CHAPTER TWENTY-EIGHT
Check-mate

"My idea of an agreeable person is a person who agrees with me," pronounced the formidable Tory, and the leader of the conservative party in England. Benjamin Disraeli, the Earl of Beaconsfield, wore green velvet trousers, a canary-colored waistcoat, and large silver buckles on his shoes. Copious lace protruded from underneath his sleeves. His salt and pepper hair fell in ringlets around his elongated face. It was difficult to believe that this man was a particular favorite of the queen, who was known for her conservatism.

Disraeli's office in no way softened the blow. Green wallpaper in ornate designs was offset with maroon velvet curtains which bunched at the top of each window like a lady's skirt which had become tangled in her corset.

"And to what do I owe the honor?" Disraeli asked politely while he positioned himself upon a pale green velvet fainting couch situated upon a turquoise and ivory oriental carpet. The furniture was in a light oak and a chess set was laid out and ready for battle. Unlike Gladstone's office which consisted almost exclusively of books, resembling a library, this room had the appearance of an English parlor, with numerous knick-knacks, wall candles, and a crystal chandelier overhead.

"Someone wishes to take you down, sir," said Mycroft without further adieu, nodding approvingly at the chandelier.

"I'm sure most of England and all of the rest of the world fall into that camp," replied Disraeli unapologetically as he brushed the curls out of his eyes. "Do you refer to our honorable prime minister in particular?"

"Interesting, he suspected you as well of wishing him ill," said Sherlock.

"The difference between myself and Gladstone is that, though our illustrious prime minister might wish to 'take me down' as you put it, he would never attempt it. William Gladstone has not a single redeeming defect," remarked Disraeli, studying the chess board before him and motioning Sherlock to play a game with him, who moved his chair forward. The Great Detective's mind was never sharper than when engaged in several activities at once.

Sherlock rubbed his chin before moving his knight to form an invisible "L".

"Whyever do you dislike Gladstone so, sir?" asked Watson, studying Benjamin Disraeli with more than polite interest.

"Must I explain everything? All right, I will do so," stated Disraeli as he fanned himself without waiting for a reply, "The distinction between a misfortune and a calamity is this: if Gladstone fell into the Thames, it would be a misfortune. But if someone dragged him out again, that would be a calamity."

"There are much greater forces at work than our illustrious prime minister," said Mycroft.

"Very true. Finally you understand." Disraeli moved his queen and leaned back into his couch.

"Forces that could see you in jail, Lord Beaconsfield," added Sherlock in a low tone, moving his bishop diagonally across the board.

"On what grounds?" demanded Disraeli, the amusement gone from his expression, as he sat up straight on his fainting couch.

"I'll be blunt, sir," stated Mycroft. "Gross indecency with other men."

"Tactless way to express it," said Watson uncomfortably, suddenly studying his hands.

"Tactless but accurate," said Sherlock, his eyes still on the chess board. "Lord Beaconsfield would be imprisoned if convicted. I don't think the seriousness of the situation can be overstated."

"Who has told you these things?" demanded the Earl of Beaconsfield, the personal favorite of the queen.

"It's all through your writing, sir, love affairs with . . ." Mycroft cleared his throat. "*Men*."

"Oh, so you've read my books, Mr. Holmes?" Disraeli smiled.

"Yes, sir," replied Mycroft, stretching his long legs out before him. "Very good books. But that begs the question."

"And what is the question?"

"The question is, 'How can we keep these fiends from bringing down England?' You are a brilliant statesman, and your loss would be felt."

"Most of all by me," Disraeli replied.

"Interesting move, Your Excellency," considered Sherlock. "You don't seem to have a care for the king."

"Indeed. I live for the Queen." Disraeli laughed, taking one of Sherlock's pawns.

"Never forget that a pawn can become Queen," cautioned Sherlock, looking the Conservative MP straight in the eye.

"I never have," replied Disraeli, his lips forming a sensuous smile. "And as for your unfounded accusations, I barely spend any time with men. To be sure, I hate men parties, except for the food—generally quite good. Can't tolerate male clubs. Moreover, you have no evidence of any such affairs on my part, do you?"

"No." Mycroft shook his head. "I do not."

"And my heterosexual affairs are no secret—along with my happy marriage to Mary Anne of so many years. I miss the countess terribly." He bowed his head reverently.

It was true by all accounts. Disraeli's three-year affair with Lady Henrietta Sykes beginning in 1832, all with the apparent knowledge of her husband, was much remarked on, as was Disraeli's devotion to his wife, Mary Anne, until she died in 1872.

"How much easier it is to be critical than to be correct," remarked Disraeli.

"I hardly think it matters if we are correct or not," said Watson.

"Quite true," agreed Sherlock, glancing at the fancy box on the MP's desk. "What matters is that you could be convicted with the right testimony—paid for or not. Your own testimony is all in black and white."

"It is true that there are many with the desire to see me convicted," considered Disraeli, his amusement still apparent even as he opened the box and took a chocolate while offering the box to his guests. His love of food, wine, music, art, literature, and socializing, all to excess, was well known. He was also a published author of fiction as well as a government official, an unusual combination to say the least.

Sherlock pocketed his chocolate. "And was this box delivered by Countess Florentine?"

Disraeli raised his eyebrow. "And how did you know?"

"And did you eat any in her presence?"

"Naturally."

"So no one has contacted you demanding blackmail money?" asked Mycroft, rubbing his chin in apparent concern.

"Certainly not!" replied Disraeli, leaning back into his couch. "And if they did I would be frank and explicit. That is the right line to take when you wish to conceal your own mind and confuse the mind of others."

"Hmmm," considered Mycroft, tapping his strong chin with his forefinger. "Either our culprit is merely in the information gathering stage, or he has a purpose other than blackmail."

"This is very bad," Sherlock shook his head, as the enormity of the problem became clear. *Bigger than blackmail could be very big indeed.*

"Bad is relative," Disraeli said with a smile.

"Your Excellency," Mycroft said, "I suggest that you learn to work with our P.M. instead of against him. He could be a powerful ally."

"Checkmate," Sherlock added, taking the Tory MP's queen.

Disraeli looked at his opponent in astonishment before tipping back his head and laughing with abandon.

CHAPTER TWENTY-NINE
A Private Affair

"Such a performance." Sherlock smiled, reaching for his brandy. He had unbuttoned his white cotton shirt and was leaning back in his wing-backed chair in front of the fireplace. After taking a sip of the brandy he loosened the blue and white striped ascot tie around his neck. "I am both dazzled and fatigued."

"The conservative MP is indeed better suited to the stage than to politics," Watson said.

"There is very little difference," Mycroft said in a low tone.

"Ah, but he was entirely false, only interested in manipulation," Sherlock said. "An accomplished brown-noser, to be sure."

"Many find him charming. However, I can see why you would find someone with social skills intolerable, Holmes," said Watson, glancing up from the *Illustrated London News*.

"It is true that the conservative MP and liberal prime minister are as different as night and day, as one might expect. Gladstone essentially does what he believes to be good and right," Mycroft said, "whereas Disraeli only does that which pleases him. Though I venture to say he often uses his talent for good."

"Much like yourself, brother dear," Sherlock reflected.

"True, so it might not be surprising that I find Gladstone to be insufferable, a dead bore," Mycroft added. "And indispensable to the country."

"Boring?" Sherlock laughed. "I think not. Gladstone has been known to keep his audience entranced with a *six-hour* speech on the country's budget. Has any other person in the history of the world been able to accomplish this? If so, it has not been documented."

"Most politicians are able to hold the interest of the listener with lies and slander, but rarely with facts," Watson muttered before returning his eyes to the paper, his brown top hat placed beside him on a mahogany marble end table.

"And yet—Disraeli would be a great deal more fun at a party," said

Mycroft.

"Not all of life is a party, my esteemed sibling."

"Isn't it?" Mycroft asked.

"At any rate, I can see why some find Disraeli foppish and annoying," Sherlock added with a shrug.

"You find most people foppish and annoying, Holmes," stated Watson, still perusing the paper. He added under his breath, "If I didn't know better, I would say that you are simply threatened by men of that persuasion."

"Not at all. Not my business. And the least of my worries, I might add," Sherlock said. "At any rate, I only said *some* would find him so."

"Hmmm, I do like Disraeli's taste in women, I must say," mused Mycroft. "Mary Anne, the Viscountess of Beaconsfield, was delightful. She referred to her husband as 'Dizzy' and often scandalized one with her uninhibited conversation."

"And you are one who likes to be scandalized, Mycroft," Sherlock said.

"Most assuredly."

"Why did you call Disraeli a brown-noser, Mr. Holmes?" Mirabella asked as she entered the room with a tea tray.

"If you had met him you would not need to ask." Sherlock shook his head. "And you may recall that Disraeli had the queen crowned Empress of India, which put her on par with the Russian czar. It was a veritable pageant that ensued."

"Which naturally put Disraeli in great favor with Victoria," conceded Mycroft as Mirabella set the tea tray before them, pouring their tea in the ornate Mandalay blue china set.

"Ah, now we're on a first name basis with the queen." Sherlock's lips formed a slight smile.

"Did you like him, Dr. Watson?" Mirabella asked. "The Tory MP?"

"In general, women like him, but men do not," remarked Watson, adding under his breath, "He is flamboyant to a fault."

"I don't know whether you insult the Tory MP or the male sex," said Mirabella. "Ah, not a manly man, a 'tall?"

"I shouldn't think he would know which end of the gun to point forward," Sherlock said.

"But he certainly had no trouble sending many men to their deaths," Watson said. "Disraeli supported British imperialism all over the world and initiated the invasion of Afghanistan."

"Now I see why you don't like him," said Mirabella.

"I did not say that I don't like him," replied Watson, rubbing his wounded leg.

"It was a brilliant move—the acquiring of the Suez Canal, I must admit," remarked Sherlock.

"Far from insignificant," said Mycroft, seated in the purple velvet couch while the other two gentleman sat in their wing-backed chairs in front of the fireplace facing each other.

"And what of you, Mr. Holmes?" asked Mirabella, turning towards Mycroft. "You are unusually quiet on the subject of the conservative MP."

"Am I? . . ." asked Mycroft, straightening his pale grey silk tie, a flash of gold passing through the air as the light caught his cuff-links. Unlike his younger brother, Mycroft had not loosened his crisp white shirt and, in fact, was without a single wrinkle that she could detect. The characteristic lock of dark hair fell into his forehead, which was more seductive than disheveled.

"Whatever one might feel about him, Disraeli is a great politician," Mycroft stated after a long silence. "It shall come in very useful in this circumstance. Only consider, aside from the Suez Canal, all in the course of two years Disraeli's government enacted an astonishing amount of reforms."

"To be sure," Sherlock said. "The Artisan's and Labourers' Dwellings Improvement Act 1875, the Public Health Act 1875, the Education Act 1876, a factory act to protect workers, the Conspiracy and Protection of Property Act of 1875 which protected peaceful picketing, and the Employers and Workmen Act allowing workers to sue employers for breach of contract." He cleared this throat. "To name a few."

"Sounds more liberal than conservative," said Watson.

"You're not the first to say so." Mycroft nodded. "The liberal-Labour MP Alexander Macdonald went so far as to say that the conservative party under Disraeli did more for the working classes in five years than the liberals did in fifty."

"Well deserved, it seems to me," Dr. Watson said. "If not baffling."

"In his youth, Disraeli was a member of *Young England,* Tory idealists who both revered the monarchy and held a humane regard for the poor," Mycroft said. "They felt that the gap between the rich and the poor could be resolved through the monarchy and old-fashioned religion."

"Disraeli is a reformer? How can he then be the leader of the conservative party?" asked Mirabella.

"How indeed?" said Mycroft. "Gladstone has balanced the budget, never done before or since, and is utterly devoted to both God and country, all conservative issues. Disraeli enacted laws that benefited the working man, is a lateral thinker, and has, shall we say, a questionable orientation, all liberal concepts. These are all labels, what does it matter? What matters is that we are all British—and that we move forward in a way that benefits all Britons."

"Rather than focusing on our differences, we might thank our lucky stars for the cumulative work of these very different politicians," Dr. Watson added.

"I still say Disraeli must be a great person." Mirabella poured the elder Holmes brother a second cup of tea.

"He can't be trusted," Mycroft said absently. "Though I find him great fun, he will sacrifice anything or anyone for entertainment value. But that's not the point."

"What is the point, then?" asked Mirabella.

"Disraeli is the only one of our victims who could be legally disposed of rather than discredited by the public," Sherlock said. "All it would take is a trial and a few witnesses who were paid to lie if no one creditable could be found. If someone is attempting to take down the government, they will start with Disraeli."

"Is, in fact, Mr. Disraeli a *pansy*?" asked Mirabella.

"Life is difficult, my dear," Mycroft said softly. "Let us not begrudge anyone whatever love he can find in this cold existence."

"Here, here!" Dr. Watson added, rubbing his wounded leg.

"For the last time, Miss Belle, it's none of our deuced business," Sherlock exclaimed, unable to hide his anger. "What matters is if the court could be convinced. And the even bigger question is what someone intends to do with those suspicions."

Oh, for goodness sake. One can never say the correct thing around here! But insult women or deny them an education and that will be entirely acceptable. Her head was spinning from all that she had been exposed to this week and the assaults upon her excellent upbringing and estimable family. One must have time to assimilate and consider.

She raised her chin. "Mr. Disraeli has done a great deal of good, that is clear. I can love the sinner, but I do not approve."

"As many do not. And for that reason, Miss Hudson was correct to ask if the Tory MP has a preference for men," stated Dr. Watson. "That is the question we are dancing around—and the question we do not wish to have answered in the press. For that reason and that reason only, we must find the answer before the press does."

"I was sensitive, I was jealous." Mirabella had pulled a book from the bookcase, *Contarini Fleming* by Benjamin Disraeli and begun reading. "I found a savage joy in harrowing his heart; I triumphed when I could draw a tear from his beautiful eye; when I could urge him to unaccustomed emotion; when I forced him to assure me, in a voice of agitation, that he loved me alone, and pray me to be pacified."

"Oh my," she whispered. "This is describing the relationship between two boys."

"And yet, if this were a man and woman being described, you would find no fault in it, Miss Belle," Sherlock suggested.

"Not at all!" she objected. "It is utterly capricious! I cannot tolerate coquetry and affectations in anyone! I find it most disagreeable."

"You have much to learn about the art of flirtation, Miss Mirabella," John Watson, chuckling.

She continued reading. "He is a sensitive child who looks pretty and loves the theatre. He does not have real friends, especially boys his own age. . . He uses witty phrases and unusual sayings to control his schoolfellows."

John winced, but glancing at Sherlock and Mycroft, she saw that they were utterly unaffected to the point of boredom.

"In the first place," Mycroft began, "this writing may be his personal fantasy and have nothing to do with his actual actions. The Earl of Beaconsfield is a shrewd politician above all else and I don't believe he would jeopardize his illustrious position which is far more important to him than any fling."

"Why, then, did he have this *published?*"

"The heart demands self-expression." Mycroft shrugged.

"Indeed," said Sherlock. "Disraeli is not entirely likable to my way of thinking—a charismatic but manipulative type—but it has nothing to do with whether or not he prefers sex with men."

"But it isn't . . . it couldn't be . . . *normal,*" Mirabella objected.

"When you find these normal people, Miss Hudson, I should like to meet them," Sherlock said sternly.

"Disraeli makes his preference for female companionship obvious," considered Watson, returning to the subject at hand.

"Again, very wise," advised Mycroft.

"Except for his intense relationships with very young men," stated Sherlock. "Lord Henry Lennox comes to mind."

"A very disadvantageous relationship," stated Mycroft, shaking his head. "Lennox is enchanting, diverting, impulsive, superficial, as foolish as the typical heir to a dukedom and as enamored of gossip as the Ladies' Canterbury Quilting Association."

"And yet, there is no evidence of any male affair," Mycroft considered.

"That *is* a bit arrogant, old chap, to say that, if it were so, you would know about it." Watson chuckled.

Sherlock cleared his throat. "Mycroft would know about it."

"So, is Lord Beaconsfield . . . a *mandrake?*" whispered Mirabella.

"Oh, no," replied Mycroft, shaking his head.

Mirabella breathed a sigh of relief.

Sherlock raised his eyebrows at his older brother, all eyes turning to Mycroft.

"Whether or not the Earl of Beaconsfield has acted on those impulses, there is no doubt in my mind that Disraeli is not attracted to men exclusively," said Mycroft.

"Are you quite serious, Mycroft?" Watson demanded.

"Certainly. He likes both sexes," Mycroft said definitively. "I don't see how you could have missed that."

"What does that mean . . ." gasped Mirabella.

"He likes *both*. Sexes." Watson explained, nodding with sudden understanding.

"No!" she exclaimed. "Is it *possible*? I don't understand!"

"Very admirable to my way of thinking to avoid showing favoritism," Mycroft stated with a smile.

"Agreed," Holmes added, tipping his hat to the group. "The Tory MP does not discriminate. And it is completely irrelevant to us or to his ability to perform within his station."

"But it is completely relevant to someone," said Mycroft. "Who has made it our business to care."

CHAPTER THIRTY
The Gift

"Miss Hudson, I have something for you," offered Sherlock, unwrapping his handkerchief to reveal the chocolates. Dr. Watson had left the flat, and it was obvious that Sherlock had waited until the good doctor had departed, clearly saving these delicacies for her.

How strange. Uncharacteristic, to be sure.

"Oh, my," she exclaimed, her eyes glued to the beautiful handcrafted delectable before her. "How divine."

Why on earth is Sherlock being nice to me? She eyed him with suspicion. "Let me be certain I understand. You wish me to take one of these creamy chocolates and consume it? Or are you simply showing it to me?"

"Yes, naturally I want you to ingest it, Miss Belle," he replied. "Make us a pot of tea and we shall sit and chat for a moment while you enjoy a confection which I know you to be partial to."

Contrasting with Sherlock's elegant and polite manner was his appearance. The Great Detective looked as if he had been wearing the same outfit for two days, which he no doubt had. His recently acquired goatee was neatly trimmed but his hair was completely disheveled, going every which way. He was wild and uncontrolled under a disciplined exterior.

"Let me get this straight, Mr. Holmes. You want me to sit rather than work? And you want me to *talk?*" she asked. Generally Sherlock would move heaven and earth to get her to cease talking. She backed up towards the kitchen with caution, keeping her eyes on him. Could this personality change be the result of drug use?

She didn't think so. Ordinarily Sherlock avoided drugs while working on a case. The work was his drug.

Mirabelle squinted her eyes suspiciously. There was nothing in Sherlock's manner to indicate that he wished to enjoy a tea time with his assistant—or with anyone for that manner. Instead he seemed as one who wished to run wildly into the forest in search of a wild boar armed only with a spear.

"Do not make me repeat myself, Miss Hudson. Go make a pot of tea," he replied sternly. "*Now.*"

That is the Sherlock Holmes I know.

"And use the gas ring. I don't have time to wait for the stove to heat the water." She longingly returned her eyes to the beautiful chocolate held in his outstretched palm as she continued backing up towards the kitchen.

What possible harm could there be in a tiny morsel of confection? she asked herself as she entered the kitchen.

That we shall soon discover.

Her mouth began to water as she pictured the beautifully formed chocolate moving towards her mouth. *Smooth with flavor.*

Looking around the corner to view the rigid outline of Sherlock's jaw and the intensity of his gaze burning a hole into her skin even from this distance, Mirabella knew what harm there could be if she did not comply with his wishes.

Mirabella picked a shilling out of the bowl next to the gas ring and inserted it into the apparatus that had been refilled only this morning by the man who came round. Immediately the pot of water began heating.

It was true, it would take at least twenty minutes to bring the pot to boiling on the wood stove. Sherlock had wished to install a gas stove, but Aunt Martha would have none of it, as with the gas lighting. As far as Aunt Martha knew, the gas ring was for his experiments of which, for some reason, the landlady was more accepting. In pursuit of criminals and such. In Mirabella's estimation, Sherlock's experiments posed a much greater danger to the building than did gas cooking and lighting.

As for the water, she had brought it up from Aunt Martha's rooms that morning. Aunt Martha had installed indoor running water—but for the first floor only. Just as the only toilet in the building—which, by necessity required running water—was on the first floor and was shared by all the building's tenants, including the Russian gentleman on the third floor opposite Dr. Watson's bedroom.

The water boiling, she moved her head around the corner to peer at Sherlock from the stove. Instead of an expression of warmth and kindness, which was rare in Sherlock Holmes but identifiable, he had that wild look in his eye that he had when he was on the verge of solving a case. An excitement that seemed more unbearable to him than pleasurable.

She reached into the cabinet and retrieved Sherlock's favorite tea, a custom-Adagio blend, placing it in the teapot.

"Bloody hell!" Sherlock exclaimed as she re-entered the room with the tea tray.

"What is it?" she asked.

"An article on our Russian diplomat. As you revealed to me—though I no doubt would have eventually discerned it for myself—I guarantee that Mr.

Perminov will not be here to pay his respects to our queen as described. He is coming to acquire the submarine plans from Moriarty." Sherlock threw the newspaper on the floor. "Everything is *too late*! Damnation! I need to get those blueprints! At the same time I need to discern Moriarty's full plan and thwart it. Even without selling the plans to a foreign government, he could conceivably bring down the British government on another front. I have to work both sides and I cannot be two places at once. More information is essential!"

"I wonder if this means that Moriarty has deciphered the key?" Mirabella considered.

"He has not been seen much about town. He is still working on the key."

"Without the key, the plans are worthless," Mirabella said. "I expect the Russians know that."

"It is only a matter of time before Moriarty solves the puzzle. Once he applies himself, he has remarkable success."

"Mr. Holmes, do you know that you are never more insane than when on the crest of discovery?" Except, perhaps, Mirabella reflected, when he didn't have a case. But that was a different type of insanity—lethargic, unreasonable, self-destructive, and despondent.

"I am never insane, Miss Belle, only single-minded. That is why I succeed where others fail," Sherlock said with a forced politeness. Despite his being seated, at the moment she knew very well that Sherlock was bursting with energy. He added softly, "Let us hope I may succeed in this instance."

"Just so. It is not yet tea time, Mr. Holmes," she stated in a last attempt to understand the enigma before her as she moved into the drawing room with the tea service. "Why are you here?"

"I need to run a little experiment for the sake of the case we are working on and for Queen and country," he muttered distractedly under his breath. "But first, I need data."

She shook her head and shrugged, placing the tray on the table before them. *There is no deciphering Sherlock Holmes.* She had learned that a long time ago.

The tea poured and cream and sugar added, she bit into the delectable chocolate marzipan.

"Oh, it is *heavenly*," she exclaimed, for once the realization as good as the anticipation. "I think I must save some of it for later—at least to give a morsel to my aunt."

"No, you must finish it now, Miss Hudson," he replied sternly. "And, as I think about it, I am not so hungry. Would you like mine?"

"So thoughtful, Mr. Holmes," she murmured. *So unlike you.*

"Oh, no, it's not from me. It's a gift from the prime minister."

"The prime minister of England," she repeated, astonished. "Who would have ever thought a country girl would be given chocolates from the P.M.? . . ." She watched him place the sweet morsel carefully on her tea saucer.

Who indeed?

CHAPTER THIRTY-ONE
The Experiment

The beautiful and soothing chimes of the Westminster clock, sounding like the cross between a bell and a harp, struck two o'clock.

Sherlock Holmes and his assistant sat for twenty minutes discussing the various elements of the case, the Great Detective asking for her input on occasion. At this point he began to notice that some of her replies seemed a bit too unguarded, even for Miss Belle.

He felt his excitement rising. *Precisely what I need to know! Proof of Moriarty's foul plan!*

"It's quiet in here without Prinnie," she remarked, looking about her as she sat in Watson's chair across from her employer sipping her tea, clearly enjoying her improved status.

"Watson has taken the bulldog for a walk. Or rather the bulldog has taken Watson, if I'm not mistaken." Sherlock reached inside the coal scuttle beside him for his pipe and a bit of tobacco.

"Miss Belle, I would like to pose a question to you, if I may?"

"Of course," she replied amiably, without the usual look of apprehension and distrust that she reserved for him when he drilled her.

"I suppose I am in unchartered ground," he said, leaning back into his fireside chair as he lit his pipe. "Very well, I shall proceed. What is your plan for the future, Miss Belle?"

"To which plan are you referring?"

"All young girls have a plan of some type. Marriage, perhaps?"

"I am saving my funds for university, you know that, Mr. Holmes." She giggled with some amusement. Miss Belle was not a fragile girl, but there was a softness in her expression.

He felt a twinge of disappointment. *So she meant what she said. She truly does intend to go to university.*

Despite her youthful enjoyment of life, Mirabella Hudson was in possession of a maturity beyond her years, he thought not for the first time. This he had often seen in spite of her naivety.

"And then what do you plan to do, Miss Belle?"

"The pursuit of knowledge is my goal. I had not thought much beyond that, to be honest, Mr. Holmes. I could become a nurse, or work in a forensics lab. And yet . . ." She placed her finger to her lovely lips as if considering her own words. Miss Belle was, in fact, delightfully attractive in a simple white lace blouse, a blue linen skirt, and a black velvet choker adorned with a pale blue cameo. Her chestnut brown hair was loosely piled atop her head, wispy tendrils escaping, her appearance subdued and genteel. Her golden brown eyes, perhaps his favorite feature, were characteristically bright and curious.

"Yes, Miss Hudson?" He sighed heavily, making no attempt to hide the impatience in his voice. He should be commended for maintaining his composure.

"I must say I am enjoying the detective work. It seems to combine everything of interest to me."

"I'm surprised to hear that you enjoy your position with me, Miss Belle," he said. "You give every indication to the contrary."

"*Enjoy?*" she gurgled, adding softly, "I love it with every fiber of my being."

Exhilaration welled up in him, not unlike the feeling he had when he solved a case. But in this situation it was unexpected, sudden, surprising. Unknown.

Terrifying.

Sherlock almost dropped his pipe. He was surprised—and gratified—to learn it. He had always assumed that Miss Belle was destined for the ivory tower as it were.

For the first time it occurred to him that perhaps Mirabella's academic nature was her gift and not necessarily her interest.

Sherlock chided himself for feeling some happiness—an unusual emotion for him—with the utterance of her words. His was a mental existence, not an emotional one, so even the experience of happiness carried a sense of awkwardness and disturbance with it.

"Indeed. An insatiable curiosity is your motivation, Miss Belle, is that so?" he asked. *Combined as it were with a fearless character.*

She sighed. "I can't seem to help myself, in the face of all danger and in spite of all the alarms which go off in my head."

"You never shared this with me before, Miss Belle."

"I certainly don't wish to increase your hold over me—or your arrogance, Sherlock." She smiled mischievously at him while placing a bit more cream in her tea. The drug clearly had the effect of dissolving the social barriers as well. She almost never slipped and called him by his first name. He found that he liked it.

"Arrogant? Me? Do you consider me arrogant, my dear?" The girl had positively the most peculiar notions.

"Is there anyone who doesn't, Sherlock?"

"It cannot be considered arrogant to know that one is a genius—if one is," he replied matter-of-factly.

"I have no doubt that is your opinion."

"Curious that you've never said it quite that way before, Miss Belle." He took his pipe out of his mouth and laboriously began to re-fill it with tobacco, frowning. "Your optimism is astonishing. You are always behaving as if the job—and me, in particular—are entirely frustrating."

"You would take terrible advantage of me if I did not." She smiled shyly. "And you *are* entirely frustrating, Sherlock Holmes!"

"Let me ask you, Miss Belle . . ." He hadn't planned to ask the question, but it was in the name of science, after all. "Do you have any plans for marriage, as other young girls do?"

"There is a young man," she sighed, leaning back in her chair and placing her arms around her waist. "whom I positively adore."

"Is there?" Sherlock felt an annoyance which surprised him. "What a fortunate young man he is to have won your affections, Miss Belle."

"Oh, it's not like *that*." She glanced at him sideways, giggling. "Though he is delightfully marvelous. Kind, warm, funny, everything one would like."

"Could it be our dear friend, Watson?"

"Shhhh!" She nodded. "Don't tell him."

"I wouldn't dream of it, my dear." *You are telling me everything I need to know.* His former elevated mood was somewhat suppressed. It was completely illogical: he had always known that Miss Belle was infatuated with Watson. It didn't take a master detective to see that.

"But, truthfully, I know very well that he is not right for me." She sighed, pulling at one of the tendrils escaping from her coiffure, a surprisingly provocative gesture.

"Oh?" Sherlock asked, leaning forward, somewhat ashamed of his own intense interest. *This is a scientific experiment. I need to—no, I must!—know the extent of the drug to formulate an intelligent conclusion.*

"In the first place, John Watson cannot be right for me because I am not right for him. He likes the ladies, if you know my meaning."

"I do." Sherlock cleared his throat. "And he does."

"No doubt he will someday meet a woman to whom he wishes to devote himself. But that is not all. I want to be in the middle of the action, at the head of the line." She shook her head, melancholy in her expression. "John is content to be on the sidelines, assisting his friends in their interests."

"I can find no fault with that," said Sherlock. "John Watson is the loyalest and the best of men."

"He is. And I do not think we should suit. It is rather inescapable: I think

I should be with someone of my own temperament."

"And what temperament would that be, Miss Belle? Driven and ambitious? Creative? Curious? And with an uncontrollable thirst for knowledge?"

"Something like that," she replied, her eyes resting on him, her expression one of surprise and perplexion. It appeared as if she had only just come to a conclusion. "Someone like *you*, Sherlock."

Surely she doesn't mean . . . he had never dared to hope.

"But not you, of course," she added decidedly.

"Of course not," he replied stiffly.

"Someone *like* you," she said, taking a sip of tea. "But without all the craziness and spinning out of control."

"Elaborate, Miss Hudson," he commanded gruffly.

"Someone who has the capacity to be happy without indulging in drugged substances and without the constant need for stimulation."

"I see," he replied, his mood suddenly dark.

"And yet," she sighed, taking his hand impulsively, "I wouldn't change a thing about you, Sherlock. I suppose if you weren't demented, you wouldn't be the *Great Detective*."

CHAPTER THIRTY-TWO
Work is Life

"A truth serum! You injected me with a truth serum!" Mirabella exclaimed, appearing to be a touch on the angry side if Sherlock was not mistaken, and he rarely was.

"As I said," he replied simply, looking up at her as he lounged comfortably in his maroon velvet dressing coat. "I shall never understand why you repeat what I say, Miss Belle. I know what I said, and clearly you do as well or you would not be able to repeat it."

"I am the most forthright person you could ever know!" She moved towards him and poked her finger in his chest.

Extraordinary. She had never touched him before and this bordered on attack. "You might have simply asked me anything you wished to know!"

"It was necessary to the case," Sherlock replied, taking her wrist to stop her from poking him. "And anyway, it was your own lack of attention that determined your fate. I told you everything while we were sitting here— everything!—but you were too enamored of the chocolates to hear it. If I had been a criminal, I would have had you entirely in my power."

"You are a criminal, Sherlock Holmes!"

"I gave you all the clues, so I cannot be faulted, Miss Hudson."

"You scoundrel! You low-life . . . !" she exclaimed, her fist clenched inside his hand though he was seated and she was standing. "You have truly gone too far this time Sherlock Holmes!"

"Miss Belle, contain yourself!" he commanded, thrusting her hand away.

"I will not!" She threw her head into her hands, more strands of hair coming loose. "I tolerate every manner of insult, I learn whatever knowledge and skill is required, and I place myself in dangerous situations. But at least in all that I am consulted before you enact the death threats against my person."

"Not always."

"Usually."

"I needed to find out the effect of the serum," he said unapologetically. "And, in all honesty, I did not know there was a drug in the chocolates. It was mere speculation on my part."

"There is some part of my mind and my body which you are not entitled to, Mr. Holmes!" She began to pace the room. "Why not take the serum yourself?"

"You disappoint me, Miss Belle. I could not very well be both the subject and the investigator. It's not scientific. Speaking of which, I now need to know how much of what you told me you remember."

"You want me to assist you at this time?" She turned on her heel to face him.

"This is very crucial to the investigation." He stared at her, disbelieving. "Surely you must understand how serious the matter is after the articles in the newspapers and the theft of the submarine plans."

"I would not help you, Sherlock Holmes, if you were the last man on Earth and the fate of the world depended on it."

"I would say it does." He sat up in his chair. "I am sorely disappointed in you, Miss Belle. This is not the time to be selfish when the future of England is at stake."

"Let me tell you this, Mr. Sherlock Holmes." She blew a lock of hair out of her eyes. There was an intensity in her eyes he had not seen before. "You will never again experiment on me without my consent. That is, if you wish to keep the head which is attached to your neck. Your fate in this world depends upon it!"

"Do I understand that you have just *threatened* me, Miss Hudson?"

"Do you not see? Do you not see how wrong this is?"

He had seen Miss Belle angry many times—but not like this. She was positively hysterical. It was beyond anything. How could she not understand that all this was *necessary* to the case? And that *nothing* was more important than the case? Particularly this case. "No I do not. At any rate, there is a sedative in my room in the first drawer of my chest of drawers which I advise you to take."

"I will never again take anything at your hand, Mr. Holmes!"

"I suggest that you do. You are ruining my appetite for dinner."

"Is everything about meeting your needs?" Her face was pink with rage as she threw her arms in the air. It was the most astonishing thing.

"Quite wrong, Miss Hudson. This has absolutely nothing to do with my needs. It is all for England. For *the Queen*. Your lack of patriotism is disturbing."

"This is entirely about you and your perception, Mr. Holmes. You are the only person in your world and no one else exists."

"I assure you that is not the case or the world would be a far better place."

"Immeasurable arrogance!"

"Miss Belle, I implore you to have a sherry." He didn't have much hope that this would aid her female histrionics, but something had to be done. He could clearly see that the blood was rushing to her face, particularly obvious in the white lace blouse she wore.

"Don't you see that your actions make you no different than Moriarty?" she exclaimed, ignoring his commands for the first time in her life. "Only you are worse!" It was beside anything.

"I am worse than Moriarty?" He laughed, amused now. "Miss Hudson, you are positively illogical at times."

"Professor Moriarty knows who he is. He knows he is not the Messiah! You think you are the savior of mankind!"

"Not of mankind, merely of the London populace." He shook his head. Reflecting for a moment, Sherlock added, "Well, in this case, most of the world."

"There you have it in a nutshell, Sherlock Holmes! You consider yourself to be above mere mortals, thereby allowing you to disregard everyone but yourself. But I have news for you: the Messiah was a servant of the people."

"As am I."

"You must know where you end and where others begin—and where your rights end." She moved to the door and turned to look at him, her expression one of pure devastation, as if she had lost everything that mattered to her. "And I assure you, Mr. Holmes, that you have crossed that line."

"Stop right there, Miss Belle! This is very important!"

"Yes?" she asked, turning to face him, her eyes beginning to water, her rage appearing to turn to sadness.

"I need to know! Do you recall any of the conversation? The answer is very important to the case."

"The case. Is that all that matters to you, Sherlock Holmes?"

"Of course," he replied matter-of-factly.

"Then that is what you shall be left with."

CHAPTER THIRTY-THREE
The Final Withdrawal

She did not slam the door. This was the part that concerned him. Miss Belle always slammed the door when she was angry.

She had resigned her position and left, gently shutting the door.

She has left me.

And the worst part was that she hadn't even answered his question. *Insupportable insubordination. Selfish, incorrigible girl.*

She'll be back, the Great Detective attempted to reassure himself. She had threatened to leave before.

But something about this was different, and he knew it. Sherlock Holmes was not one to pretend.

Bloody hell. Something about the idea of losing Miss Belle made him want to pretend for the first time in his life.

"You leave me no choice but to resign my position, Mr. Holmes," she had said calmly.

Quiet. Refined. Miss Mirabella Hudson was rarely refined and *never* quiet.

"What ho, Holmes!"

"Snort!"

Slam! The door slammed shut. Watson was back with Prinnie.

"And where is Miss Mirabella?" Watson asked, throwing his hat on the table beside him as he sank into the chair, looking about him.

Blazes! The first thing Watson had noticed was Miss Belle's absence. This did not bode well.

Gffaw! Grump! The bull pup plopped down in front of the fire.

"Miss Hudson has left my employ."

"God save us!" Watson stopped mid-way in removing his wool scarf from his neck. "Holmes, what have you done?"

"There's the good faith. I see that you assume me to be at fault, Watson." Despite the look of consternation crossing the good doctor's expression, the news didn't appear to surprise Watson at all.

"Of course it is your fault, Holmes. What did you do?"

"What did *I* do? What did Miss Hudson do which was completely illogical and unreasonable, that is the question."

"What did you do just prior to her resigning her position, Holmes?" Watson repeated patiently, moving to sit in his chair.

"I attempted to persuade Miss Hudson with logic, which naturally failed."

"Holmes, what reason did she give for resigning her post?" emphasized Watson, leaning forward in his chair.

Sherlock raised his eyebrow at his friend. "The incident in question involved my drugging Miss Belle with a truth serum. Unaccountably, she took exception to that, even though I afterwards explained the necessity of my actions for the future of England."

"Good God, man! Holmes, you didn't!" exclaimed Watson, disbelieving.

"Mind you, as far as I knew it was only chocolate. I had no way of knowing with a certainty. That's why the experiment was necessary."

"I thought you capable of anything, but—"

"I had no choice. I needed to see if the chocolates were drugged." Why could no one see that? "And naturally it had to be someone I know, otherwise, how would I comprehend the full extent of the drug?"

"Naturally." Watson stared at him as if he were a cannibal or a Blackleg. "For God's sake, Holmes, you don't appear to have any remorse!"

"Of course I don't. Why is everyone so blasted upset? Don't you see that it was crucial to the case?"

"Thank God I wasn't at home," reflected Watson.

"This is a matter of national importance," Sherlock explained, disbelieving the lack of understanding. Of course, it wasn't truly necessary to ask all the questions he had asked Miss Belle, but the answers were indeed interesting. "The future of England and the Queen is at stake. How can you take the side of a histrionic young woman?"

"Holmes, you're an idiot."

"Actually, I am a genius," Sherlock corrected him. "And Miss Hudson is a selfish young woman at that."

"So you're saying, if the case demanded it, you would drug me?" asked Watson, standing and moving towards the fireplace.

"Not you, old chap!"

"Why Miss Hudson and not me?"

"Well, it wouldn't be quite right, drugging my friend and . . . Dash it, Watson! I wouldn't have, but the case demanded it!"

"Holmes, I don't know if you will be able to get yourself out of this one," mumbled Watson, stoking the fireplace. "This time you've gone too far."

"Odd," said Sherlock.

"What, old chap?"

"That's precisely what Miss Belle said."

"Not odd at all, Holmes."

"Explain it to me, Watson." Sherlock sighed. He knew Watson to be an expert on women, so no doubt the good doctor could shed some light on this puzzle. But it fried one's goat that one had to be wasting time in attempting to understand the workings of an assistant's illogical mind when the assistant in question should be assisting her employer.

"You disrespected Miss Mirabella, Holmes," Watson said, moving to pour each of them a brandy.

"Disrespect?" He laughed. "Are you serious? I have the greatest respect for Miss Belle."

"You used her, Holmes," Watson said.

"Of course I used her! But it wasn't for me personally. And don't all employers use their employees? She provides a service."

"You experimented on her without her permission, as if she were a laboratory rat." Watson returned to his fireside chair, the drinks on the table between them. "How do you know the drug won't inflict permanent damage?"

"I suppose if you put it that way . . . but I was careful to keep an eye on her, to ensure she had it in very small doses."

"You showed an utter disregard for her feelings and her person." Watson seated himself.

"Dash it all, Watson! What do her feelings have to do with it when England is at stake?"

"Holmes, you can certainly treat people however you wish to serve your purposes," Watson considered, taking a sip of his brandy. "But don't expect them to hang about for your next move."

"Do you seriously think Miss Belle has gone?" Sherlock swallowed all of his brandy in one gulp.

"Holmes, every relationship is a series of deposits and withdrawals. And I fear you may have just made the final withdrawal."

CHAPTER THIRTY-FOUR
The Need for Improvements

"Mr. Bloody Sherlock 'Olmes, you get your sorry ass out of 'ere!" Mrs. Hudson stood at the entrance to her Baker Street suites on the first floor, not allowing her tenant entrance. One hand was firmly planted on the waist of her lavender silk gown, revealing that she had not lost her youthful figure. The other hand gripped an ornate brass doorknob framed by a freshly polished five-panel butternut wood door. "I 'ave stood for every manner of noise, for criminals on the bloody premises, for bullet holes in me walls, and for being awakened at every hour of the night, so it is, but I won't stand for your breaking me niece's heart! She 'asn't 'ad the mockers put on cryin' since she came home!"

"The young are inclined to exaggerate, Mrs. Hudson, as you know."

"Auch, that's rubbish, that is! Mirabella ain't the type! She be as patient as a saint. Takes after me side of the family," Martha Hudson replied indignantly, leaning against the solid wooden door with a golden sheen. "And no doubt you are gettin' a dose of your own medicine!"

"Whatever do you mean, Mrs. Hudson?"

"Sherlock 'Olmes, you are dull as dishwater if I 'ave to tell you!" She sighed heavily. "Which I won't."

"Singular," he said. "You are the second person to insult my intelligence within the course of the past half hour, Mrs. Hudson. I have had many insults hurled at me, but never of that nature."

"Two is more than never, so it is," she replied simply, tapping her foot.

"May I please see Miss Hudson?" Sherlock asked impatiently.

"Heavens to Betsy, if you aren't in a fine fettle, Mr. Sherlock 'Olmes. I have seen me niece angry many a time, but nothing to match this. My recommendation is that you eat a hefty piece of humble pie."

"I am prepared to do so, Mrs. Hudson, even though Miss Belle is being overly sensitive. I did it for the greater good. But I am nothing if not accommodating. However, I must see Miss Belle in order to make amends." He bowed to his landlady.

"You may *say* that you are sorry, Mr. 'Olmes, but your attitude says otherwise. You be more like one who has thrown his hat in the ring, and that will n'er do." She crossed her hands in front of her chest. "Aye, I know me niece."

"I have come to depend on Miss Belle, and I need her," he said. "She is an excellent employee."

"An excellent employee? So she is. And is there anything else, Mr. 'Olmes?"

Staring at his landlady's angry expression, for a long, painful minute Sherlock considered the idea that he might have actually lost Miss Belle. He felt a sudden terrible emptiness and a weight upon his chest.

Now that you mention it, I can barely imagine life without her. She is sunshine, intelligence, and beauty wrapped into one. Sherlock cleared his throat, the realization both distasteful and terrifying. "For the injury I unwillingly caused in attempting to serve God and country and to save the world, I am truly sorry. And I am sorry that I am the only one among us who is willing to serve England without reserve."

"Well there's an iron hand in a velvet glove. Tell me this, Mr. 'Olmes, what did you do?" Mrs. Hudson demanded. "Mirabella won't tell me."

"Nothing of consequence," he replied, straightening his tie.

"Auch, then, what is it that don't matter to the likes 'o you but does to her?" Mrs. Hudson repeated.

"I merely administered a truth serum to Miss Belle," he stated in his typical monotone voice. "I suspect there are no lasting effects, and the process itself she seemed to enjoy, in fact. Painless, as it were."

Mrs. Hudson slammed the door in his face, almost resizing his Grecian nose.

Women. There positively was no understanding them.

He knocked on the door again, which was not opened, but he heard Mrs. Hudson's voice from the other side of the door. "Go away. I 'ave nothing else to say to you now or ever until it's time to collect the rent."

"That is fine, Mrs. Hudson, as I have something to say and wish you to listen. I wonder if we might re-visit our discussion about installing gas lighting in the building. I appreciate your installing plumbing and running water on the first level—none for the rest of us, mind you, but Watson and I enjoy the Turkish baths and a smoke, so no matter—but don't you think it's time to install gas lighting? That is where I would appreciate a bit of courtesy on your part. We light our flat with candles and oil lamps, it's positively antiquated."

He heard nothing tangible from the other side of the door, only mumblings and something that sounded remarkably like cursing him into the pits of Hell.

"Mrs. Hudson? Did you hear my request? What do you say? When can

I expect the installation?"

"Go away, Mr. 'Olmes, before I open the door and shoot your head off!" That she said quite clearly.

"Ah, I see. Very well then. Once you have talked some sense into Miss Hudson and have approved my request for improvements to the building and would like to inform me of same, I'll be in my quarters."

CHAPTER THIRTY-FIVE
A Heart-to-heart

"I know about the chocolates laced with a truth serum. You distributed them, Fantine, and obtained the information for Moriarty."

"What makes you think so, Sherlock? How was it done?" She wrapped her silk robe around her naked body, adorned with only a diamond necklace, and sat up in bed.

He raised his eyebrows at her. "In my studies of South American herbology, I came across a powerful drug made from the borrachero tree, odorless and tasteless. It is almost impossible to tell a lie under the influence of the drug, an effect increased with morphine."

"If this substance is odorless and tasteless, how did you know, Sherlock?"

"I have learned it at great personal cost to myself." Mentally he contrasted the seductress before him with the most pure, ethical, and intelligent woman who had ever entered his life. *Now gone.* "Once I had an idea of the direction I was headed, I examined one of the pieces of chocolate, matching it to the white and yellow blossoms of the borrachero tree, where I found a match. In addition, we found morphine in the blood when we examined Hamilton."

"I had no part in any murder! I only distributed chocolates—and I guarantee that no one died afterwards! Everyone was in perfectly good health!"

"Hamilton died of a heart attack, which too much borrachero can cause. The borrachero was in the chocolates."

"I don't know anything about borrachero!"

"It is despicable, Fantine. The absence of knowledge does not erase your part in it." He stared at her. She had—almost single-handedly—allowed for the execution of a devious plan.

He had been transported by Fantine's passionate music—and her other expressions of passion—but he felt nothing but coldness for her at this moment.

In fact, he felt . . . *nothing*. Which is precisely what he preferred. A confirmation that affairs of the heart were a waste of time. Perhaps Fantine had given him something after all.

"Let us not talk of such things," she said.

"An excellent idea. There is nothing left to talk about, Fantine." Sherlock threw his tie around his neck, grabbed his jacket, and left the suite.

CHAPTER THIRTY-SIX
Unfinished Business

"As wrong as he was in his treatment of me, Sherlock was right about one thing, Aunt Martha: the case is all-important to the future of England. I must finish what I begin." Mirabella applied dark circles under her eyes as well as a gray pallor to her skin as Sherlock had taught her. She sat at the mahogany dressing table on the blue and red oriental carpet in her aunt's bedroom. "Did you see the newspapers today?"

"Aye, o' course I did! But you are no longer bloomin' working for Mr. 'Olmes!" Mrs. Hudson exclaimed, pacing the room.

"I am not. And I don't intend to work for him again. But that is a separate matter from the case."

"And I heard you to say the man is a bludger! And so he is!" Despite her anxiety, Martha Hudson looked characteristically fine in a long, fitted jacket in a striped satin of silver and lavender with a profusion of white lace at her neck, an outfit more suitable for visiting than keeping to their apartments.

But that was Aunt Martha, ever a fashionable woman. Nervously she smoothed her white hair swept to the top of her head, meeting at the forehead with frizzied hair, the current style. Mirabella was not one to follow the new fashions unless they allowed one more freedom.

"He is."

"Auch then, what are you thinkin' girl? He ain't payin' you." Mrs. Hudson moved to glance out the window of the street level rooms, elegantly appointed with pale blue curtains draped across the windows accented with beige tassels.

Mirabella sighed, looking up momentarily from her mirror. "If Sherlock says the future of England is at stake, the future of England is at stake." She added softly, "And I have to help."

"God save us," exclaimed Mrs. Hudson, moving to fall into her chair beside the window where she kept a watch for anyone approaching the main doors.

"I, for one, will put my faith in Sherlock Holmes," said Mirabella, placing her battered hat on top of her head with satisfaction.

"Mirabella Hudson, I will not allow such blasphemy in my home! Besides that, you were ready to kill him not two days ago."

"Yes, but there are more important things at stake than my feelings." Mirabella stood and twirled before the mirror in the worn burlap skirt and battered hat. She giggled, aware that she looked completely out of place in her aunt's quarters which were much more elegant than Sherlock's quarters. Tasteful, they were: pale blue and cream wallpaper, cream-colored walls, and mahogany furniture.

"Why are you dressed like a pauper and behavin' as if you're Cinderella, Mirabella Hudson? I begin to think you have lost your mind."

"I feel like Cinderella." She was very proud of her disguise, though whether or not she would succeed, she did not know. Of all her lessons, disguise was the most difficult to master. Even more difficult than knife throwing. As Sherlock had often chided her, an effective disguise encompassed much more than simply changing one's clothing, make-up and hair. It involved speech, the way one moved, and even one's attitude. A girl on the lower rung of life who had been beaten down by society would not move or speak with confidence.

"You'd best take care before the clock strikes twelve."

"Do I look like a flower girl, Aunt Martha?" Mirabella asked, studying herself in the mirror.

"Aye. Or a dollymop," said Mrs. Hudson, raising her eyebrows in disapproval.

"A lady of the night?" considered Mirabella, returning her eyes to the mirror, astonished. "How appalling! *Unless . . .*"

"Mirabella Hudson! I don't like that look in your eye! You could be killed pretending to be a ladybird. Or *worse . . .*"

"Oh, I won't be killed." She smiled at her aunt. Mirabella opened a drawer and placed a revolver in her makeshift pocket, along with a truncheon and some other items which looked harmless but were, in fact, weapons in her hands. "Or anything else."

I have learned from the best how to protect myself.

"Now I know you've lost your mind, Mirabella Hudson!" exclaimed Mrs. Hudson, putting a hand over her mouth as she sank deeper into her chair. "Take care you don't lose something else, foolish girl."

"I don't intend to lose anything," replied Mirabella, fingering the gun as she moved towards the door. "But I do intend to find out the truth."

"Auch! And once you find it, what will you do with it?"

"Save England, naturally."

The door shut and Martha Hudson shook her head, muttering to herself,

"That's too bad, so it is. The girl has lost all her sense in the company of Mister bloody Sherlock 'Olmes—and has become almost as cocky as he is in the bargain."

A dangerous combination.

CHAPTER THIRTY-SEVEN
The Poorest Among Us

Catherine Glynne Gladstone, wife of England's prime minister, ran the wet cloth along the girl's skin, the welts and sores horrible to look at but undoubtedly more horrible to endure.

"Shhhh!" Catherine whispered though the girl was asleep, still wincing when the cloth touched her skin.

The lesions were past the stage of being pink in color and pus-filled and were now copper-colored. This meant that the disease had now moved to Emily's brain, liver, lungs, and muscle.

Still, there were ways to make the sweet child more comfortable. The final application would be the chamomile cream to ease the discomfort and incessant stinging.

Take command of yourself! Catherine admonished herself. She wiped a tear from her eye with the sleeve of her blouse. *You are no stranger to service! Why is this proving to be so difficult?*

Indeed, she had borne eight children, and was the founder of orphanages and convalescent homes in addition to lending her home to prostitutes. Her primary concern was the support of the poor, in whatever form that might take. Currently her mind was heavy over those suffering from cholera, near-starving mill girls and homeless orphans.

According to Henry Mayhew's 1862 publication, *London Labour and the London Poor*, the prostitutes were the seducers, using their charms for immoral purposes and preying upon the industrious and the thrifty.

And the public believed him. Blaming prostitutes for the diseases spreading throughout society rather than attributing any blame to the men who sought their services and to the society which provided poverty wages and few professions for women.

Even her own husband would never blame the ladies themselves. Above all, William Gladstone accepted responsibility: not only for himself, but for the whole of England.

Catherine glanced at her husband, the effective leader of the free world, now in his parliamentary best dress. He sat next to Emily, the poor girl, so disfigured now. In an effort to stop the wagging tongues and to dispel all doubt, Catherine had resolved to always be present when William was in the room with one of the girls.

As if any man, devil or saint, would ever be attracted to or wish to take advantage of such a creature in this state.

It made her livid with anger that someone who never did anything good for anyone had attacked William Gladstone, who had done as much good for England as anyone ever born.

"Yip yip yippeee!" She heard the children's feet hit the expensive black and white checkered marble on the floor below, stood upon by every British prime minister since the first.

"Come and get me!" she heard one of the children yell. Glancing at the precious child in the bed, Catherine knew these words to be the wish of Emily's heart as well.

It was a wonder Emily was able to sleep through the din. When Mary, Catherine's beloved sister, had died in the year of our Lord 1857, Catherine had gladly acted as the mother to her sister's children as best she could. At times there were upwards of seventeen children in the house downstairs, between her eight children and her sister's nine, while those ill with the diseases of prostitution were in the upstairs rooms.

Catherine smiled as she wondered, not for the first time, what Sir Robert Walpole and Pitt the Younger would think of their home at 10 Downing Street being used for such purposes.

"Mrs. Gladstone, what do you say?" William asked. The girl they had most recently picked up on the streets moved quietly about the room without speaking. The new girl was replacing the wet rags, assisting with applying the creams, and keeping the room clean. She was a good girl and a hard worker.

"I don't believe Emily has very long, dear," Catherine whispered to her husband, her eyes returning to the girl in the bed.

"They rarely do," he said.

"But you knew that, William," Catherine added, returning her attention to her husband and partner in life. "Emily has come here to die."

Catherine's eyes moved to study her new helper.

The new girl said she did not have the disease, which her energy bore out, but her skin was pallid and grey, unhealthy, which was not a match to her movements. Bella, as she called herself, was a great help, though, and Catherine would have offered her a home regardless.

Bella was also very intelligent and never had to be told anything twice, very rare among these girls. Another odd thing about her was, though the girl was quiet and never intrusive, Catherine sensed a confidence in her that was not consistent with the other girls here. And though Bella had an affected accent, the structure of her language was that of an educated person.

Nothing fit. But that was no matter. Anyone who needed help was welcome here.

***

William Gladstone, the leader of the free world, wiped his eyes. Little more than his youngest daughter's age, Emily was dying of the diseases of prostitution. She was so cold and clammy it was difficult to believe the child had ever been warm.

Possibly she hadn't.

"Stoke the fire, my dear," Catherine beseeched, as if to read his thoughts, as she was wont to do.

Bella moved to stoke the fire before he could rise and do so. The new girl always seemed to be a step ahead. This one they would be able to find a position for, whatever her past.

William knew it was unprecedented that the prime minister of England should have prostitutes living under his roof, or that any lady of quality would allow such a thing in her own home, but Catherine was unlike any woman he had ever known.

That's why he married her. She was, indeed, the love of his life and the most admirable woman he had ever known. A *true* lady of quality.

Catherine took his hand momentarily even as the new girl continued applying the creams. Funny how Miss Bella had become a fixture so quickly, so much so that they tended to carry on as if she weren't in the room. "I do wish you could smile sometimes, William."

"Believe me, my dear, I wish there was something to smile about."

"I am so grateful the country has you."

"That may be short lived," he said.

"Where would we be without you?" Catherine asked.

"Where am I?" Emily stirred.

Catherine took Emily's hand while Bella continued applying the creams, doing all the work that she used to do, allowing her to administer to the patient's emotional needs.

William smiled appreciatively at Bella, and she smiled back at him through sunken eyes, her skin grey. He had never seen a girl who looked so sickly with so much energy. *God save her.* He hoped with all his heart she didn't have the disease.

As for Emily, it was too late for her.

"Hello! Hello! Where am I?" Emily was stirring, looking into Catherine's eyes as she smiled back at her. Thank the heavens the hallucinations had not yet begun. Though the wild imaginings signaled the end and therefore a much better place, it was the most difficult part for him. "Have I left this world yet?"

"No, not yet," Catherine replied. "We're still here, dear."

"Bella, would you call for tea?" William asked. "The warm liquid will be good for Emily."

"Yes, sir," she replied quietly, almost in a whisper. Bella moved from the fire to pull the chord, once again saving him from the duty.

Once the tea had arrived, William could almost see the warmth reviving the invalid. Emily glanced at the pink roses on the nightstand he had personally picked for her, so like the complexion she had once had.

"Don't ye haf t' work, Mr. Gladstone?" Emily turned her head on her pillow towards him. "Runnin' the country 'an all."

Bella moved to refill all three of their tea cups and then moved to the doorway, seeming to know when to remove herself from the room. She began sweeping in the hallway, within earshot if she was needed.

"I am expected in Parliament soon, yes," he replied somberly. "But if there is anything at all we can do for you, Miss Emily, that is our first priority."

Emily smiled becomingly at him before returning her eyes to his wife. The feather of a girl always seemed to prefer the company of women, though she could not help but attempt to charm when there was a man in the room, it was second nature to her.

The child knew where the power was in this world.

Better that he should leave and allow the poor girl her rest—and the rare luxury to be completely at her ease.

Cursed diseases! If only they had been able to help the girls find other employment. But the fact was that the girls hardly ever turned from the life. There was limited other employment and most required certain skills, certain manners, and a certain address—not always attainable. A mistress could turn away a maid on a whim.

Things would not change until society changed.

Still, he and Catherine had to try. Even though it had cost him his reputation.

What do I care of that? Let them say what they will—and may they all go to Hell! Or more to the point, better that I should go to Hell for not following the conviction God put in my mind and heart.

"Did ye 'ave a fancy dinner party last night?" Emily asked shyly. "I 'eard voices."

"To be sure, we did," replied Catherine, suddenly laughing. "As fancy as we get around here."

William began chuckling, in spite of his sadness.

"Why do ye laugh?" asked Emily, beginning to smile herself in anticipation of the story.

"Mrs. Gladstone was up to her usual tricks," he said.

"There was no trickery about it at all!" replied Catherine with feigned indignation.

"Wha' did the grand lady do?" asked Emily.

"What she always does!" William smiled. "Mrs. Gladstone was shameless in asking our dinner guests to support her causes—despite her audacity in placing the guests together who most disliked each other and had the least in common."

"And yet they keep coming to our door, longing for an invitation to the prime minister's table," said Catherine. "It seems to be the place *to be*."

"And who was at the party?" Emily asked, her eyes holding an uncharacteristic brightness, as she managed to pull the white-and-blue checkered quilt up to her neck.

"Well, Princess Alexandra, to be sure," said Catherine, tapping her forehead as if to recall.

"Married to Prince Edward, the future king?" exclaimed Emily, almost sitting up.

"Delightful woman," replied Catherine. "She often comes for tea."

"Who else came?" asked Emily, regaining her composure as she fell back into her pillow.

"The Duke of Cambridge, the Marquess of Ailesbury and his wife Louisa Horsley-Beresford. Also, Archibald Primrose the Earl of Rosebery and his wife the famed heiress Hannah de Rothschild, among others," Catherine replied matter-of-factly.

"Oh, my!" exclaimed Emily. "Such fancy names they 'ave! And the ladies—were they dressed butter upon bacon?"

"Indeed they were!" replied Catherine. "It is most unfortunate, however, that the Marchioness of Ailesbury's hairstyle does not suit her *at all*!"

Emily giggled before turning to face the prime minister, suddenly serious. "You're a man o' God, Mr. Gladstone. Do ye think I will go to Hell? You know, for what I 'ave done?"

"Have you confessed your sins to Jesus?" he asked.

"Yes."

"Have you accepted Him as your savior?"

"Yes."

"Then, no, Emily, that is a promise made by one far greater than me— you shall go to Heaven." He shook his head, placing his hand on the Bible beside the bed. "But I think that there are those among us who may go to the other place for allowing this to happen."

"Will you pray for the forgiveness of my sins?" she persisted.

"Forgiveness for being poor and attempting to feed yourself," said Catherine. "No one would willingly go into such a life."

"Yes, I will," he replied, as Emily's eyes were glued to him. "But you must promise never to let sin stand between you and God. *Never* let your guilt separate you. He welcomes you with open arms."

"True. Do not let anything stand between you and God's love—that is the only sin," said Catherine. "As much as we love you, your Father loves you one thousand times more."

"Can you tell me a story Missus Gladstone?" Emily asked, her eyes now alighting upon his wife.

"What do you wish to hear, Miss Emily?" Catherine asked, nodding to her husband even as she appeared to have difficulty composing herself.

Emily smiled at the polite inquiry. She had clearly not been accustomed to being treated respectfully.

"The same as las' time." Emily's powder-blue eyes were large in her sunken head, her long black hair thinning.

"Jesus was in the house of Simon the leper . . ."

Emily glanced at her skin, covered in welts visible through the cream. She asked the question as she had many times before. "Jesus kept company with the lepers?"

"Yes, he did," interposed William. "Not with government officials any more than he could help. Then as now Jesus couldn't tolerate the company of politicians nor of the high and mighty religious."

Emily giggled, even as she looked through the doorway to smile at Bella. They seemed to have a special rapport, the two girls. William had seen them whispering before, though Bella was ever professional in his company.

"They were dining when a woman approached Jesus with an alabaster box of a very precious ointment," Catherine continued.

"What is an ointment?" asked Emily. "Like the cream Miss Bella puts on me?"

"Yes, but with a different scent. This was a very expensive oil—and scented, with the smell of licorice and cinnamon," Catherine replied. "And while Jesus dined the woman poured the oil on his head and on his feet, even wiping his feet with her hair."

"Should Jesus like that?" asked Emily, confused. "Having oil poured on his head while he ate?"

"Jesus never says," replied Catherine. "Though I must agree, Emily. I don't think I would like it at any time, but certainly not while I ate."

"It was a thing that would only have been done for kings and prophets," stated William.

"All that we learn is the disciples saying that the money could have been better used," considered Catherine, opening her King James version and scanning the pages. "No where do we read that anyone says it is an odd thing to do — this woman walking into their dinner and anointing the guest with oil — or that Jesus didn't like it."

"The oil in the alabaster jar — it cost a lot of money?" persisted Emily.

"About a year's wages," nodded Catherine, placing the book back on the nightstand. "The disciples were very indignant, "saying that the ointment might have been sold and the money given to the poor."

"Don't it seem odd?" asked Emily, perplexed. "So this woman just walks into the dinner with the oil, and anoints Jesus as if he were a king."

"Why do you think she did it Emily? Why did she take a year's wages, buy this jar of expensive oil, and anoint Jesus with it as one might a king?"

"Because . . ." Emily wiped her eyes. "Because she loved 'im."

"Yes," Catherine nodded, looking at her with compassion. "Sometimes the love in one's heart is so great that it is impossible to resist it. She did the only thing she could think to express that love. Maybe she had heard Jesus speak, maybe He had changed her heart forever, maybe He had healed her or someone close to her, but, for whatever reason, *she loved Him.*"

"An' why did Jesus let her do it? When it went against His teachings'?"

"I think because He felt her love and knew how much it would hurt her to reject her gift. She was a woman already rejected by society. She may have been a lady of the night," considered Catherine.

"*Like me?*" whispered Emily.

"Like you," nodded Catherine, looking up and glancing through the doorway at Bella.

"And Jesus—did He love her too? As she loved Him?"

"Much more," replied Catherine softly, kissing her forehead. "So much so that the Son of God, the Creator of everything, rushed to her defense to protect her. It is a beautiful moment when He realizes her love and her sacrifice—and it is like the ugly gossip which attempts to spoil that beautiful and pure moment."

"Maybe He didn't care one way or 't other about the oil, but did care that she loved Him," Emily said.

"Most certainly. To love someone so much, even once in one's life, is the most meaningful thing that can ever happen," added William somberly. "It should not be diminished nor betrayed."

"Now sleep child," Catherine said.

"Let us leave the room, sweetheart," William said, glancing at her. "It makes you too sad to do this, doesn't it my dear?"

"It does make me sad. But it also makes me happy to take some of Emily's sadness away," Catherine shook her head, her lips trembling even as she smiled at him. "She has so little happiness compared to mine."

"And mine." He took her hand.

"I can spare a little," Catherine added, closing the door quietly behind them.

CHAPTER THIRTY-EIGHT
In the Shadows

Someone is following me. Mirabella looked behind her. *Someone is after me.*

Carrying her packages, Mirabella was en route to her new job, which was a fine sight better than her prior employment. Yes, her last position was working for an escapee from the lunatic asylum who was determined to gain her admittance as well.

She now lived with the Prime Minister of the United Kingdom of Great Britain and Northern Ireland!

For the time being, that is, until a vote of *no confidence* in the parliament replaced the brilliant William Gladstone, kicking them all out of 10 Downing Street. Which could not be long away.

It is a fine job, she told herself. Though perhaps a trifle boring. Not being shot at or poisoned, no one trying to kill one with tigers. No mad scientists.

She turned a corner and hugged the brick wall, carefully setting the packages at her feet while awaiting the arrival of her companion.

An old woman, who had been limping a bit and going along slowly as the elderly would, turned the corner. Mirabella grabbed the ivory cane in the feeble lady's hand and began beating the elderly woman with the walking instrument.

"Yeeeee! Arrrrrrr! Save me! Oh me God! Help me!" the old woman was screeching.

"You shut up, old woman, or I'll do worse by you," Mirabella replied, taking the old hag's arm and twisting it behind her back while covering her victim's mouth.

The arm was surprisingly muscular and it soon spun Mirabella around, capturing her chin.

"Hello, Sherlock," Mirabella stated. "Why are you following me?"

"And why are you beating old women?"

"I am late to work, Mr. Holmes, and I have a fine position, I don't have time for this nonsense," she stated, attempting to breathe despite his firm hold on her. She managed to gulp, "I repeat, why are you following me?"

"I have to make certain you are safe, Miss Belle." He tightened his hold.

"So you have attacked me in order that I might be safe?" she managed, gasping. "Cutting off my air supply is an odd way to ensure my safety."

He held her close to his firm body. *Too close.* It was entirely unnecessary, though she felt her breath increasing.

"Forgive me," he stated as he loosened his grip somewhat, his voice suddenly soft.

"For attacking me just now?" she demanded.

"For the other thing. Earlier."

"Never!" she replied, indignant, listening to his tone for even the slightest hint of remorse as she studied his eyes. "And as you can see, I can take care of myself."

"As you can well comprehend, I have you in a lock hold from which you cannot remove yourself, Miss Belle," he remarked.

"You are correct as usual, Mr. Holmes." She jammed her foot into his kneecap as she dropped to the ground, releasing herself from his grip. "Though I believe you have overlooked a fine point in this instance."

"*Bloody hell!*" Sherlock wailed. "Really, Miss Belle, there was no need to kick me so hard!"

"That is a matter of opinion." She shook her head in disappointment. "And you must stay in character at all times, Mr. Holmes. That did not sound like the exclamation a woman would make."

"Your point is well taken, Miss Belle," he said as he rubbed his knee.

"Naturally, it was what you would have said to me."

"I shall endeavor in future to add a feminine touch to my shrieks of pain and torture."

She shrugged as she recovered her packages. "It might conceal your true identity and thereby save your life. A matter to which I am indifferent, I am sure."

"You are in a hurry to get to Cadbury's I see," Sherlock's silver eyes, peering out from under layers of wrinkles, were smiling with approval as she stole a glance at him. He was not one to reveal his opinion in either expression or tone of voice, but she had learned that his eyes revealed much. "Your new position."

"My second position." She turned away from him and began walking at an admirable pace before he managed to entwine his arm in hers. "I also work for the illustrious Prime Minister Gladstone! And I obtained both of these positions without any assistance from you, I might add."

"Two jobs, eh? And you would rather work for two employers than for me, Miss Belle?" he asked. It seemed to her that there was a hint of insecurity in his manner, something she had never observed before in the great Sherlock Holmes.

"Absolutely!" she replied through gritted teeth. "Ten jobs would be easier than working for you, Mr. Holmes."

"But not as interesting, I daresay." He smiled at her, and she observed the blackened teeth. Very convincing. So convincing that she was surprised she was able to take him seriously. She bit her lip. *How I wish I could master disguises as he does.*

"Not at all," she replied indignantly. "I love it. My employer is wonderful. In fact, his employees all love him."

"Cadbury?" Sherlock asked.

Mirabella nodded. "Both Cadbury and Gladstone. But, yes, I am speaking of Mr. Cadbury at the moment."

"Hmmm . . . I expect I might like him too, if he built a home for me," suggested Sherlock. "Unprecedented."

"Could you . . . would you . . ." She felt her heartbeat increase as her hand brushed his.

"Yes, Miss Belle?" He looked into her eyes, his breath on her cheek.

"I must go, Mr. Holmes," she whispered, attempting to increase her pace. "It has been so lovely being hunted by you and exchanging these meaningless pleasantries, but I must be off. Mr. Cadbury does not tolerate tardiness."

"Ah, a strict taskmaster," Sherlock said, maintaining a tight grip as they walked together.

"Not at all." She swallowed hard. "All Mr. Cadbury ever does is think of his employees, *unlike some*, who only ever think of themselves."

"I wouldn't know," Sherlock stated somberly. "I am here to serve."

"Serve *yourself*. In the first five years, when Mr. Cadbury thought he might lose the business, he gave up even his morning tea and newspaper," she explained. "And yet, he always thought of his employees. Even after his two brothers died, along with his young wife, leaving him with three children under six years of age."

"A very sad set of circumstances which would have turned a man of less strength," considered Sherlock.

"There is absolutely no possibility that Mr. Cadbury had anything to do with the chocolates being drugged. He would not let his morals falter even when his own survival was on the line. He will do what he believes to be right every time—just so with Mr. Gladstone."

"I see you have been busy amassing information, Miss Belle. Excellent work."

"I am not working for you, Sherlock Holmes, and I require neither your praise nor your condemnation."

"And yet, you shall have it." Sherlock's voice lowered. "How did you know, Miss Belle?"

"How did I know what?"

"That it was me in disguise."

"It wounds your ego, does it, to be found out by a mere girl?" She glanced sideways at him.

"Not at all," he replied with a self-satisfied smirk she found annoying. "It proves me to have been an excellent teacher."

"Everything proves your superiority, I understand." She kept her eyes glued to the passers by as they walked. "It was your height at first. You are a bit tall for a woman."

"Actually, I'm not. I have a height that could pass for either a man or a tall woman. I am quite grateful for my perfect height."

She raised her eyebrows at him. "Although you no doubt think that everything about you is perfect, Sherlock, you had to hunch over considerably to give the illusion of being shorter."

"But that wasn't the most telling clue was it?"

"True. I couldn't seem to lose you—very odd that you should be going precisely the same way. Naturally, I took a detour to be sure, and there you were."

"Anything else?"

She cleared her throat. "I recognized your cane."

"Ah, now we have the clincher. An unfair advantage," he mused. "But I give you credit for the other deductions."

"How kind of you, Mr. Holmes."

"Presuming they came before you observed the cane and not after. In the case of the latter, that would be bending the facts to match the conclusion, which is insupportable."

"Most assuredly." She cleared her throat. "As I said, I do not believe that Mr. Gladstone is guilty of the accusations made about him. He is a good man. An exemplary man."

Sherlock nodded. "Tell me more about Mr. Cadbury."

"It is astonishing, frankly," considered Mirabella, tapping her finger on her cheek with the loose arm that was not being held in a gorilla lock.

"What is?" asked Sherlock politely as he limped along beside her, maintaining his cover.

"Rather than causing him to be bitter, Mr. Cadbury's hardships appear to have caused him to be more devoted to his religion than ever," considered Mirabella.

"It is astonishing that one should have a spiritual base?" asked Sherlock, looking at her with interest as they continued to walk. She had missed their conversations.

"Life kept going wrong for him, but he kept doing the right thing," considered Mirabella, adjusting her hat as she walked with him, not having the option to stop.

"It appears that his faith and morals are unshakeable. This is very important information," said Sherlock. "But we have to know if Cadbury is a co-conspirator or if Moriarty is working on his own. Haven't you always told me to make no assumptions?"

"*Impossible*! Cadbury is not involved, I'd stake my life on it." She turned to glare at him. "There are plenty of people who talk of religion, but then do evil behind the backs of others. *Or to their faces*."

"Why are you looking at me, Miss Belle? I never talk of religion."

"Except in a negative light. The Quaker religion is different, though," considered Mirabella. "There is not as much focus on 'Do what you will and Jesus will forgive you', but rather on service and lifestyle. *Accountability*, if you will."

"And yet, Mr. Cadbury is a very fun sort, not continually serious as you might expect," remarked Sherlock.

"Which makes me trust him all the more."

"Fun-loving, you say?" Sherlock mused, glancing sideways at her. "So you trust a person with a sense of humor, Miss Belle?"

"It rather bespeaks a genuine nature, don't you think?"

"Do you consider me to have a sense of humor, Miss Belle?" Sherlock asked.

"If you mean a cruel and biting wit coupled with a nasty and habitually pessimistic demeanor? If so, yes I do, Mr. Holmes." Mirabella giggled in spite of herself. "On your good days, that is. The rest of the time you are unbearable."

"There's no need to have a care for my feelings, Miss Hudson. Tell me the truth."

"I wouldn't think of doing anything else." She glared at him. "So there is no need to drug me for it."

His expression was genuinely remorseful. "I am sorry, Miss Belle."

"Are you, Mr. Holmes?"

"I did not realize it would be so offensive. I always assume that everyone has the same devotion to the case which I have."

"That sounds dangerously like a justification rather than an apology."

"I am truly sorry to have hurt you, Miss Belle."

"Probably because it has impacted you."

"Undoubtedly."

She found herself enjoying walking arm-in-arm with Sherlock, despite not having any other choice. Studying him, she saw that he was looking more thin and haggard than usual, his disguise completely believable.

How I have missed him.

"I don't know if I could work there forever," said Mirabella.

"Whatever do you mean, Miss Belle?" His tone was a bit too anxious, even for Sherlock Holmes.

"I don't particularly care to be obliged to go to prayers every day before work."

He stopped abruptly. "You astonish me. I thought you said prayers every day."

"Of course I do. But having them imposed upon me strikes me as paternalistic, the employer as the boss in all things."

"Naturally no employer should expect to be your boss, Miss Hudson." He shook his head in feigned sympathy. "They must work *for you.*"

"Did you ever think of me for even one second of your life, Sherlock Holmes?" she retorted, turning to look at him.

"*Often,*" he replied somberly. "Many seconds I should say."

"One has one's own mind, you know, and I think that should be encouraged."

"In that light," Sherlock said, "no one can be better than Cadbury. Quakers believe that, rather than looking to church officials, or even to the liturgy for guidance, one should look to oneself, a personal relationship with the Holy Spirit."

"Men may say so, but, in the end, they always choose to dominate."

"Tsk! Tsk! Miss Belle, that is a very negative viewpoint. Very sad. You are sounding more like a New Woman every day." His expression was one of grave disappointment, but she did not miss the upturned corner of his mouth. "And I always thought of you as religious, Miss Belle."

"I should hope that I am! But I cannot tolerate the type of religion which is used by men to subjugate women." She shook her head. "This is not what God intended."

"Though I do agree, it is most unappreciative of you towards those who have taken you under their wing when no one else would have you. Recall that both Mr. Gladstone and Mr. Cadbury employed you under deceitful circumstances: under the premise that you were needy, not because of a particular skill. They showed a great kindness to you, and look how you repay them: with your insults and aspersions and attacks on their motives."

"Heavens to Betsy! If I blaspheme their gender, it is due to you, Sherlock Holmes, and not to them." She grew pensive. "I wonder if it is a characteristic of men to believe that they know everything. Even Mr. Gladstone insisted that Emily must accept Jesus as her Savior."

"You do not agree, Miss Belle? I confess I am shocked."

"Not under the circumstances, no. Jesus already knows her heart. Emily is already in His care."

"And did Miss Emily feel better after the P.M. spoke the words?" Sherlock asked softly.

"That poor, dear girl covered in welts," she murmured. "Yes, I think it was a comfort to her, and no doubt Jesus entered her heart, but I think Jesus loved her either way. How could anyone not? I could not have sent that poor child into Hell, and God is a much more loving God than I."

"Forgive me if I'm wrong. I recognize that you are the expert, being the daughter of a curate, but I believed the idea of prayer was not to persuade God but to allow oneself to receive what God has always been willing to give. Perhaps being told by a powerful man in a male-dominated society that she was saved was just what Miss Emily needed to hear."

She turned suddenly to stare at him. His words were indeed profound, but she could not let Sherlock Holmes know that he had impressed her—or that she had missed their talks and his plain speaking. Certainly not at this time.

"This lesson in theology from a man who drugged me!" she exclaimed. Odd that a man who professed not to be religious could be so spiritual. "I will say that, though Mr. Cadbury forces me to go to the prayer service, he has never attempted to poison me."

"Ah, so that is your conclusion, Miss Hudson?" he asked, rubbing this chin as an old woman might.

"It is," she pronounced. "Mr. Holmes, are you eating?"

"On occasion."

"You do not look well." She shook her head with concern. "But do not think to elicit my sympathy. You are still a scoundrel and a blackguard." She studied him more carefully appreciating that he appeared to have a mouth full of decay along with the welts and wrinkles. She added, "And a snaggletooth."

"Tsk tsk!" said Sherlock. "I believe I know what you are saying, Miss Belle."

Mirabella raised her eyebrows. "I should think so, I said it very clearly."

"You are merely asking if you may return to my employ."

She burst into laughter. "For such a great detective, I have to ask myself how you came to this conclusion, Mr. Holmes?"

"It is elementary, my dear. Because not everyone is so fortunate as to have such a wonderful, intelligent, and encouraging employer as you once had."

CHAPTER THIRTY-NINE
Mr. Cadbury

They walked along for some time in silence before Sherlock turned sideways to look at her. "I missed you, Miss Belle."

"I'm sure you did."

He frowned, but his eyes never lied: the Great Detective was amused. "In fact, I would be willing to make a number of concessions if you would return to my employ."

"Promises you don't intend to keep?"

"I always keep my promises. I am not like other men in that regard."

"True." She glanced in his direction. His expression was one she had never seen before: almost pleading.

"You are more than an employee to me, Miss Belle."

"Oh? And what am I?" She trembled as she spoke the words.

"A cohort. An advisor. A confidante. A *friend*."

This is what she had longed for, to see that he had some awareness of her presence. For a man so often living in his brain, it was monumental. As much as she fought it, a smile formed on her lips. "Things will be different than they were before, Mr. Holmes."

"They always are where you are concerned, Miss Belle."

"And may I ask—where are we going?"

"To see your former employer, of course." Sherlock tipped his hat to her.

"Richard Cadbury?"

"Ah, yes. We're almost there. And I see Lestrade has beaten us here. That cannot bode well."

Sherlock took the steps to Mr. Cadbury's home two steps at a time, with Mirabella not far behind.

As they were admitted into the home, she heard Lestrade in the parlor. They lost no time in joining him. As much as Mirabella hated the reason for their visit, she could not help but be grateful for the excitement that had been missing from her life.

Have I reached the point of no return? Will I never be able to return to a normal life again? Or will I forever feel something is missing if I am not in the proximity of that madman?

She glanced at Sherlock. *What have I become?*

"You are under arrest, sir," Lestrade said, motioning to his man.

"I have committed no crime," Richard Cadbury replied, an old man in his chair.

"Other than poisoning everyone at the top levels of government," huffed Lestrade. "Including the *Queen.*"

"I most certainly have poisoned no one!" replied Cadbury, aghast. "It would be against every principle I hold dear."

"You are much too hasty, Lestrade," Sherlock rebuked. "I told you that we merely wished to speak with Mr. Cadbury."

"Did you? Well, I'd say the time for speaking, as you put it, is done, when the Queen of England is being defiled."

"Whatever are thee speaking of?" asked Cadbury.

"Recall, Lestrade, that Richard Cadbury's contributions are many, the most progressive labor laws ever known," Sherlock said. "The Saturday half-day, even a doctor and dentist on staff. Does this sound like the actions of a poisoner?"

"We are not here to discuss your progressive politics! None of that matters when we are speaking of the Queen of England!" exclaimed Lestrade, blustery. "I'd say Cadbury's *contributions*, as you put it, are one too many!"

"What are thee speaking of?" pleaded Cadbury.

"Someone is drugging the top layers of government," Lestrade interjected.

"*God have mercy!*" managed Cadbury in a whisper.

"Through your chocolates," stated Lestrade.

"The fancy box to be precise," added Sherlock.

"Cadbury chocolates? Contaminated?" exclaimed Cadbury with uncharacteristic emotion, his long white beard almost quivering, as he clutched his heart. Mirabella gasped, afraid that the old man's heart might fail him.

Richard Cadbury found his voice again in full force. "I refused to put red paint and other fillers in my chocolates when everyone else was doing it at the risk of losing my business! I even took the matter to Parliament! Thee must be mistaken—or quite mad!"

"I am not mistaken," replied Lestrade. "There were narcotics in your chocolates!"

"That cannot have happened in the factory, I'd stake my life on it," Richard Cadbury protested in a state of shock.

"You may be doing just that, Cadbury!" Lestrade retorted.

"Do sit down Lestrade," ordered Mycroft, suddenly joining in the conversation. He took a handkerchief out of his pocket, patting his forehead while turning to Richard Cadbury. "I don't suppose you have any refreshment? Perhaps we should all sit down together and have tea."

"Of course," replied Richard Cadbury, ringing the bell on his desk. "I hope thou will forgive me. I quite forgot myself in being accused of the attempted murder of the queen."

"Poison yes. Murder, no," replied Mycroft.

Richard Cadbury looked quite befuddled—and ashen. "I am of the Society of Friends. We are pacifists."

"There was no attempt to kill—yet," remarked Lestrade.

"I beg thou will tell me the particulars. What is the poison thou speak of?"

"It was in the chocolates," replied Mycroft. "The poison was a truth serum. To be precise, the drug derived from the leaves of the borrachero tree. It inspires the one who consumes it to tell the truth."

"One should always tell the truth," replied Cadbury.

"So you admit that you did it?" demanded Lestrade, moving forward.

"I didst not!" Cadbury protested.

"It's at the highest levels of government," Mycroft explained. "Someone is attempting to obtain state secrets, which, as you can see, could easily lead to ruined alliances—even war."

"Or to blackmailing individuals, to overthrowing the government, and for power and monetary gain," Sherlock added.

"That my chocolates should be used for this purpose I am most aggrieved!"

"We will have to interview all of your workers," interjected Lestrade.

"Of course," agreed Cadbury. The tea had arrived and, as he appeared to be unable to hold the teacup, Mirabella poured the tea for Mycroft and Sherlock, Lestrade abstaining. Richard Cadbury gladly took the cup of tea she offered to him. "I know my workers like I know my own family. None would be engaged in this."

"I am inclined to agree." Sherlock nodded, studying Richard Cadbury. "I believe the poison was added after the purchase."

"We'll need a list of the names of all your sales of the fancy box," Lestrade said before turning to Sherlock. "And why do you think the poison was added after the chocolates left the factory, Holmes?"

"Well, for one thing, there was the dead body," Sherlock said.

"What the devil are you talking about, Holmes?" Lestrade said.

"Hamilton. We did an autopsy on the body. True, we found borrachero in the blood stream, but we also found morphine. The man died from morphine poisoning."

"What man?" Lestrade demanded.

"Hamilton, of course," Sherlock replied.

"You did an autopsy of Hamilton's body . . . Are you the grave digger? . . . You had no right! I'll see you in jail, Holmes, I will!"

"Uh-hmm." Mycroft cleared his throat. "My brother performed the autopsy under the direction of my office."

"And what does the foreign office have to say to it?" demanded Lestrade.

"Classified information," Mycroft replied without pausing, staring down the police inspector.

"W-what did you find out, then?" Lestrade asked indignantly.

"Yes, the truth serum was administered, but the fact that there was morphine present as well clears Mr. Cadbury of all wrong-doing."

"And how's that?" Lestrade demanded.

"There is no morphine in the chocolates," Sherlock said. "But there was morphine in the body. Whoever did this was experimenting on a victim—and got it wrong. Furthermore, I know who is behind this."

"Of course you do." Lestrade narrowed his eyes at Sherlock. "Don't keep us waiting, Holmes."

"Professor Moriarty."

"Of the London University?" Lestrade laughed. "Holmes, you're a lunatic. Why would the chair of the mathematics department be mixed up in this? And why do you keep wasting my time with your crazy theories?"

"I have proof."

"And what is that?" Lestrade asked.

"I smelled *La Intimidad* on Hamilton's suit," Sherlock said.

"What the deuce are you talking about?"

"Professor Moriarty smokes *La Intimidad*."

"That doesn't mean a damn thing!"

"There's not a handful of men in London who can afford that cigar, Hamilton not being one among them. He was a cleric in a politician's office. Besides, there was nothing to indicate that Hamilton was a smoker. His teeth were white."

"His teeth were white," Lestrade repeated, sneering. "So the murderer was Professor Moriarty of the University of London because you smelled cigar smoke on the victim's clothing and because his teeth were white?"

"Correct. Though I have no doubt one of Moriarty's henchmen actually administered the drug that killed Hamilton."

"*Bloody hell*," Lestrade muttered. "I've landed at the asylum."

CHAPTER FORTY
A tête-à-tête with Moriarty

VICTORIA NOT THE LEGAL HEIR TO THE THRONE

Even though Sherlock had been expecting it, the headline splattered across the *Irish Democrat* sent chills down his spine. The London newspapers weren't likely to print anything like this, but the queen was no favorite of Ireland. The slander would spread like wildfire.

"I know what your plan is, Professor," Sherlock remarked casually as he tossed the early edition of the newspaper on the table between them with a feigned indifference.

"I should think you do, Holmes." Moriarty leaned closer to him, stating under his breath, "It's in black and white." The professor took a sip of his hot chocolate as they sat across from each other at Cadbury's. The academic clearly did not consider Sherlock Holmes to be a threat to his plan.

Good. I might have precious little on my side, but this is a start.

"Don't try to stop me, Holmes," Moriarty said. "Or it would be most disadvantageous to you."

PM CARES FOR CHILD OF ILLICIT LOVE AFFAIR
AT 10 DOWNING STREET
Our country's leader!
In his own home with wife in attendance

Victorians did love a scandal and this was proof of it. But was it enough to break the government? There was no proof, no witness, no one to testify in a court of law.

Yet.

Still, it was more than a little alarming and the effects were, as yet, unknown. But possibly disastrous.

The sunlit room of beige walls and black lacquered furniture was both inviting and professional, conducive to the exchange of information between gentlemen. Or between a criminal mastermind and the world's first consulting detective.

"I would think it to be obvious even to the slow of wit," Moriarty added. "How lovely that we should finally understand each other."

BENJAMIN DISRAELI NUMEROUS LOVE AFFAIRS! WE KNEW THIS – BUT WITH MEN?? IS THE TORY MP ENGAGED IN CRIMINAL ACTS? *Read about it in Lord Beaconsfield's own words*

Sherlock glanced at the headline. And yet, still, there was no proof. The government could be severely hurt by such gossip. Many an election had been won with ridiculous claims and without proof of the slander to the other side.

"I have understood you for a long time now, Professor," stated Sherlock casually. In an effort to stall for time he attempted to hold his companion's interest, one whom he knew to be easily bored, much like himself.

"And what do you understand, Holmes?" Moriarty inquired politely, stroking his neatly trimmed auburn beard. He appeared more curious than threatened, clearly confident in the outcome of his plan.

"It is clear that you wish to overthrow the monarchy. I should say that is a fairly great discrepancy in our *raison d'être*," Sherlock stated without further ado, taking a sip of tea while leaving the cocoa for his companion, his eyes glued to the professor.

"Are you suggesting that I have something to do with these headlines?" Moriarty's eyes glistened with the pleasure of a predator on the hunt.

"Someone wishes to discredit the government of England—perhaps to destroy it." Sherlock slapped the paper on the black lacquered table, making no attempt to hide his annoyance. "So naturally I believe you to be behind it, Moriarty."

"You wound me, Holmes," the professor said. "Someone is only reporting the truth."

"It is far from the truth," retorted Sherlock.

"The public shall be the final judge of the truth, as you well know."

Moriarty moved as if he were about to rise, which alarmed Sherlock more than he cared to admit. *I must keep Moriarty here.*

"I have no idea how you collected this information," Sherlock lied. "I admit that it was ingenious." Sherlock hoped his delivery conveyed sufficient admiration. In addition to craving adoration, Moriarty's Achilles heel was to overestimate himself and to underestimate everyone else.

"I take that as a great compliment coming from you, Holmes." He returned to his seat, much to Sherlock's relief.

"Yes, you are the master of destruction, Moriarty." The time for flattery was past. Sherlock knew that, at this point, his anger would please Moriarty and egg him on. The professor was so certain of his eventual success that he was getting sloppy.

That is not a mistake that I will make.

"I do what needs to be done."

"But is it so very clever?" considered Sherlock, taking his pipe out of his pocket and loading it with tobacco. "To slander and destroy another person is the simplest thing on Earth—it can be done to a saint."

"Fortunately there are no saints in government. You know that very well, Holmes."

"There are none of us perfect, we all have faults, and one need merely find that negative quality about a person and play it up out of proportion, twist it and expand it."

Moriarty smiled. "With only a grain of truth it can be made to look remarkably bad."

"And yet those who are, in truth, remarkably bad, can look snow white while pointing the finger," added Sherlock, staring pointedly at his companion. He purposely kept his tone low. A certain conviviality must be maintained. "If you don't care about our queen, do you care nothing for England, the land of your birth?"

"I think of little else, I assure you," Moriarty replied, taking another sip of cocoa.

"You think of how the queen may best be used to your advantage, not of how you may serve her," Sherlock stated in a low voice through clenched teeth.

"It shan't be long, and you will bow to me, Holmes."

"Over my dead body."

"I guarantee that can be arranged."

One of the waitresses approached the table and Sherlock ordered another pot of chocolate.

"I warn you not to proceed, Moriarty," Sherlock said softly, making no attempt to hide the threat in his voice. "You are already rich. You already run the criminal underground in London. How much more power do you need?"

"We must act now, Holmes, before it is too late." Moriarty leaned in closer to him.

"What the devil are you talking about?"

"I can see how things are going, and I know you can too: the vote for the everyday man—it is insanity!"

"It is inevitable," said Sherlock.

"Newspapers and books available to everyone!" Moriarty continued without pause. "Literacy increasing, education for children—even girls. And shorter working hours? We have to turn all that back before it changes the world forever. If we don't stop it soon, there will be no turning back."

"I see your point, Moriarty," Sherlock nodded, feigning complete agreement. "Once a man learns to read, that skill cannot be unlearnt."

"Precisely! We cannot let the everyday man become enlightened, you know that Holmes, you know how superior you and I are to the common man."

Ah, yes, but to be common is not necessarily to be inferior.

"Superior," Sherlock repeated. "But that will always be the case, Professor. I shouldn't worry. Even if the average man learns to read, he will not be your intellectual equal."

"You miss the point entirely, Holmes!" Moriarty enunciated in a sharp whisper. "Once everyone can vote and read, how will we control the masses? Now is the time to take control, there is no better time."

"Indeed. An enlightened populace is a grave threat."

"Do you know many country folk, Holmes? They can't vote, they can't read. They believe whatever their local parish vicar tells them, they never leave the farm. If you meet one, you meet them all."

And yet, education has not much improved you, has it Professor?

"And the factory workers are not much better are they, Moriarty?" Sherlock goaded him.

"We have the common man where we want him in the cities. They work every breathing moment. We control *everything*: the wealth, the land, the technology. *The information.*" Moriarty smiled broadly, the gleam in his eye grossly disturbing. "Above all, we control the *information.*"

"So everything is perfect, why agitate yourself, Professor?" Sherlock asked with dry nonchalance. "Take another sip of cocoa and calm yourself."

"Because by 'we' I mean 'I'—I must control it all. And it's not going to last if something isn't done!" Moriarty was, by now, in an uncharacteristically impassioned state. "Today's people are different. Curiosity, a fascination with science, the belief that they deserve as much as the wealthy—can you fathom that, Holmes? They no longer accept their station in life! There is, in the population, a willingness to question both assumptions and the class structure. There is even intelligence in the rare one."

"We must stamp that out at once."

"Precisely my thought," said Moriarty.

"And how do you propose to put yourself in power, Professor?" Sherlock asked as nonchalantly as he could muster given his current view into Moriarty's derangement. "With the expressed purpose of both owning the technology and putting a halt to education and the vote for the everyday man?"

"Take a stab at it, my enemy."

"It is easily deciphered." Sherlock leaned back in his chair. "Here we have possibly the most extraordinary government England has ever known: Gladstone, Disraeli, and Queen Victoria. They may be at odds, but, in the comical fashion of life, together they are pure genius."

"Precisely."

"And you intend to discredit them all, the most extraordinary government we have ever had."

"Obviously. Really, Holmes, I make it too easy for you. It is child's play."

Holmes leaned towards his opponent. "But what can be the purpose unless it is to be the prime minister yourself?"

"Aha!" exclaimed Moriarty, smiling broadly, his pleasure obvious. "Sometimes even you astonish me, Sherlock! Yes, the P.M. is even more powerful than the queen."

Sherlock had hoped against hope that he was wrong. "But no doubt, being a man of genius, you have a secondary plan. A backup, as it were."

"Do you expect me to tell you?" Moriarty finished off his cocoa just as the fresh pot arrived. Sherlock glanced at the body-guards who had grown bored with their employer's harmless coffee shoppe conversation and had their eyes on one of the pretty waitresses. The timing was perfect.

"Actually I do." *And why should you reveal your plan to me, threatening its very success? Despite all logic to the contrary, I certainly do expect you to tell me.*

"I hate to disappoint," said Moriarty. "A moratorium by the people, showing their lack of support of the government. But don't you see, Holmes? There are so many scenarios, and I emerge victorious from them all."

Beholding Moriarty's unfettered ego with such intimacy was darkly terrifying if unsurprising. He had long understood Moriarty's character but to be emerged in such darkness was both ominous and disturbing. It was as if all pretense of social appropriateness had dissolved, leaving only the true nature of the man before him: deception, manipulation, self-worship, and a lust for power.

There was a certain satisfaction in using Moriarty's own weapon against him.

I must keep Moriarty's interest. The government—even the queen—discredited by a moratorium would be disastrous. Sherlock returned his eyes to his nemesis, forcing himself to remain nonchalant. "You either wish to destroy the government—or to be the power behind the throne. Both ingenious and despicable."

"Indeed. If I cannot win as P.M., I have a bright, young charismatic man in mind whom I have a certain hold over." Moriarty's lips tightened like one who had eaten a tart lemon.

"Alsop?"

"He is very promising, is he not? Turns heads wherever he goes." Moriarty nodded. "I have his ear."

Moriarty's plans *might work*. Moriarty's plan to be—or control—the P.M.

was definitely not outside the realm of possibility. Just because Moriarty's insanity was obvious to Sherlock did not mean that it was to everyone. Moriarty was indeed a genius at staying in the background and not revealing his true self to anyone. He knew how to keep his mouth shut. Today was a notable exception, but Sherlock had assistance on this one occasion.

Moreover, Moriarty could throw the country into anarchy while attempting to enact his plan. The professor could very well oust both Gladstone and Disraeli while discrediting the queen, which could do no end of harm to Britain.

Sherlock knew the best way to keep Moriarty talking was to stroke his ego. "But, tell me, Professor, wouldn't your first choice be to rule yourself?"

"Of course." He sighed. "I wish to be elected to the House of Commons. Anymore, the prime minister is more often than not from the House of Commons rather than the House of Lords. I had initially thought this to be a terrible state of affairs, but one can utilize even misfortune to one's advantage."

"You are a plethora of inspiration and platitudes, Professor," Sherlock muttered.

"Aren't I?" Moriarty smiled. "Even I could be the prime minister. Completely legal."

Heaven help us.

"It occurs to me that your genius could be put to better use, Professor. Improving the world perhaps?"

"I will control the government," Moriarty stated in a low tone. "That is the relevant point, Holmes. To be in control of Britain, the most powerful country in the world, is to wield enormous power. Whosoever rules England rules the world."

Sherlock leaned forward. "I'll stop you, Moriarty, as I always do."

"I had already thought of that." He frowned. "I wouldn't, if I were you, Holmes."

"Or?"

"Or I'll go after your girl."

This is news indeed.

It was Sherlock's turn to laugh. He knew Moriarty wouldn't lay a hand on Fantine Noel. Not just because she was his sister, but because the countess was much too useful to him. And Moriarty couldn't handle the bad publicity amidst his own people. Someone as visible as Fantine could not be disposed of easily.

Sherlock was surprised to learn that, even under the influence of the serum, Moriarty was attempting to manipulate him. *I should have known! I should have predicted the outcome since the serum was designed to reveal one's true character.*

"You do that, Professor, and may God save you from her wrath," Sherlock replied, rising to stand.

"She is harmless," Moriarty stated matter-of-factly.

"You surprise me, Moriarty. She is a dangerous woman," Sherlock tipped his hat to his rival. "I don't think you have any idea how treacherous she can be."

CHAPTER FORTY-ONE
Buckingham Palace

The King of Denmark escorted Queen Victoria into dinner at the supper-room of Buckingham Palace. The princes were in their royal uniforms, and the princesses wore their most elegant and beautiful ball gowns. The table, shaped like a large horseshoe, was set with gold plates and afire with candles. Everything sparkled and glittered.

Victoria had ruled for forty-four years. It was largely a family affair, not being a jubilee or a diamond year, though still a momentous and significant occasion, with many members of the House of Lords and House of Commons present. Some ten former prime ministers were in attendance.

The queen wore a crown atop her head from which a lace veil emerged. She was dressed in black satin in mourning for her late husband, Prince Consort Albert of Saxe-Coburg, who had died at the age of forty-two in 1861, over twenty years prior.

Queen Victoria was covered in lace from head to toe, and she wore the ceremonial blue sash across her torso, along with the Crown Jewels on her ears, neckline, and fingers. The Royal Family Order of George IV was pinned to her sash, a portrait suspended from a white silk bow and framed in oak leaves and acorns.

Certainly everyone present and all of Great Britain understood the importance and significance of this occasion. Queen Victoria ruled four hundred and fifty million people worldwide; the sun never set upon her empire. Since 1870, Britain had added Zanzibar, Fiji, Cyprus, Bechuanaland, Somaliland, Kenya, the New Hebrides, Rhodesia and Uganda to her colonies.

When the imperial ruler had been seated at the center of the horseshoe, the others present were seated. The Duke and Duchess of Coburg, the Prince and Princess of Wales, and the queen's cousin, Prince George the Duke of Cambridge, were present. The queen's cherished youngest daughter Princess Beatrice and her fiancé, Prince Henry of Battenberg, in the opinion of many the handsomest prince in all of Europe, were, of course, present. It had seemed Beatrice would never marry, and here she had nabbed the best catch of all.

Clink! Clink! The master of ceremonies tapped on his crystal glass, rising to address the party. "We are gathered here in celebration of our illustrious queen's ascension to the throne."

"Long live the queen!"

"The British government is the best and most successful since Queen Elizabeth I," the master of ceremonies added, perhaps in response to the recent headlines.

Some of the foreign notables in attendance were the Archduke Franz Ferdinand of Austria, The Grand Duke and Duchess of Hesse, the Crown Prince Danilo of Montenegro, and Prince Amir Khan of Persia. One of the princes of India was present, a dashing and handsome young man. Many of the queen's generals were present, including General Kitchener. And, of course, Mr. Perminov, the Russian diplomat, was present. He had been closely watched by Mycroft's men and had been unable to meet with Moriarty—as yet.

Among the guests were several unexpected guests: Dr. John Watson, Miss Mirabella Hudson, and Mycroft Holmes. Mycroft was known to many and he cut a dashing figure. Also present were certain members of the British army, the British navy, and the horse guards.

Sherlock Holmes was absent. Or was he? In truth, he was disguised as a footman that he might move about the party. It was important that Sherlock both be able to keep his eye on the party and have unfettered mobility, which the seated members of the party did not have, both due to their elaborate costumes and the rules of decorum.

Victoria's countenance is unusually severe this evening, Sherlock thought to himself as he took Mycroft's cane. Sherlock had not informed Watson and Miss Belle of his disguise as he could not afford that there should be any recognition. He and Mycroft had, however, spoken to the queen, Gladstone, and Disraeli, imploring them to set aside their differences and to unite against a common enemy.

"The supreme monarch is known to enjoy a good laugh, but there is no amusement in her eyes on this occasion," Mycroft murmured to his party, sharing the same thought as his brother.

With difficulty, Sherlock averted his eyes from Miss Belle, which would have been considered an affront by a footman. It was clear that she was absolutely astonished to be included in such illustrious company and paid little notice of him, though she generally erred on the side of being too polite to the staff.

All were seated and the meal commenced. The scent of the curry, lemon, and meringue, combined as it was with the vanillin scent of a sea of white snowdrops, Prince Albert's favorite flower, ornamented the room, casting an exotic ambiance. With so many foreign nationals, and so many exquisite dishes, the sights and smells were intoxicating.

The dishes were never ending. Twenty-four French chefs prepared, with every manner of sauces, Normandy sole, roast beef, venison, quail, tongue, potato soufflé, asparagus tips, green beans almandine, and even curry, a particular favorite of the queen's. Having acquainted himself with all the details, as was his custom, Sherlock knew that dessert included rice cream and cherry sauce, pineapple fritters, strawberries in meringue, and another of the queen's favorites, lemon jelly.

Sherlock's party might not recognize him, but they all knew that they were there to protect the queen. He glanced at Mirabella, who kept her reticule containing her pistol close to the fingertips of her left hand. *Good girl.*

Mirabella was seated between Dr. Watson and Mycroft, but she kept her eyes on the guests and on all the doors. If there were to be an intruder, perhaps he would come from the outside.

Or perhaps not.

Given that the enemy was Moriarty, it was guaranteed to be both unpredictable and remarkable.

"I am a woman of the night." A beautiful young woman, elaborately dressed, entered from the kitchen door and exclaimed with a smile and a twinkle in her eye, "And I have been with your prime minister, the great Gladstone. Emily, whom he cares for in his home, is our daughter."

The entire party held their breaths in a collective gasp. Sherlock looked to Queen Victoria, who frowned.

This is the proof. No doubt the accuser would be willing to be both interviewed and to testify in a court of law. It was her word against Gladstone's. Sherlock could see the headline now

MOTHER OF ILLEGITIMATE CHILD HAS COME FORWARD

This is a disaster. It might be a closed occasion, but there were many servants present, and the recounting of an event like this would spread like wildfire. A terrible scandal which could only discount the prime minister.

"It is a lie!" Gladstone rose from his chair. There was no hesitation in his expression, his anger evident and uncontrolled as one might have expected from a hotheaded evangelical. "I have never broken my marriage vows. I demand to see the birth records!"

She laughed. "For a prostitute's baby? There are none."

"Most convenient, madame!" There was authority in Gladstone's delivery, a born orator, and sounds of approval within the party. It was almost as if Gladstone had known it was coming.

Even as the loud murmurs and shocked expressions began to create a commotion of disorder, one of the young servers dropped his silver tray, everyone turning to him.

Everyone except Sherlock Holmes, who kept his eyes rotating about the room. He noticed there was a cane in the corner of the room where there been none.

The server who had dropped the tray was unusually handsome, with a charismatic presence and a baritone voice.

"That is nothing, I myself have been with the Earl of Beaconsfield," the server exclaimed in a silky voice.

Lord save us! There was now a witness, someone who could substantiate the gossip. Sherlock glanced at Mycroft, who looked quite discomfited. If Disraeli wasn't nervous about this development, the Holmes brothers were. They saw the headline in their mind's eye as if it were in print:

MALE PROSTITUTE WILL TESTIFY!

All eyes moved to Disraeli, some ladies covering their mouths with their hands. It looked as if Princess Beatrice might faint, and the Prince of Wales appeared utterly disgusted. Queen Victoria, however, was as cool as a cucumber.

Disraeli, seemingly unaffected, took a handkerchief out and dabbed his mouth with it. He then lifted his monocle to his eye, examining the young man from head to toe, perhaps a bit longer than was necessary.

No one so much as breathed.

"Sadly, it is a lie," Disraeli asserted after a long pause, a smile on his lips.

Some gasped, forks dropped, and faces turned red, but all eyes turned to the queen, whose expression was particularly cold and hard.

After interminable seconds, a smile crept into the supreme ruler's expression.

"*Hee! Hee!*" Victoria began laughing, unable to stop.

This naturally led to the laughter of many in the party. It was difficult to know if the amusement sprang from joining in the joke—or in reaction to the spectacle the queen was making.

Sherlock was not so naive as to be unaware that, in a gathering such as this, there would always be those who would ape the reactions of the most powerful person in attendance.

With the queen's sudden amusement, the disturbing situation was transformed into a play staged for the amusement of the guests.

"As for the prime minister," Victoria pronounced once she had regained her composure, obviously discounting the claims against Disraeli and proceeding to those against her adversary, "he is many annoying things, but he is not a liar."

Excitement ran high and the guests were fixated on Queen Victoria. Sherlock slowly began moving to the corner of the room. He noticed that Mr. Perminov had stood and was moving in the direction of the cane as well.

"Stop!" As the guards proceeded to remove the two intruders, the woman playing the harp stood up and exclaimed, "She has no authority. I am the niece of Baroness Louise Lehzen, Victoria's nanny. I do not say queen because Victoria—or 'Drina', as she is called among the family—is not the legal heir to the throne. Her father is Sir John Conroy—not the Duke of Kent. Victoria is an impostor!"

There was a general moan among those present. Princess Beatrice fainted, followed by her maid administering smelling salts.

All eyes—almost all—were on Victoria, who rose from her chair, her expression remarkably unperturbed. To those present, she did appear to be the Queen.

"We are a country of elected officials and a country for the people," Victoria said. "We are the strongest nation on Earth and we have the best government on Earth."

"It doesn't change the facts," the woman retorted, holding her chin high.

"I have no objection to the expression of legitimate concerns," she continued, "but out-and-out lies and slander are a different matter. However, I am a fair and just sovereign. Let us put it to the people. For that reason, I have only just resolved to introduce the Representation of the People Act, which will extend the vote from the boroughs to the countryside. This act will extend the voting populace to fully five and half million Britons. Let the people decide. If they do not wish me to rule, I shall oblige them."

Victoria placed her hand in front of her mouth as if yawning, and motioned for her aids, who assisted in her departure. In truth, she appeared nothing more than bored by the interruption. "Let us proceed to the ballroom for dancing."

The attendees looked once more upon the accusers, but the charged air of horror and shock had turned to disdain and disgust.

The invited guests rose and leisurely followed the queen into the ballroom, their every movement indicative of their continued allegiance.

As the party moved into the ballroom, with so many people moving about the room, Mr. Perminov moved to the corner and retrieved the cane.

"Your cane, sir." The footman handed Mycroft his cane.

"How did you know that I was ready to depart, my good man?"

The footman bowed and removed himself.

"Such a delightful party," Mirabella whispered in near shock. "And who is that footman? He looks familiar."

"I couldn't say. That was not as dull as most state dinners," Mycroft agreed with nonchalance. "But I fear I must go. I have a busy evening ahead of me. Good night."

And with that, Mycroft motioned to his underlings and exited the room.

"Lord save us!" Dr. Watson exclaimed, as Sherlock approached them in full tuxedo. "Where did you come from, Holmes?"

"I've been here and there." Sherlock was patting his mouth with his handkerchief. "Indeed. And what did you think of the proceedings, Miss Belle?"

"As my father would say, 'that would make a stuffed bird sing'." She caught her breath.

Sherlock broke into a rare display of amusement.

"Do you think, Mr. Holmes, that the government is safe? Was it *enough?*"

"The voting act will go a long way in the government's favor," Watson said.

"We shall see." Sherlock nodded, frowning. "But the truth of the matter is that, despite the obvious benefits to Moriarty of the slander, it was all a ruse."

"A ruse? Whatever do you mean, Mr. Holmes?"

"A distraction. To veil the true purpose. It has been Moriarty's plan all along to sell the submarine plans to the Russians for an enormous amount of money—and to gain a powerful ally."

"The most advanced military plans in the hands of the world's largest country—also a potential enemy to Britain—would not be a good development," Dr. Watson said.

"I could not be in greater agreement, my friend."

"And did Moriarty succeed in his plan?" Dr. Watson asked with apprehension.

"No. The actual blueprint is now with Mycroft." Sherlock said, shaking his head. "But thanks to Miss Belle's basic understanding of the key and my not inconsequential abilities in the forging of a blueprint, it may be some time before that is discovered." Sherlock smiled.

"The Hebrew and trigonometric symbols I gave you are nonsense, Mr. Holmes. I hope you understood that."

"Naturally. But they gave the blueprint the appearance of legitimacy." Sherlock turned to Mirabella and held out his hand as he stood. "In the meantime, Miss Belle, may I have this dance?"

CHAPTER FORTY-TWO
The Queen's Ball

Her arm in Sherlock's, Mirabella stepped into the adjoining ballroom trailed by her long white silk ball gown. With her elbow-length white gloves and her hair adorned with orange blossoms, she had never felt so elegant. What could promise more delights than a ball? And this was no ordinary ball.

Mirabella had only been to one other ball in her life: the Christmas ball at *Miss de Beauvais' Finishing School for Distinguished Young Ladies*.

As elegant as that was, this was stunning by comparison in its attention to every detail: the candlelight, the chandeliers, the flowers, and the incomparable attire.

Most important was the quality of the music. These musicians were like none she had ever heard. There was a quadrille band, a harpsichord player, a flutist, and even bagpipe players, Scotland being near and dear to the queen's heart.

There was yet more food: a table laid out with tea and coffee, ices, biscuits, cakes, bonbons, and sandwiches.

"What did you do while you were under cover to thwart Moriarty?" She raised her eyebrows at him.

"Miss Belle, do you remember the last time we danced?" Mirabella felt Sherlock's hold tightening on her waist. She looked into his steel-grey eyes and knew that there would be no further discussion of the case at this time. She didn't blame him, but she was dying to know what he had been up to. Judging by his good mood, he had been successful.

"Of course I do, Mr. Holmes. At Miss de Beauvais'."

"You shall call me 'Sherlock' tonight, Miss Belle."

She smiled up at him. Sherlock could be the perfect partner when he wished.

It was no secret that Sherlock Holmes was a great lover of music. Outside of the successful resolution of a case, music seemed to be the only thing which calmed the savage beast.

Indeed, something about music and dance transformed Sherlock Holmes, bringing out a side to him which was irresistible. He was no longer her critical employer and an intellectual highbrow, but, instead, simply a charming man.

A *delightful* man. A handsome man.

And an exceptional dancer. The music began for the first waltz. "Ah, Johann Strauss Jr. if I'm not mistaken. *Morgenblätter.*"

"The Morning Papers," she said.

He led her out onto the dance floor with his right arm, her left hand on his right. When they reached the dance floor, he effortlessly spun her about twice as they began to circle the dance floor with the other dancers.

All dancers now on the floor, he stopped and bowed, and she curtseyed, before he moved to firmly place his right hand on her waist, his left arm extended, which she took. She felt the strength of his muscular arm holding her.

His grey eyes were almost silver tonight, alive with amusement as well as their usual intensity. He raven hair framed his strong features.

As the waltz began, they rotated several times to his rear and then again forward before he spun her again, her white dress spinning about her. The waltz alternated with slow, romantic sections and fast, invigorating phrases.

Just when she thought he could surprise her no more, he dipped her to the side.

"You are such an exquisite dancer, Sherlock."

"And do you find that astonishing, Miss Belle?"

She giggled. "I do. You hold so many social niceties in disdain."

"It does not follow that I do not know how to execute them, however." He pulled her closer. "I can assure you that my mother would fall into her grave if her sons were not able to show themselves to advantage on the dance floor."

"Your socialite mother who married a country squire in Sussex?" Being a curate's daughter, she was sufficiently impressed. The country squire was the most important man in any country parish, owning a good portion of the land, having at least one tenant, and living in a large house. The manor house, which would someday pass to Mycroft. Obviously a country squire was not a peer, but all country folk looked up to the squire as the most important local person.

"Indeed, she married the lord of the manor," Sherlock raised his eyebrows haughtily, but there was amusement in his grey eyes.

"And the local justice of the peace." She sighed. It explained a great deal about Sherlock and must have been the perfect upbringing for his temperament. He would have experienced the criminal justice system and the law from a young age—and in a manner which was close to the people.

Court was often held in the local pub, which explained why Sherlock was comfortable with those from every walk of life.

"And my mother is related to the Vernets of Paris—famous painters all."

Mirabella giggled. "The queen has nothing on you, Sherlock."

"Indeed, not." His eyes grew soft. "But then, we are all famous in our own world, are we not, Miss Belle?"

He held her in his arms and she wished they might dance forever as he maneuvered her expertly about the dance floor. She felt some guilt for forgetting about all the important matters of state in just that moment.

Although Sherlock had no difficulty negotiating the other couples, by this point all eyes were on them, and a larger space began to form around them.

Her heart was beating so rapidly, but it was that of joy and pleasure rather than of exhaustion. During one of the refrains with the clashing of the symbols, he lifted her off the ground by the waist, while maintaining the spin of the waltz.

There was a general applause, even in this subdued environment.

Mirabella glanced at those seated to see the Queen of England smiling in delight. She knew that Victoria had been a dancer in her youth as well. Mirabella wondered if the older woman might be reliving her dance with a young Prince Albert. Surely we are all youthful in our hearts.

She glanced at Sherlock. No, he was as complex as ever.

"I must thank you, Mr. Holmes—"

"—Sherlock."

"I must thank you, Sherlock, for this wonderful life I have. I never imagined to meet such people or to learn so many fascinating things."

He spun her about. "The pleasure is all mine, Miss Belle. If things were different . . ."

"If what were different?"

"If the work we did was not so important, if there was not so much danger, if any attachments did not put all parties in grave peril, if I were a different man . . ."

Yes, if you were not so afraid of emotion and of love. If you were not so ruled by your logic . . .

"Tell me, Sherlock . . ."

"Yes?"

"Do you take after your British father or your French mother?"

He frowned at her. "The British side, of course."

"Naturally."

He then placed his right hand on her back so that they were side by side. They began spinning, side by side, across the dance floor. The beautiful music surrounding them, the chandelier overhead, Mirabella felt as if she were floating across a lake in the moonlight.

"Mycroft is more French than British, I think," he added.

"I agree," she said quietly. "And I wish you might be."

When the music was over, she thought she might cry, so beautiful a moment had it been.

And she realized something else. At Miss de Beauvais' ball she had been jealous watching John Watson flirting with her fellow debutantes.

She looked up at Sherlock. This evening she had not wished to be anywhere else.

Even for a moment.

CHAPTER FORTY-THREE
An Historical Turning Point

QUEEN VICTORIA VOWS TO EXPAND THE VOTING POPULACE
Representation of the People Act put before the House of Lords
WE COUNTRY FOLK MAY SOMEDAY VOTE
LONG LIVE THE QUEEN!
LONG LIVE GREAT BRITAIN!

Mirabella held the *London Times* out to Sherlock, revealing the headline on the front page. "How ingenious," she reflected. "Extending the voting populace, making the country more democratic."

"Agreed," Sherlock said. "Giving the country to the people that the people might not overtake the country."

"A brilliant move." Watson chuckled, reading the headline. "That alone might have won support for our queen."

FREE ALE AND TOBACCO DISTRIBUTED TO ALL
Celebrating Queen Victoria's forty-four year reign

"I shall lay that act of genius at Mr. Lipton's door," said Sherlock.

"Was it not your idea, Mr. Holmes?" Mirabella asked.

"I called in a favor," said Sherlock.

Watson nodded in agreement. "The people are so thrilled with the queen and her policy to extend the electorate that the negative propaganda being spread is having little to no effect."

"Besides making the initiators look ridiculous," Sherlock added.

"There are still those who are dissatisfied," Mirabella considered.

"True, but dissatisfaction does not make a government fall," Sherlock mused. "If that were so, there would be no governments anywhere."

"And what will the act do precisely?" asked Mirabella.

"It will extend the concessions from the boroughs to the countryside," said Sherlock. "All men paying an annual rental of ten pounds or all those holding land valued at ten pounds will now have the vote."

"But all women and forty percent of the males still will not have the vote," Dr. Watson said.

"Very true, it is not universal suffrage. Far from a democracy."

"Still a vast improvement and enough to prevent an uprising," Dr. Watson said. "The pertinent point is that we have deflected the fate that befell the French."

"Ah, no French Revolution on English soil," Mirabella considered.

Dr. Watson frowned somberly. "I wonder how close we came."

ARE WE BRITONS OR ARE WE SHEEP?

"Those who would accuse our beloved queen of tyranny are not to be mimicked," read Dr. Watson. "Are we Britons not better than that?"

GLADSTONE RENOUNCES ALL ACCUSATIONS
Claims he has never defiled his marriage vows

"The mother of the supposed daughter was paid to lie," Dr. Watson read from the article. "Gladstone claims the deception was created as an attempt to discredit the government."

"How willing people are to believe slander, to condemn and to criticize," Mirabella said.

QUEEN CONDEMNS RUMORS AROUND DISRAELI
all lies initiated by the liberal party
Do you trust the word of a prostitute over the Queen?

"All know that Disraeli is the queen's favorite, but she goes further," Watson chuckled as he continued reading.

"And what about the rumors of Disraeli's . . . uh . . . *criminal acts?*" Mirabella asked.

"Our beloved conservative whip is keeping a low profile." Sherlock shrugged.

"That must be very difficult for him," Watson said with a chuckle.

"Disraeli is nothing if not a politician."

"And the queen?" Mirabella asked anxiously. "What about the rumor that she is the daughter of Sir John Conroy rather than the Duke of Kent? Could it be *true?*"

"My dear girl, have you ever seen a picture of the Duke of Kent?" asked Sherlock, moving to his library and pulling out a book.

Returning to his seat, he retrieved two photographs and handed them to Mirabella. Dr. Watson glanced at the photo from over her shoulder.

There before her was a photograph of Victoire and the Duke of Kent.

Add a wig to the duke's balding head and he might have been Queen Victoria's twin.

CHAPTER FORTY-FOUR
Somewhere A Voice is Coming for Me

"What are you saying? That Victoria is the rightful heir to the throne?" asked Mirabella, standing next to the fireplace mantel while leaning over Sherlock's shoulder, presumably to view the picture in his hand.

Her proximity was somewhat disturbing.

"Of course I am." Sherlock looked up into golden brown eyes studying the photograph, completely impervious to the closeness of his presence. *How can one person feel so much and the other so little?* Particularly alarming since he was a person not accustomed to feeling anything. He cleared his throat. "Can there be any doubt after seeing this photograph?"

"A mere photograph is not entirely scientific," said Dr. Watson, studying his friend with amusement as he puffed on his pipe. "Although convincing, I find it surprising that you consider it to be sufficient proof with your obsession with the mathematical and scientific, Holmes."

"And yet there is no doubt in your mind as to Victoria's parentage is there, Watson?" Sherlock raised his left eyebrow, glancing up from the photo.

"Not in the least," said Watson.

Somewhere a voice is calling, calling for me. In the background a record had been placed on the new phonograph. The popular melody was a deviation from the usual classical music and Strauss waltzes Sherlock generally favored.

"Even his countenance and expression is the same," said Mirabella, continuing to study the likeness of the Duke of Kent. Sherlock could feel her breath on his cheek. "If you were to put a dress on Prince Edward, it would be Victoria."

"Precisely," agreed Sherlock, handing the picture to Miss Hudson that she might not stand so close. "The only thing that was ever at issue was *not* the queen's legitimacy—but if the public could be persuaded that Victoria was not the legitimate heir to the throne."

"But hemophilia—and the improbability?" Mirabella asked, obviously perplexed. She set the photograph down on the table beside him and moved to dust the mantelpiece.

"Alas, it is possible that the gene was newly mutated, despite the extremely low odds," said Watson. "To be sure, genetic mutation accounts for approximately one-third of all cases of hemophilia. And the percentage is higher among older parents. The Duke of Kent was fifty-one when he presumably fathered Victoria."

"Over thirty-three percent doesn't seem like low odds." Mirabella turned to look at Watson.

"The chances of an individual developing the hemophilia gene through genetic mutation is one in twenty-five thousand. But amongst those cases of hemophilia, one third are attributable to genetic mutation. Which is to say that hemophilia doesn't occur through virus or bacteria but through genetics." Watson appeared thoughtful. "In addition, the mutated hemophilia gene could have occurred with Victoire or with her mother or her mother's mother. The gene is carried on the X-chromosome. So focusing on the father is somewhat misplaced since the father is never a carrier: he either has hemophilia or he doesn't. A woman can be a carrier without having the disease."

"And the porphyria?" asked Mirabella.

"Possibly the queen favored fortune with that one," Sherlock shrugged, stretching his legs out before him.

"Though it is my guess that porphyria will turn up again and is only temporarily out of sight," suggested Watson. "And, if not, it is possible that porphyria stopped with her father. Not all traits are passed on, it is the luck of the draw."

"Victoria defied the odds in so many ways becoming queen to begin with," Mirabella considered. "It appears to be her lot in life to defy the odds. I suppose it is not surprising that she should then defy statistics in other ways."

Dusk and the shadows falling o'er land and sea, the tenor crooned. Sherlock glanced out the window, but, in a rare moment, heard and saw nothing. He knew there was something wrong with him—something *terribly wrong* which he did not like. His mind kept returning to holding Miss Belle in his arms at the Queen's Ball.

"What are the traits of porphyria, Dr. Watson?" asked Mirabella, moving to dust Sherlock's laboratory. Sherlock's eyes followed her.

"Seizures, anxiety, itchy skin, flatulence, constipation, colic, and discolored urine," stated Dr. Watson.

"Maybe King George wasn't mad at all," considered Mirabella, that peculiar half-smile on her expression that was so appealing. "Maybe he was simply exceedingly uncomfortable."

"Or maybe it was the arsenic administered by the king's physician attempting to cure the porphyria which made King George mad," posed

Watson.

"At any rate the photograph, it does not lie," stated Sherlock, waving his hand.

"And yet—it is a very fickle public," Watson said.

"A moot point," Sherlock stated, closing his eyes momentarily. "The public has rallied around the queen after she proposed the Representation of the People Act. It may take a few years for the proposal to be enacted, but there can be no doubt of its eventually being put into law given the political muscle behind it."

"You speak of Gladstone, Disraeli, and the Queen of England?" Mirabella asked, peering over her shoulder.

"Precisely." Watson studied the photograph. "I'm ever so grateful that Victoria took after Prince Edward rather than the tall and graceful Princess Victoire. Otherwise Moriarty might have gotten away with it."

Dearest, my heart is dreaming, dreaming of you.

"Yes, most fortunate," Sherlock said, his mind wandering, a state to which he was unaccustomed.

"Not to insult the queen," Watson interjected. "Alexandrina Victoria was a pretty if somewhat plain girl in her youth, but nothing to compare to her mother."

Sherlock raised his glass, nodding reverently. "To the Queen."

"To the Queen," toasted Watson.

"What's the matter Mr. Holmes?" asked Mirabella, eyeing him suspiciously. "You don't seem yourself."

"Nothing is the matter," he quipped. *The devil take it! I will recapture my mental focus. I simply need another case.*

"You're sad because she's gone, aren't you?"

"Who's gone? The queen is safe on the throne."

"You know very well who, Mr. Holmes," replied Mirabella, pointing to the photograph on his laboratory table. "The countess who was with Miss Adler, the perfect woman."

"Yes, I suppose I do miss Fantine a little. But it's for the best that she is gone."

"Why?" asked Mirabella, more interested in his response than he had expected.

"Fantine is never up to any good," Sherlock said. "It is a shame to see someone with that much intelligence and cunning always put it to ill use. Most disheartening."

"Funny. You didn't seem gloomy when you were with her," Mirabella suggested.

"Most assuredly not." Sherlock's already melancholy mood became pensive. "If one could take Fantine's qualities, her drive and ambition, her cunning, her dynamic attraction, and imbue it with a motivation other than pleasing herself—teaching her right from wrong, as it were—she might be worth pursuing."

"Yes, only that small change of entirely reversing her character, and she would not be a deadly viper after all," Watson said under his breath.

"I understand." Miss Belle's gaze was suddenly intent upon him. "It is difficult to love someone and to see what that person could be."

Why do I torture myself when it is a ridiculous thought to begin with and would never work—for her or for me?

"Speaking of the female sex, have you heard Henri Poincaré speak on the theory of chaos, Watson?" asked Sherlock, desperate to change the subject.

"A bit over my head," Watson said, smiling. "At any rate, I would not compare female behavior to chaos theory."

"Perhaps. The theory of chaos forwards that there are no random elements involved in the initial conditions despite the chaotic outcomes. This could never describe the female sex."

"I heard Poincaré speak." Mirabella turned to face them both, her duster in hand. "I was not convinced. Chaos theory is simply another way of saying 'we don't know why'".

Sherlock added in his most sympathetic tone of condescension, "There is a mathematical formula attributed to the theory of chaos, Miss Belle, it is not as simple as that."

"Of course. And what is the equation you speak of, Mr. Holmes?" She bit her lip, quite provocative actually.

"There are many, of course, but the equation of particular interest is $X = V - E + F$, where V is the vertices of the shape in question, E is the edges, and F is the number of faces in three dimensions." He cleared his throat.

Mirabella appeared to run the formula round in her mind. "If we understand the theory and the mathematical model is in place, why have we not then adjusted the formula and learned to predict the weather, as well as epileptic seizures and random numbers? I shall tell you why. Could the chaos formula be incorrect? It is absurd to say that we have a formula which can predict chaos—but which doesn't actually work because we don't know all the variables."

"No doubt you simply don't understand it, Miss Hudson," Sherlock said consolingly. "The theory states that minute differences in the initial variables dramatically impact the outcome. Hence the error."

"Something does not fit the scientist's model," she continued, "so the experts call it 'chaos' and call it a 'theory' instead of admitting that it is outside their realm of understanding and that their models are therefore useless—or, worse, incorrect. That's like saying that I am a violin virtuoso— except I don't have a violin and have never learnt."

"I fear if you wish for a theory which correlates to our everyday life, you should study chemistry or biology, Miss Mirabella," Dr. Watson said. "Physics and mathematics are used to study phenomena on the level of the universe—and the things we cannot see."

"Excellent, Watson." Sherlock took a puff on his pipe as he turned his attentions to Miss Belle, encouraged that she appeared to be rebelling against ivory tower academia in favor of a study more applicable to the detective. "Though I fear your words have fallen on deaf ears. Miss Belle appears to believe that chaos theory is the result of a wounded male ego, an explanation she attributes to many conditions."

"That, or possibly a bias towards intellectualism."

"You are opposed to the intellect, Miss Hudson? I would have thought you destined for academia," inquired Dr. Watson, amused.

"I am not at all opposed to the intellect. But part of being intelligent is being able to admit when you don't know," Mirabella said. "It is the first step towards knowledge. Moreover, why is it such a revelation to realize that one cannot predict the future with mathematical models? Any average working fellow on the street knows that. Scientists are saying 'It is a complex system with too many variables.' The fellow on the street is saying 'It is life'."

"Ah, so you don't believe that life, as you put it, can be explained with science, Miss Belle?" asked Sherlock.

Somewhere a voice is calling, calling for me.

She moved towards the laboratory, dusting the jars. "Personally I think that life will always seek to live, it is a spiritual phenomenon and not a scientific one."

"Not scientific?" asked Sherlock, disbelieving.

"The brain can shut us off to wisdom. You know that very well, Mr. Holmes, or you would not use illicit substances. It is the only way you know to shut your mind off to the things you do not understand."

"Quite the opposite! I only use mind-enhancing aids—such distasteful terminology that you utilize, Miss Belle—when there is no other course open to me."

"Or when you are bored, Holmes," said Watson. "I must agree with Miss Mirabella on this one."

"And yet it is still the brain which solves the mystery," said Sherlock, undeterred, polishing his pipe. "Chaos theory is not about chaos. It is about the idea that there is order in seemingly chaotic behavior. The study of the criminal mind is a perfect example of the application of the theory of chaos."

Knock! Knock!

"We take a completely unstable—and subsequently unpredictable—mind and predict both his behavior and the outcome. He can never allude or escape us. If there were no method or predictability, we would be unable to capture him—and *yet we do*. Or, rather, *I* do. The London police are relatively unsuccessful."

Mirabella moved to answer the door amidst the climactic finale of the phonographic record. Sherlock closed his eyes and attempted to lose himself in the music still playing. He longed to be in a drugged state so disconcerting were his thoughts.

It was some seconds later when Sherlock realized that Miss Belle had not returned from the door. He opened his eyes abruptly and jumped from his chair. The door to the flat had been left open and she was not in the room.

Sherlock ran to the window to see a carriage escaping at full speed. "What a fool I've been, Watson!"

"What is it?" Watson came out of his reverie.

"Miss Belle, she's gone! Did you see who came to the door?"

"Why, no, I was resting my eyes at the time."

"*Bloody hell!* As was I! It can't have even been a minute!" *Attempting to remove myself from this world, in fact.* Sherlock reached for his coat and his cane which concealed a sword. "Get your revolver, Watson!"

"What the—!" Watson came to his feet in a rush, throwing his pipe on the table. "Why? Who?"

"When Moriarty said 'the girl,' he didn't mean Fantine! He meant Miss Belle! Watson, we've got to go—*now!*" shouted Sherlock, heading for the door at full speed, with Watson not far behind him.

Somewhere a voice is calling, calling for me.

CHAPTER FORTY-FIVE
Revenge

"You're going to kill me?" Mirabella exclaimed, tied up while seated in a chair. "But why?"

"Because it will annoy Holmes." Professor Moriarty scowled, his expression one of fury, filtered through a perfected persona of superiority.

Because Sherlock outwitted you and foiled your plot. "That's it? You're going to take another life simply because it will annoy Sherlock Holmes?"

"Essentially, yes, that's correct."

"I guarantee there are many, many things that will annoy Sherlock Holmes that do not require such drastic measures!" She swallowed hard, her hands shaking now. "Simply put me in a room with him. That never fails to annoy him."

Professor Moriarty moved closer, and she could feel the hatred oozing from him.

He is uncomfortable with his hatred. She determined to pay attention to her observations, despite her fear: the professor was repelled by his own emotion.

Much like Sherlock. Moriarty felt intense anger, but he did not like feeling the emotion. Perhaps the professor was not a true psychopath, who would have felt nothing to hurt another.

"Stop!" she exclaimed. "Why do you think Mr. Holmes will care at all? He might be decidedly relieved to have me done away with."

"I do not think so, Miss Hudson." A wry smile came to Moriarty's lips even as his eyes shone brightly.

Perhaps she had given James Moriarty too much credit. He seemed to have turned a corner and now appeared to be enjoying himself.

"I'm not certain Mr. Holmes even likes me," she insisted.

"Ah, but that which appears to be hatred is often love, I have observed. At any rate, it would upset Holmes that I should take something of his."

"I don't belong to him," she replied indignantly.

"In his mind you do." Moriarty frowned. "But enough talk. Hippo, get the knife. I wish it to be particularly gruesome."

"Oh my goodness! Please no!" Mirabella exclaimed as the horrible, grizzly man with the glistening six-inch blade came toward her. She willed herself to keep her wits about her at the same time she hoped she might faint.

"Stop!" Moriarty commanded.

Thank goodness. She managed to catch her breath, her heart beating so fast she thought it would depart her chest.

"Kill her quickly. I want her to be cut up in a gruesome fashion, it will destroy Holmes, but I don't want to hear the screams. Most uncivilized."

That's very kind of you. You're going to murder me and you think it civilized. This gave her a clue to Moriarty's motivations. "Please, please don't kill me! A gentleman would never do such a thing!"

He twisted his lips, and she knew she had hit a chord. But in a mere instant the professor appeared to have regained his resolve. "Kill her, cut her up—but not so much that the her identity is in question—and then dump the body somewhere where it will be found."

"Sure, boss," the grizzly man replied, his expression one of anticipation.

"No! No! Please don't, Professor. It is inhumane!"

"Don't worry, my dear. Death will occur very quickly, and you won't suffer for long. Hippo is an expert at this type of thing. I hate unnecessary violence, don't you?" The professor smoothed the plaid vest of his three-piece suit, his appearance completely incongruent with his command.

"Blimey! I daan't." A middle-aged, thin woman entered the room. "Lawd above, I could do i' fer you."

Moriarty suddenly looked even more furious, if that were possible. "Jeffries! What are you doing here! I never told you about this place."

"I 'ave me methods."

"You are out of bounds, madame!"

His face was now turning pink. Mirabella forced herself to keep her wits about her and to analyze this relationship, even if these were the last two minutes of her life. Sherlock had taught her this: *work until there is no other option.* It was her only chance for survival, however slim that chance might be.

Mirabella was relieved to see Hippo, ever astute to his employer's emotions and desires, turn the knife toward the intruding woman and away from her.

"I wouldn't advise it," the woman called Jeffries said. "I have a sealed letter with me lawyer to be opened if I should be found dead."

"So I have heard. Why are you here, Jeffries?" Moriarty demanded, but his expression revealed that he knew the answer. "Can't you see I'm occupied at the time? I'm not exactly having a good day."

I'm having a much worse day, if the truth be told, Mirabella thought.

"I wish t' know if yew 'ave come to a decision," Jeffries said.

"Most certainly I have. We shall never be partners."

"Not good enough fer you, am I?"

"Nothing of the sort, madame." But Mirabella could see that she had hit the mark. "I work alone."

"I was good enough fer yew at da beginnin' when you needed bread and honey. I'll give yew until next week, Professor—or I'll go to da authorities, mate." And she left the room.

Moriarty's complexion was now red, which did not bode well for her, Mirabella thought. He had not been that pleasant to begin with.

Hippo stood, knife in hand, his eyes glued to the door where Jeffries had just exited. Time was frozen for an instant, which was just the interval Mirabella needed.

Think! Think! Mirabella looked about the room, trying her best to stumble across anything that might assist her in staying alive.

Her eyes landed on the chalkboard where she observed trigonometric functions combined with Hebrew.

Heaven help us! Those were not the formulas she had utilized on the copy—this was the key to the original blueprint!

This told her two things: Moriarty had succeeded in making a copy of the blueprint and *he hasn't solved the key.*

The knife was only now six inches from her throat.

"If you haven't solved the key yet, Professor, how did you plan to sell the submarine plans without it?" she asked. "Don't you think that would have angered the Russians?"

Moriarty spun on his heel towards her, an expression of complete surprise in his ice green eyes. Just as quickly Moriarty held up his hand in a gesture which told his henchman to stop, from whom a heavy sigh erupted.

"Clever girl. I suppose I should have known that Holmes kept you around for a reason."

She had impressed him with her intelligence, but that wasn't enough to keep her alive. She knew that she had to be of use to him.

"Could you solve the key, Miss Hudson?" he asked, ever polite even as he intended to cut her into pieces. He motioned to Hippo to leave the room, that very act allowing her to return to breathing.

"Of course I could." *Not a bat's chance in Hell. I would rather die than betray my country.* In fact, she had every confidence that she could solve the original key, but she would never give the key to Moriarty. Still, it might buy her time until Sherlock found her.

"I have surmised that the key is in trigonometry and in Hebrew," Moriarty said nonchalantly, as if he didn't need her.

"Of course it is." She smiled. "And yet, you obviously haven't been able to solve it."

He frowned at her, with a gleam in his eye which was frightening. "I can tell from your expression, Miss Hudson, that you have an idea how to solve it."

No doubt the Hebrew connotes a Biblical verse with a hint to unlocking the trigonometric function. And no doubt there is no one here—either you or your henchmen—who is overly familiar with the Bible.

"I do," she said simply.

Moriarty sighed heavily, glancing in the direction of Hippo's exit, as if he intended to recall the thug, sending a lightning bolt of fear through her body. *Like Sherlock, it was as if Moriarty could read her mind.* "I don't believe you have any intention of helping me, Miss Hudson. As interesting as I find you, I do not think we would suit. One thorn in my side is enough."

He began walking to the door, obviously to procure Hippo. And his knife.

"Oh, but I do!" In a panic, she remembered Moriarty's dislike of being called "ungentlemanly" and his even greater dislike of the unsophisticated Jeffries. She concluded that his façade—and most likely his title of 'professor'—were important to him. Her eyes returned to the chalkboard.

"Ah, I see you are studying chaos theory, Professor Moriarty," she stated as matter-of-factly as she could with the image in her mind's eye of a knife coming towards her chest. She made a futile effort to keep her voice from expressing her panic.

"And how do you know that, Miss Hudson?"

She swallowed hard. "I attended the lecture of Henri Poincaré."

"And you were able to extrapolate enough from that talk to recognize the formula on my chalkboard?"

No. But I remember it from a recent conversation with Sherlock Holmes.

"Naturally," she managed to utter. *Use your brain girl!* Suddenly an observation occurred to her. An appeal to the professor's morality had been useless. The only thing that appeared to impress the professor—and, more importantly, postpone the gruesome murder of yours truly—was the intellect. *I must impress him in order to keep myself alive.*

In an instant she knew how to save herself. Sherlock Holmes' comparative intelligence was the only reason Moriarty had not yet attempted to kill his arch foe, in her estimation.

Moriarty would find the world lonely—and unbearable—without a worthy adversary.

Professor James Moriarty frowned. "I believe we are done here if that is all you can add to the conversation, Miss Hudson." He opened the door. "Wait until I have left, Hippo. Then kill her. I abhor savagery."

"Do you agree, Professor Moriarty?" she asked in a high-pitched voice as Hippo returned to the room with the six-inch blade.

"Do I agree to what?" Moriarty demanded, turning on his heel, his back to her, but his head turned sideways.

Hippo stopped in his tracks, sighing heavily.

"Do you agree that every simply connected, closed three-manifold is homeomorphic to the three-sphere?" She swallowed hard. "The Poincaré conjecture."

She had, in fact, understood much of the lecture if not remembered the formulas, even as Sherlock had refreshed her memory. She had simply disagreed with the conclusions. Now might be the time to re-think her disagreement and proclaim the genius of the conjecture as it appeared to be of interest to the villainous mastermind in the room. An expert in trigonometry and Hebrew he could find, but the Poincaré conjecture had outwitted every mathematical genius in the world.

Moriarty raised his eyebrow in interest. He turned to his henchman. "You may leave us for now."

Hippo moved to the door with the knife in hand, scowling with disappointment, but not before handing a pistol to Moriarty. The henchman's exit did little to slow her heartbeat, which alone might kill her given enough time.

"And what is your opinion of the Poincaré conjecture, Miss Hudson?"

As if it were a gift from the angels, Mirabella suddenly saw an image before her, and she thought it might be the key to her survival.

Scheherazade. The storyteller who dissuaded the King from beheading her with a new story during every encounter, her only weapon being her ability to entertain and to engage her captor's curiosity. Every evening, the clever Scheherazade completed the story from the previous night and began a new tale, only to leave it tantalizingly unresolved as she yawned and fell asleep.

You must pursue this tactic, she told herself. *Listen to your instincts.*

And listen to Sherlock. *Do not be intimidated by the criminal. Do not let your fear control you. You must understand the criminal and know where his weaknesses are.* Staring at Moriarty, the intensity of his gaze terrifying, it was difficult not to be afraid.

Even Satan has his weaknesses. You must understand your enemy.

She swallowed hard, pretending confidence, just about the most difficult acting she had ever attempted. "The conjecture seems intuitively correct, but it has not yet been proven."

"Can you prove it?" Moriarty insisted, leaning forward, the cold calculation in his eyes having turned to excited interest. She had gained enough of his confidence with the key to the submarine to make this ridiculous scenario seem feasible to him.

Mirabella contained her laughter. If none of the top scholars of the world had solved the conjecture, why on earth would Moriarty consider that she could? Mirabella knew very well that someone who could prove the Poincaré conjecture would be incredibly famous.

But the truth was immaterial; against her upbringing, *she must lie.* Her key to survival was convincing the professor that she could solve the conjecture. She must be a better actress.

"Perhaps," she said, the closest to a lie she could muster. She hadn't the faintest idea how to prove the conjecture. "I am working on it. The proof has enormous implications for the theory of chaos. A particular interest of mine."

All right, that was the complete truth. She had a sudden intense interest in the proving of the Poincaré conjecture.

"Indeed." He sat down across from her, studying her with escalating regard. "And what are those implications?"

Mirabella took a few breaths, attempting to both regulate her breathing and to clear her head. Simply because she couldn't prove the conjecture, didn't mean that she didn't understand it—or at least well enough to fool someone.

But the chair of a mathematics department? Even Sarah Bernhardt wasn't that good of an actress.

Stop it! That type of self-doubt is not helping. *I must try.*

"Given a wedding ring and a round sphere—such as the planet Earth—the implication is essentially that one can lasso a ring but not a sphere. The lasso would fall off the sphere. And because a sphere cannot be made into a ring without cutting the sphere, the two shapes are not homeomorphic, that is to say, one shape cannot transform into the other."

Moriarty's eyes grew wide, his interest apparent. "Very good, Miss Hudson, but you have explained the Poincaré conjecture, you have not proposed its significance."

"Naturally." She pretended to feel indifference when, in fact, she felt terror. "I could not explain its significance until I had defined it. And—I find that the pistol you are holding is not conducive to my thought processes."

"Quite so. Most impolite."   He placed the gun beside him, thereafter staring at her for a long period. She knew Moriarty was calling her bluff, just as Sherlock would have.

Finally he spoke. "Even so, most people who listened to Poincaré's lecture would not have understood a word of it." He sighed with reluctance. "It seems a shame to destroy a promising mind such as yours."

"I agree wholeheartedly," she whispered.

"A mind that might be of considerable professional and economic benefit to me." He smiled, suddenly appearing as sweet as a grandmother in her Easter bonnet, the pale eyes of a madman examining her. "You see, Miss Hudson, I am very interested in the proof—and I am very interested in chaos theory."

You are interested in prestige and power, Professor.

"I surmised as much."

"Someone who could prove the Poincaré conjecture would be invaluable to me—so valuable that I might forego other considerations."

"Considerations such as—killing me?"

"Yes, as satisfying as that would be toward my ends."

"I would certainly wish to be valuable given my situation," she managed to utter, the tightness of the ropes that bound her particularly uncomfortable.

By this time she had concluded that Professor Moriarty had a great hatred for Sherlock Holmes. And yet, he was willing to forego revenge upon Sherlock for a mathematical proof.

Moriarty truly wants that proof.

Either he was intensely curious, possibly even addicted to the workings of the mind and the uncovering of a puzzle—or he had nefarious plans for the equation.

Possibly both.

"And what, Miss Hudson," he began, "do you think is the basis for the proof?"

Think. Think very carefully. Please help me Lord Jesus.

"Naturally it would be the Euler characteristic," she replied in a whisper.

"Ah." He studied her with interest. This one was not easily fooled. "And what is that formula?"

Don't miss this girl! Recall Sherlock's words.

"$X = V-E-F$."

He frowned.

"I mean of course . . . $X=V-E+F$ . . . where V is the vertices of the shape in question, E is the edges, and F is the number of faces in three dimensions." Working with Sherlock had taught her to think on her feet (or tied up as it were) and to perform even in an atmosphere of criticism. And terror.

This lesson had thus far saved her life today.

"And what is the Euler characteristic for each the sphere and the ring?" the professor asked. His voice was quietly peaceful, but she knew that could change in an instant. Violence was as close to Moriarty's nature as the desire to live was to hers.

Scheherazade. The image nagged at her, begging for attention amidst her fear. *What was the picture trying to tell her?*

"Y-y-ou know, Professor, I am feeling quite tired and I will not be able to continue this conversation until I have eaten and rested for the night," she said as nonchalantly as she could manage.

Anger flashed in his eyes. He glanced at the gun. Then he picked it up, the light glistening off the polished metal.

"You are refusing to answer me, Miss Hudson?"

I am. I am refusing to die today.

She smiled sweetly even as her heart pounded inside her chest. "Naturally I am not. My brain will function much better after rejuvenation."

He knew she was lying. But more importantly, *he believed that she might know the answer to his question and was refusing to answer him.*

That was the funniest joke of all.

Why am I not laughing?

In an instant Moriarty seemed to resign himself to the fact that she was playing the only card she had—and very well indeed. Perhaps he respected her for it.

Or perhaps he wanted the answer and would wait until the morrow to kill her.

"Very well, Miss Hudson. We shall speak tomorrow. Early."

I pray to the heavens Sherlock gets here before then.

CHAPTER FORTY-SIX
Moriarty's Hidden Lair

"You shouldn't have interfered with my plans, Holmes!" exclaimed Moriarty, pulling the sword from his ivory cane. "I don't know how you found me, but the day won't be a complete waste once I've left you face down in a pool of blood."

Sherlock and the Baker Street Irregulars had spent the night scouring the abandoned buildings and warehouses in and near Holburn since Mirabella was not to be found at the warehouse in Old Bailey Newgate. It had to be assumed Moriarty had pieced it together and moved his headquarters.

For his part, Sherlock had something of Moriarty's—his cane—which was presented to the bloodhound Toby, who then went in search of the new warehouse location.

Once Sherlock had found the new warehouse on St. Paul's Pier, which appeared to be a soap factory from the strong stench of the lye, he spotted Mirabella, gagged and tied to a chair in the corner of this sizeable building near the River Fleet. Rage filled Sherlock as he wondered if any harm had come to Belle—and if she had been compromised in any way.

James Moriarty is now my sworn enemy. Sherlock was re-born in fire in this moment. His knowledge of Moriarty's criminal connections had always given him many a reason to detest the mastermind, but it was this instant in time when Professor James Moriarty became his arch foe. Prior to this the crime lord was a mere annoyance, part of a puzzle to be solved, a criminal to be pursued and stopped.

Now Moriarty will pay. Glancing at Mirabella, Sherlock did not trust himself to refrain from killing the man before him. Even if he hung for the crime.

And I do not wish to stop myself.

"Whether you will have a good day remains to be seen, Moriarty." Sherlock pulled the sword from his walking stick. "You're a poor sport indeed to have taken my assistant. She had nothing to do with your failed attempt to bring down the throne—an ill conceived notion at best."

"Don't be ridiculous, Holmes. All governments are controlled by someone—industry and wealth—and never by the people. The machine wishes for someone to be the front man while the monied interests control the populace." Moriarty's expression was fiercely angry. "It should have been me."

"You see the fine conclusion to those plans. You are made to look like a fool, Moriarty." When Sherlock's eyes rose to meet his adversary's he felt no trace of the English gentleman left to his being. His very existence was engulfed in the blackness of hatred. He might emerge alive and he might not, but he would be damned if Moriarty would survive.

Moriarty laughed, slicing the air with his sword. "We shall see who is the fool in the end."

Swish! Swish! Sherlock moved his sword back and forth, preparing for what he expected to be the final battle.

Moriarty lunged forward with his sword.

That tells me what I need to know. Sherlock made a mental calculation, now knowing the length of Moriarty's lunge.

I intend to kill you now. But not for the crimes against your own nation, but because you dared to harm Miss Belle.

Better that Moriarty should not know the full truth. Sherlock had already revealed too much of his feelings or Miss Belle would not be here. As much as Sherlock hated himself for the existence of those feelings, even worse was the obvious fact that he had allowed them to be seen.

Mirabella was in his range of vision, situated behind Moriarty as it were, and she shook her head, as if to tell him not to fight Moriarty. She created an odd picture, shaking her head vehemently, Moriarty's black umbrella leaning against the wall beside her. It was difficult to know what she wished to communicate since she was gagged, but there was clearly something she wished to convey.

"Untie Miss Hudson now, you devil!" Sherlock commanded.

A sinister laughter was Moriarty's reply. "And you thought I believed Fantine to be your soft spot. You believed that I could kill my own sister."

I still do.

"En garde!" Moriarty sliced the air with his sword again although the air was clearly not his intended victim, missing Sherlock altogether as he jumped back.

The Great Detective took another half step back, raising his blade in a classic fencer's salute, normally a gesture of respect, but in this instance communicating that the fight would now begin in earnest.

The meaning was not lost on Moriarty. The professor, as one might expect, was not easily intimidated. He initiated a lightning quick lunge towards his opponent's heart.

Sherlock parried, deflecting the tip of Moriarty's blade with the bell guard of his own weapon, barely avoiding the deadly maneuver.

But Sherlock was now in a position to strike back, which he did not hesitate to enact. He replied with an equally fast riposte, brushing his enemy's shoulder with the point of the sword.

Moriarty anticipated the move and twisted his upper torso.

"Damn you, Holmes!" Moriarty screamed when the blade grazed his shoulder. For all the gentlemanly manners which were a source of pride for the professor, the fight soon became what it truly was: a savage quest to spill each other's blood. Sherlock Holmes, because his opponent had dared to violate one of his own, and Moriarty because his opponent had destroyed his plans to be the man behind the throne.

For the time being. Sherlock knew very well that, were Moriarty to live, he would try again.

Instead of attempting to reply instantly with his steel as expected, Moriarty grabbed Sherlock's sword arm, an affront to the rules of swordsmanship, and attempted to drag the detective onto the point of his blade. And the professor might have succeeded had Sherlock not utilized his own unconventional methods and head-butted his opponent, drawing on his boxing talents.

Ah, two can play at that game.

"I have tolerated you up until now, Moriarty, because I am not the law, I am an investigative detective. I wrongly left it to the law to deal with you," Sherlock said. "I should not have. You are a scourge upon London."

Though I may hang by the neck for my good deed.

Sherlock made a particularly strong lunge and Moriarty's defensive parry half collapsed. But the university man was more successful on the counter-attack.

"Arghh!" Sherlock felt the sting as the sharp blade sliced the skin over his upper bicep, just missing skewering his ribs by a hairsbreadth.

Good Lord! I've been an idiot! Sherlock was losing blood now. He couldn't take time to stop the bleeding with his cravat or Moriarty would finish him off.

Clank! Their swords interplayed even as Sherlock spoke. "I don't suppose you'd allow me to tie a rag round my upper arm, Professor?"

"Don't be ridiculous, Holmes! You're finished!"

"I didn't think so. Sportsmanship is not your calling card."

Sherlock evaluated his prospects. He was the better swordsman, and in better shape, but once he lost enough blood, he would become dizzy, his reactions slowed—and it would be over. Sherlock glanced at Miss Belle. He had to make sure she was free and could escape before he died.

Sherlock rallied everything he had. He then took the offensive with a series of thrusts and slashes, hoping that his enemy's poorer physical condition would be the end of him.

No such luck. Moriarty blacked and jammed his rival's blade, kicking

Sherlock in the stomach. The detective staggered, moving backwards.

This seeming false step was actually a stroke of good fortune because Sherlock's momentum carried him to a point behind Mirabella, who was seated in a wooden chair. With a single slash, her bonds were cut. The cords fell into her lap, and Miss Belle jumped to her feet, even before untying her legs.

"Run!" he commanded. "*Run!*"

Her movements were lightning fast, but she did not flee. She had apparently been watching for just such an opening.

She threw the chair at Moriarty, creating just enough delay. Quickly and expertly, she pulled the handkerchief from her mouth, tying it around Sherlock's upper right arm in a matter of seconds, the chair still between them and Moriarty. Once Sherlock was engaged with Moriarty again, she removed the ropes from her feet.

"Get out of here!" Sherlock ordered. But instead of heading for the factory door, she ran for the umbrella. That would surely be of little use.

Sherlock's attention was quickly returned to keeping himself alive. Moriarty moved forward, and the swordsmen found themselves in a classic clash, swords jammed together, neither able to withdraw without exposing themselves to disaster.

Sherlock was still feeling faint, but he knew he might now have a chance with the bleeding stopped. A slight chance, but still a chance.

The young detective lunged. As it was, the point aimed for Moriarty's ribs instead found the professor's left tricep muscle.

Still not a bad move. And Sherlock might feel faint, but he noted how heavily his enemy was breathing.

"I say, Moriarty, a man must keep his body in a certain degree of fitness. Or it will be the death of him."

If he could increase Moriarty's fear or alter his concentration, it would be in Sherlock's favor. To his disadvantage, he was on Moriarty's turf.

No doubt someone was waiting in the wings ready to finish Sherlock off, if by some miracle he were to win. If he lost, he would lose his life. If, instead, he won, Moriarty's minions would take revenge and he would lose his life.

But if he rid the world of Moriarty in the process, that would be his reward.

As he fought, Sherlock's eyes scanned the warehouse, looking for signs of other people, and found none. A strong indicator that Moriarty had something else up his sleeve—the master criminal didn't trust anyone, least of all his own men. The professor managed things through an intricate web which made him difficult to trace.

And clearly Moriarty wished this to be mano a mano. The professor wanted the satisfaction of killing Sherlock *himself*, or it already would have been over.

Moriarty's desire to inflict pain and to be the one with the power would someday be his own demise.

Add this is to my advantages. Sherlock reminded himself that being an expert fencer was not just about being fast, or even entirely about having good aim. It was about continually fooling one's opponent as to one's next move.

Fencing is much like poker.

Sherlock lunged, indicating where his next attack would be. Moriarty played into the ruse, slashing viciously at the supposed location of Sherlock's throat had he not dodged the attack.

Good. Sherlock looked over to where Miss Belle had been and saw that she was no longer there. This gave him some newfound energy.

Clink! "Although our acquaintance is of a short duration, Professor, it is clear that you are leading a double life and are not utilizing your mathematical genius solely in academia."

"Whatever was your first clue, Holmes? And I thought I had done an excellent job of covering my tracks."

"Indeed you have, to the untrained eye, thereby encompassing all of the London constabulary, but you leave a detectable signature, Professor."

"Ah, and what might that signature be?"

"It is apparent that you are protecting many of the major criminals in London in exchange for their obedience and a share in their profits."

Crash!

"And, for another, the trail of bodies is difficult to overlook," said Sherlock. "Those who are not a part of your network of criminals soon come to regret it."

Moriarty lunged forward, apparently not liking the tables turned. "I never kill anyone unless it is absolutely necessary. Sadly, it is now necessary."

The professor flashed his thin blade in a rapid figure eight, followed by an aggressive thrust at Sherlock's seemingly unprotected chest. The Great Detective sidestepped with remarkable speed, catching his enemy's blade against his own, followed by a slight turning of the wrist. This miniscule move deflected Moriarty's sword past Sherlock's right shoulder with half an inch to spare.

"You have improved," remarked Moriarty with a feigned superiority, but his breathing was shallow and there was a concern in his eyes which Sherlock had heretofore not seen.

Moriarty also began to glance about the warehouse, whose eyes Sherlock followed.

Sherlock slashed at his opponent as Moriarty concentrated the entirety of his energy in disengaging himself from the onslaught. It was only the devil's luck that the professor was able to duck the blow.

And then Moriarty grew angry.

This did not bode well for Sherlock. Up until now, Moriarty's hatred had been in Sherlock's favor, causing the professor to make ill-conceived decisions. Generally Moriarty relied on his henchmen to enact his evil deeds, not being in as fine a physical form as his adversary or as accomplished a swordsman.

But despite the odds, Moriarty's corrupted nature, his hatred and his desire for vengeance, had spurred him on against his better judgment as the avenger of his supposed misfortunes.

"Burn in Hell, Holmes!"

Sherlock knew very well the power of fury. "I should think Hell would be your domain, Moriarty." He was enjoying the attack upon his person in a demented sort of way, savoring the battle as a competitive boxer does, setting aside the fact that this match could end in his death. "My dear Professor, it is so rare to see you lose your temper thus."

Clink! "You have spoiled my plans and for that you shall perish, Holmes!"

Whoosh! He determined to use Moriarty's fury to his advantage. Sherlock ducked and just missed the sword aimed at his neck. "It is a great source of disappointment to me, I assure you. But one acknowledges that one can't always have that which one wants. *As should you,* my dear Professor."

Blazes to Hell! Sherlock could see behind Moriarty that Belle had merely moved closer to the door. She still had not left. He screamed, "I command you to leave Miss Hudson!"

Moriarty looked around for her, and Sherlock took advantage of the distraction, slashing the professor's fencing arm.

"EOOOW! Holmes, you bastard! I might have ruled England!"

"You have a criminal empire in London, surely that is enough."

"Enough! It is never enough!" exclaimed Moriarty, still reeling from the pain. But his emotional pain seem to override anything his body was feeling.

"And what would you do, my dear Professor?"

"Rule! Control the technology! Initiate wars!" Spittle was developing at the edges in Moriarty's mouth as his voice rose.

Crash! The swords met each other.

"It is a sad day indeed," said Sherlock. "You have no purpose other than the exercise of your power. Is there no higher goal to your madness?"

"I guarantee, Holmes, I will destroy something that matters to you as well." Moriarty glanced in Mirabella's direction.

"I shouldn't go there if I were you, Professor." The Great Detective's motions instantly grew more direct, channeling his own sudden influx of rage. "You would pay dearly, I assure you. *No more games of shadow, no more intellectual exercises.* I promise I would hunt you down and kill you if any harm comes to Miss Hudson. . . . In fact, there is no better time than the present."

"I agree, Holmes."

Despite being engaged in a sword fight with Moriarty, he had never forgotten that Belle was in the room with them. *Why had she not left the building?* Now that she was free she should have left with haste! His command had been clear.

"This is between you and me, Holmes!"

In an instant understanding dawned. *It is the umbrella.* She kept pointing the tip of the umbrella at them.

She was looking for an opening to fire. *The poison dart.* Moriarty had used the method of the poison dart on more than one occasion to kill a victim, death ensuing some two days after the dart was embedded in the skin, making the perpetrator impossible to isolate and identify.

Now Sherlock knew how it was done—with an unassuming umbrella that any gentleman might carry.

Just as quickly as awareness dawned, he stepped away from Moriarty to give Miss Belle the opening she needed.

But in that same moment one of Moriarty's goons had the same idea and was aiming his pistol at Sherlock.

It is too late. In a split second Mirabella took it all in and aimed the umbrella at the would be shooter. The dart landed in his chest.

"You damn whore!" The effect of the drug would not be instant, but the shooter understood the significance of the dart in his skin. Without an antidote, he would die. This created just enough distraction for Sherlock to shield his body behind Moriarty. But it wasn't necessary; the shooter departed the scene, obviously in search of the remedy.

In the meantime, Miss Belle had pulled not one but two—one in each hand—of the patented expandable truncheons from her corset and was twirling them rapidly.

"Professor Moriarty, I'd advise you to step back from Mr. Holmes," Miss Belle commanded.

Impressive. She must have been practicing.

Moriarty backed up to the center of the room. He took a cylinder tube out of his jacket and threw it.

A copy of the submarine plans, in all probability. This was not good news, but it would have taken a great deal of painstaking effort to copy them. There wouldn't have been time for more than one duplication.

CHAPTER FORTY-SEVEN
Girl Fight

Fantine appeared out of the shadows and caught the cylinder. Mirabella raced after her, grabbing Fantine's arm in an attempt to dislodge the cylinder.

Mirabella was a strong country girl, having been raised on a farm in Dumfriesshire, and she'd been training in the eastern arts of self-defense for several months now. She assumed that the concert violinist would be no match for her.

She should have known better: Fantine surprised her. What's this? The musician dropped the supposed plans on the floor and grabbed Mirabella's wrist, twisting and rotating her wrists ninety-degrees to the outside. The stress on her tendons forced Mirabella to fall to the ground.

Why would a violinist have developed her combat skills to such a degree? It was a very stupid decision in Mirabella's mind: Fantine's hands were her livelihood, her profession.

Or perhaps Mirabella's ego was as wounded as her throbbing wrists, not to mention her embarrassment at having been caught off guard.

Fantine stooped to recover the cylinder, thinking her opponent stunned.

No you don't, Countess! Mirabella thought to herself, this time utilizing the element of surprise to her advantage. Still lying on the ground, she threw her entire body towards Fantine, feet first. Mirabella kicked out and hooked the woman's right leg, sending Fantine's leg skyward.

Fantine Noel, Countess of Florentine, fell in a most unladylike fashion, impacting the floor with a sudden *thump*.

Fantine's lovely face was much less beautiful when twisted into a snarl.

Both women struggled to their feet and Fantine rushed at Mirabella, hands outstretched.

Mirabella winced, assuming that Fantine was going to claw her face, but instead, her assailant grabbed the collar of her outfit and pulled it tight in a painful choke.

The countess has been trained! Time and again she used both skill and the element of surprise, but Mirabella's vision began to be occluded by spirals and flashes.

Realizing that she was going to be on the floor unconscious in a moment, Mirabella unleashed a flurry of Chinese boxing punches into her enemy's face. Fantine staggered and sank to her knees. Mirabella turned toward the cylinder. She grabbed the cylinder and was moving towards the door when another of Moriarty's big thugs overtook her.

"I've got it, boss!" One of Moriarty's goons emerged behind Mirabella, gun in hand.

***

"No! God no!" Sherlock didn't know if the man was aiming at him or at Mirabella. In the meantime Moriarty had re-engaged him, so he was helpless to know what to do, yelling, "*Move!* Miss Belle!"

BANG! But it was too late. A shot had been fired.

"Belle!"

His heart racing, he saw that the body now lay on the floor.

Moriarty moved forward, and the swordsmen found themselves in a classic clash, swords jammed together, neither able to withdraw without exposing themselves to disaster.

Moving towards the body as they fought, they arrived at the body of Babbitt, who had taken aim at Belle. Babbitt's gun lay beside him.

In the corner of the warehouse was Watson, holding a smoking gun.

Damn if Watson wasn't a capital shot—and if he didn't always show up at just the right time. Sherlock dropped his sword and went for the gun.

Fantine had opened an escape door through the floor and proceeded to enter.

"I'm hurt, boss!" Babbitt exclaimed, clutching his leg, bleeding profusely.

Moriarty moved to grab the cylinder, leaving Babbitt's body lying on the floor.

"Drop it!" Sherlock commanded.

Moriarty slammed the secret door shut, followed by the sound of a clock ticking.

"Watson, it's a bomb! We have to get out of here! Where is Belle?"

"I'm out here, Mr. Holmes!" They looked through the warehouse door to see Mirabella driving a small wooden cart with a horse. "Hurry! Run!"

"Help me!" Babbitt yelled. "I can't walk!"

Sherlock and Watson exchanged a glance of annoyed resignation before rushing to Babbitt and picking him up. Babbitt placed an arm on each of their shoulders as they ran as best they could to where Miss Belle waited with the cart. For a long moment, Sherlock wondered if he had exchanged Babbitt's life for Miss Belle's.

They threw Babbitt in the cart, accompanied by his screams, and jumped in after him.

"Hyah!" Mirabella snapped the whip and the horse took off just as the warehouse exploded into flames behind them.

CHAPTER FORTY-EIGHT
A Not so Fond Farewell

Once they managed to stop the runaway horse, which did no small amount of damage to their skeletons bouncing about in the wooden cart, they applied their efforts to stopping Babbitt from bleeding. The four then sat quietly watching the warehouse burn as the firemen and police arrived.

Babbitt was turned over to the police, but the captive's eyes remained glued to Sherlock like a dog who had found his lost owner. "I'll never forget 'ya, gov'ner."

"I'm sure you'll have an opportunity to repay me, Mr. Babbitt."

"I wish he might buy me a new suit," John muttered under his breath. "And anyway, I was the one who stopped the bleeding."

"We're still alive," Mirabella murmured, as if she were surprised by that fact.

"I guess that's something," Sherlock said reluctantly.

Mirabella turned to stare at him. "Whatever is the matter, Mr. Holmes? We barely escaped with our lives, and here we all three sit!"

John rubbed his hips. "In a manner of speaking."

"Honestly, you two need to cultivate a feeling of gratitude."

"I'm ever so grateful," Sherlock said. "We might have saved the British monarchy, but we condemned the world to disaster. Moriarty still has the submarine plans. Essentially we got Babbitt and Moriarty got the plans. I wouldn't say we came out ahead on that one."

"Not quite accurate, Mr. Holmes." Mirabella reached into her corset and pulled out some papers. "The professor has an empty cylinder."

"Miss Belle!" Sherlock exclaimed, taking the plans in his hands. "You've officially saved Britain from the threat of foreign invasion!"

"It's all in a day's work, Mr. Holmes, at the Baker Street Detective Agency." She smiled.

John Watson laughed. "And how did you do it, Miss Mirabella?"

"Quickly, very quickly," she said. "Honestly between Moriarty and Mr. Holmes' sword fight, your watching them, another of Moriarty's henchmen focused on setting the bomb, and Fantine executing her escape, there was a small opening. I merely kept my body between Moriarty's view of Babbitt, and made haste." She winked at Sherlock. "I did learn something at the queen's banquet, you see."

"I am most pleased, Miss Belle!" Sherlock's expression held a rare smile.

"May I have a raise in my salary then?" Mirabella asked.

"Absolutely not." Sherlock put the plans inside his jacket and handed her the reins, re-seating himself in the wooden cart. "And now, if you would do the honors and drive us to the nearest cabbie, that would be much appreciated. We still have work to do."

"Honestly, Holmes, we just saved the world from tyranny, is that not enough for one day?" Watson asked.

Sherlock shook his head, the smile removed from his expression. "If you think Moriarty will not retaliate, you are sadly mistaken," Sherlock added somberly. "And particularly now that Miss Belle is in his sphere of detection. This is most unfortunate."

"I have to agree, Miss Mirabella, this is a very bad turn of events," Watson agreed.

"I may be able to make a bargain with him," Mirabella murmured. "I believe I have a bargaining chip."

"You are to do nothing of the sort, Miss Belle! You are to stay away from Moriarty, do you understand?"

"Absolutely right," John agreed.

"You are on Professor Moriarty's radar, Dr. Watson, and that doesn't seem to worry you," said Mirabella.

"What do I have to live for? Nightmares, memories, pains in the night. All of that keeps my mind off the past. I need the excitement—to live."

"Maybe I need the excitement, too," she said softly.

"Not at all. Why should you need excitement, Miss Belle?" demanded Sherlock crossly.

"Because I'm a girl?"

Sherlock shook his head, a rare expression of fear crossing his countenance. "You don't truly understand his depravity."

"HYAH!" She cracked the whip, recalling the six-inch blade coming towards her chest. "I might understand it better than you think, Mr. Holmes."

CHAPTER FORTY-NINE
The Bargain

Sherlock thrust the advance newspaper copy underneath Moriarty's nose.

RESPECTED PROFESSOR HEAD OF CRIME SYNDICATE
London's web of crime traceable to unassuming mathematician

"If I am forced underground and lose my professorship, I will kill your friends, Holmes," Moriarty said, throwing the paper on the oak desk of his university office.

"If you're alive to do so, Professor." Sherlock's soft voice was unmistakably threatening. "If you don't know yet how dangerous I can be, you shall soon learn."

As Sherlock observed Moriarty's pale green eyes turn to ice, there was no doubt in the Great Detective's mind that the stakes were incomparably high for Moriarty—his esteemed reputation and gentlemanly façade meaning everything to him. A cornered animal was a dangerous animal.

"I sincerely hope so," Moriarty said. "But rather than continuing to escalate this battle, let me make a proposal."

"I don't make deals with criminals."

"Hear me out, Holmes. We are, both of us, *gentlemen*."

"Ah, yes, the gentleman executioner." Sherlock leaned back in his chair, studying the professor, who had a remarkably pleasant countenance given his recent defeat.

"We shall let bygones be bygones if you do something for me, Holmes."

"I already have the submarine plans. So far as I can see, you don't have anything to bargain with, Moriarty."

"Indeed I do. The lives of your friends." The professor tapped his finger on the paper.

It would be to everyone's advantage to call a truce. Sherlock frowned, demanding, "What do you want, Moriarty?"

"You are to stop this from going to press. And I have another favor to ask. And I, in return, will both leave your friends be and drop my plans to run the government."

For now.

"Coming from you, Moriarty, it almost seems as if you are showing me a kindness, which is bothersome in and of itself. You must want something of enormous magnitude from me."

"Never fear, Holmes. It is a good deed and a service to society. Entirely up your alley."

CHAPTER FIFTY
The Proposal

"Come work for me and I'll put you through university."

Walking down the stairs to her aunt's flat, Mirabella recalled her last conversation with Professor Moriarty. Her hands had been tied up and the pistol with which he had threatened to kill her was in full view.

Not the most appealing job offer she had ever received.

And then she remembered that Sherlock had purposely tripped her and attempted to injure her during their interview.

"No, I'm not working for crime," she had replied to Moriarty, even tied up before him.

"Not at all. You will be my student assistant. We will discuss higher mathematics together. Completely separate from a crime machine, imaginary or otherwise. This is *academia*, my dear. That Holmes is an imbecile compared to us."

She had now reached the first floor and was standing outside the door, staring at the hallway to the front of the building. *To life.* To dreams come true.

"Mr. Holmes is simply more interested in practical matters than in academia."

"As I said, he's an imbecile. He can't even name the planets in the solar system," Moriarty had said.

Because he has no need of them.

"You must work for me, Miss Hudson. Imagine what two minds such as ours might do."

To work with a mathematical genius would have its rewards. "I wouldn't have to be involved in crime? Only in education?"

"Mathematics," he had whispered, like the voice of the devil in one's ear promising the world. "Precisely. You would be the first woman *in the world*, in all of history, to graduate with a bachelor of science degree in the sciences."

"You know a great deal about me, Professor Moriarty."

"Indeed."

"And would you kill me if I did not perform to your satisfaction?"

"I am not stupid. Whatever people may think, one cannot go about killing one's employees. No one would wish to be in one's employ. Word does get about for that sort of thing."

"You were going to kill me yesterday." How well she remembered Hippo holding the six-inch blade in front of her chest.

"And yet I didn't." He smiled sweetly as if the memory were a pleasant one. "But once you are seen with me, it will be much more difficult to kill you, Miss Hudson."

"That is a great incentive." She swallowed hard. "I am warming to the idea."

Moriarty laughed. "You are a clever girl, Miss Hudson." He grew suddenly somber. "Do think quickly. The position will be filled soon."

"And, if I don't agree, will you let me go and let me live? What if I prefer to work for Mr. Holmes?"

"I did not realize that you were that unambitious, Miss Hudson."

Nor am I so unintelligent as to play with fire.

"At any rate, I believe that position will soon be closed."

"And if I don't agree? Will you kill me?"

"I make no promises there." He smiled like Cheshire cat.

"And, if I do agree, will you allow Mr. Holmes to be safe? At least until the Poincaré conjecture is solved?"

He studied her for a long while. "You are even more clever than I thought, Miss Hudson."

"And the answer, sir?"

"I would enjoy watching Holmes suffer, knowing that you were working for me. In fact . . . I might enjoy that even more than killing him. I could see that you obtained your degree, Miss Hudson." He leaned close to her. "A university degree."

Her faith in Moriarty was growing in leaps and bounds. She believed him. He could do it. To be around Moriarty was to believe he could do anything.

I would be respected beyond imagining. I would have access to knowledge beyond imagining. I would not be working with the professor in his criminal capacity — only in his academic capacity.

And all I must do is sell my soul. The idea of the devil whispering in her ear loomed greater.

A wave of guilt ran through her. Such an action would be anathema Sherlock. But Sherlock was allowed to pursue his dreams and his interests—why shouldn't she?

And did she really have a choice? Moriarty said he wouldn't kill Sherlock — and her — if she agreed.

And, in fact, Sherlock was still alive. Nothing was an accident where

Moriarty was concerned.

Above all, I cannot let anything happen to Sherlock. It would break my heart.

And if I were to drop in on Professor Moriarty on occasion — to discuss mathematics — I am quite sure he would not turn me away. And perhaps I might do some spying on your behalf, Mr. Sherlock Holmes.

CHAPTER FIFTY-ONE
Karma leaves her Calling Card

Accompanied by her bodyguards, Mary Jeffries was leaving for home after a profitable night in her posh child brothel in Church Street.

She smiled to herself. The torture chamber had been a stroke of genius if she did say so herself. She had installed rings in the ceiling for hanging women and children by the wrists, as well as other means of securing them.

Between the flagellation house in Hampstead, the "chamber of horrors" in up-market Gray's Inn Road (she smiled to herself, pleased with the reference), and the Church Street brothel, not to mention the house in Kew which was used for smuggling kidnapped children abroad, she was kept busy.

Reaching the front door of the brothel, the silence was disturbing. All of the screams were nothing more than a cash register in her head. The quiet made her insecure.

Jeffries heard footsteps behind her and looked about. Nothing out of the ordinary. And she had two large bodyguards who always accompanied her home at these late hours.

"Where is the cab?" she demanded of Albert, the hulking bodyguard who generally sat with her while the other man sat next to the cabbie. The second bodyguard had his back to her as he was looking down the street for the cab. "I shouldn't be kept waiting out here in the cold."

SCREECH! At just that moment the hansom cab came round the corner.

It was not long before she was in a hansom, one of her bodyguards riding up front with the cabbie; Albert was seated beside her. Not that she had to worry: she owned the police on this street. She smiled to herself. *I have too much on them.*

"I 'eard you were down at the courthouse, ma'am. For the rape of that thirteen-year-old girl, after the nob whipped her with a belt. Looks as how you've set 'em straight." Albert was a big, brawling man. He rarely spoke, which was the way she liked it. Still, she didn't mind gloating about her successes on this occasion.

"Stead has been after me. Blasted journalist. And that inspector spent a year garn after me — only t' turn in 'is badge when da bloomin' Metropolitan gavvers refused to prosecute me. As I knew they would! Har har!"

"The jokes on them, ma'am. What happened at the courthouse then?"

"I plead guilty and paid a fine of two-hundred pounds to ensures all the evidence remained undisclosed."

"Ah, you bought 'em off!" She could see a faint smile on his lips in the darkness, with a light in his eyes which appeared to relish something—no doubt her success. He added in a whisper, "*with the blood money.*"

"O'course! What else is there but money?" In truth, there was reputation, which all those high level 'public' officials was fightin' to save. Didn't want anyone to know the truth about them. "And me young ladies formed a ring around me as I left the chuffin' courthouse. That showed that gavvers inspector wot fer! Har har!"

They crossed King's Road continuing on Old Church Street towards the Battersea Bridge Road where they would cross the Thames, near the location where she had sold many a child and stupid white woman to slavery. That was a profitable business: to get them out of the country where no one could help them. Always stupid, naïve girls who thought they were superior because they were chaste.

There was nothing new about selling women into prostitution; it was the middle class who took a particular dislike of *white* slavery.

"Where're we goin'?" Jeffries commanded as they drove along the Chelsea Embankment. "You should 'ave crossed at the Battersea Bridge."

"The bridge is closed ma'am," the driver yelled.

"I 'eard nothing of it!" She fingered her pistol in her purse.

"We'll go a bit further east and cross over at the Albert Bridge."

"*Whoa!*" Some minutes later the carriage stopped at the Albert Bridge where she saw a small tugboat at the dock.

"Why 're ya stoppin' you imbecile!" She fingered her gun. The cabbie alighted from the driver's seat and opened the door for her.

"I don't think it's anything ma'am," he said, holding his hand out to her.

She didn't recognize him. He was stinkin' ugly, his hair overlong, and his teeth missing.

She pointed her gun at her guard standing outside the door, her back to Albert, the body guard who had been riding with her. "Tell the driver to get driving again and to take me home."

In a fell swoop, Albert covered her with a burlap bag, dislodging her gun in the process which fell to the floor of the carriage. "You've got a new home now, ma'am. I ne'er liked this line 'o work. The cabbies is one thing, but chil'un is another. I got chillin' 'o my own."

He picked her up screaming and kicking, and threw her to the ground where the other two assisted in binding her with rope.

"Tsk tsk! Do try to be more ladylike," she heard the voice she recognized as her driver say. "I fear we won't get much money for you at all."

"I disagree, Holmes," the other body guard muttered. "Some enjoy the fight. And no one will put up more of a fight than Mary Jeffries."

"She's going to have to be shipped very far away, Watson. We won't hear her screams."

"That is no problem. I have studied the routes she has used in the past."

"What are you doing?" she yelled from inside the burlap bag.

"I'm cleaning up London," the one referred to as Holmes explained. Could it be . . . ? "We were unable to win in court, so we're closing down your businesses the only way we know how."

"*Oh, no!* You ain't Sherlock Holmes is you?"

"At your service."

"What does you 'ave to say to it, you bloody vigilante!"

"We're attempting to save your soul, madame," he added. "Clearly you're entirely devoid of empathy. I've taken it upon myself to fill that empty chasm. Perhaps I will yet save you from the fires of Hell."

"I doubt it, Holmes, but it is our Christian duty to try. We never give up on our fellow man—or woman."

"You bastards! Wot the bloody Gypsy Nell 're ya talkin' about?"

"Calm yourself, madame!" the one named Watson intervened.

"The professor will kill you!" she screamed.

"Strangely enough, Professor Moriarty and I have reached an arrangement we both agree upon," Holmes continued. "We've formed a partnership of sorts in this regard—healing an ugly break in our formerly tight friendship. I've done something for him, *he's done something for me.*"

"How?" she demanded in muffled tones from underneath the burlap bag. "How did you turn my body-guards?"

"I owed the professor a favor. He was a bit miffed with me as I had ruined his plans on another matter, and I did wish to be in his good graces due to an upcoming exchange. And, though we often do not see eye to eye, on this matter we were only to happy to assist," Sherlock explained. "The professor has offered our friends here more profitable employment—and, in the process, gained our appreciation. He was surprisingly willing to assist, I must say."

They threw the burlap bag into the tug boat which began traversing down the Thames, the screams gradually not so painful to the ear.

"Ah, another happy ending," Sherlock said. "It warms the heart, does it not? Let us go home, Watson."

CHAPTER FIFTY-TWO
A Broken Promise

"Do you feel some remorse for our part in this, Holmes?"

"Certainly it would have been preferable for the English judicial system to have put the woman in jail. But, in the absence of justice, I can't think what other options were available to us outside of murder. I only wish we might have done it sooner, saving the innocent from unspeakable suffering." Sherlock settled into his easy chair. "The police are, even now, freeing those held captive in her brothels."

"I can't say the punishment was equal to the crime," Watson said.

"No. I'd say it fell far short." Sherlock filled his pipe with tobacco. "I took the liberty of inviting journalist William Stead to the party. Once the public gets wind of it, it won't matter if Stead goes to jail again. The public outcry will have the last word."

"What are you speaking of?" Mirabella asked, entering the room with their evening sherry.

"Reparation, Miss Hudson. In some situations, justice will never prevail. Still, we do our best to provide a window of insight to those who would inflict pain upon others."

She raised her eyebrows. "Are you a vigilante, Mr. Holmes?"

"If you mean, Miss Belle, do I take matters into my own hands, I admit that I do. Naturally I would prefer for our elected government officials to take care of the problem rather than being part of the problem."

"Corruption is rampant, it seems." She shook her head while handing him his sherry.

"It is very unwise to associate with those of immoral character," Sherlock said pointedly, taking a grip on her fingers while the sherry was still in his hand.

Mirabella giggled nervously. "That's funny. My father always says that."

"Oh, and why is that funny?"

"You seem so different, that's all."

Sherlock stared at her, his gaze intense as he released her fingers. "Are you keeping any secrets from me, Miss Belle?"

"Nothing outside of the secrets a girl has." Her father had not raised a liar. Her hand began shaking and she was relieved she had already handed him his drink. She began backing up.

"You must always discuss any concerns you have with me." He added softly, "Let there be no secrets between us henceforth, Miss Belle?"

"Of course, Mr. Holmes."

CHAPTER FIFTY-THREE
Jack of all Trades

"I am a fortunate fellow of great renown!
It is so marvelous to be me!
Men who are gallant call for my talent.
Here is a gentleman craving a shaving.
Or maybe a gent has a note to be sent,
Or it's cleaning a wig, or dancing a jig,
I can do it all!
Figaro, Figaro, Figaro . . ."
--The Barber of Seville by Gioachino Rossini

"Ha ha!" Sherlock laughed, turning to Mirabella. "It's a very good opera, don't you think, Miss Belle?"

"Oh, indeed I do, actually my favorite," exclaimed Mirabella. But how could she not be pleased with anything performed in the Theatre Royal of Drury Lane in Covent Garden? The theatre was stunning, with an arched dome overhead and rows of opera boxes five stories high!

She was likewise pleased with her maroon silk gown which she thought did some justice to all the elegancies of the opera.

Not that long ago she was slopping pigs. Now she had met the prime minister—and the queen! It was unfathomable. Mirabella smiled at her aunt Martha.

"Auch then, this opera is fine, so it is. What is the name of it?" Mrs. Hudson asked.

"The Barber of Seville."

"A very interesting choral arrangement," Dr. Watson said.

"Yes, there are eight distinct melodies, not harmonies, but *distinct melodies*, and yet they all sound lovely together. Remarkable," Sherlock said.

Mirabella was scanning the audience, delighted to be in one of the box seats. "Oh, my."

"Hmm, I see."

"Who is it?" asked Watson.

"The Countess of Florentine," said Sherlock. He added tersely, "with Professor Moriarty."

You mean that window . . .
How exceedingly lucky.
This fits together like cheese and macaroni!
Inside there, I am their barber, their coiffeur.
I cure them all, their dogs, their little kittens;
I handle all their business.

"Fantine Noel," muttered Watson. "I thought she had left London."

"I believe she did," replied Sherlock.

"Auch then, she's awfully close for someone who ain't in London, so she is. That's too bad, so it is."

"It appears that she came back for something," said Mirabella, glancing sideways at Sherlock. "Or *someone*."

"I wonder if Moriarty suspects betrayal," considered Dr. Watson. "Did Miss Fantine reveal the plan to you, Holmes—in one of her weaker moments?"

"I assure you that Countess Florentine has no such moments," replied Sherlock. "She has moments when she wants something, and moments when she wants something badly."

She's all I live for!
I simply have to see her!
Daytime and nighttime I wait beneath her window.

"Is there is no other state of being for the countess besides wanting something?" Mirabella asked. "Enjoyment, pleasure, delight, perhaps?"

"One who has everything and takes little delight in any of it because it is never enough," said Sherlock non-committally, most uncharacteristic. "Much like her brother."

"Much like you, Mr. Holmes," Mirabella said.

"Aye, that's so, so it is." Mrs. Hudson added.

"As to her betrayal, even if she didn't reveal the plan to you—Moriarty doesn't know that," suggested Watson.

He's a snake full of guile.
A very crooked fellow.
Oh, the very thought of money
Sets his genius in rapid motion!
He responds with unbelievable devotion
When he knows that there is money on the way!

"It's not so difficult to discern," replied Sherlock. "That part of Moriarty's plan—the acquiring of secrets—did not fail. It was, in fact, an astounding success. The part of his plan which had problems was swaying the public against the monarchy and those in power."

"It was successful—just not successful *enough*," Mirabella added.

"Indeed. I have no doubt Moriarty will try again. He still has access to many state secrets he should not be privy to."

"Unfortunately, nothing is final in life—until it's *final*," said Dr. Watson.

"But what about the service you performed for the professor?" Mirabella asked. "Do you think he will now leave you alone?"

"I think, Miss Belle, that the professor does not wish to kill me—for the time being. But no doubt his attention is turned elsewhere." He turned to look at her, a feeling of concern brushing over him. He did not care for the feeling at all.

"Countess Florentine is waving at you," said Mirabella.

"I'm quite sure I can discern that for myself, Miss Hudson."

"Aye, no doubt you can, Mr. 'Olmes. So you ain't goin' to join her then?"

"Absolutely not. There will be sufficient time for chaos, disruption, and discord on some other occasion."

"She's quite beautiful, is she not?" asked Mirabella.

"Quite," replied Sherlock, glancing in Fantine Noel's direction.

Dr. Watson chuckled. "No more beautiful than you, Miss Mirabella."

"Do not tease me, Dr. Watson." Mirabella looked at him aghast, adding in a soft voice, "It is unkind."

Sherlock's eyes turned to her. "Watson does not tease you, I assure you, Miss Belle."

"Please be serious, Sherlock. Me with my plain brown hair and plain brown eyes."

"Chestnut-brown hair and golden-brown eyes." Sherlock cleared his throat.

"And warm inviting smile," added Watson.

"A smile is a dime a dozen, but a tall, lovely figure—" began Sherlock. Mrs. Hudson cleared her throat.

"Did I say something amiss, my dear Mrs. Hudson?" Sherlock asked.

"He did not! Let Mr. Holmes finish, Aunt Martha!" admonished Mirabella.

"Mr. Sherlock 'Olmes!" Mrs. Hudson exclaimed, staring disapprovingly at her niece before turning her disapproval upon Sherlock. "I'll thank you, sir, not to address me niece in that fashion—not now, not *ever*."

We must figure out a way to answer the lady.
Why not serenade her?
Make up a song
To tell her the things she wants to know

"No, quite right," Sherlock smiled, winking at Mirabella. "No, it certainly would not do."

CHAPTER FIFTY-FOUR
A Sweet Country Girl, Gently Bred

"I have nothing to offer a maiden
Save love overladen
All I can measure
To add to my treasure
Is my heart's devotion with fond love's emotion
Ah, could ever a lover do more?
Day and night it is you I adore."
--The Barber of Seville by Gioachino Rossini

"What would not do?" Mirabella asked.

"Auch, Mr. 'Olmes means an older man should not address a younger woman in such a fashion unless —" Aunt Martha began.

"Unless matrimony were his object," Dr. Watson completed the sentence.

"Aye, so it is," Aunt Martha added. "You're a'right, Dr. Watson."

"Oh, for heaven's sake!" exclaimed Mirabella. "I must endure continuous insults from Sherlock Holmes, and on the rare occasion when he chooses to say something nice to me—it is inappropriate? No wonder the world is in such a state of affairs."

"Do not trouble yourself, Miss Mirabella," consoled Dr. Watson. "Here we are in the glorious Covent Garden with two beautiful ladies. I insist upon enjoying myself."

"Very true. There will be time enough for things to go to Hell in a hand basket," Sherlock said.

"Aye, and very likely they will," Mrs. Hudson agreed.

"Then let us enjoy what time we have," Sherlock said, smiling as he patted her gloved hand, his silver-grey eyes sparkling with an unspoken amusement.

She felt that familiar electricity when he entered the room, only this time it passed through her hand. And, uncharacteristically, it was not altogether unpleasant.

Coming into womanhood was posing a danger to herself—and the world.

"Me? Oh, nothing. Nothing at all." *Except that I lost my mind for a moment*, probably an indicator of both an early demise and an immoral character.

Or of poisoning, one of the two. I always knew my mother should not have used that old dishware set she found in that abandoned mine in Dumfriesshire.

"Not to worry, my dear." He patted her hand. "There are far more important things than beauty. Such as brains: a necessity for the world's first lady detective. And it is my fondest hope that, for your own safety and mine, you will learn to use yours to its full capacity."

Whew! Things are back to normal. She breathed a sigh of relief, smiling up at him, and he returned her smile.

"My beauty or my brains?"

The Great Detective had a wicked smile on his lips which was startlingly attractive, framed as it was with his wavy raven-black hair. For the first time, there was something new in his slate-grey eyes, as if they shared an understanding, an unspoken agreement that things were not as they seemed.

She glanced across the opera house at Fantine Noel, who had her head bent towards Professor Moriarty, continuing to look at her.

Mirabella felt a shiver. The man scared her. As did Countess Florentine, if the truth be told.

I am quite well behaved,
As sweet as honey.
My disposition is bright and sunny.
For I am gently bred
When I am gently led.
It all depends on what you do.
But if you push me 'round
Then I will stand my ground,
I'll get you in the end
I'll have the last laugh, my friend.
No matter what you say,
I'll get my own sweet way.
The final joke will be on you.

Mirabella knew now that she was strong. She had come so far and learned so much working for Sherlock Holmes. Even he acknowledged her to be a 'lady detective.' He might couch it in insult, but he would never admit it if he didn't believe it to be true.

She was afraid when she looked at Moriarty, but she knew the path she must take. Everything in her gut told her that it was important and that she was the one to do it. *I must keep my eye on him.* Certainly Sherlock did not have access to Moriarty's lab!

Mirabella resolved to visit Moriarty's lab on a regular basis. Perhaps on her day off? She knew very well that she would not be turned away, particularly if she appeared to be working on the equation the professor wished solved. She didn't have to be working for Moriarty *per se*, but he would be more than willing to steal her conclusions.

But how to keep it from Sherlock Holmes? There was *nothing* he could not discover. And now she was proposing to keep a secret from the greatest detective who had ever lived.

I must employ the methods he has taught me.

Sherlock was watching her with an odd expression of discomfort on his face. He seemed to be experiencing an emotion he didn't wish to feel.

Perhaps he was not alone in that. He was so handsome in his tails and crisp white shirt, his dark curls framing his strong features and stormy grey eyes, now alight with laughter and amusement.

Why should she care so much what happened to Sherlock? Because . . . because . . . they now shared the same purpose.

To keep London—and the world—safe from evil doers.

She was, in fact, a sweet country girl, gently bred, with a shrewd talent for detective work. His eyes penetrated hers.

And maybe because she could no longer imagine her life without him.

The End

Of one life
And the beginning
Of another

EPILOGUE
A Worthy Foe

"I have a new plan, Colonel Moran," Moriarty said. His new muscleman, Underhill, stood at the door out of earshot. Moriarty liked Underhill already; he was not much of a talker.

"Yes, Professor? Shall I kill Sherlock Holmes?" Colonel Moran, formerly of the 1st Bangalore Pioneers and Moriarty's chief of staff, asked. When an assassination requiring an expert long-distance shooter was needed, Moran was the man for the job.

"Patience, Colonel. I'd like to torture him, first. Much more satisfying."

"Seems a waste of time to me," Moran muttered, leaning back into his chair as he took a sip of sherry. Educated at Eton and Oxford, as well as being the son of the Minister to Persia, Moran presented a debonair and aristocratic demeanor. "You wouldn't have wanted me to take that tactic with Mr. Reynolds."

"Madame Jeffries' lawyer? Ah, and Mr. Reynolds. Where is he?"

"In Australia. I gave him an offer he couldn't refuse."

A slight smile formed on Moriarty's lips. "We went a bit soft on that one, didn't we? Mr. Reynolds is a very fortunate man."

"He has children. I don't like to kill a man if there's another way. Actually I do, but I made an effective bargain with Reynolds." Colonel Moran's lips formed a terse smile. "I'm quite sure Reynolds is happy in the Outback."

"It warms the heart to know that. What about the letter Jeffries left with Reynolds to be opened in the event of her death?"

"Funny thing about that. There's no proof that Jeffries ever died. The letter still sits in Reynolds' safe on Chelsea Street."

Moriarty smiled. "So that was the bargain. There might be an explosion on Chelsea Street in the near future."

"I thought you'd say that, Professor."

"You see what I mean, Moran—you're a thinking man. A lack of patience was precisely my error in this interlude. I was too bold and open. I can run things from the shadows. I simply need to be a bit more subtle." I must embrace my situation. *If everyone thinks I am a dead bore, I must use their stupidity to my advantage rather than bemoaning what idiots think of me.* I must punish them with their own ineptitude.

"I can appreciate the value of duplicity. It is necessary to have a façade, but that doesn't mean we must move slowly."

"Indeed. I have a plan in mind."

"May I inquire?"

"The girl. She impressed me." Moriarty smiled to himself. "And I'm not often impressed."

"She's a bright enough girl, I'll give you that. And pretty." Moran shrugged. "A dime a dozen."

"Miss Hudson is much more than she seems, Colonel. She surprised me with her bravery, her deception, and, most importantly, with her intelligence. She kept herself alive long enough to obtain assistance."

"She outsmarted you," Colonel Moran pronounced, his expression critical. Moriarty let it pass; Moran was his most important man. Irreplaceable. No one handled a rifle like Moran.

Moran finished his sherry in one gulp. "But don't ask me to kill her, Professor. Killing women is not in my line. *Usually.* There are always exceptions."

"Killing the girl is not my immediate goal." Moriarty glanced at Moran.

"So you want her to solve your equation, is that it?"

"The Poincaré conjecture? That's only part of it. Although that would come in very useful to me." Moriarty laughed. "I think the girl could solve it. She thinks she was pretending to be able to solve the equation to save her skin, but she doesn't know her own abilities—and neither does Holmes. She doesn't have confidence in herself. *I can give her that.*"

"Yes, but why would you?"

A smile formed on Moriarty's lips. "I may win this round after all."

"Forgive me, Professor, but I don't think the girl will have anything to do with you after you tied her up and threatened to kill her. It tends to make one unreceptive to further advances."

"An ordinary girl wouldn't, no. But Miss Hudson is anything but ordinary. The pursuit of knowledge is a drug for her."

"Ah, like the game is to Holmes."

"Precisely. Even better than that, her devotion to Sherlock Holmes is complete. She doesn't yet know that, and Holmes doesn't either, but if she believed there was something she could do to help him, she would face her worst fears."

"How do you know that, Professor?"

"She already has." Moriarty stared pointedly at Moran. "I saw her face the tigers, you must remember. There are very few who will face a tiger."

Moriarty knew that Moran understood his meaning. In addition to being an expert marksman, the colonel was the author of *Heavy Game of the Western Himalayas* and had once descended into a drain after a wounded man-eating tiger.

"True," Colonel Moran agreed. "*True.*"

Moriarty smiled. "Miss Mirabella Hudson, like Holmes, is a *worthy foe.*"

END NOTES

Thank you for reading this book. If you enjoyed it, this alone means the world to an author.

If you enjoyed this book, please consider writing a review. Reviews are the magical amulet of authors today: without reviews, our books have no visibility on Amazon – and readers do not find them. If you like a book, the surest way to insure that an author can continue writing for a living is to write a review. Readers today have a power they never had before. This cannot be overstated: ONE review is worth several hundred dollars in advertising spent. This is because every time a review is posted, there is a small window when Amazon gives the book visibility amidst the sea of books which generally render one's book invisible. Posting a review is a great kindness to an author and SINCERELY appreciated.

Personal notes are always appreciated! Certainly I wish to correct any errors as well as hear from my fans.

http://suzettehollingsworth.com/contact/

Also by Suzette Hollingsworth

Sherlock Holmes and The Case of the Sword Princess
Sherlock Holmes and The Dance of the Tiger
THE PARADOX: The Soldier and the Mystic
THE SERENADE: The Prince and the Siren
THE CONSPIRACY: The Cartoonist and the Contessa

To be released in 2017:

Sherlock Holmes and The Vampire Invasion

AUTHOR'S NOTES:

This is a work of historical fiction, meaning that some of the settings and characters are based on actual historical fact and that some of the characters and settings, as well as the plot, are fictional but possible given the right set of circumstances. In the best of worlds one wishes to time travel through books.

"It is a lamentable fact if, in the midst of our civilisation, and at the close of the nineteenth century, the workhouse is all that can be offered to the industrious labourer at the end of a long and honourable life. I do not enter into the question now in detail. I do not say it is an easy one; I do not say that it will be solved in a moment; but I do say this, that until society is able to offer to the industrious labourer at the end of a long and blameless life something better than the workhouse, society will not have discharged its duties to its poorer members." *The Times* (12 December 1891), p. 7., William Gladstone

Truth serums are, in fact, used in modern society, so someone clearly believes they work. I actually spoke to someone who was administered a truth serum in an alcohol-treatment center. He was then asked many questions and taped. He said himself that he was "unable to lie". The tape was then played back to him.

Scopolamine is used widely in Columbia because it is odorless and tasteless. Snopes writes that some of the stories passed around facebook are urban legends – but admits that Scopolamine is used widely in Columbia with the intent to rape or steal. http://www.snopes.com/crime/warnings/burundanga.asp

"There is controversy as to how much of their free will victims ultimately surrender under the drug's sway. While there is little dispute that datura alkaloids do cause significant disorientation, there are those who believe burundanga's supposed "brainwashing" effects are better understood in terms of disinhibition which causes people to act in ways they later regret."

The account of Mary Jeffries given here is true—with the notable exception that she was never punished for her heinous crimes, which included the kidnapping of children for the purposes of sex trafficking. It is true that Jeremiah Minahan resigned from the Metropolitan police force when senior officials refused to prosecute Jeffries. It is true that Minahan compiled information and gave it to journalist William Stead, who went to jail for three months for bringing Jeffries' crimes to light. In fact, Mary

Jeffries was never prosecuted; and those she harmed protected her. One can hope there is justice somewhere. Even the kindest of interpretations of what happens when we die does not envision an afterlife without consequences. In the meantime, I envision a world in which Sherlock Holmes brings justice to the wronged.

"The Nordenfelt-designed, Ottoman submarine *Abdül Hamid*
The first such boat was the *Nordenfelt I*, a 56 ton, 19.5 metres (64 feet) vessel similar to Garret's ill-fated *Resurgam*, with a range of 240 kilometres (150 miles; 130 nautical miles), armed with a single torpedo, in 1885. Like *Resurgam*, *Nordenfelt I* operated on the surface by steam, then shut down its engine to dive. While submerged the submarine released pressure generated when the engine was running on the surface to provide propulsion for some distance underwater. Greece, fearful of the return of the Ottomans, purchased it. Nordenfelt commissioned the Barrow Shipyard in England in 1886 to build *Nordenfelt II* (*Abdül Hamid*) in 1886 and *Nordenfelt III* (*Abdül Mecid*) in 1887. (So it is conceivable that the plans could have been in existence in 1882). The submarines were powered by a coal-fired 250 hp Lamm steam engine turning a single screw and carried two 356mm torpedo tubes and two 35mm machine guns. They were loaded with a total of 8 tons of coal as fuel and could dive to a depth of 160 feet. It was 30.5m long and 6m wide, and weighed 100 tons. It had a normal crew of 7. It had a maximum surface speed of 6 knots, and a maximum speed of 4 knots while submerged. ***Abdül Hamid* became the first submarine in history to fire a torpedo submerged**.
However, the solution to fundamental technical problems, such as propulsion, quick submergence, and the maintenance of balance underwater was still lacking, and would only be solved in the 1890s.
https://en.wikipedia.org/wiki/History_of_submarines

When one thinks about early submarine designs, the names H.L. Hunley, Wilhem Bauer and John Philip Holland naturally come to mind and not that of a late 19th century British clergyman. Yet, Reverend George W. Garrett should be listed among those more famous names. Garrett approached Swedish arms manufacturer Thorsten Nordenfelt with a proposal that he should take over the development of Englishman's submarine patents. Nordenfelt recognized the potential and viewed this type of craft as the ideal platform for the Whitehead torpedo. So, in1881, the two came to a formal agreement, with Garrett becoming Nordenfelt's assistant, which led to the production of a series of steam powered submarines. At this time, an arms race was heating up among Balkan and eastern Mediterranean countries and Greece agreed to purchase Nordenfelt I. Not wishing to fall behind, the Ottoman Empire, Greece's arch rival, agreed to purchase the next two submarines. Nordenfelt II was built at the Barrow Shipyard in England in 1886. It was dismantled and shipped to Constantinople, where it was re-assembled at the Taşkızak Naval Shipyard under the supervision Garrett himself. The submarine was renamed **Abdul Hamid**, after Sultan Abdul Hamid II. Nordenfelt III, renamed **Abdul Mecid**, was later delivered to the Ottoman Navy.

http://www.steelnavy.net/UBoatLabCombrigAbdulHamidFBustelo. html

It is true that Victoria introduced hemophilia into the royal family and that porphyria apparently ended with her.

"Although genetic mutation accounts for around 33% of all cases of haemophilia, the chances of it occurring in any one generation are between 1 in 25,000 and 1 in 100,000.

Acute porphyria is now often attributed as the cause of George's 'madness', triggering the famous discoloured urine, flatulence, constipation, colic, itchy skin, seizures and anxiety. This diagnosis suggests that the king may not have been mad at all; rather the incessant discomfort, severe pain and nervous exhaustion caused by porphyria may have literally driven him to distraction, creating the impression of a man who had lost his mind and all connection to reality. It is extremely rare for men to exhibit such extreme symptoms of porphyria, leading some researchers to speculate that it may have been caused by exposure to arsenic. An examination of a sample of George's hair found traces of arsenic at 300 times the toxic level, likely as a result of the arsenic-laden James' powders medicine the king is known to have been given."

http://cultureandstuff.com/2010/02/02/how-do-you-solve-a-problem-like-victoria-was-queen-victoria-illegitimate/

I was astonished to read about Richard Cadbury and all that he suffered (the loss of his brother and wife, being so poor that he had to give up his morning tea, raising four children alone under the age of six) and yet that he continued to do what he thought to be right in spite of religious persecution—and was rewarded. It is encouraging to know of a righteous person who was enormously successful on this earthly plane.

"Above all we believe in the equality of God's presence, that no person, church, or religion enjoys exclusive access to God."

"When George Fox, the founder of Quakerism, was imprisoned in 1656, he sent a letter to Friends urging them to 'walk cheerfully over the world, answering that of God in every one.'"

"'We Friends believe the Light of God is in every person of every faith, and even present in those people who profess no faith. **God's presence in us has nothing to do with anything we've done.** It isn't something we've earned. God's presence in us isn't something we've achieved because we've followed a certain ritual or believed a particular doctrine.'"

Cadbury's shop was actually located in Birmingham, not in London.

http://www.cadbury.com.au/about-cadbury/the-story-of-cadbury.aspx

In 1824, 22-year-old John Cadbury opened his first shop at 93 Bull Street, next to his father's drapery and silk business in the then fashionable part of Birmingham.

In 1831, John Cadbury rented a small factory in Crooked Lane not far from his shop. He became a manufacturer of drinking chocolate and cocoa, laying the foundation for the Cadbury chocolate business. In 1847, the Cadbury brothers' booming business moved into a new, larger factory in Bridge Street in the centre of Birmingham.

See "The Chocolate Wars" by Deborah Cadbury, which I found to be as enjoyable to read as are Cadbury's chocolates to eat, https://amazon.com/1610390512.

"Some of the duties Gladstone intended to abolish in 1860 were the duties on paper, a controversial policy because the duties had traditionally inflated the costs of publishing and **thus hindered the dissemination of radical working class ideas**." - Wikipedia

We live in a world that is so, so different from earlier times. Imagine a world where most people could not read. How would that affect personality, education, learning over one's lifetime, achievement, disparity in income, and the ability of the privileged to control the poor?

In the 14th century, 80 percent of English adults *couldn't even spell their names*. When Johannes Gutenberg invented the printing press in 1440, only about 30 percent of European adults were literate. Gutenberg's invention flooded Europe with printed material and literacy rates began to rise. In the 17th century education became an emphasized part of urban societies, further catalyzing the spread of literacy. All told, literacy rates in England grew from 30 percent of about 4 million people in 1641 to 47 percent of roughly 4.7 million in 1696. As wars, depressions and disease riddled 18th century Europe, the pace of literacy growth slowed but continued upwards, reaching 62 percent among the English population of roughly 8 million by 1800. In 1820, 53% of men could read. In 1870 76% of men could read; I believe the figures were about half that for women.

The relevant point is that, in a society which can read, newspapers—and information—represent the power to shape ideas. **Once an idea is in place, change happens.** Particularly in the Victorian age when everyone who could read, read the newspapers.

"The New Journalism reached out not to the elite but to a popular audience. Especially influential was William Thomas Stead, a controversial journalist and editor who pioneered the art of investigative journalism. Stead's 'new journalism' paved the way for the modern tabloid. He was influential in demonstrating how the press could be used to influence public opinion and government policy, and advocated "government by journalism". He was also well known for his reportage on child welfare, social legislation and reformation of England's criminal codes.

Stead became assistant editor of the Liberal *Pall Mall Gazette* in 1880 where he set about revolutionizing a traditionally conservative newspaper 'written by gentlemen for gentlemen.'" - Wikipedia

"The Representation of the People Act" actually passed in 1884.

Mr. Lipton did, in fact, hand out free beer and tobacco at the Golden Jubilee.

Formerly, the **Representation of the People Act 1867** enfranchised part of the urban male working class in England and Wales for the first time. Before the Act, only one million of the seven million adult males in England and Wales could vote; the Act immediately doubled that number. Moreover, by the end of 1868 all male heads of household were enfranchised as a result of the end of compounding of rents. However, the Act introduced only a negligible redistribution of seats. The overall intent was to help the Conservative Party, but instead it resulted in their loss of the 1868 general election.

Peers can only be tried by other peers, and they cannot be tried for anything except treason or a felony. Only one peer has ever been convicted by his peers (for murder), and he was mad.

So Prince Earnst, the Duke of Cumberland, would have never even been tried for assaulting a woman, much less convicted. But that doesn't mean that the general public approved. Lord Lyndhurst put something in the paper regarding the rape of his wife, which the Duke of Cumberland insisted be removed, but Lord Lyndhurst refused to do so.

The Victorians by A.N. Wilson

http://royalfoibles.com/tag/lady-lyndhurst/

"Throughout most of the Victorian era, however, syphilis was blamed on prostitutes, imaging them as a kind of womb of infection and implying that syphilis was a product of the degenerate female body." – Health, Medicine, and Society in Victorian England by Mary Wilson Carpenter

By the mid nineteenth century it was becoming more and more difficult for women to find work in more desirable professions, and this lead to a rise in the number of women holding jobs with long hours and little pay, such as agricultural gangs, shop girls, domestic servants, needle-trades and factory workers (Sigworth et. al, 81). Subsequently these women sought other means of supplementing their incomes, and increasingly turned to prostitution as a way to do so. With the passing of the Contagious Diseases Act of 1864, 1866 and 1869 (Acton, iii), which legalized prostitution but entailed legislation enabling the police to arrest women suspected of being prostitutes and the subsequent examination of them for signs of venereal disease, it became a matter of public controversy and the era of "The Great Social Evil" was born.

"A few weeks ago we mentioned a ghost story that had attracted the special attention and interest of Charles Dickens. This was the narrative of Mr. Thomas Heaphey, the artist, who stated that he had seen the apparition of a lady thrice - first in a railway carriage, then in a country house, and again in his own studio, where she asked him to take her portrait, and gave him an engraving that was considered to be very like her."

http://www.guardian.co.uk/theguardian/2012/jan/18/archive-1883-ghost-story-dickens

Crack a safe:
https://www.google.com/search?q=how+do+you+guess+the+combination+to+a+safe&ie=utf-8&oe=utf-8

How to guess the combination:
http://surrey-shore.freeservers.com/VicCrime.htm

Hammering on the handle:
https://www.youtube.com/watch?v=SZ3oOVZJ2Y8

Blowing up a safe:
https://www.youtube.com/watch?v=qn79_I41UmM

The Poincare Conjecture was one of the Millennium Prize Problems (7 math problems), the ONLY one of the seven which was solved. The prize for solving it was One million dollars. The Poincare Conjecture was proposed in 1904 by Henri Poincare, it stumped the brainiest of the brainiacs for 100 years, it and was solved by Russian mathematician Grigori Perelman (who, incidentally, refused the prize money as he didn't feel he deserved it. Perelman lived until recently on his mother's pension without a job in St. Petersburg). So far, I have spent two days just attempting to understand the question. At this point I am not concerned about understanding the answer, but I am determined to understand the question. So I went onto u-tube, since the problem is essentially one of geometry, I thought maybe a visual would help me. If you have some spare time, there are still 6 unsolved problems, worth $1 million each.

https://www.youtube.com/watch?v=p4FtN3FN3XY

"The Poincare Conjecture or: How I Learned to Stop Worrying and Lock my Bike"

Kate Poirier at Nerd Nite East Bay #8, The New Parkway, 27-May-2013

A BEAUTIFUL performance can be seen on YouTube of The Stanford Viennese Ball Opening Committee in full tux and white ball gowns dancing to the Morgenblätter, or Morning Papers Waltz by Johann Strauss Jr.

https://www.youtube.com/watch?v=AYBwaFkbSdw

The University of London in 1878 was the first university to admit women and University College London laid claim to be the first institution to run co-educational lessons.

http://www.london.ac.uk/history.html

University of London

Senate House

Malet Street

London

WC1E 7HU

In 1878 London became the first university in the UK to admit women to its degrees. In 1880, four women passed the BA examination and in 1881 two women obtained a BSc.

In 1900-1, there were 296 women students at Cambridge and 239 at Oxford. Women did not become full members of the university in Oxford until 1919 and in Cambridge until 1948.

In line with Arthur Conan Doyle's depiction of Sherlock Holmes and John Watson:

January 6, 1854: Sherlock Holmes' birthday. Mycroft 7 years older

John H. Watson's birthday on July 7, 1852   1.5 years older than Holmes

Mirabella's birthday: Nov. 7, 1863

Many of the characteristics depicted in this book were introduced by Arthur Conan Doyle, e.g., the description of John Watson's campaign in Afghanistan and resultant insomnia, the description of Mycroft as a lazy but brilliant mid-level bureaucrat, the description of 221B Baker street, and the statement of Sherlock's parents as being country squires. Although not explained by Arthur Conan Doyle, it is a fact that a country squire might live on the largest manor, and would very likely be the local Justice of the

Peace. All the explanations surrounding this is consistent with the history of the day. The location of Sussex as the family home is my own invention, but is in line with Doyle saying that Sherlock retired to Sussex. Arthur Conan Doyle made very little mention of Sherlock's family, parents, home, and no mention of siblings outside of Mycroft. These additions were in line with the framework established by Arthur Conan Doyle and were written with the idea of "making sense" within that framework. Mirabella Hudson is my own creation.

It does seem very likely that Sherlock Holmes would need a female operative, doesn't it? He cannot play every role. Some readers who are avid fans of Arthur Conan Doyle do not want a feminine presence in any books containing Sherlock Holmes as a character. There cannot be giggling or emotions, and the feeling must be somber and intellectual because, naturally, there were no women in Victorian times.

I have attempted to write a book which is true to the original characters and to the Victorian ambiance. I understand that some readers want to read a book which was written exactly as Doyle would write it, but those works are still all here. This is a *pastiche*. Nothing can diminish Doyle's genius. That is why the Jane Austen and zombie books do not take away from or diminish Jane Austen: she was a literary master and nothing can detract from the greatness of her works, which stand on their own.

Author Bio

Suzette Hollingsworth grew up in Wyoming and Texas, went to school in Tennessee (Sewanee), lived in Europe two summers, and now resides in beautiful Washington State with her cartoonist/author husband Clint, Barney D. Barncat, and Tinkerbelle the dachsie.

Visit Suzette's website at www.suzettehollingsworth.com. You can contact her http://suzettehollingsworth.com/contact/. If you enjoyed this book, please write an honest review and post it on Amazon, which enables the author to continue writing for a living.

Suzette's writing style combines wit with elegance and has been described as "Sherlock in Mr. Darcy mode" by a reader.

Her goal in writing historical fiction is that you, the reader, will engage in a magical journey and time travel through her books. She is very excited about her current Sherlock Holmes series in which Mrs. Hudson's niece is a potential love interest amidst these Victorian mysteries. Sherlock Holmes is a great, fun hero to write because he is liked from the get-go despite being pompous and insufferable (or perhaps because of it!), something which might result in an unsympathetic hero in another narrative. The series draws on the imagery surrounding the beloved Sherlock Holmes and Dr. Watson (Robert Downey Jr. and Jude Law, in particular, though the author is a fan of all versions, including Jeremy Brett and Basil Rathbone), incorporates the witty banter into the relationship between Sherlock and Mirabella, and lends itself well to Steam punk, blending the "Age of Invention" with something old-fashioned, elegant, and slower-paced.

Enjoy. *The game is afoot.*

Printed in Great Britain
by Amazon